EPILOGUE

EPILOGUE

Lily Lashley
aka Etzoli

Podium

Published in 2022 by Podium Publishing, ULC
www.podiumaudio.com

EPILOGUE

DELLFORD COUNTY, OR. SHERIFF'S DEPARTMENT   CASE: 2010-44674
INCIDENT REPORT   DATE: 10/06/2010
                                             PAGE: 1/1

DESCRIPTION: Missing Person

Date/Time Reported: 10/06/2010 19:42
Location Occurred :   2342 Darlton Rd.
Reporting Officer :   PORTMAN, D.   2251

Primary Investigating Officer:
10/06/2013   PORTMAN, D.   2251
Primary Investigating Officer:
10/06/2013   WEST, C.   2325

Case Status: Open   Offenders: Victims: 1

SUBJECTS:

Missing Psn.
      PRIMARY : SVARTHOLM, BLAKE   PHONE: 971-555-0162
    HOME ADDR: 2342 Darlton Rd.
               Mellbridge, OR 97012
      RACE   : WHITE   SEX: MALE D.O.B : 10/23/1992 AGE: 17
      HEIGHT : 6'3"   WGT:180   HAIR : Blond   EYE: Blue
      BUILD   : Medium   COMPLEXION : Light
  DR. LICENSE : None   OTHER PHOTO ID : Student ID
                                          (attached)

  Occupation : Student   Location: Mellbridge High School
                                    (604205)

  Notes   : Minor. No history of abuse. Last Seen:
                                          Cyraveil Forest
  Reported by : SVARTHOLM, ADELA (parent)

CHAPTER 1

MATT

When I woke up, I was seven years younger.

"Disoriented" didn't even begin to describe my mind at that moment. My lungs rasped for air. I swallowed a long, deep breath, finally opening my eyes to the dark ceiling above. I sat up, leaning against the wall. Soft bedsheets wrapped snug around me, a stack of pillows propping me up. Everything felt wrong.

None of this should be here. *I* wasn't supposed to be here.

I felt groggy and confused. My brain was still pulling itself together, trying to shape what was in front of my eyes into a coherent picture.

It was almost pitch-black in the room—*my* room, I reminded myself. *This* is my room. The only light source was a street lamp near the house, streaming through a curtained window. Long, dark shadows stretched the length of the floor, casting the room into segments of color and accentuating the voids filling the nooks and crannies. Everything looked familiar, exactly where I'd left it, as if I'd just stumbled out of a dream.

Had it all been a dream?

A strange feeling filled the air, something I hadn't felt in a very long time. The faint hum and crackle of electricity. My computer. An *actual* electronic PC. I'd left it on that night. When we left, I'd been chatting with someone . . . Her face brushed against my mind, but it was a vague shape, an outline I couldn't form into a complete picture. It had been a lifetime since we'd last spoken—or maybe no time at all, as it suddenly occurred to me.

I got out of bed and hurried to the computer. The chair rolled as I sat down. I'd forgotten it had wheels. I jabbed at the space bar on the keyboard, tapping impatiently. It was a cheap machine, something I'd gotten secondhand from Carl, and it always took a while to wake up. I hadn't even turned it off, but I still had to wait while the disks inside rumbled to life and the fans spun back up to speed. The monitor gave a sharp crack, then finally sprang to life, colors washed out as the backlight slowly warmed up.

Right in the corner of the screen, exactly what I wanted. It was 1:32 a.m., on the sixth of October, 2010. It was a Wednesday.

Now I was even *more* confused. Years had gone by, right? I brought a hand to my face, very carefully. Something was missing. Everything felt smooth and foreign. It wasn't my face anymore, not as I remembered it. Suddenly, my arms and legs felt so much weaker.

Was it all just a dream? A sickening, terrifying near-decade of my life, wholly imagined by the random quirks of my brain in a single night? All those life-and-death encounters, adventures, betrayals, romances? Battles and campaigns spanning years? Was that even possible?

I pulled up the browser window. I was still struggling to recall exactly what we'd been doing that night. I had to trust that the old me hadn't cleaned up behind himself, had left clues that a skilled tracker could follow. Electronic clues this time, but it was the same basic idea. It was the closest thing I could think of to having a record of what had happened so many years ago . . .

No. It was just the night before. It had only been a few hours ago. I needed to remember that now.

The map to Cyraveil Park was still open. I remembered that much. I'd driven us out there in the truck Dad left me, the day he disappeared. We'd parked right on the edge of the woods, after I picked up our friends. I hadn't wanted to go, but Blake's enthusiasm was infectious. He'd seen something out there, and we had to see it too. Jen, listening in on the line downstairs, persuaded me to go.

Then Blake spotted a shadow flitting through the trees, and we followed.

Blake sprinted through the woods, and we followed as close as we could. He kept having to circle back around, shouting at us to follow him down a path only he could see. It was just like when we played ball together, and Blake was the one sprinting ahead of the play. He was always five steps ahead of where he was supposed to be.

When we crossed over, he was exactly the same . . . except he turned it into an asset. He was always five steps ahead of the enemy, doing things nobody else would dare. I'd used his insanity to win more than a few battles.

How much of that actually happened? How much of it was true?

More memories flooded my mind, along with the creeping poison of dread. The weight of what I'd done began to press harder on my mind, threatening to crush me entirely. I'd become something horrible. I'd been forced to make decisions with the lives of hundreds, thousands, tens of thousands hanging in the balance. I'd sacrificed allies, I'd lost friends. I'd come right to the edge of losing everything. Everyone. We'd only barely made it out the other side. I hated what I'd done, who I'd been.

Was there a way out?

The answer came. It was so simple and easy that I laughed aloud. I was home now. I was safe here. No one was hunting me anymore. Barely anyone even knew me. Nobody here would know what I'd done. If I'd even done it, for that matter.

There was a beautiful, golden path stretching out before me, one I could walk without delay. Without regret. I could finally return my life to the normal, simple place it belonged. No more fighting. Just normal life. I could hang out with friends, play basketball, let other people take control for a change. All I needed to do was . . . forget.

Even as I thought the words, I felt weight lift off my shoulders. I closed the map to Cyraveil on the screen, symbolically wiping it clean. The browser returned to the conversation I'd been having with a girl on the next tab. She had a reserved face, a guarded expression, like she was always hiding something behind her smile—but her eyes had that friendly intelligence, the kind that begged you to hang on to every word she said, even when they might be few and far between. Her voice was warm and passionate, the sort that could inspire armies to go to war.

We'd been talking in a private chat she'd invited me to. Scrolling back through the conversation, I'd been so casual and relaxed. I'd forgotten how to talk like that. These days, everything was either prepared and stuffy for the court, or rousing improvised speeches in the midst of a heated battle. I had no idea how to talk to someone just one-on-one anymore.

I shrugged it off. I'd figure it out. I could play anything awkward off as a joke, or just let her do all the talking. I could work around it.

I'd work around all of it. Everything would fall back into place. Nothing happened last night, after all. My life was perfectly normal. I was just some guy, a senior in high school. Nothing more.

I put the computer back to sleep. I figured I'd follow it to bed; after all, I had school in the morning.

After everything else, school sounded downright easy. I was almost looking forward to the mundanity of plain old classes. I was just about to hop back into bed when I heard rustling downstairs. Someone was moving around. My mother, I assumed—home late from work yet again. Her being late wasn't exactly unusual, but I had a sudden desire to hug her. I'd missed her a lot.

I had forgotten how cold it got in our house, especially this late at night in October. I dug through my closet for my jacket. My favorite jacket. I savored how soft and warm it was. Another thing I'd missed for years.

Hours, I reminded myself. It's only been a couple of hours.

I opened my door, flinching as it clicked loudly in protest. The handle had always done that if it was turned all the way. I usually remembered to stop before turning it too far. Just another item on the list of things I needed to remember. I'd have to start writing them down if this kept up. I closed the door behind me and headed downstairs, where the light in the kitchen had just clicked on.

Walking down the stairs felt like an eternity. I spent every step thinking through what I would say. If I'd even say anything. If I'd just pretend to come down for a drink, if I needed an excuse for being up so late on a school night. My mother wasn't exactly the kind to get mad over us staying up late. She did her best to provide for us, but this was exactly the sort of evening where I'd be making dinner for all three of us, leaving hers in the fridge for whatever late hour she got home. I used to hate having to put away leftovers for her, and that she couldn't be around to cook for us.

Tonight, I appreciated so much more what she'd done for us over the years. Mom might not have been there for dinner five nights a week, but what did that matter when she was working two full-time jobs every week to keep my sister and me healthy and in school? I don't think I could have done as much. I'd learned a lot about cooking on the other side. Come the weekend, I'd treat her to a real feast—and tonight, I was going to remind her how great she really was.

I turned the corner to find not my mother, but the long brown hair of my little sister, Jennifer, poking over the door of the pantry she was digging through. She looked up surprised as I walked in. Bits of snack cake fell out of her hand and sprinkled the floor. I'd actually managed to sneak up on her somehow.

"Uhh . . . Hey, Jen," I started awkwardly.

" 'Hey, Jen,' " she repeated slowly. " *'Hey, Jen?'* That's it?"

". . . Did you expect a speech or something?"

Jen frowned. "No, but . . . after all of that . . ."

"All of what?"

Jen's mouth fell open, and I spotted a bit of the same snack cake dusting her teeth. I winced. Her eyes widened to the size of dinner plates. "You . . . you don't remember?"

Her words were a sledgehammer. Even as the wall I'd hastily thrown up started to crumble away, I still wanted to deny it all. If only for a few more moments, I wanted to stay in that bliss. "Remember what?"

"God, Matt. *To dou evv erreth kapavas, vis duralav.*"

"*Dou nara kapavas,* Jen."

The snatch of Etoline sprang unbidden from my mouth. Jen's insult demanded some kind of answer. I couldn't let it go. But as her face twisted in satisfaction, I felt the structure of comfortable ignorance I'd so hastily built crash down around me like a crumbling fort.

If Jen remembered . . . if she could speak Etoline . . . then it was real.

Cyraveil was real.

"That's what I thought," Jen said smugly. "Your pronunciation still sucks, by the way." She picked up her snack off the floor and hopped onto the kitchen counter, inspecting it carefully. After a few moments, she bit into it. Her face lit up. "This tastes amazing. Matt, we need to buy like two hundred more of these. Right now."

I leaned against the refrigerator, pressing my hands into my forehead. A headache was pounding into being, like a drummer building up to a crescendo in my temples.

"Headache?" she asked.

"Yeah."

"How long have you been awake?"

"Only a few minutes. You?"

"Half an hour, maybe? Don't worry, it'll pass—yup, here it comes," she added, right as a *massive* wave of pain cascaded through my brain.

My skull felt like someone was trying to chop it in half repeatedly with a dull axe. I gripped the handle of the refrigerator door tight. I felt like I might collapse. My vision faded away, the kitchen light vanishing into a void of black terror. A faint voice followed me down, farther and farther as I descended into oblivion. It called to me, and I desperately wanted to answer, but all I could do was fall. I felt an impact that might have been a small earthquake, miles away, sending shivers up through my core.

I snapped back into being. The lights had returned. I was on the floor staring directly into the pale, buzzing bulb. I smelled chocolate. Jen's snack. Her face was inches away, peering closely. As soon as I opened my eyes, she moved away to give me space.

"You good, Matt?"

I coughed, trying to clear my throat which was suddenly dry and raw. "Think so. Need a drink."

"Any preference? There's no *sylvandine*, but I could probably get you something harder if you want. I think Mom keeps some stuff on the top shelf in the garage."

I sat up, grateful for the warm, hard exterior of the refrigerator. The pain had subsided a bit, and logic and reason were beginning to return. "Jen, we're underage."

"You're twenty-five."

"No, I'm eighteen. You're sixteen. Didn't you notice?"

Jen sighed. "Yeah . . . Like we never left."

"Yeah."

Neither of us spoke for a minute. I stood up, rummaging through the cabinets. I found the little bottle of ibuprofen and pulled out a pair of tablets. A quick glass of water later, and I was already feeling a little better. I sat down at the kitchen table and rested my head against the wall, waiting for the effects to kick in.

"Wish I'd thought of that," Jen muttered.

"Huh?"

"Painkillers." She held out her hand, and I passed her the bottle. "I kinda forgot they existed."

"The wonders of modern medicine," I murmured. I closed my eyes. The pain was still all too real. My brain felt like it was trying to push its way out of my skull with every huge pulse. I heard a car start up outside, and the engine noise felt like it was rattling through my eardrums from inches away.

My eyes flew back open as the realization set in.

"Jen, you can't—"

"Nope. I tried as soon as the migraine hit me. No dice."

She sighed and sat down across from me, bringing another pair of glasses filled with water. She slid one across the table, and I gulped it down gratefully. My throat still felt dry and parched, and the water was only doing so much to help.

"I guess that didn't make it across." Finding out Jen could no longer heal was a bit of a shock. It had been so useful. If Jen couldn't cure us and keep Blake from getting himself killed in his crazier stunts . . . I'd have to plan around that limitation.

Wait. No, I wouldn't. That part of my life was over. If I could help it, I'd never get into a situation again where I might need her abilities. I was going to live a peaceful, normal life—no matter what it took.

"I think it's starting to die down now," she spoke up, gulping down more water. "Are you as ridiculously thirsty as I am?"

Despite downing the entire glass, my mouth and throat still felt like the surface of a desert. I nodded.

"More water?"

"Sounds good." I backed my chair into the corner, where I could lean against the wall more comfortably, and improvised a pillow by bunching up my jacket and propping it against my shoulder—just like I'd done a thousand times on the campaign. "You still seem better off than me."

Jen shrugged, returning with another refill of water. "Maybe just 'cause I've been up longer. I got something to eat too."

"Snacks." I frowned. "You should be eating something more substantial."

"Do you *know* how long it's been since I had something chocolatey?"

"Yes."

Jen sighed. "Stop being so down, Matt. We're home. We've got electricity again. Running water!" As if on cue, a heavy truck drove past outside. The loose windows in our house rattled slightly. "Cars, Matt. *Automobiles!*" She stretched out the word, excitement laced in every syllable. "Planes, trains, hair dryers. Shampoo. Oh god, showers. Matt, we have *hot showers* again."

"I get it, I get it." I forced a smile onto my face. "It's good to be home."

"*There* you go." Jen smiled. She gulped down the rest of her water and let out a satisfied breath. "Even the water tastes better."

"It's not like they had water filters."

"Well, the Sylves did. We had this whole thing where they—"

I cut her off. "They filtered it with magic, yeah. You told me." I didn't want to hear any more than I absolutely had to. The sooner we returned to normal, the better. I'd indulge her for now, but it couldn't last.

"Yeah. Cool shit," Jen added, returning to the pantry to find another snack. My headache was steadily declining, freeing up more of my conscious brain for processing.

We could do this. Integrate back into the world. It would be tricky for a while, remembering exactly who we were seven years prior. There was no visible trace of our journey, but there were so many little things we had to watch out for. As far as I could tell, my body was exactly the same as the night we left—underwhelmingly so. I felt so much weaker and smaller, the finely toned muscle I'd built up vanishing overnight. Still, I remembered everything I'd been trained on, every single battle I'd bled through. If I had to get into a fight, I could hold my own.

I wasn't getting into any fights though. I'd never been in one before we left and I definitely didn't plan on starting a fight club now.

"Pass me some cookies, will you?" I asked. Jen tossed me the box, and I dug into them. She was right. I'd missed chocolate just as much. The cheap box of cookies tasted like heaven. I ate my way through a third of them, realizing how hungry I was with each fresh bite.

Jen filled up two glasses of milk and brought them over without even being asked. Compared to her reputation as a self-centered chatterbox, the Jen I knew was almost the inverse. She was incredibly perceptive; she just didn't always act on it. We ate in silence, savoring the snacks. Jen kept glancing around the room as if she'd never seen it before, taking in every detail.

"So," she started, finishing off the last cookie.

I nodded. "You're right, we should get more of those."

"More urgent things to talk about, Matt."

I sighed, resigning myself to fate. Better to have it out now than later, I suppose—but Jen had other things on her mind than the events of the last week.

"Is this real?"

"Yes."

"How can you be sure?" she asked, eyes squinting at him. "What about the time we had those visions, back in Helsevar?"

"Do you remember the pact I made?"

"Selnou."

"Then you know as well as I do, this is for real."

Jen nodded. "Okay, yeah. Guess the old bitch wasn't lying."

"I'm sure you meant to say witch."

"You didn't know her like I did," Jen replied, grinning. "So . . . we're home . . ." A melancholy look filled her face. ". . . Forever."

I didn't dare contradict her. Luckily, I was saved from having to answer as Jen leaped out of her chair and darted to the other side of the kitchen. I twisted around, confused, and saw the home phone lit up and about to ring. Jen picked it up just as the ringer was about to intrude on the peace and quiet.

"It's Carl."

This was another unwelcome development. I steeled myself for confrontation. "Can you put it on speaker?"

"Yeah, one sec." Jen fiddled with the phone. "Crap. I don't remember how."

"What?"

"It's been a while, okay?" She held it up to her ear. "Hey. Yeah, Carl, it's me. Hang on. Shut up a second. How do I put this on speaker? . . . Button on the . . . okay, yeah." She fumbled with a few buttons, and the faint white noise of the phone speaker filled up the kitchen. Jen set the phone down on the table. "Matt's here too."

Carl's voice crackled out of the speaker, very low. He was avoiding making too much noise, lest he wake up his temperamental father. "We're alive."

"No shit, Carl," said Jen. "Trying to be profound?"

"Shut up." I could practically hear his face turning red through the phone. "Matt, you there?"

"I'm here." Dread filled my entire mind, cascading as if a dam had suddenly burst wide open. I knew exactly what was coming next.

"Have either of you heard from Blake?"

Jen looked at me, her expression grim. She was waiting for me to answer.

I shook my head very slowly. "Carl . . ." I started.

"Hang on. Hear me out. We came back unchanged, right? So maybe—"

A sliver of hope. I didn't dare entertain it. I was afraid—of what it might grow to become, and of how quickly it would be snuffed out. I had to take control, fast.

"Did you try calling him?"

"He doesn't have a cell. I tried his house once, but no one answered. I didn't want to try again. I don't want to wake anybody up." Carl was right. Blake's parents were the nicest couple in the world, and every time I hung out there I felt jealous of his home—but his dad absolutely would not be okay with getting woken up at two in the morning.

"Then that's all we can do for now."

"But—" Carl's voice rose slightly, getting louder.

"Carl," I interrupted sharply. "Remember where you are. You're eighteen. It's a school night, and your dad's asleep down the hall." I tried to inject as much calm into my voice as I could muster. As it had so many times before, it worked. When Carl spoke next, his tone was low and subdued.

"So what do we do?"

"We go to school. Meet up at lunch tomorrow, like we always do. Jen, you'll come sit with us."

Jen nodded. "Okay. Sara can live without me for one lunch."

"Good. Carl?"

"Yeah?"

"Cyraveil doesn't exist."

There was a pause. I waited, hoping Carl would understand and follow without question. There was only one way we'd all get through this without being locked up in an asylum. We had to fit back in as if we'd never left. Tell absolutely no one. I could do it. Jen could probably do it too, with some help—but Carl had changed so much more than I had, and in the opposite direction. I was ready for a challenge like this. The new Carl? If he still had his sword . . . I couldn't be sure.

He finally answered. "Got it."

I let out a breath I hadn't realized I'd been holding in. Jen noticed it, looking at me curiously. She didn't say anything, leaving Carl in the dark.

"Okay. Then we'll see you tomorrow, Carl."

"Tomorrow," Carl acknowledged. "Hey, Jen. You still there?"

"Dov?" Jen leaned forward over the phone.

"Vei savi ilu dou, desve ta nal erreth. Syldae se valenda, selnou?"

". . . Sure, Carl." Jen looked slightly embarrassed, but it faded quickly. "Will do."

"Okay. Night, guys." The phone clicked off. I watched Jen carefully as she put the phone away, looking for her reaction.

"What was that about?" I asked. I only had a vague idea of what Carl had said. I'd never learned the language like he had, just a few useful phrases (and a few insults), and of course neither of us came even close to Jen.

"What? A guy can't be nice and be concerned about me?" Jen replied.

"O-o-o-kay, forget I asked." There was something there, but Jen made it clear I didn't need to know it. As long as it didn't affect us, it was her business.

"So . . . we just go back to school, then?" Jen changed the subject for me, to which I leaped gratefully.

"Yeah. Just be normal. Not that you ever were."

Jen punched my shoulder in response. "You can do better than that."

I laughed. "Give me a few days. I'll bring back *all* the bad jokes."

Jen grinned. It already felt like we were returning to normal. A few more little pushes and maybe we could slide completely into perfect mundanity. "So, what do you want for dinner tomorrow?"

"I dunno. What are you in the mood for?"

I shrugged. "Why don't we just go to the grocery store after school and play it by ear? We can get anything you want."

"Ooh. I might abuse that." Jen's face turned mischievous, but I'd meant what I said.

"Abuse all you want. It's a special occasion."

"The day the bad jokes returned?"

I laughed again. It felt warm and comforting, like the sun rising out of the darkness. I hadn't had much to laugh about for a long while. "Sure, let's go with that."

"What on earth are you two doing up?" A groggy voice echoed from the hallway, followed by the front door clicking shut. Our mother had wandered in finally, her face looking like it was melting away from exhaustion. Her eyes were sunken and drowsy, and she was leaning against the wall. She dropped her bag on the floor.

"Mom!" Jen leaped out of her seat and rushed over, wrapping her in a bear hug. I stayed put, watching them both—but in truth, I felt the same joyous reaction as Jen in that moment. I'd never really been much for hugging her before . . . but everything was different now.

"What's going on?"

"Nothing, Mom," Jen replied, and as her face pulled back, I saw tears forming in her eyes. "I'm just glad to see you."

"Did something happen?" Mom's eyes widened, becoming alert and adept. Even as tired as she was, the mere possibility something might be wrong with her daughter brought her to life. It was a trait I'd come to recognize in all three of us now, the adrenaline rush and the hyperaware state we all had mastered. Mom, like the two of us now, could be ready for anything, even on the brink of collapse.

"Nothing happened, Mom," I answered. "We were just waiting for you to come home. I couldn't sleep."

She frowned, but with reassurances from both of us, her fatigue was beginning to win out over the adrenaline. Her eyes drooped again. "All right, Matthew. If you say so."

"We're fine. Time for bed for everyone, I think."

"Come on, Mom," Jen added. "I'll help you upstairs."

"Thanks, Jenny." I'd forgotten, Jen was still going by Jenny seven years ago. She'd long since decided she hated it. As Jen half-carried our mother back down the hall, she twisted around and shot me a pained look. I grinned.

"Good night, Jenny," I called. She rolled her eyes, before turning back to the stairs as they began to climb.

I cleaned up after our snack, putting away the milk and tossing the empty box of cookies.

I was actually looking forward to school tomorrow, as crazy as that might have sounded before we left. There were friends I hadn't spoken to in nearly a decade, after all. Classes would be a bit harder to get back into. I was having a hard time remembering things like what rooms they were in, or where my locker was. I'd have to trust in physical memory to lead me to the right spots.

I could do it. I *had* to do it. The only way I could get my life back on track was if no one ever figured out what happened. Cyraveil was in the past, and if I could help it, it would stay there. Forever.

As I turned out the lights and headed back to my room, I saw Jen's light click off as well. I closed my door, remembering to avoid the click this time, and crawled back into bed. Exhaustion had returned with a vengeance. I began to drift off almost immediately, but one nagging memory pushed its way back to the surface, keeping me awake just long enough to remember the ramifications.

The witch had told me a secret after we'd made our pact. Something I'd kept hidden deep inside my soul, that I dared not reveal to anyone. She'd told me how we could return to Cyraveil.

On my life, if I could help it, I'd never let any of us see that wretched land again.

CHAPTER 2

CARL

"Portman, what is this?"

"Sir."

"You two got the call, you two take the case. You know the rotation. It's that simple. Do you have a problem with that?"

"No, sir."

"Look, I get it. It's a teenage runaway. Pain in the ass, but someone's gotta take care of it."

". . . Sir, if I understand correctly, the father is a personal friend?"

"I'm busy. Get to work."

———————

I tapped on the screen, ending the call with Matt's last words still echoing in my ears. He was a dick sometimes, but he was usually pretty smart, and he was in charge for now. I wasn't about to get answers at this hour. I definitely wasn't sleeping anytime soon though—especially with the migraine that had plopped its ass down on my head.

I set the phone down and plugged it in to charge, leaning back in my chair and closing my eyes while the headache washed through my skull. The glow of the screens in front of me shone through my eyelids, irritating as hell. I lifted a foot and turned them off with my toe, one by one. Blessed darkness returned to the room, the only sound being the white noise of the case fans from my desktop. Any other day, they'd annoy me just as much, far louder than they needed to be—but today, I wanted something to blot out all the background noise.

I was back, and I hated every damn second of it. This world sucked.

Even the smell was wrong. It all smelled too clean, too *fake*. I already missed the deep forests and huge mountains, the castles and villages, the market square and the festivals. Yeah, it might've smelled like shit for a while, but eventually, it was actually kind of charming. It had way more character than my dusty room. And it had real people.

God, the people. At best, they were actually *interesting*, with stories to tell and lives that actually mattered. At worst . . . I had plenty of ways to deal with them.

Tomorrow was *really* going to suck. I'd never liked school much in the first place. It always seemed like a huge waste of time. I knew everything I needed to know already, but I had to sit through lectures and lessons, while teachers droned on and on. I had to wade through mounds of bullshit for the few nuggets of actual, useful information. The internet taught me more than they ever could.

There was a redeeming note in the despair settling into my mind. I had the internet again. Once you've lived without electricity for years, you really come to appreciate just what an incredible and awe-inspiring invention it really is. With a few taps on a plastic keyboard, I could communicate with virtually anyone, anywhere in the world, instantly.

Having just returned from a world where the fastest method of communication (barring risky and draining magical talent) was by horse-back, the idea was mind-blowing. Coordinating groups of soldiers hundreds of miles apart into an effective fighting force was difficult enough on its own, and horses tire out faster than you might expect. The lands I'd helped conquer could attest to that.

While I was busy reminiscing about old campaigns, a fist rapped on my bedroom door.

Oh shit.

"Carl?"

Oh *shit*. It was my dad.

"Carl, what the hell are you doing up this late?"

Could I just pretend I was actually asleep? The lights were all off. I doubted he'd actually come in. It seemed like the best option.

"I heard you talking. You know you're not allowed to be up this late."

Just ignore him. Just keep ignoring him.

"We'll be speaking about this tomorrow, young man." I heard him walk away, heavy footfalls receding into the night.

Young man? Did he realize who he was talking to? I could—

No, wait. I couldn't. I didn't have that anymore.

Without warning, tears were already forming in my eyes. I was crying, silently. I'd been feeling it ever since I woke up. It had built up, slowly but surely, like the tide rolling in and the waves rising up the shore higher and higher. Everything I'd worked for, all the training I'd sweat and bled through . . . it was gone. I'd gone overnight from one of the most feared men in multiple kingdoms to . . . this.

I lifted an arm up and opened one eye, examining it. It was so skinny and frail. Sure, I could still lift a fair amount. I wasn't exactly *weak*, but comparatively . . .

Something to work on, I decided. I brushed the tears out of my eyes. I leaned forward and turned the screens back on. It was time to get to work. I needed information. I needed to know exactly what had just happened.

I began jotting down notes. We'd apparently disappeared in one place and returned in another, with only a few hours passing in between. Seven years went by in that short time. We'd grown older, we'd changed physically and mentally, but the physical changes were totally gone. This could all be easily explained away by magic, for better or worse. Magic was real in Cyraveil, and had somehow leaked over and ensnared us in its web for seven long years—the seven best years of my life.

Dammit all.

I headed to the search engines, but as I suspected, it was mostly fruitless. Every variation on "Cyraveil" I could think of only brought me the results I expected: articles on the park and the forest inside. I skimmed them briefly, but nothing jumped out as a clue. I started assembling a folder of bookmarks anyway, just in case they were relevant in the future. I branched my searches out, adding in small details of the world on the other side, and received empty results, or vague connections to fantasy novels and games I already knew held nothing useful.

In a way though, I was glad. Despite years of neglect, I still knew my way around the internet. I might not be finding anything, but at least I knew *how* to not find anything. I delved deep into old forums and ancient message boards, hunting down posts from years past.

It almost felt like working with Reynir again, uncovering old scrolls deep in the castle vaults. That was one of the first things we bonded over, a deep fascination with the history of the Cellman Empire and the Saenvaland. We traced history back through the ages—*his* history, following his family back through the centuries to the first Cellman who finally broke the bonds of slavery and freed their country.

My country.

I was getting more desperate now, and with the desperation came a dose of paranoia. Matt was right about our need to be careful. If people didn't believe us, we'd get locked away in an asylum for sure. I shuddered at the thought. The idea of being trapped in a colorless, faded building, clean and sterile, with no freedom and the world believing you to be a jibbering mess? I'd sooner kill myself.

But there was the other extreme. What if they *did* believe us? We could be hunted down by anyone. There were plenty of governments that might leap at the chance to exploit a whole new world full of valuable resources. And magic? What world power wouldn't want magic on their side?

No, I had to cover my tracks. I kicked on every security measure I had available at the moment, routing my connections through multiple private networks and ensuring end-to-end encryption on everything. No one would know where my posts were coming from.

I started leaving replies to those abandoned posts on old fantasy message boards, those people who claimed to have truly traveled to other worlds. Few had any replies, most users assuming they were crazy or just trolling. I didn't discount them just for having the wrong name of the world, or a few incorrect details. They might have been hiding themselves too, just as I was, or they could have gotten their information from ill-informed peasants and savages. On the truly ancient boards, those dating back past the turn of the millennium, I also sent emails when possible.

Having set everything in motion that I could, I turned the screens off once more and slid back into bed. My mind was still whirring as furiously as the fans in my machine. Even though only a few minutes had passed, I became irrationally irritated that my phone wasn't immediately buzzing with results, emails flooding in from fellow travelers grateful and eager to connect with me. Sure, I could logically remind myself that it was past two in the morning here, and five in the morning on the East Coast where most of those boards were situated. Few of those respondents, if they even maintained their accounts anymore, were likely awake and trawling the boards at this hour.

I couldn't help it. I *needed* to find anybody like me.

I tossed and turned for what felt like hours, as my phone remained stubbornly silent. Then, with a buzz and a jolt, I heard my phone slip off the desk and fall to the floor.

I leaped out of bed and grabbed it eagerly.

It was 7:00 a.m., and my alarm was going off.

*   *   *

I didn't spend any time getting ready for school. I only had a little time, and I had plenty of other things I wanted to get done before I left.

Right away, I got back online, checking every post I'd made. No replies or updates yet, but that wasn't surprising. I really just wanted the reassurance that I'd actually put the word out, that I hadn't just dreamed it all. The internet didn't lie.

Well, it did—frequently, and with gleeful malevolence—but it couldn't just erase my postings from existence. Nothing could ever truly be deleted, after all.

My mind a little more at ease, I pulled out my phone and tried to compose myself for the one message I couldn't send the night before. I scrolled through my contacts until I found Blake, far down the list thanks to his last name. Svartholm was such an awesome last name. I was jealous. Way better than *Stokelson*.

Hell, even Jen and Matt had better last names than me. "Matthew Westin" was plain, but with the right person behind it, you could be intimidating as shit. Having watched Matt at work, believe me, he was that right person. I was pretty good in my prime, but even if I were still at my best, I *think* I could take him to a draw. Not so much now, obviously.

Despite being Matt's little sister, Jen had a different last name. Silverdale, same as her mother's. Jennifer Silverdale. Even her name was beautiful. I didn't know the story behind the discrepancy, but to be fair, I barely knew Jen existed before that night, and I didn't meet the *real* Jen until about six years later.

I definitely regretted not getting to know her sooner. Hindsight's a bitch.

Blake's name matched his accent, born and bred in Sweden. He was my best friend, all the way back to the day his family had moved to Silicon Forest when he was ten. We met through an event at a tiny video game shop, when we'd both shown up for the new expansion on the same day. I'd spent years searching for him when we got split up, and now it felt like I was right back to those days again.

Blake's father went to work pretty early in the morning, and his mother was a graveyard-shift nurse. Neither would be home in the early hours before school. I pressed call, and my phone started to connect through the wires to reach their home phone.

I imagined it ringing, echoing through their house. I could picture it perfectly—every step in the staircase, every twist and turn of the hallway upstairs. The carpet was dark green, the couches were pale blue. Blake's cat was likely lounging on the landing halfway up the stairs, soaking in the sunlight. Sometimes I felt like I knew their house better than my own.

Blake never made it to the phone. As the ringer gave up in futility, I heard Adela's voice through their answering machine.

"Thank you for calling the Svartholm residence. We aren't in at the moment, so please leave a message and we'll get back to you soon. Thanks!"

I reminded myself over and over that it meant nothing. Blake could have left already. I should have left for school myself by now. I was going to be late if I didn't pick up the pace.

I had to leave a message though. I'd be dealing with more follow-up if I just left a blank message and my number in their caller-ID log. Better to just deflect it now.

"Hi, it's Carl. I just needed to ask Blake something, but I guess he already left for school. Don't mind me."

I stood and went to pick up my bag. As my hand grasped the strap and tugged, I felt a sharp pain in my arm. I recoiled, staring at it blankly. My face grew hot as I realized what was happening. It was embarrassing, even if no one had witnessed my mistake.

Of course I couldn't lift it. I wasn't strong anymore. My brain hadn't registered the loss of my muscles yet, the return to my weaker, younger body. I was trying to pick up a bag stuffed with multiple textbooks, my laptop, school supplies, notebooks. I had to put a lot more effort into it than I was used to.

The heat in my face turned into frustrated rage. I didn't deserve this. I'd fought and bled for my accomplishments, for the power I'd gained.

I'd been thrust back into the pathetic life I'd gotten so far away from. I shouldn't be here. I don't belong here anymore.

My father was already gone for work. My mother was in the back-yard, weeding her garden. She'd left a lunch for me on the kitchen table. She waved at me through the window. I grabbed the brown paper bag and waved back, before turning to head out the door. I only had fifteen minutes to get to school now, and it was going to be a long jog.

Out the door, down the driveway, and onto the sidewalk. Suburbia was all around me, in all its bland glory. Garbage trucks billowed thick black smoke. A news chopper with heavy beating blades passed over-head. Hundreds of cars rumbled in the distance, filling the rush hour with their incessant moans. Every bit of noise annoyed me just a bit more. The few pleasant sounds, like the birds chirping and the wind rustling through the leaves that hadn't fallen yet, were drowned out by a man doing woodwork with a table saw in his garage, with the door wide open. I glared at him as I walked by, but he didn't look up. Blake, always proud of his own woodwork, would have given the man an earful over how much he was wasting.

Blake.

I'd been doing my best to avoid thinking about him. I'd voiced my vague hopes to Matt the night before, but I knew I still had to pre-pare myself mentally for the alternative. I didn't expect to see him any-time soon. He rode the bus from the far side of town every day, and I wouldn't likely see him until at least second period. Matt should run into him first, in first period. Matt would be able to coordinate him on the plan, and what we'd be doing next.

What was the plan, anyway? I hadn't gotten that far yet. I'd checked while pulling on my clothes that morning, but I hadn't gotten a response yet. Tonight I'd be able to do more digging, but the internet seemed to have failed me so far. The library would be my next stop. Something, somewhere, would have the answer for what had happened—and more importantly, how we could reverse it.

The walk to school was going more quickly than I expected, or wanted. Every turn and every street was still burned into my brain from the last few years I'd spent going to this stupid place.

As the school came into view, it became a symbol of everything I'd most hated about this world. My eyes scanned across the entire campus, taking in the sight once more. I thought I'd been rid of it forever. It had only been a nightmare, and even then it had faded completely over the years. To be confronted once more by the hell I'd escaped was almost overwhelming. If it wasn't for Blake, Jen, and Matt, waiting inside, I wouldn't have taken another step.

"Hey, Carl!"

I stiffened, but the voice wasn't unfamiliar. It was Kyle, someone I used to consider a friend. Someone I'd forgotten, and definitely not the first reunion I was expecting today. I turned to greet him, and was handed a large thick book—a *Dungeons & Dragons* manual.

"Sorry it took so long to get this back," said Kyle, panting. He'd apparently been sprinting to catch up with me. "Thanks. Having a hard copy was great for our session."

"Sure." I took off my backpack and slid it inside. It barely fit, but compared to some of the magic tomes I'd perused over the last seven years, it was practically a featherweight. Of course, with the arm strength I had now, it brought the weight on my shoulder to a threatening load. I'd have to ditch some of them when I got to my locker. I closed it up and kept walking.

Dungeons & Dragons. It seemed so . . . trite now. No amount of imagination and role-playing could possibly conjure up how terrifying a dragon was in reality. The searing heat of their breath, or the concussive bursts of wind with every wing flap. Awesome, in the most traditional sense of the word.

As for dungeons, I'd been in a few, and been the owner of a few more. They tended not to have any treasure, just the other notable T-words: torture, terror, and tyranny. Really not fun places to be. I avoided them whenever possible.

"You okay, man?" Kyle asked, falling in line beside me and jolting me out of my memories.

"What?"

"Nothin'. You're just usually way more talkative."

I didn't respond for a moment. Was I? I'd tried to build up such a completely different image in Cyraveil. I had to struggle to remember who I was. Talking was something I usually let advisers and servants take care of. Silence was an incredibly versatile tool as a leader, and I'd mastered it over the years. Matt's reminder crept back into my mind. We didn't know if we were safe yet. I had to maintain some level of normality. "How was the session?"

"Load of crap. They got bogged down in arguments over rules during a single fight. Took us hours just to get through it. But having the book on hand helped. It was way easier to flip between actual pages than scroll around on an e-book."

"Why not just open the e-book in multiple windows?"

"Because the software's a piece of shit and wouldn't let me?"

"You can override that, you know."

"You can?"

"Selnou."

Kyle stared at me. "Huh?"

Crap. Wrong language. I was used to talking with Jen. I'd slipped into the shorthand Etoline I'd picked up from her. "It's easy. I'll show you how sometime."

"Cool." Kyle glanced around, looking at the other gaggles of students heading in. The buses were pulling away already, and most of the kids who rode them were already inside. "Hey, you seen Blake anywhere?"

My throat tightened up. It took me a few seconds to pull it back together. "You know he rides the bus, right?"

"He does?"

"Yeah. He lives way out over on the other side of Mellbridge. Just off the exit ramp."

"Oh. Huh. I just assumed he lived near here. I always see him walking this way."

I shook my head. "He comes over to my place a lot."

"Ah."

We continued walking in silence for a bit. Kyle kept glancing around in random directions, like he was uncomfortable around me. It bothered me more than a little. We'd been friends for years, hadn't we?

But I'd changed. I wasn't me anymore. I'd gotten rid of that pathetic kid a long time ago. I'd replaced him with someone stronger. Someone worth being.

He reminded me of what I really needed to be doing. Who knew where my next clue might come from? No matter how unlikely, I had to pursue every possible avenue that came up.

"Hey, Kyle . . ." I started casually. "You know Cyraveil Park?"

"Yeah? What about it?" He didn't sound suspicious, but I could tell instantly. I'd interrogated a thousand people. I'd negotiated with the best diplomats and nobles in the country. It was all in his body language. The way his head subtly turned, how his eyes sped up just so. His posture slipped just a little, got defensive. He had something to hide, and he was terrible at it.

"You ever go down there at night?" I asked benignly.

"Uhh, why?"

"Just curious."

Kyle swallowed audibly. He glanced around again. "Yeah, sometimes."

Bingo. I was circling my opponent now, preparing to strike. Kyle was a pushover. He'd talk in seconds. I lowered my voice just slightly. *Imperious.* That was the tone, that's what Reynir called it. "Spill it, Kyle."

". . .You won't tell anyone, right?"

" 'Course not." What good would that do?

Embarrassment flared up in his face. "Me and Kersey sneak out there to . . . umm . . ."

Disappointment crashed into me like a mace. I'd hoped for

something more than that. Now I just had a stuttering lovestruck kid, with nothing useful to tell me.

"Ah." I clapped him on the shoulder. "Nice. She's pretty cute. Good for you."

I'd meant it genuinely, but I guess it came out condescending. Kyle became prickly. "Like you've done any better."

"Oh, you have no idea," I answered wistfully, remembering the woman in question.

Kyle rolled his eyes. "*Three-dimensional* females, dude."

"More three-D than you. Hair like a glowing hearth and more curves than a roller coaster." Also a killer with a spear and overwhelmingly racist, but he didn't need to know that.

"What was this imaginary beauty's name?"

"Aud Onundottir."

He raised an eyebrow. "Fantasizing about Viking women?"

I laughed. To be honest, I had no idea how the Cellmans ended up with so many Nordic-style names. It wasn't like they spoke anything besides English there (or as they referred to it, Linguen). It was one piece of their history I still wanted to uncover, probably buried in the pile of scrolls I'd taken from Reynir's cellars before I left, waiting under my estate in Candir. "Nah, I'm over her."

"Too odd for you?" Kyle grinned.

I sighed. "That pun got old years ago."

"Nice to see you're so loyal to your fantasy woman you stuck by her for years."

"Hey, when I commit, I commit." It was true, even if it did come back to bite me in the ass. Aud ended up leaving me, not the other way around. I was just grateful she hadn't decided to put her spear through my spine before she'd taken off. "But we got off topic. Kersey, eh?"

Kyle's expression twisted back into embarrassment fast. "Yeah."

I couldn't really remember the girl besides just her looks, but that wasn't any reason I couldn't be supportive. Kyle could use the boost. "She seems great for you. Congratulations."

"Thanks, I guess?"

"You guys had sex yet?"

I didn't think his face could get more red, but he proved me wrong. ". . . The hell, Carl?"

"What?"

Kyle shook his head. "Never mind." He looked up as the five-minute bell rang. "Shit. I needed to get to class early today. See ya." He sped off and passed through the front doors in a hurry, leaving me alone again.

Oh, right. I was part of the collective of nervous virgins again. I wasn't supposed to be this confident or self-assured. To Kyle, I must have sounded like a completely different person at the end there.

Still, it went better than I'd expected. Maybe I *could* pick up right where I left off, without anybody noticing. I'd keep it cool at least until we figured out how to get back. I reached into the bag slung over my shoulder, thumbing through books and papers. I'd left everything in there the night before, ready for the next day. I was eternally grateful to my past self for the foresight, as I wouldn't have had a clue what to bring today. Between that and my (admittedly vague) recollection of what classes I was taking seven years ago, I was reasonably confident I could bullshit my way through at least a few days of classes—just long enough for us to leave, I hoped.

I walked through the front door, and realized that was a ridiculous notion. Where the two wings of the school met, classrooms lined both sides, with only a room number to provide me any information. Every single one of them looked exactly the same to me.

I had absolutely no idea where my first class was.

CHAPTER 3

JEN

"Long day, West?"

"This shit was awful. Give me good news, Portman. What's the verdict?"

"We'll be taking the Svartholm case."

". . . Goddamnit. Do we have anything to go on, at least?"

"Not yet. The first twenty-four hours are the most important in an abduction though. We should get going."

"You think it was a kidnapping?"

"We can't rule out anything yet."

Thank every single star in the sky and the realms beyond for texting. No, seriously, text messages on cell phones are the bomb. Might seem obvious to *you*, but being able to talk silently and quickly, and without all that mess of face-to-face expressions and emotions? That can be really wonderful sometimes.

More to the point, it's all recorded.

I spent the entire morning combing through old text messages one-handed, while I chowed through a few pieces of toast. Sure, I still remembered (most of) my friends. I was never like Matt; I actually *liked* talking to people around me. But it was good to center my memory on where everything was at right now. Kersey was going through her "I hate all men" phase, Jane was going out with Steve, who Kari had a crush on (not that I'd ever tell him). Mitch's band was breaking up over some stupid fight. My best friend, Sara, had been texting me all night and even now about some guy she met, and Aivallei Syldarei was getting married to—

Wait. That one didn't fit. Aivallei didn't go to my high school. For one, she was something like eighty years too old. Even if she still looked gorgeous. She insisted I was prettier, but we all knew that was an outright lie. I couldn't possibly measure up to a Sylf princess. I couldn't even measure up to half the girls in my grade. Pity she had to marry such a slob, but hey, nobody ever said political marriages were easy.

But that wasn't my business anymore.

"Hey, Jen," my brother's voice echoed from the front hallway.

"Dov?"

"I'm heading out early. Can you wake Mom up?" I could hear him slipping on his shoes, squeaking against the wooden floor by the door.

"Okay. What's up?"

"Told someone I'd meet up with them before school today."

"Oooh, got a girlfriend?" I teased, still scrolling through my old texts.

"None of your business."

"Aww," I pouted. I got up and leaned around the corner to give him a look. "Won't you tell me, duralav-hila?"

"Nope."

"You know that means you *do*, right? You're just making it obvious," I snickered.

"If you say so. And, Jen?"

"What?"

Matt stood up straight, bundled up in his favorite jacket and with a backpack slung over his shoulder. He reached forward and pulled me into a hug. I stiffened, discomfort quickly rising. I pushed it away, even as the nausea clawed up through my chest, urging me to free myself from his arms. I consciously reminded myself he was just trying to be comforting and kind—that he was my brother, that he would never hurt me, that he was on my side—but the feelings remained. Not that I could ever tell him.

I leaned into his hug, putting my arms awkwardly around him in return. After a few seconds, he let go, and my anxiety slowly ebbed away.

"You know I never stopped looking for you, right?"

"Selnou," I whispered.

He smiled, but it was in a sad, lonely way. It echoed my own feelings so exactly, I almost burst into tears on the spot. I'd gotten pretty good at hiding my emotions though, a vital tool of my profession. Emotions weren't coming anywhere near my face. For now.

"Remember," Matt intoned in his calm and careful voice, "Etoline doesn't exist here either. I know it's harder for you, but stick to English, yeah?"

I nodded. He opened the door and stepped outside, the world beyond waiting for us both to finally reemerge after so many years gone. "Don't forget about Mom!" he called as he reached the sidewalk and vanished around the fence border.

He was right: it *was* harder for me. Let me be clear, I don't mean that resentfully in any way. But after all those years, Linguen just didn't feel like my native tongue anymore. Being surrounded by this now foreign language was the weirdest feeling after being plunged back into this world.

Yeah, I could *understand* things written down, words people said, whatever. Mostly, anyway. But I hadn't spoken it much in nearly seven years. I had a harder time getting to the meaning sometimes. Linguen might have been my childhood language, but Etoline was the language of my heart—and more importantly, my brain. Even now, I was mentally translating those text messages into Etoline. It was just automatic.

Nothing like getting dropped into a place where not only does no one speak the same language as you, but where they're actively hostile to Linguen. It was like the worst immersion learning possible. Or the best, I guess, since I did learn pretty quickly. I had a good teacher. Linguen disappeared for me practically overnight and didn't return for a very long time.

You should have seen my first interpreting session between the Sylves and the rebellion reps. That was a hoot. First time I'd spoken or even *heard* Linguen in nearly six years.

It didn't end well.

My phone buzzed again, bringing me back to reality. If I didn't get a move on, I might end up late. I hurried upstairs to my mother's room, pressing my ear to the door. No sounds. She must still be asleep. Ugh.

I rapped on the door with my knuckles lightly.

"Mom?"

"Nnnnngh."

I rolled my eyes. "Mom, you gotta get up."

"Wha' time's it?"

"Time for breakfast. Come on." I smelled coffee beginning to waft up the stairs, and wrinkled my nose. I'd never liked coffee, and even less so now. It messed with my head too much. "I'm coming in, okay?"

I pushed the door open, with more force than I'd intended. It swung wide and bounced off the wall audibly. My mother twisted around under the covers, raising a hand to shield her eyes from the sunlight that streamed in behind me.

"Jenny, let me sleep."

I brushed aside my irritation at the wrong name. I'd been called much worse. "Mom, if I do that, you'll sleep past work. Come on."

"What?"

I sat down next to her and helped her sit up. She leaned heavily on my shoulder, blinking through the fatigue. "Did you forget to set your alarm again?" The question bounced through my mouth unbidden, but it felt instantly familiar. It was a weird feeling, like I was acting out a play I'd performed a hundred times, but never read the script for. I just knew what was supposed to come next, although I was playing the part normally meant for my brother.

"All right," she said, her eyes finally opening properly. "Go on, let me get dressed at least."

"Nuh-uh. Up you get." I took an arm over my shoulders and helped lift her out of bed. She wobbled slightly, but steadied herself quickly enough. Now that she was standing, she was way less likely to fall back asleep. "Look on the bright side. You only have to go to one job today, right?"

". . . Yeah." She smiled. "Go on then. I'm up."

"I'm going to heat up your breakfast. If you want it warm, you'd better be down soon." I went back downstairs and found the plate Matt had prepared, and tossed it in the microwave.

By the way, microwaves? Pretty awesome. Even if they usually made food taste worse, convenience trumps that—a lot.

Refrigerators too. I'd learned how to live without one, how to preserve meat and live off the land, but hell if I wasn't about to use one now.

I heard my mom thump down, down the stairs just as the microwave dinged. I pulled the plate out and set it at the table for her with silverware. I was weirdly proud that I remembered where the silverware drawer was. It made me feel comfortable and warm inside. The little successes were adding up, okay? I was feeling almost like I was back at home, so much so that I forgot what planet I was on.

"Vei pol nara susvyla ta nara bylar, selaval," I said, gathering up my own dishes and rinsing them in the sink.

"Huh?"

I glanced up to see my mother looking *very* confused. Whoops. I mentally slapped myself a dozen times. Linguen—err, *English,* dammit.

"I'm just practicing. Your food's on the table." I gestured toward the steam rising from her food. It was bothering me that I couldn't remember the Linguen name of her meal. I could give its Etoline name (kelbasal, for anyone playing along at home), but that didn't really help much. I began pouring her coffee into a mug as she sat down and dug in. I set the mug next to her and gave her a peck on the cheek.

"I didn't know you were taking a foreign language," she said, picking up the newspaper Matt had left. Having now dealt with a lot of high-level politics myself, I suddenly found Matt's habit of keeping up with the world at large a lot less strange.

"Well, why not? Might be useful." To my undying relief, she didn't ask what language, just returned to her food. I pulled my bag off the table and onto my back. It felt balanced, but it didn't hold a candle to the quiver I usually wore around my shoulder. The quiver had been a light but remarkably sturdy material, hand-made by Tethevallen Syl-nanden for my twenty-first birthday.

My throat choked up a bit. My heart sank at the memory bubbling up to the surface. I missed him dearly.

"Are you okay?" Mom's voice punched through the veil that had suddenly fallen over my eyes. I looked at her with a smile at the ready.

"Of course," I replied, very deliberately in Linguen this time.

"You've been acting weird."

"You're just tired. I'll see you tonight, okay? Matt's making dinner."

Mom perked up at that. Matt was definitely the best cook in the family, plus it saved us a bunch of money. He managed to make even the cheapest ingredients taste pretty great, and he'd picked up a lot of new tricks while hiding from the Cellman legions. I was looking for-ward to that grocery trip after school, weird as that might sound. It'd help me out in more ways than one.

"I gotta go now. You good?"

"I'm fine, Jenny. Have a good day at school." She threw me a little wave, before returning to her kelbasal.

I gave her my best smile, then pulled on a dark coat and headed out the door.

The world opened up around me, and it was good to see the sky again (even if it was mostly covered by layers of puffy gray clouds, rolling steadily in with an angry look that predicted an imminent downpour), but all of that was completely ignored in favor of the girl waiting impatiently on the sidewalk. Her name was Sara, and she was my best friend in this world.

She was also the reason my phone hadn't stopped buzzing all morning.

"Jenny, what took you so long?" she called out. I practically skipped my way down the sidewalk. I was so happy to see her I almost glazed over the fact she'd called me Jenny.

Sidebar: I stopped going by Jenny a long time ago. In the other world, anyway. And if you're wondering if I used some fancy Etoline name, the answer's no. Tethevallen translated my last name directly for royal meetings and formal occasions, but mostly I just went by Jen. For one, it sounded cooler, but really it just felt more like me. Stronger, I guess? I dunno, it's just how I felt. Sorry I can't give some sort of profound explanation that digs into my identity or soul or whatever. I used to be Jenny, now I'm Jen. It was a thing.

I decided I might as well start trying to change that now. I *really* didn't like Jenny.

"Hi, Sara." We started walking toward school, which was only a few blocks away. Because our house was so close, my friends usually gathered here whenever we decided to walk together. Normally, there were at least three or four of us, but today it seemed like it was just Sara. I was a little glad. I was worried about dealing with too many people at once right now. I wanted to ease back in, so to speak. "This is gonna sound weird, but can you call me Jen?"

"Uhh, okay?"

"I dunno, I just feel like Jen now."

Sara looked at me funny. "Did you have an epiphany overnight?"

"Sure." I wasn't quite sure what "epiphany" meant, but I figured it'd do.

"All right. Jen." She nodded. "Okay, remember how I've been hanging out with a guy online?"

"Yeah?"

"Well, he's pretty cool. I talked to him a few times in person too, if you're wondering, so this isn't a chat room romance or anything. Anyway, I was thinking about asking him out, 'cause I don't think he's ever going to ask me."

My eyes were glazing over just a little. I only vaguely understood what she meant by "chat room romance." I felt so tired from everything I'd just been through, and my mind was wandering away to memories of nights in the deep woods. Sitting around the fire wrapped in furs, watching a blanket of stars envelope the sky, listening to Ruvalei play us a gentle tune as we drifted off to sleep.

"—your permission, because it's your brother."

I snapped back into reality. There was no way I'd just heard her right. "Dov?"

"Huh?"

Dammit, not again. "You want to go out with my brother?"

"Yeah." Sara bit her lip nervously, waiting for my reply.

I pondered for a minute. I understood why she was asking me, since my brother and I had always been pretty close, even before all of this. We'd grown up taking care of each other, since Mom didn't have a whole lot of time, and we became pretty protective of each other. More than once, I'm pretty sure I deliberately got in the way of people trying to hang out with my brother, if I thought they were a threat or something. Now it all just seemed so silly. He was plenty capable of making his own decisions and taking care of himself. I'd seen that firsthand.

"That's up to you," I replied. "I'm just a bystander."

"You sure?"

"I'm sure." I affixed a smile to my face that felt entirely too fake. "Just as long as nothing changes between us, right?"

"Right." Sara smiled too. Hers looked genuine.

I wasn't lying to her—well, not *entirely*. She and Matt could be totally happy together. Who knows? They didn't seem like a *bad* couple. What really bothered me though, besides all the other crap on my mind, was that she'd never told me. Sara and I didn't keep secrets from each other. That was our thing.

Except . . . she *had* kept a secret, and now I had a massive secret of my own. What a way to start my human life back up again. I couldn't deal with this yet. I had plenty of other concerns to deal with once school started, as Sara was about to demonstrate.

She'd just said something I didn't comprehend at all. I knew every word, and it wasn't exactly a long sentence, but the meaning was completely lost to me. I felt panic rising in my chest, sending shivers through my limbs. I tried to steady myself mentally. Maybe I hadn't been listening close enough.

"Sorry, what?"

She repeated herself, a little slower. I listened carefully. It didn't help one bit. My brain struggled to process the words into something, fatigued as I was.

Full confession: I didn't actually sleep last night. Might have dozed off a couple of times, but I was too scared to actually let myself fall asleep. Between that and the hectic events of the past few days (weeks, really), I was seriously running on empty.

I desperately tried to decipher Sara's words. Context didn't help at all; she was switching topics. How much of it was idiom, and how much was literal? It wasn't a question. Maybe I could just brush it off. No . . . Sara was waiting for an answer.

"Sure," I ventured hopefully.

"Do you need help with it?"

Crap. Crap, crap, *crap*. What did *that* mean? I was too afraid to answer incorrectly. That question could go *anywhere*. I wracked my brain, but the best I could come up with was that she was talking about something to do with technology. Computers, probably. I never used them much in the first place. That was her thing.

"Hello?" Sara waved a hand in front of my eyes.

"*Vack,*" I swore under my breath. "Vackal daphut vack." My face was heating up. I suppressed it with every ounce of will I could muster. I wasn't about to look embarrassed, not right now. I might have felt it, but damned if I was going to look so stupid in front of my best friend.

Not that I had any other options at this point. I sighed.

"Look, this is gonna sound weird again . . . but I have no idea what you just said."

Sara raised an eyebrow. "Uhh, what? And why are you talking like that?"

I realized I had stopped trying to correct my accent. Sara was way too attentive. Usually something I loved about her, but right now it was *really* problematic. I tried to affect the more plain Pacific Northwest speech again. "Don't make fun, okay?"

"I'm not," Sara replied. "But we were just talking about this yesterday, and the day before . . ." She trailed off.

". . . Can you keep a secret?" No, I'm not about to tell her. Don't be stupid. But I had to come up with something.

"Of course." Sara leaned close, expectant.

"I'm not so great with memory right now. Forgetting little things a lot." Sara looked *really* concerned now. "Don't worry, I'm fine. I went to the healers; they checked me out. Nothing wrong with me." I might not have been lying earlier, but I can do the deception game when I have to. Like I said, former diplomat.

"Healers?" Sara pointed out dryly.

"Like I said, forgetting things." And looking like an idiot while I did. Doctors. That's the word. Doctors, nurses, surgery, hospitals. Ambulances and 911. Not healers and rituals and magic. "So anyway, what were you saying?"

"Your laptop. You know, your computer?"

"Right, what about it? You said something about sound and broken records?"

Sara shook her head. "What on earth happened to you? Did you have an aneurysm or something?"

"Assume yes, okay?" If I weren't feeling so awful, I'd have laughed at her choice of words. This definitely didn't happen on Earth.

"Fine, whatever." She took a deep breath. "What I said was: I'm sorry if I'm repeating myself a lot, but uhh . . . you need to improve your laptop's . . . protection." She sighed. "Did you get that?"

"Yes." I winced. I felt like I was being spoon-fed by her. It was mortifying. But I had no idea what a record was, or a laptop until she'd just explained it a moment ago. And "firewall" meant something *very* different in my book. More literal-wall-of-flames. I looked away as my face turned bright red. I felt a hand on my shoulder. Sara was taller than me, which only added to the effect. She was older, taller, smarter, everything-er.

I was just . . . inferior.

"Jen, are you okay? Seriously?"

I nodded. "Yeah, I'll be fine." I put a smile back on my face, and turned around to meet her concerned expression. "Just feeling wonky today."

Sara frowned. "Text me if anything else happens, okay? I'll see you at lunch?"

"Yeah. Wait, no."

"No?"

"I promised Matt I'd have lunch with him today. He needed to talk about something."

"Oh." Sara looked relieved. "Okay, that's fine."

A car buzzed by us, breaking up the conversation for a moment. It startled me—the first moving car I'd seen in nearly a decade. I managed to hide my surprise, thankfully, or else Sara would have probably gone to full emergency mode.

"Hey, Sara," I added quietly. "Don't mention any of this to Matt?"

Now she looked even more worried. "Jenny, what's going on?"

"Promise me, all right?"

"I promise." I could tell she meant it. Good old Sara, always reliable. I felt a rush of affection for my best friend.

I'd missed her a lot too.

"I'll see you in journalism," I said, trying to reassure her.

"Okay." I wasn't sure if it had worked, but she looked a bit better now. Meanwhile, I just felt awful. I felt guilty hiding myself from my best friend. Maybe Sara ought to know at least a few things. I couldn't possibly tell her *everything*, even if I wanted to—but if she just knew a few details, it might make our lives a whole lot easier. I was sure I could get her to believe me.

I just had to get Matt to agree.

After that long detour of head-pounding panic, our conversation reverted to safer topics. Things I had a way better handle on. By the time we reached the school, I was back to my normal self. Or as close as I could be, anyway.

I waved goodbye to Sara, who had a class on the opposite end of the school. My first class, something-something-algebra, was only a few steps inside. Funny how I couldn't remember the name of the class, the teacher, or more than two fellow students, but I knew exactly what room it was in and where it landed in my schedule.

Things you appreciate when you aren't very comfortable with a language: Math is pretty much universal. Different symbols, but everything else carries over. I could breeze through this class without a sweat. Meanwhile, as more Linguen filtered through my brain from snatches of conversation around me, the memory of the language flowed back in as well. It still didn't feel *right*, but at least I wasn't going to look like an idiot again, as I had in front of Sara.

I'm not a huge math nerd or anything, but I don't have trouble with it. And with the day I was having so far, it was almost relaxing to deal solely with symbols and logic puzzles. Of course, my satisfaction only lasted a few minutes before I remembered this was still work, and I was still stuck in a class full of people I mostly didn't care for. The class seemed to drag on forever after that. I probably fell asleep three or four times, little micro-naps that nobody noticed. Coming out of the last one though, I was instantly awake again.

My vision seemed to flash slightly, and suddenly everyone looked . . . different. I couldn't say why. Nothing had changed. Physically, everybody was exactly the same as the moment before. But everyone seemed just a little off-putting. Hostile, even.

Their faces were blank masks. They could be hiding anything. Planning anything. They outnumbered me twenty to one. They could take me, if they wanted.

My chair was up against one of the walls. I turned slowly, as subtly as I could manage, orienting myself toward the crowd.

If one of them made a move, I was ready.

I might not be armed, but I knew dozens of ways to escape a hold, or quickly knock down someone larger than me, and I felt confident I could outrun most of them.

They wouldn't ever take me again.

What the hell am I doing?

The moment passed. Nobody in the room was looking at me. No one had any designs on me. My mind was playing tricks. Relief ebbed back into my brain, but it was still tinged with lingering dread. I'd been completely gone for a minute, sunk back into the corner of my mind where I'd never wanted to go again.

The moment the bell rang, I was out the door. Second period was journalism; that one I remembered for sure. Again, not a huge journalism nerd, but this class had a lot of my friends—and most importantly, Sara was there. Friendly faces. I needed some friendly faces. People I could relate to, of my own age.

Relatively speaking. Naeflin was way older than me by any sane measurement. But that didn't matter right now. She was a world away, and I had to get to the journalism room.

The crowd of students pouring into the hallway formed a teeming maze, seemingly impossible to navigate. I hugged the wall, avoiding the main body and sticking near the banks of lockers on the edges. It meant running into more individual students, but I could get around them more easily than trying to move through the constantly shifting pattern in the center of the hall.

Why was this suddenly so difficult for me?

Oh, right. I haven't been to high school in over seven years and I'm suddenly in the body of a sixteen-year-old again. That sort of thing would probably throw anyone off balance. Literally, actually. More than once. My brain expected me to be just a little bit taller, a little bit stronger. I'd nearly tripped over my feet a few times, which was deeply unsettling for a Sylf-trained huntress like me.

There. The doorway to the journalism room was in reach. I was inside, and in the corner we usually hung out in, long before the class bell rang. Consequently, I was one of the only people in there. A few of the normal early-comers shot me odd looks, but I was mostly left alone. We were a tight-knit group back here, the ace reporters, the cream of the crop. Or something like that.

Let's be real. It was high school journalism. We mostly just hung out and screwed around.

I felt exhausted from my trek across the school to get here. Not physically exhausted, apart from lack of sleep; I might not be in peak shape anymore, but sixteen-year-old me still kept herself fit. I was mentally drained. I closed my eyes and laid my head down on the countertop, carefully orienting myself so the corner was behind me. I could still pick out the sounds in the room, the slight currents in the air from people moving around.

At least that hadn't been taken from me. I'd trained myself to pick up every clue I could, from every sense my body had. I could keep a perfect mental picture of the room and everyone in it, and even keep it up to date with my eyes closed. It was very, very hard to sneak up on me—as Sara was about to find out.

"Shasi, vis hila," I said, throwing my hand up to catch hers. She'd been about to tap me on the shoulder to wake me up. "What do you totev dou to tolal? Dov litev dou seddeka evel naland vei."

I opened my eyes, grinning. I expected to see her frustrated, maybe make fun of her a bit before we got back to class, but all I got was confusion. In my sleep-deprived state, it took me a few seconds to realize I'd dropped the ball on Linguen again.

"My turn, I guess," she said slowly. "I have *no* idea what you just said." Sara's worried expression from the morning crept back into place, like an annoying pest that just wouldn't leave us alone.

Not that I think Sara's annoying. That was poorly worded. I just really wasn't doing well in general.

"Oh, uhh . . ." I scrambled around for a moment, picking the first thing I could come up with that sounded halfway believable. "It's a fake language I made up."

"Huh," Sara replied, clearly unconvinced. I flinched. My best friend was not having it. I really, really didn't want to lie to her.

Matt would understand. I hoped.

I sighed, mostly to myself, and took a deep breath. "Okay, Sara. Look. Something did happen. I can't tell you what. Not yet."

Sara raised an eyebrow, as the final bell rang and students started to filter in. She glanced toward the classroom door. I could tell we both had the same thought. The other two members of our little group in this class would arrive soon. I liked them both plenty, but Sara was my best friend. *That* sort of friend, you know? The only person I could even *consider* telling my story to.

"I assume you've got a good reason?" she asked quietly, edging closer so we wouldn't be overheard.

"I promise I'll tell you. I just can't yet."

"Are you okay though?"

"Yeah," I replied. I took a few seconds before I spoke again. I had to compose exactly what I wanted to say in Linguen, make sure I got everything across. "Honestly, I'm fine. Not dying or anything, and I'm not in any trouble. But my head's gonna be in a weird place for a while. I'm having trouble remembering a lot of things. I'm sorry to dump all this on you, but I'm going to need a lot of help for a bit, and you're the only one I can really trust."

I waited, impatient, as she appeared to consider my words. Her face was an unreadable mask. I was never that great at reading *other* people, I was just good at hiding my own emotions. Finally, she spoke up again.

"Okay." She nodded. "I believe you. But I do want that explanation."

"I promised, didn't I?"

"Still waiting on that pony you promised," she added with a forced giggle. It worked though, despite being an ancient joke that neither of us even thought was funny at the time. I started to laugh too, and soon we were both doubled over even as Kersey and Mirai showed up, eager to hear a joke neither of us could explain.

But finally, things were starting to feel normal again. We settled into class, and broke into groups, and everything was going okay. Kersey and Mirai were still calling me Jenny though.

I'd have to fix that.

It wasn't long before I started feeling it again. Discomfort, and the inklings of adrenaline pumping into my system. I felt like I was getting overwhelmed by something I couldn't actually see. There were too many unfamiliar faces in the room. They shouldn't have been unfamiliar. Seven years ago I would have known the name and face of every single person here. Today . . . they may as well be complete strangers.

This time, though, I had an out.

I poked Sara. "Hey. Let's go out for a walk?"

"Sure."

Two minutes later, we were wandering the grounds behind the school, supposedly to go interview a staff member with a free period right now—but really just to get outside for a while. Press passes, aren't they the best?

Even better, I didn't have to explain it to Sara. This was totally normal. We used this excuse to head out all the time. We were talking about nothing in particular, joking and laughing like usual. Luckily, the rain I'd expected had already rolled right on by. Patches of sunlight swam across the well-kept rain-soaked lawn, growing larger as the clouds were swept away. A few birds were swirling above the trees at the end of the field. It looked like it might be a beautiful day after all.

I was so busy watching the sky as we walked that as we rounded the corner behind the portable classrooms, I almost missed Carl, sitting in the shadows with his face in his hands.

CHAPTER 4

CARL

"Clark, man. Callin' me West makes me feel like I'm fifty years old."
"Right. Well, have you ever done an abduction, Clark?"
"No, but I sure as hell know some kids who deserve it."
"I meant—"
"Yeah, no, never landed a kidnapping case. This'll be my first."

The fields were much better. The school was way too squeaky-clean. Even if this was too even, too maintained—it was still *nature*. The clouds loomed ominously in the distance, but I figured I'd have plenty of warning if the rain picked up.

I was lounging behind one of the portable classrooms situated around the back half of the school campus. The classroom made a nice L shape, which blocked me from view in every direction from the main school building. The only window in the classroom faced away from me, high enough on the wall that someone would have to deliberately look down toward my corner to spot me. I didn't think that likely for any teacher, and what student would bother to report a loner kid hanging out?

With my luck, I'd probably get that one stickler kid. Or even worse, it'd be Matt, and then I'd *really* be in for it. Normally, I'd never take that crap from him . . . but I couldn't take Matt on anymore.

At least I had the internet again. I had one of the first phones with an actual 4G connection available on the US market, with speeds that blazed circles around everything else. It sucked compared to my home connection, obviously, but it was way, way better than the school's shitty wi-fi. I was checking through the forum posts I made last night. It was obsessive and unnecessary, as I well knew. I'd double-checked them this morning. Here I was, just an hour or two later, trying it again. I doubted I'd get any responses even by tonight. Most of these boards were sinking ships by now.

At the same time, I had my private IRC logged in and running too. Kyle and a few others were signed on . . . as was Blake. That didn't mean anything though; he always left himself logged in. I'd bugged him about it a few times. He'd been marked away automatically by my bot days ago—after the last time he'd sent a message. I scrolled back through the log, but there wasn't anything I didn't at least vaguely remember. Then it hit me.

One of the logged-in users was Jacob. Jacob was in the same class as Blake right now, unless I was remembering wrong.

I opened a private message with him and started poking him for a reply. Nothing came back. I waited anxiously, watching the cursor flick on and off in the text box as if I were hypnotized. The screen stubbornly refused to print a new line.

"Dov lavack?"

Her voice was way closer than I'd have expected. Startled, I brought my hand up in a defensive posture instantly, but I needn't have worried. There was only one person on this entire planet who'd be cursing in Etoline.

There she was, standing just slightly askew on the balls of her feet. She was ready to move in an instant. Her eyes were alert and burning with intensity. If I closed my eyes, I could picture the first day I saw her clad in hand-crafted elven clothes, quiver over her shoulder, stumbling her way through broken English like she'd just immigrated from overseas. She could barely make herself understood—but at the same time, I could tell how graceful and powerful she was. Even now, seeing her as she'd been so many years ago, I could still see the fierce, brave hunter hiding inside.

Her hand was clapped over her mouth, as if she'd said something wrong. I thought that weirdly out of character, since Jen had never been reluctant with the more colorful parts of the elven lexicon—but then I noticed her friend a few steps to the side, looking very concerned.

"Hi," I greeted her awkwardly, shifting back to relaxed again.

"Carl, why are you out here?" asked Jen. She seemed to be calming down quickly enough.

"Felt like a walk. You?" I was too embarrassed to admit the truth— that I couldn't find one measly classroom of mine. In response, she pulled out a laminated piece of paper from her pocket, showing me the press pass.

I smirked. "Ahh, shirking class. Nice."

Jen rolled her eyes.

Her friend finally spoke up. I struggled to remember if I'd ever met her before. My instincts leaned toward no. "Jen, you know this guy?"

"Uhh, yeah. This is Carl. Carl, Sara." Jen gestured to each of us in turn.

"*The* Sara?" I interjected.

"What does *that* mean?" Sara asked pointedly. Jen looked confused as well.

Shit. I hadn't gotten the whole story. Back in the first year or two, before we'd gone our separate ways, Matt used to go on for hours about Sara, a girl he'd had a crush on. Whenever girls came up in a conversation between us guys, Blake and I would talk the whole field, but Matt only had eyes for her. He'd just been too uncertain to ask her out when he had the chance, and (this being the old Matt) I'd called him out for it. I hadn't realized she was Jen's friend. Suddenly, his reluctance made a lot more sense.

This was getting tricky.

"Nothing," I said quickly. "Never mind."

"Nuh-uh," said Jen. "You don't get out of it that easily." She lowered her voice a little, enough that it wouldn't carry, and leaned in so Sara wouldn't hear. *"Tol la nalv tola ta Cyraveil?"*

My Etoline was never that great. I struggled with learning the wider vocabulary, and I was too busy to study it in detail, when there were so many more interesting things I could be doing. When I spoke it, I always felt like I sounded ridiculous. Anyone who wasn't an elf sounded stupid trying to speak it, in fact. There was a windlike quality to it that just couldn't be taught, the way the sounds moved through a sentence. I could never grasp it.

Jen was a natural. As far as I knew, she was the only human to ever become fluent in Etoline. She sounded so perfect, and every time she used the language it tickled my ears with joy. Jen had spaced out the words a bit so I could more easily understand them, but normally it flowed like a river through the woods. She'd once tried to explain to me how it connected to the wind and the trees and something-or-other nature nonsense. I didn't really pay attention—until she started to sing.

I cannot possibly describe what it was like to hear Jen sing in Etoline. "Transcendent" is probably the best word we've got for it in English. I could have died happy right then, if not for the fact that I never wanted the song to end.

Jen's expectant stare pulled me back out from reminiscing. Oh, right. She'd asked me a question. I glanced pointedly at Sara, still watching the two of us curiously. Jen sighed, and turned to her friend. "Hey, Sara. Can you give us a minute?"

"What's up?"

"Remember what I was telling you?" That brought me a shock. What the *hell* was Jen up to? Behind our backs? She might not have been a part of society nearly as long as the three of us . . . but still.

Sara nodded. "You owe me big here, Jenny."

"Jen," both Jen and I corrected automatically.

Sara frowned, but turned and walked a few paces away, keeping watch around the corner for any students or teachers. A good friend, it seemed. Jen came and sat down next to me, smoothing out the grass. She leaned back against the portable wall and closed her eyes. Her mouth twisted into a frown.

"So what was that about?" she asked, eyes still closed.

I hesitated. "I don't know if I'm supposed to tell you."

Jen cracked an eye open, giving me a death glare. "Do I gotta remind you what I can do to you with just my pinky?"

I laughed, but there was a kernel of truth to what she said. I'd seen what Jen could do. Not with her pinky, but still. She'd earned those titles slapped onto her name. They weren't just for show.

". . . Matt had a massive crush on her. I assume it's her, anyway."

She looked genuinely surprised. "He *told* you?"

I shrugged. "In that first year, we had a lot of long nights stuck in barn hay lofts or stables. We didn't have a whole lot to do. Blake and I got it out of him, and after that, he just wouldn't shut up about her. You know how he loves his speeches. The description matches up, so I'm pretty sure that's the right Sara. She was always the one for him, at least for the first couple of years."

"Oh," Jen answered noncommittally. There was a troubled look haunting her expression, but I couldn't be sure what caused it. She closed her eyes again, slouching a bit. She looked like she was exhausted beyond belief.

"*To dou valensel?*" I asked tentatively.

"Ugh, no. Well, yes, I'm okay, but stop that. Sorry," Jen added, rubbing at her temples. "English, please. I'm having a hard enough time remembering to use it already. *Ala dou daendalasas valensyl masadalel, snekkiva litashav.*"

". . . So's your mother."

She giggled. "You don't have a clue what I said, do you?"

"Something-something squirrel brain?"

"Glad you picked up on the insult. Wouldn't want it to go to waste." She yawned, leaning against the corner of the building. "What's up with the migraines, anyway?"

"Consequences of magic?" I ventured.

"Doesn't usually feel like that."

"You're the expert."

Jen must have noticed a tinge of regret in my response, as her eyes reopened. "I'm sure you would've felt it someday," she said quietly.

"I dunno."

I looked up at the sky, watching a bird fly down and land on the rooftop near us. The clouds had rolled away, leaving an empty expanse of blue above us, hiding the endless void of space. I picked off a blade of grass and threw it at the bird. It caught the air almost instantly and fell to the ground, defeated. The bird cocked its head, as if it were mocking me. If we were still in Cyraveil, it probably *would* have been, as the eyes of an elf magician.

If we were still in Cyraveil, it would have had an arrow through it a second later. Couldn't take any chances. But we weren't, and that meant I probably wouldn't ever get to learn magic. "I couldn't even acquire a single *etolen* . . ."

"*Etolendei,*" she filled in. "And that was the problem, you know. You thought of it like you were taking something. Like there were single pieces of spells you could just pick up out of the blue."

"I've heard this lecture," I muttered.

Jen's eyes slid shut again, the frown returning to her face. "I wasn't the best teacher."

No, that's not what I wanted. I never wanted Jen to feel sad. I instantly regretted my words. I had to walk it back somehow. "You were a fine teacher; I was a terrible student."

"My one and only student never learned a thing," Jen pointed out, laughing. "Nice try though."

"Eh," I said. "Maybe I just wasn't meant to learn magic."

"*Anandelv sed anlev etola,*" Jen intoned.

"I think I've heard that one before," I said sarcastically. It was Jen's turn to pick up a few blades of grass. Hers found their way right into my face, of course, and right at the moment my mouth was open. I spluttered, spitting grass and dirt from my lips.

"Thanks." I barely heard her whisper, just above a gust of wind that rolled through. We sat silently for a few moments, just enjoying the sunlight and the light breeze.

Jen opened her eyes again, glancing skyward. "It's almost midday."

"Yeah," I agreed, looking up. It took me a moment to remember the significance. "Right! Your . . . uhh . . . what was it called again?"

"Something else you can't pronounce." Jen smoothed out a patch of grass in front of her, then knelt on her knees. "Do me a favor?"

"Go away?"

She smiled. "Sorry. It'd normally be fine, but I'm exhausted, and I really need this right now. A little privacy would probably help me concentrate better."

"But . . ." I started to ask the obvious question, but Jen cut me off.

"No, I have no clue if it'll still work. I haven't had a chance to try it yet, obviously." Jen looked determined, anxious, a little annoyed. I was worried for her, but I had to step aside and let her work through it. Good or ill, she had to give her ritual a try.

"Before you do," I interrupted. She opened one eye, having just begun to raise her arms to the starting position. "Sara's still here, you know."

"Oh!" Jen looked like she'd honestly forgotten. I peered at her more closely, and realized just how debilitated she really was. Her eyes were reddened and drooping, and her entire posture seemed drained and subdued. Had she even slept last night?

"What did you tell her?"

"Just that something happened. And that I couldn't say anything else." Jen bit her lip, opening both eyes to look at me.

I sighed. "Matt's gonna give you hell for that."

"I know," she said nervously. "He'll understand though, right?"

I didn't answer. Both Jen and I were thinking about the same event. Matt could become a pretty scary guy when his orders weren't followed. Yeah, he usually had the best plan, and sometimes it was necessary for him to shout his men down—but still. It was a far cry from the guy who just took everything for granted and never liked to get involved in anything serious. I can't believe it took more than a year before I finally ditched him.

"I'll go hang out with Sara then," I added awkwardly, after a few moments of silence. I stood up and walked away to join Sara, who was leaning against the far corner of the portable. She'd been watching kids running around the track for gym class, eyes glazed over.

Sara was a pretty good-looking girl. Blond, tall, all the right curves. I could see why Matt had obsessed over her for so long. She'd been the only girl in his life before we'd left, to hear him tell it. Kind of strange I'd never met or seen her once though. His little sister's best friend too (so I assumed), and she had no clue? Weird relationship, in my opinion.

But who was I to judge? Especially after some of the relationships I'd had . . . Yeah, Matt was free to love whomever he liked. Not my business.

"You just gonna stare all day?" asked Sara, still watching the track.

I gulped. How'd she notice me?

Was I really that bad at moving around now? Even outside on rough ground I should have been able to sneak up on a lone, ordinary teenager. This was just sad.

"Sorry." I pointedly stopped next to her and watched the track as well. As far as I could tell, nothing interesting was happening down there. Sara seemed to agree, and at the same moment we both turned around to look back at Jen.

"What is she doing?" she asked, stupefied.

"Just stay here and don't talk too loud, okay?" I touched her arm lightly as she started to walk back toward Jen. She stopped, twisting around to look at me strangely—with hostility. Did I do something wrong? I let go immediately, and she returned to leaning against the portable without comment.

I couldn't fault her curiosity. Jen was currently sitting on her feet, knees pressed into the grass. Her arms weaved a curious dance around her entire body, regularly tapping specific points. There was no apparent pattern, but there was an elegance to how her hands moved through the air. Her mouth kept uttering short phrases, bursts of Etoline I couldn't make out from this far away.

One of the few times I'd persuaded her to explain in more detail, she'd described it as something like meditation. I knew it had something to do with her magic, but beyond that, I was clueless. I had to admit, from an outsider's perspective, it definitely looked weird.

"But seriously," Sara asked, much more quietly, "what is she doing?"

"She's concentrating." It was as close to an explanation as I was willing to offer right then.

Sara raised an eyebrow. "Are you guys all on drugs or something?"

"God no. I'd never touch them. Waste of my brain," I snapped. A bit more harsh than I'd intended, but it was a sticking point for me after a certain . . . incident in the Sylkaedr market.

"Jeez, sorry. Forget I asked." Sara turned back to watch Jen.

"Sorry," I added. "I'm having a weird day."

Sara sighed. "You and her both. It's like she got replaced with an alien overnight. But she still knows me, and she's *definitely* still my best friend. I still love her to death." She shook her head. "Why am I telling you this?"

"Because I'm here, and because I'm one of the very, very few people in the world who knows what's going on," I answered honestly.

Sara looked at me oddly. ". . . Yeah." She shrugged. "And about that. Jen refused to tell me anything. I'm guessing you're going to say the same thing?"

I paused, considering my answer. "It's not my place to tell you."

"What kind of crappy non-answer is that?" she snapped. She was fiery, didn't take any shit. I could see why they liked her. Well, Jen at least. Old Matt probably liked that, but I wasn't so sure he'd feel the same way anymore.

"Okay," I conceded. "I *could* tell you, but Jen could tell you more, and do a better job at it too. And there's a lot more of it I don't know, and some of it I'm not sure she'd want anyone to know. And besides that, we're not the only two people involved."

"Matt too, right?"

My eyes widened a little. "She told you?"

"Not exactly. Close enough though." Sara frowned. "Look, I can keep secrets. Jenny—"

"Jen."

"Goddammit. Okay. *Jen* knows that about me. So take the time you guys need," Sara continued, "but remember you've got friends. Right?"

". . . Right."

"Okay then." Sara brightened up a little. "So what's up with . . . whatever is going on over there?" She gestured vaguely toward Jen, who had sped up by now to the third stage.

"Again, Jen's business."

"No fun at all." She sighed. "Your name's Carl, then?"

"Yeah."

"Sara." She extended a hand.

"Nice to meet you." I shook it firmly. Of course, Jen had already told me her name a few minutes ago, but apparently she liked to be formal about it. I appreciated that, actually. It was protocol. It reminded me of the court, and all the nobles I needed to get back to playing off one another.

Greetings done with, we both turned to watch Jen's ritual continue. It should have only taken a few minutes to complete, but she was still going. That meant something was wrong. I took a few steps toward her.

Instantly, her eyes flew open, her hands dropping to her sides. She adjusted herself so she wasn't sitting on her feet, which looked horribly uncomfortable to me in the first place. I sat down across from her, just outside the circle she'd formed in the grass. "Jen?" I asked, uncertain.

"Vei toldeka litev," she said slowly. Her head swiveled left and right, searching for something I couldn't see. *"Vei totevas vei vaselvas etola, dasa . . ."* She looked like she would keep muttering all day in Etoline if I didn't interrupt.

"Sylajen," I said sharply, using her title with as much emphasis as I could. Jen immediately snapped out of it, staring at me in confusion. It took her a few seconds to come back to her senses.

". . . Sorry. I'm not sure what happened. I *thought* I felt something, and I kept going at it, but I guess it might've just been the wind . . ." Jen trailed off again. Sara glanced at me quizzically.

"Don't look at me," I answered, shrugging.

Jen started. She looked like she'd forgotten where we were again. "Sorry. Hi."

"Hi yourself," said Sara. "You back from cloudland?"

"Cloudland?" Jen asked, puzzled—then her face lit up. "Cloudland!" She grinned. "How did I forget about Cloudland?"

I was feeling left out. "Cloudland?"

"None of your business," Jen and Sara said in unison. It sounded rehearsed, like they'd said it a thousand times. Clearly an inside joke I wasn't ever going to get.

Whatever. As long as Jen wasn't so mopey, I could live with that. I hated seeing her like that.

"Class has gotta be almost over, right?" asked Jen, with a sidelong glance toward the main school building.

I pulled out my phone to check the time. "Nope. Plenty of time left."

Jen was looking at my phone with an odd expression. I had no idea what she was intending, and that worried me a bit. I didn't understand half of what she said, but I usually knew what she was going to do when we were out in the field. "What?"

"Can I borrow that?"

"My phone?"

"It can go on the . . ." Jen's face contorted in frustration.

"Internet."

"Yeah." Her face flushed in embarrassment again. Is it horrible of me that I found it cute? She was so clearly struggling, yet I found it endearing, and I was happy to help her. Did that make me a horrible person, enjoying someone's discomfort solely because I was one of the very few people who could help?

While I was getting introspective, Jen was getting impatient. She snatched my phone from my hand.

"Hey!"

"Calm down, *kapar-basal*," Jen snapped. "I just need a minute." She scurried back into the corner, scrolling through menus. I was deathly curious what was so urgent, overriding my annoyance at the casual insult.

"What are you doing?"

"Don't worry about it." She started to type something. I resigned myself to finding out later. I doubted she remembered how to clear a browser history.

Sara seemed to have given up entirely on trying to understand. She stood off to the side, watching us in silence. I wished more than any-thing that she would just disappear. Sara didn't belong here. Not with us. She wasn't part of our group. She hadn't earned the right to be here. She hadn't been through the pain and suffering, or felt the power and magic. She was just an ordinary person.

We were special, Jen and I. Sara couldn't possibly understand. She didn't *deserve* to understand.

But she was Jen's best friend, and maybe that was something Jen needed right now. I could understand that, I guess. I had a best friend too, and I was desperate to see him.

"All good," said Jen finally. She handed the phone back, and I pock-eted it without looking at the screen. *"Vannen dou,"* she said, giving me a small smile.

"No problem."

Sara cut in, killing the moment. "So are you gonna explain the whole new language thing? Or why you suddenly talk with an accent I've never heard before?"

Jen swiveled around to face her. "Sara, I . . ." she started, but I cut her off. I wanted to save her the effort.

"We can't. But act like Jen's only just learned English, and you'll be doing her a huge favor."

Sara's eyes widened. "That bad?"

"No," answered Jen, rolling her eyes at me. I shrugged. Her accent was greatly diminished as she continued. "I still know English. Just not as well as Eto—"

"Jen," I interrupted warningly. She stopped in time. It might have seemed harsh, but any terminology, any details, anything at *all* leaked to the wrong third party would mean trouble for all of us. I was just looking out for her.

Sara's eyes narrowed. "Hey, let her talk."

"No, he's right," said Jen quietly. "Sorry, Sara. Seriously. I'll tell you if I can. Soon."

She hesitated, but she nodded. "I'm holding you to that. Getting *really* tired of that line."

The patter of raindrops started up again. A moment later, it opened up into the layered roar of a shower crashing down on the rooftops all around us. We all looked up, shocked. The sky had been practically clear moments before. Was this just a normal Oregon downpour? I glanced at Jen, who seemed just as surprised. I'd seen her do amazing things before. Shifting the weather to favor us in a battle was even in her repertoire . . .

"Jen?"

She answered me instantly. "Nope." We'd been thinking the same thing, as usual. "Come on!"

Pulling on our coats, we hurried to the nearest entrance. The rain was coming down in buckets. We made it inside before we got soaked. It was lucky the portable had a slight overhanging cover, or else we'd have been drenched almost immediately.

Sara glanced at the nearest clock. "We should probably get back to class."

"Yeah," I replied.

"What will you do?" Jen asked me. She had a point. I could hardly hide outside in that downpour.

"Class is almost over. I'll just head to the cafeteria now, say I was let out early. I'll grab us a table in the corner."

"*Selnou.* See you there." Jen started walking away, and Sara hurried to catch up. I didn't envy Jen now. Sara seemed like she'd be hard to shake off. There was no way Matt would be okay with her joining our conversation at lunch though. Once we met up with Blake, we had some serious planning to do.

The food wasn't as bad as I remembered. Sure, it was mostly bland generic American foods, but it could have been worse. To be honest, I'd kind of missed pizza, even unremarkable pizza like this. Pizza and soda were things Cyraveil could definitely use. I had no idea how I might carbonate water and flavor there, but maybe Jen and I could devise something using magic.

Magic, right? We had *magic.* Who'd want to live on this stupid planet when you could have magic?

My ideas of improving our quality of life would have to wait though, as the only human to ever achieve anything with elven *etola* walked into the cafeteria. Or, more accurately, she jogged in. Jen looked like she was trying to get through the room as quickly as possible without drawing attention to herself, weaving through the crowd. She didn't have much skill in it, to be honest. She mostly just stuck to the edge of the room, for better or worse. Cities and crowds were my turf. Jen was at home in the forest.

I spotted Sara a few steps behind her, trying to get Jen's attention and point her in the right direction, but evidently failing. I stood up and waved at both of them.

Jen spotted me immediately and beelined for the corner where I'd found a table, abandoning her route entirely. It was an unpopular corner for the sole reason that it was farthest away from the serving line. Most kids didn't care where they sat, as long as they were with friends, so they'd unconsciously gravitate toward the opposite end by default. Great for people like me, since we got the other half of the cafeteria to ourselves. Relatively, of course. It wasn't like we were alone. But there was a clear amount of space between groups here, so we could talk without fear of being overheard too much.

Jen sat down across from me, Sara right next to her. They both pulled out home lunches in those ubiquitous brown paper bags, practically in unison. I raised an eyebrow.

"Not to be rude, but Sara can't be here."

"She knows th—" started Jen, but Sara interrupted her.

"I know that. I'm gone as soon as Matt gets here. But until then I'm sticking to Jen, so deal with it."

I raised my hands defensively. "Okay, okay. Sorry." I finished off my lunch, glancing around the cafeteria to seem uninterested. As Jen pulled out her food, she made a few brief hand motions, muttering something under her breath. She did this every time she ate, but had never explained the significance to me. I just passed it off as some elf ritual. Not worth my time to figure out.

Sara, of course, had no idea what she was doing. After a few dumbstruck moments, she returned to her own lunch. Jen took a bite out of her sandwich, frowned, but kept eating it regardless. Her face fell just a little.

I was worried. Jen seemed to be slipping farther and farther away from the strong girl I'd known. I didn't want to lose that unique beauty, that confident and fearless warrior. But what was I supposed to do to help her?

Jen and Sara ate in silence, Sara still throwing the occasional concerned look Jen's way. I wondered what that was about. Had something happened between us separating and meeting up here? Or was it just Sara's continued nosy intrusions? God, I wished she'd just go away now.

Something to ask Jen about later, I suppose. I didn't have time now because Matt was walking toward us.

Alone.

It took every ounce of self-control I could muster to not rush him down right then and there. Questions exploded in my mind one by one like fireballs. Where was Blake? Why wasn't Matt with him? Why had Matt left Blake behind?

What was I supposed to do now?

I only vaguely heard Sara make up some sort of excuse to Matt and quickly disappear. He sat down in her place and pulled out his own lunch, identical to Jen's. Matt asked me something, but I didn't hear it. I couldn't hear anything. The noise of the room had built up to a dull roar, a rushing sound that threatened to overwhelm me completely.

A sharp kick to my shin. I spluttered back into existence.

"The hell was that for?" I snapped.

"Stay focused," Matt answered firmly. "We need to talk."

"No kidding," Jen said mildly. "Carl, you with us now?"

I glared at Matt. That kick was completely uncalled for. I could still feel it on my leg. "Yeah, I'm here. So talk."

Matt frowned. "Carl, if we're going to do this . . ."

Jen cut in. "No, we're not. Carl, *se develd* and let Matt talk, *selnou*?"

"English, Jen."

"Dammit." Jen slapped herself in the face lightly. "Sorry, Matt."

"It's okay. Has it been a problem?"

"Kinda," she answered with a remarkably straight face. She didn't want him to worry. No way was she going to let him know the full extent of trouble she'd been having all day. She and I would keep that secret. "Mom thinks I'm taking a foreign language now, but other than that . . ." She trailed off.

"Well, good enough." Matt sighed. "She ate the scrambled eggs, right?"

"Eggs!" Jen exclaimed, sitting up rigid. Embarrassment flooded her face, and she relaxed a second later, eating her food with a guilty look.

"Huh?" I asked, genuinely confused.

Matt grinned. "She couldn't remember the name for eggs," he explained. Jen picked up a grape and threw it at him. He ducked it easily.

"Syldavacka," she muttered, but a smile crossed her face as well.

They were both so casual. I couldn't understand it. We had way more pressing things to deal with here. Life-and-death things. I dropped my fist in the middle of the table—a bit louder than I'd meant to, but I didn't make excuses. They both fell silent.

". . . Kind of dramatic, Carl," said Matt. The words were a joke, but his tone was suddenly icy. I didn't care though. I was fed up.

"Blake," I snapped.

"I haven't seen him," Matt replied, in that same infuriatingly calm voice he'd been using all day. He put up his hand before I could answer. "Doesn't necessarily mean anything. Could be he just didn't come in today. You know he skips morning classes all the time. Our first two periods are pretty worthless."

"I called this morning though, and I didn't get anything," I said slowly.

"Not even his parents?'

"No. But that's not surprising, they're never home in the morning. His dad's already gone and Adela's shift doesn't end 'til nine." Maybe there was still hope. I couldn't consider the alternative. Not yet.

"He would come in today of all days though," said Jen.

Matt nodded. "Yeah, he would. Which leads to the other possibility."

"Don't say it," I said.

"Carl, we have to figure out what we're going to do if he's—"

"Don't you fucking say it," I snarled. A bit too loud. People at a nearby table looked over, startled. I lowered my voice again. "He's just at home."

"Carl . . ." Matt began, but I was done with this. I stood up and walked away, taking my tray and tossing it into the nearest trash can. Some busybody started in on me about recycling and how the tray shouldn't be trashed and some other crap. I walked straight through them and out the front doors.

My best friend was alive. He had to be.

CHAPTER 5

MATT

"So who's up first?"

"The parents of the reported missing."

"Any tips from the academy's finest Officer Portman on this interview?"

"Keep it clean."

"No shit. But what about talking points?"

"Same as anything else for now. We need to establish a timeline, suspects, motives. Most importantly, if this was an abduction or a runaway."

"I dunno, kid sure seems clean from the basics we've got. You think he rabbited?"

"You never know with some. Doesn't matter how nice or smart someone looks. Everyone's got an animal instinct inside, you just never know how deep it might be buried."

"I thought we were talking about runaways, not murderers."

"Fight or flight. Runaways usually start with some kind of fight, with parents or guardians."

"Then flight?"

"Don't get cute. Pay attention to the road."

Carl stormed off, and all I could think about was how much I wanted to do the same.

Not seeing Blake was a hammer blow to my chest, even with what I already knew. I guess some small part of me had hoped—same as Carl—that Blake would just be there this morning. I'd run into him on the way to school as he got off the bus, or in class since we had all the same classes on Wednesday. After first period, doubt crept in.

After second period, it crushed my hopes into dust.

Blake was really, completely gone. I'd expected it, but I hadn't wanted it. Of course I hadn't. Blake and I were good friends. We should have been playing basketball together tonight. It was a regular thing, basketball in the park on Wednesdays. Blake was never going to play basketball again.

Carl . . . I felt so awful for him. He wasn't going to have an easy time. If Blake and I were good friends, he and Carl were closer than brothers. When we'd gotten split up at Skyldr, Blake got me to keep searching for Carl for weeks. So much wasted time, but Blake couldn't ever give up—just like Carl couldn't give up on him now.

As he snaked through the cafeteria tables, it was clear just how little he cared about life here on Earth. He nearly knocked over some poor freshman on his way out the door. I couldn't blame him for wanting to leave. I'd leave too, if I could. I was the leader though. I had responsibilities. I don't know why it fell to me. Maybe it was just my bad luck, to be the only guy with a car that night.

Whatever it was, I ended up in charge. Decisions were dropped in my lap. No matter how huge or life-altering, they were entrusted to a kid from the suburbs in Oregon. Everybody in that whole country was insane. Every last one of them. They trusted *me* to make the hard choices.

Like now. If Carl didn't accept Blake's death soon, I was going to have to make another hard choice.

"Matt?"

My sister's voice brought me out of my daze. She was still gazing at the spot Carl had vacated, her face etched with worry.

"Yeah?"

"What do we do?"

I sighed. I'd really hoped I'd never hear that question again. "He needs to vent. Blake was his best friend. One day. We can handle that. One day won't hurt him."

"What if it hurts someone *else*?"

I shook my head. "Carl's not stupid. He's not going to start attacking random people. He just needs to work through his grief."

Jen frowned. "Matt, he's not *sad*. He's angry. And he thinks there's still a chance."

"Well there is, isn't there?"

"*Tol deka danedek so vei*, Matt!" Her voice was as harsh as a whisper could get. I was taken aback. What was this about? I didn't know how to answer. I didn't even know what she'd said. Jen's eyes narrowed, her expression suddenly fierce. "I know, okay?"

A battering ram against the walls of denial in my mind. ". . . Know what?" I replied, hoping desperately she was referring to something else—anything else. But I knew exactly what she'd say next.

"I was there. In the antechamber. I know why Blake died," she said, her voice cracking. I froze up, doing everything in my power not to react. I didn't answer. My eyes were fixed on the wall far over Jen's shoulder, though I couldn't make out anything I was seeing. I was trying to block out everything, everyone.

Jen had been there. She'd seen what Blake had done—what *I'd* done.

After a few moments without a reply, Jen continued. "I get it, okay? I'm not blaming you. You did what you had to do. Blake and I both understood that. The son of a bitch needed to die. He *deserved* to die. But Carl doesn't know what happened."

"Explaining it won't do anything for him," I said quietly.

"Maybe," she said, leaning forward on her elbows. "There's no chance Blake's alive though."

"... No."

"And Carl will keep trying until he finds that out for himself."

"Probably," I said, glancing away. The cafeteria continued to bustle around us, as if everything were perfectly normal. As if we weren't discussing events so brutal that I was still having nightmares a week later.

"Wouldn't it be easier to just tell him?"

"I don't think he'd believe me," I replied honestly. Carl and I weren't on the best of terms, even before we left. He only attached himself to me because Blake and I hung out so much. I'd mostly ignored him, except when he got in the way.

"Well, what if we both—"

"No."

"No?" Jen asked. She lifted her head a little, surprised.

"You shouldn't get involved."

"Matt—" she started, but I stopped her again.

"You've got your own life to get back to. A happy, normal, safe life," I said. *Where nothing ever happened to you and you're just an ordinary teenage girl,* I added in my head.

"It's not like I can just go back, Matt," she said, her expression dark.

"Why not?"

"Well, for one, *vei suselenas wenda daned Etoline valenas envil.* Or did you forget?"

"No," I replied quietly. "Of course not. That's on me."

"Dov?"

"It was my fault, Jen," I said, still determinedly refusing to meet her eyes. I couldn't bear to see her face right now, even if it was the little sister I'd grown up with, and not the scarred Sylvandar warrior I'd come to know. "All of it. You wouldn't have been there if I hadn't let you—"

"Stop. Right now." Her hand grabbed mine. I looked at her finally, at her face that had reemerged from my past, and felt such despair that it could have consumed me—except that her expression wasn't sad or dark anymore. She looked determined. "You are not to blame. How the hell could you have known?"

"But even after we got there—"

"We got split up. *All* of us. And you are not responsible for what happened to me." A few people were walking close by, giving Jen pause. My eyes were watering up with tears. I brought up my sleeve and brushed them away before Jen could notice. I couldn't afford to show weakness. I was the strong one, the center of the group. The fearless leader. I had a role to fulfill.

By the time the kids moved on, my eyes were clear, my expression controlled.

"It's okay, Matt. I'm okay. You're okay. We're home," she continued in a low voice. "I'm back to normal. Ish." She smiled. "So what if I'll be a bit *kapar-litashavec* for a while? No big deal."

"In English?"

"Oh, screw you." Jen tossed another grape at me. "Uhh . . . scatterbrained. Kinda. It's not really a direct translation."

I shook my head, amused. I'd never learned the language. I knew a few words, enough to understand some of Jen's lapses, and I knew some short phrases we'd practiced. They were useful for quick directions in combat. In a rebellion, the ability to communicate on the field without being understood was invaluable. I'd also learned how to answer a few insults, like the one Jen used the night before. I'd heard it *far* too many times from random elves, so I'd finally had Jen explain it to me.

It was . . . pretty racist. Elves and humans don't get along very well.

Carl went on and on about the language being beautiful and special, but I honestly didn't really see what he was talking about. Etoline sounded pretty much like any other tongue to me. I mean, I couldn't understand what was being said most of the time, but it was no different than listening to something like French or Spanish or Japanese. All gibberish, even if it wasn't human gibberish like the rest of them.

The language held a profound importance for Jen though. That much I got. Living with the elves had changed her in so many ways. Deep in my mind, I feared she'd never be able to return to normal. But damned if I wasn't going to try to get her there.

"Are we good?" Jen asked. *That* phrase I understood in both, but I could tell she was trying to make an effort. I appreciated it.

"Yeah," I nodded. "We're good." I returned to eating, as did Jen. We'd both gotten distracted—for obvious reasons—and the lunch hour was running down fast. I dug into the lunch I'd thrown together that morning. It wasn't my best work, but for the first meal back, it wasn't bad.

I always put together our lunches. Mom used to, a long time ago, but all that changed when our father left. Jen was too young at the time to remember him well, but I remembered him. We were better off without him. Still, that left our mother picking up a second job, suddenly never able to spend much time with us except on the weekends. During the weekdays, unless we stayed up late, we were lucky to see her at all beyond the wake-up call I grudgingly gave her at breakfast time.

But she kept the money flowing, and somehow kept the rest of the house clean and tidy on top of that (our bedrooms were another matter entirely). On weekends, after she got home in the evening, we'd always eat dinner together and do something as a family. Watch a movie or some TV, play a board game, whatever didn't cost much. When we were younger, we'd go down to the park a lot. Early on, Jen and I were mostly with the other neighborhood kids on the swings and playground. When I got older though, I spent more time just sitting on a bench with Mom, watching the others.

We'd talk about anything and everything. Mom was always there to listen to me complain. She'd listen to how school was going, or anything else that came to mind, no matter what it was. Once, I started ranting about some problem I was having with a video game for more than thirty minutes straight. Something about how I was having trouble figuring out how the enemies did a particular move, and how I couldn't beat them. I can't remember the specifics at all anymore, but Mom just sat there calmly and listened. When I was done, she asked if I had figured out the problem in the end, which I still hadn't.

She smiled, and told me, "Sometimes solutions can show up where you least expect them. Never forget that everybody in a fight has a reason they're fighting. Everyone wants to think they're the good guy in the end."

It didn't apply to the game in the slightest. I don't know if she missed what I was talking about and assumed it was a book or something. Her advice was completely useless at the time. But in Cyraveil, that simple piece of advice saved my life more than once, and helped me build an army. It saved the entire kingdom more than once.

I wished I could somehow express that to my mother someday. But I never would. It'd be far better if my mother never had to learn about that place.

"Hey, Jen."

"Mmmph?" Jen mumbled through a mouthful of pretzels.

"We should do something for Mom."

She swallowed them down before answering, thankfully. *"Anala?"* I started to remind her, but she caught herself first. "Sorry, sorry. Like what?"

"I don't know yet."

"We could bake her a cake," she added, her mouth slowly widening to a grin.

". . . You just want cake."

"That wasn't a no," she shot back.

I sighed. "Fine. We'll pick something up."

"Do se nara sevensyl, Matt."

"You're not even trying anymore."

"Masal," she said, giggling.

"You never change," I grumbled. "Speaking of which, where'd your partner in crime run off to?"

"Oh." She frowned. "She had some stuff to take care of during lunch."

"Ah," I said noncommittally. I was actually a little disappointed. When I'd walked up, Sara had been sitting next to her, and the moment she'd turned to look at me, I'd remembered exactly why I'd always wanted to ask her out.

We'd been chatting for the last week or two, all the way up 'til last night, when Blake had called and everything went wrong. She'd been Jen's best friend for years and years, but somehow we'd never crossed paths much. Jen never seemed to invite her over; they always hung out at Sara's or somewhere else. But lately, I'd started noticing her more. She was intelligent and confident, and good-looking on top of that. I'd wanted to ask her out, but I'd always been held back by something. Caution maybe, or fear of rejection.

Now that just seemed silly. Sara was worth the risk. Better yet, she was normal. Ordinary.

Human.

"Why, what's up?" Jen asked.

"Nothing," I answered quickly. She seemed suspicious, but I was saved by the bell. Lunch was over. Jen glanced up, disappointed, and started to gather the remainder of her lunch back into her bag. "You should probably finish that. It's still going to be a long day."

"You've still got the headache too?" she asked, zipping up her bag.

I nodded. "Leftovers, but it's there."

"Bunch of *keldaphut.*" Jen stood up, pulling on her bag.

"Seriously, Jen. English," I warned, but she only grinned and wandered away.

The last thing I needed was Jen spouting off curse words in a language that didn't belong in this universe. I doubted anyone would take it as anything other than gibberish, but the more she lapsed, the more she'd probably continue to lapse, and the more attention would fall on us. It was bad enough already that Blake was missing. I still didn't know how to handle that.

I watched Jen leave, joining Sara at the opposite end of the cafeteria and vanishing down the hall. My only plan at this point was to pretend we knew nothing. What else was I supposed to do? No one could prove anything about Blake's disappearance. All the evidence was safely tucked away in an alternate dimension—or whatever the hell Cyraveil was. Without any leads, and with us resuming normal lives as if nothing had happened, any investigation would just fall flat.

With that comforting thought, I finished my lunch and headed out for my next class.

My other classes went by without anything else going wrong. After the mess at lunch, I barely even noticed the rest of the day drift by. I was too busy worrying about what Carl might be up to. I wasn't lying when I told Jen he'd probably be fine for a day, but he'd lost more than I had. Could I really understand what he was going through?

I pushed it out of my mind as I arrived home. Mom was still out, although not at work for once. She had the day off today, a special occasion, and she'd only have to work tonight. She'd promised to be home for dinner though. I wondered what she was up to as I tossed my bag into my room and grabbed the keys off my desk, before heading down to the garage. I flicked on the light, and there sat my father's legacy.

It was intact, and it ran better than you might expect, but it sure looked like a hulk of scrap. The paint was chipped everywhere, the driver-side door was scratched up heavily, and the door to the bed had been stuck shut for fifteen years. Still, it was mine. After Dad had disappeared, Mom found all the papers signed over to her in the glove compartment. She had her own car, so once I'd gotten old enough, she'd taught me how to drive the truck.

Why had I been so ashamed of it? It was such a useful tool. I shuddered to think how much I'd avoided using it, out of a mixture of resentment of my father and a fear of judgment over its appearance. Why did I care so much? I was such an idiot back then. I'd walk an extra thirty minutes to get to basketball and home again rather than let anyone see my beat-up old truck. I'd only ever driven it to get groceries with Jen, or other small errands. Plus the one journey out to Cyraveil Park.

Now it looked more like a trusted old workhorse than anything. It might not be winning any contests, but it didn't deserve hate. I put a hand on the hood, feeling the solid metal under my fingertips.

For a moment, my memory flashed back, and my hand was upon not cold steel, but the warm mane of Haldammar, as he snorted loudly and pawed at the bloodied grass, while the stench of decay filled my nostrils and the sounds of the battlefield filled my ears with groans and the slick sounds of swords plunging into necks and between seams of armor.

Then I was back, and my finger jutted up against a slight chip in the paint on the side of the hood. I got in and opened the garage door. Through the rearview mirror, I spotted Jen hurrying inside, carrying her backpack close to her chest under the rain. She ran in through the front door, then came out to the garage a few minutes later, hopping in next to me.

"You remember how to drive this thing, right?"

In response, I turned on the engine and reversed out onto the street, as smoothly as if it had been yesterday. Jen raised her eyebrows. "O-o-o-kay, then." She leaned away over the side of her seat, while I drove out onto the main road. Suddenly, she disappeared from the corner of my eye. *"Daphut!"*

"You okay?"

"Yeah," she muttered. "Just forgot how twitchy that was." Jen came back into my peripheral view, inching her seat back up to a reclined position. Her eyes slid closed. "I'm gonna take a r-e-e-e-eal quick nap, *selnou*? Wake me up when we're there."

"It's only a fifteen-minute drive . . ."

"Plenty of time."

I shrugged. When I glanced over, she did look tired. From what I remembered, music had always helped her fall asleep. I leaned forward and fiddled with the radio, trying to remember how to work it while I pulled in neatly between a minivan and a delivery truck at a red light. I got static, then after some experimenting with the dials, I got some pop music to start flowing. I would have switched it immediately, but I vaguely remembered this being one of Jen's favorite songs.

As the beat grated through my worthless speakers, I rolled onto the highway and sped up. The truck groaned as it edged above fifty-five. I had one hand on the wheel and the other resting comfortably on the open window, letting the breeze waft over my arm. Periodic breaks in the clouds sent shafts of sunlight through the rain, and as I looked around I could see patches of a rainbow in the distance.

Without warning, the music shut off. I assumed it was the truck's stereo taking a particularly bad bump, but then I saw Jen's retracting hand a second later when I looked back to the road.

"What's up?"

Jen just shook her head, closing her eyes again.

"I thought you loved that song."

"I dunno," she replied, eyes still shut. "Just not feeling it anymore, I guess."

We drove the rest of the way in relative silence, filled only by the bucking of the truck and the engine noise as it bounced along the poorly maintained patches of the highway.

"Jen."

"*. . . Dasa dou vofas anala e kepar ta las shaval atel doues uveles*, Naef."

She was talking in her sleep. The only word I recognized was Naef, short for her friend Naeflin. I poked her in the shoulder, light as I could. She snapped awake, one hand flying down with lightning speed to grasp my wrist. Within a second, she'd let go, blinking furiously.

"*To suuna dona?* Oh, wait. Sorry. Dumb question." She glanced around. After a few moments to adjust, she reached to unhook the seat belt, before noticing she'd never put it on. ". . . Whoops. Why didn't you remind me?"

I glanced down and realized I hadn't worn mine either. Jen giggled. After a few seconds, I started laughing. We sat there, engine off in the parking lot of the grocery store, laughing uproariously for more than a minute. It was such a small, silly thing, but for whatever reason it set us both off. Maybe it was just fatigue. Whatever the case, it lightened the mood significantly as we got out and walked into the store. I finally felt calm again, but I did wonder what Jen had been muttering in her sleep before I woke her.

She'd always talked in her sleep, as far back as I could remember. That part wasn't new. It had always been in English though. It bothered me more than a little that she seemed to have traded it wholesale for Etoline. I could logically reason with myself that it was to be expected, but it put her just one more step removed from reality.

I didn't want to just take it away from her. I could tell how important it was to her identity. Sometimes, it felt like she'd become an adopted foreigner, with an entirely different culture and upbringing than me, even though we'd spent sixteen years together here on Earth. I'd never understand what she'd gone through, and how she'd become the huntress I'd finally reunited with on opposite sides of a negotiating table in the secret cellar of a border-town tavern.

As I walked behind her though, she seemed like a perfectly ordinary high school girl—more graceful than usual, but ordinary. More importantly, she looked like the girl whom I'd grown up with, spent every Christmas with, bought presents for, watched TV with, and cooked dinner for nearly every night. She was my sister.

I started down the aisles, following my normal cycle, picking up the usuals. Jen was in another aisle, presumably grabbing whatever she'd decided we were having for dinner. I'd promised, after all. There was no way she'd forget that.

To my surprise, I'd picked up everything before she returned. I wandered aimlessly until I spotted her, staring intently at the shelves of bread.

"Did you find something you wanted?" I called out, walking up to join her. Jen didn't answer. Her head moved slowly to the next loaf of bread in the aisle. "Uhh, Jen?"

"*Se develd.* I'm learning over here."

Curious, I leaned in, basket under my arm. "What are you doing?"

She looked around, face growing pink. "Learning. Or . . . relearning, I guess."

I examined the bread. It didn't seem remarkable in the slightest—until I noticed the loaves were all turned upside down so Jen could read the ingredients. "Names?"

"Forgot the word for bread, for one. Or cinnamon. Wheat, nuts, raisins, peanut butter." Jen sighed. "Don't make fun of me?"

"Could I ever honestly promise that?"

She snorted. "Okay, you got a point. Anyway, do you mind if I keep going for a bit? You'd be surprised how helpful this is."

I shrugged. "It's fine. Just remember we've gotta be back in time to cook before Mom gets home."

"Yeah, yeah." Jen waved me off.

I suddenly remembered what Jen had requested at lunch. I couldn't deny I had a huge craving for cake as well. This store had a bakery attached, didn't it? After a moment's attempt at remembering where it might be, I gave up and began wandering the outer edge. I figured I'd run into it eventually.

Instead, I found something else. Someone else.

I almost ran into her coming around the corner of the aisle. It was bizarrely comical as I nearly knocked her over, too distracted by the sight of the deli and the thought of fresh ham for dinner. Cyraveil didn't have pigs. I scrambled to help her back up to her feet, and realized with a shock it was Sara once again.

"Oh, hi," I said awkwardly. "Uhh . . . sorry."

She shook her head. "Totally my fault. I wasn't looking where I was going."

"Well, I wasn't really either. We'll call it a draw?"

"Sure," she laughed. Her face was the kind that lit up completely when she did, wide smile and sparkling eyes. It rekindled every spark of the crush I'd had from a smoldering ember into the flame it had once been, doused over the years as my mind got distracted by endless other concerns. This time around, I was determined to fan it into a true fire.

"Well, anyway. If it's all right with you, I'd like to run into you again sometime."

"Oh?" Her eyes flashed with curiosity, even as she suppressed a smile at my bad line. So I was never the best at this sort of thing, on either side. I didn't care anymore though. I just knew I wanted to spend more time with her.

"Are you busy Friday?" I asked, the plan already forming in my head.

"No. I don't think so. Yeah, nope, I'm free."

"Want to go out somewhere?"

Sara smiled, giving me a tiny nod. "Sure, Matt."

"Cool. I'll pick you up then."

"Uhh," Sara started, glancing around. That wasn't part of the script in my head. A little pool of anxiety began forming in my mind.

"What's up?"

"Oh! Nothing. Just, I'll be walking home with Jen anyway. I might as well meet you at your place?" she said quickly. Was she embarrassed about something? Her eyes were darting around a lot. Avoiding something. I wasn't sure what to read into it.

"All right." I smiled, trying to convey it wasn't a big deal. She returned it, and all the world seemed to get a bit lighter.

"So, you're making dinner?" she asked casually.

"Jen told you?"

"Seemed super excited. Like, hyperbolically excited. Are you some kind of mega-chef?"

I shrugged. "I dabble."

"Ah, playing it cool. Wise choice." Sara grinned. "Maybe I'll have to come over and try one of your meals sometime."

"I dunno if I can handle the pressure of cooking for someone as good-looking as you."

Sara's eyes glazed over momentarily. Her face flushed. "Save something for Friday," she murmured.

I grinned. "Don't worry. I've gotta head home now anyway." I turned to leave, but Sara caught me by the hand. Despite her sudden urgency and shift in tone, it still sent a spark through my skin, feeling that touch.

"Wait." Her voice had changed. It was the tone I'd come to dread, concerned and serious and wrought with fear and confusion. It bespoke upcoming panic and horror, terrible things bound to happen. "Look, Jen told me not to say anything, but I'm worried about her."

My fears were realized. Someone outside our group had learned what they shouldn't.

I tried to dial back my panic. Jen wasn't an idiot. Smarter than me more often than not. She'd have had some reason to bring Sara into the fold, something we'd talk about as soon as we got home. On top of that, I didn't know what Jen had told her exactly. I had to play this carefully.

"Worried how?" I asked, not too casually. The concerned older brother, that's all I was.

"Have you noticed anything lately? Today in particular?"

I shrugged.

Sara frowned. "Oh come on, don't give me that. You two are super close. Thick as thieves."

"Sometimes with actual thieving."

"Huh?"

"Nothing." That wasn't a story I could share with Sara, although it was a pretty good highlight. Carl's armory guards never saw us coming. "I mean, yeah, she's been a bit different lately. But people change. Nothing can stay the same forever."

"If you say so." She sighed.

"Talking about me behind my back? For shame," intoned Jen from somewhere nearby. Sara and I both jerked around, startled, but we didn't see her anywhere.

". . . Jen?" I asked to thin air, unsure where she was.

"Present," she replied, poking her head over the top of the shelves from the next aisle.

I frowned. "Are you standing on the shelves?"

"Don't worry about it." Jen grinned. "You two are so cute, by the way. Finally going on a date after years of crushing on each other."

My cheeks might as well have caught on fire. I'm sure I looked exactly as red as Sara became the next instant.

"Jenny, I—"

"Jen," we corrected her automatically.

Sara shook her head in disbelief. "All of you are insane."

"Also intelligent, insightful, and *insyladanal*," added Jen. "Matt, don't we need to get going?"

I nodded, grateful for the excuse to leave. "Did you figure out what we're eating tonight?"

In response, Jen held up a plastic bottle. It caught the light of the lamps above just right, lighting up the semitransparent amber liquid inside. She tossed it over and I caught it. A bottle of maple syrup.

"Pancakes it is."

CHAPTER 6

CARL

"Assuming Blake was a runaway then, where do we start?"
   "Closest friends. Whoever he might confide in."
   "Don't you mean whomever?"
   "Grammar? From you?"
   "I woke up in school once or twice, fuck you very much."

For some reason beyond my understanding, I'd ended up in class after the disastrous conversation with Matt in the cafeteria. I guess my feet took me there on muscle memory alone, because I had no idea what class it actually was. I assumed it was right though. The corkboard at the front of the room had a little green index card pinned to it with "Carl Stokelson" written on it, showing where I was supposed to sit—right near the back and by the window, exactly where I'd prefer. Somewhere I could avoid attention and zone out watching the street, ignoring class entirely.

Which, of course, is what I ended up doing right away. The rest of the room became a bland, unfocused blur and dull hum. I couldn't get the conversation with Matt out of my mind. It began with rage, waves of heat and frustration rolling through my face like someone were pressing hot pans to my cheeks. How could Matt be such an idiot about this? Blake was fine, and we were wasting time when we should be out looking for him.

And Jen backed him! Matt wasn't always right. I was right as often as he was. After everything I'd done for Jen, you'd think she'd be more supportive. *I'd* rescued her, dammit all. Matt didn't do shit for her while we were separated. If I hadn't found her . . . If I hadn't been in a position to get her released . . .

I shuddered. No one deserved to go through that hell.

The bell rang, and more students filed into the room in groups, talking and laughing. I glanced around, trying to pick up clues as to what class this actually was. I saw maps on the wall, of Europe and the Americas and drilling down to specific countries. History, I guessed? I tried to dredge up everything I could remember of their history, but I couldn't be sure which names and details were of Earth and which were of Cyraveil.

Were the Ostrogans the leaders of the revolt that overthrew the Western Roman Empire, plunging Italy into chaos? Did the Visigoths assassinate the last God-Kings of Laodrannen, paving the way for the enslavement of the Saenvaland and the economic miracle that brought the rough country back to the forefront of civilization? Was it the Cellman or the Medici family who first discovered—and were subsequently captured and tortured by—elves in the forests of the Sylvandar?

I sighed audibly. I'd figure it out on the fly. I didn't really have any better options, and improvising under pressure had brought me a *lot* of success in the past.

Our teacher, who was barely older than I should have been, began lecturing in an upbeat, cheerful voice completely at odds with the subject matter. He seemed under the impression that speaking exuberantly might keep the attention of the students—as if he could compel their interest with just his voice. Such an amateur. I would have preferred a normal drone, so I could tune him out easier and ignore the class.

My eyes remained fixed on the street outside, but I wasn't really looking at anything in particular anymore. My vision glazed over as I set myself adrift in memories. Anything that could take me away from this hell on earth—on the wrong Earth. I couldn't properly vanish from the room or the lesson, but I found myself using it as a springboard to escape, nonetheless. As the teacher began explaining something or other about the American Civil War, I remembered my own war.

No stories of battle, even from the most vivid storyteller, can prepare you for the real thing. The heat, sweat, and grime as you stand on a battlefield for days and sometimes weeks, with blood cascading down limbs from arrowheads embedded in flesh, while swords and armor clash all around you. Sword fights aren't anything like what you might expect either. No choreography or fancy, tricky footwork to be found on the battlefield. A real sword fight between two guys in full plate mail is like two mountains hurling themselves at each other. Slashing is useless, since it just bounces right off the plate. Your best bet is to try and get the point through a seam between the pieces, where it can slip through a weak point and into their flesh.

More often though, I'd just see the stronger man bash the weaker into submission with a shield, or the flat of his blade, as many times as it took. Once someone went down, then you got to the messy business of actually killing them.

Full proper armor like that was rare though, reserved for the truly exceptional or exceedingly rich. More often, you'd just see groups torn down by hails of arrows while charging, or speared by men on horseback. Once you really got into the thick of it, you were just another face in a crowd of lightly armored men with pointy objects, doing their absolute best not to get stuck by anything.

None of this applied to the Americans' Civil War, obviously. That was a war with guns, something yet to be invented in Cyraveil. I'd toyed with the idea of introducing weapons like that, but to be honest, I didn't really have much idea how to make a revolver or even something like a musket—if it were even possible in Cyraveil. Besides, the few turncoat elves we'd recruited were more than enough long-range firepower to substitute as artillery. They didn't get ruined by the rain or run out of bullets and powder either. Exhausted from overuse, but given a day and a good meal, they'd recover pretty much completely.

I could have done without the constant complaints about the *mana-vus sel setavus* or whatever though. Elves got really whiny sometimes. I'd never dare mention it to Jen, but they seemed weirdly immature as a race. Haughty, sure, in that way you'd expect, but despite their obvious abilities and overwhelming protectiveness of their home forests, the elves seemed totally caught off guard when we attacked.

It was absurd. A capital-E Empire expands to completely surround your homes and has a clear need for resources to sustain itself—and you *don't* expect them to want access to a few vast forests that grow unnaturally fast, without any apparent need for water or nutrients? Anyone would leap at such an abundant garden. I'd already started drawing up plans to conquer the region by the time Reynir formally brought my fiefdom into the Empire.

They were so naive, almost to a man. I was relieved when I found a few willing to switch sides and join us. It humanized them, for lack of a better word. I even made friends with one of them, although he was old enough to be my great-grandfather. He understood how the world worked, and how to stay near the top.

Yeah, we both might have chosen the wrong side in the end, but come on. None of us could have seen where the war was headed, the horrors that would emerge. At the time, it was the right call.

I resurfaced momentarily, feeling like I'd been swimming through an ocean of memories. The teacher was talking about the reasons the Union had won the war. ". . . and they did have the moral high ground, but it was more than that. The North just had more cash-ola. General Lee addressed this himself in his surrender in 1865. War comes down to resources. It's always been in the rules. The winners are who's got more, and who can move it around more quickly. Leadership helps, but if you've got more men, bullets, and food, and you've got the factories to keep churning them out, you're gonna have a good time."

I snorted. I didn't mean to; attention was definitely not something I needed right now. But his conclusion just didn't match up with what I knew. It was a horrible habit, but I could never resist correcting someone when they were wrong.

To my dismay, I found a sea of faces turning to await my response. I tried to ignore them, staring intently out the window, trying to avoid catching anyone's eye. The teacher smiled at me with a condescending friendly grin that demanded to be knocked off his smug face.

"Well, we've got a volunteer. All right, Carl, what's on your mind?" he asked brightly. How could he be so cheerful about a topic like this? It bothered me even more than his smile. I threw caution out the window to the cars racing by on the main road; I was determined to demolish that sunny disposition.

"Morale."

"Morale, huh?" He looked surprised. "Well, that's a fair point. Plenty of the South didn't actually believe in slavery, or the Confederacy per se. Lee himself freed his slaves, and it's believed that part of the reason he seemed to lose his edge on leaving Virginia was that he only believed in the cause of defending his home, not the country at large. Like I said, the North had the moral high ground. That helped the troops keep morale up."

He looked like he was about to continue onto another lecture point, but I jumped back in. I'd studied this war, like I'd studied so many others before. I'd always been fascinated with history and war in particular, and that hadn't changed one bit.

"Screw their morals. The North was in it for the money, same as everyone else." I took a deep breath before continuing, emphasizing my point and giving my audience time to digest. I knew how to dominate a crowd when I had to. "Wars are won by whichever side is more willing to be ruthless. There aren't any rules. The Union troops burned crops and towns. They killed civilians. They demolished infrastructure wherever they could to cripple the South's resources. They pillaged and raped." I saw a few in the room wince at the word. Oversensitive bookworms. "Scorched earth, that was Sherman's play. It worked wonders."

I should know, it worked pretty well for me too. Thanks, General Sherman. Studying all the successful American generals paid off, in a very fruitful way, and definitely not how my teacher probably expected. He'd faltered at my response, holding a whiteboard marker limp between his fingers. I was really getting into the discussion at this point.

"It's pretty common. The Soviets in Germany after World War II, or the Japanese in Nanjing. There's plenty of examples, all the way back to the Romans and the Greeks. When you're invading a hostile nation with a different culture than your own, the most effective way to pacify them is to utterly destroy their way of life. You leave them nothing they can recognize as their own nation anymore. Dismantle their society. If they can't unite under any sort of common ground, they can never hope to mount a resistance against you."

I was actually enjoying this, being able to speak from experience to a crowd of attentive listeners. Reynir and I used the strategy to great effect against the rebels in the first few months—burning crops and villages, destroying symbols and other rallying points. We were careful to never make martyrs or leave them anything to rally around.

If only Reynir hadn't taken to those lessons so well.

One kid decided to speak up. Someone I couldn't remember, if I'd even known him in the first place.

"But plenty of wars were fought over moral or religious grounds. You can't say it wasn't a big factor in them winning or losing." He sounded so naive, I was practically salivating at the chance to correct him. The teacher made no move to interrupt, leaning against the whiteboard and watching the debate unfold. He seemed unwilling to step in, which suited me just fine. Every head in the room swiveled between me and the other student as we traded blows.

"Once you're in the middle of a battlefield, morals mean shit. There's just you and the other guy, and the other guy is gonna kill you unless you kill him first. Religion's just a reminder that there's something better waiting for you if he gets you first."

"Okay, but that's low-level. What about the high-level stuff?" he countered. I realized I hadn't actually answered his question. Whoops.

"It's the same thing. Yeah, morals and shit might help you with recruitment and retainment, but you'd better hope the guys actually planning your strategy aren't hamstrung by *daphut* like that." Crap. I'd meant to say "crap." Jen's colorful collection of curses had inserted themselves into my vocabulary after all those months we spent together in hiding.

"By what?" he asked, confused, but I was already steamrolling ahead to cover it up.

"It doesn't matter what time period, what era, or if you're in an alternate fucking dimension. War's always been the same. History's just written by the winners, and everybody wants to look like a hero in the end." *It's different once you're actually out there.*

I turned back to my window, watching the cars roll by again. My face was still hot from the attention and the debate. I forced myself to calm down, focusing on tapping my fingers on the side of the desk to the rhythm of my legion's marching song in my head. One-two, one-two, one-two-three-four, one-two. After a few stressful seconds, I felt the anxiety lift away like a blanket sliding off. The cool air drifting through the open window was wonderfully refreshing. My mind was clear.

Which meant, of course, that the real pressures I was facing came back with a vengeance.

"Well, that's . . . one way to put it, I guess," the teacher finally spoke up. I briefly wondered what his name was—then remembered, I didn't care. A few kids were giving me weird looks. The teacher started to segue back into his lecture, but I couldn't stand to hear another second of the crap.

I stood up, and the room fell to silence again. Nice. I can still do that. I calmly picked up my bag and strode out of the room, not looking at a single person. I couldn't bear to be there anymore. Too many feelings were starting to tumble through my head as fresh anxieties and relapsed dread made their return known.

I began to jog as I reached the hallway, passing a concerned-looking staff member at the front desk. She called out to me by name, but I ignored it. I didn't stop for anything. I was out the doors and back in the warm sunlight, smelling the trees and the petrichor after the deluge of rain that passed through earlier. It was the first welcome sensation I'd had since seeing Jen before lunch. I needed that.

I needed to get out of this world, and back where I belonged.

"Easier said than done" is a well-worn cliché, but it became one for a reason. My first instinct was to head back to Cyraveil Forest where this all started, but the park was too far away. We'd gotten Matt to drive us that night, meeting Blake at the spot he'd called from. Today, I just ended up wandering the streets of suburbia for a while. I couldn't go home, for more reasons than one.

The endless sea of near-identical houses were taking a toll on my brain. It bothered me that they were so uniform and perfect. I could consciously tell myself this was more efficient, that economically it served a greater purpose, but I longed for the villages in the hills and valleys, or the huge port cities and the capital. They built around nature, instead of terraforming it to their whims. Sure, it was more out of necessity and lack of ability, but it gave them so much more charm and character.

I *had* to get back there.

Ten minutes later, I was on a bus headed across town. I got a few offhand looks from the other passengers, probably wondering why I wasn't in school, but I was mostly left alone. I was hoping they just assumed I was in college. I needed time to think, to strategize.

Since he wasn't at school, Blake had to be at home. There simply wasn't another option at this point. Adela would be home by now, but she'd probably be asleep. The overnight shift at the hospital was a killer, and she usually took something before retiring to a blacked-out room, where it was nighttime twenty-four hours a day. I didn't expect to run into her. I'd go in, find Blake, and we'd figure out what to do next.

I wish he'd just *call*, or send a message. Anything at all. He knew my cell number, or he could hit me up on the chatroom, or send an IM, a text, even a damn email. Anything. But it was just like him to be completely incommunicado. He was probably super distracted by something and forgot to check in.

As the bus approached the stop closest to Blake's, I reached up and pulled the yellow cord draped along the ceiling. The light up front flashed on, and the bus glided to a halt. I hopped off, thanking the driver. He gave me a noncommittal nod in return, but I didn't mind. Politeness was something to be valued, but it didn't need to be returned. It was all about the offer, not the receipt. Sooner or later, people who didn't default to being polite would run into someone who did take offense, and they'd find out just what their lack of effort meant.

A few blocks away, I found Blake's home. His neighborhood was vastly different from my own. The houses were older, and spaced out wider with much larger yards. More trees lined the sidewalks, and even dotted the center of the streets, where the road wound around them rather than through them. Despite how important it loomed in my mind, Blake's house really didn't stand out much. I'd built it up so much over the last few hours that I half-expected it to be glowing and surrounded by clouds, but it was a quiet afternoon. One neighbor I vaguely remembered was walking her dog on the opposite side of the street, and someone else was mowing their lawn, but that was it.

I stopped stalling and walked straight up to the door. I didn't bother to knock. The door was unlocked, and I'd long since stopped waiting to enter. I opened it quietly, peering inside.

The hallway stretched out before me, with a carpeted staircase immediately in front that lead up to the bedrooms. There was a short table with the house phone sitting right in the middle of the hallway, a red light blinking away with the message I'd left this morning. The empty kitchen sat at the end of the hallway, tall windows showing an empty yard beyond. As I glanced to the right, the living room was equally devoid of human presence. Thanks to the open, spacious layout, it was quickly obvious just how dead the house was.

Dread seeped into my bones, like I were a ship beginning to sink beneath the waves. My heart pounded up into my throat, even as I climbed step over step up the staircase. I was completely silent. I knew these stairs better than those in my own home. Blake and I used to have a game, seeing who could sneak up the stairs and surprise his mother. You had to know exactly where to step, since each stair had a spot or two that would creak at the slightest touch. I knew the sequence perfectly, even seven years later. It should have felt like I was coming home—but without my best friend, this wasn't a home anymore.

No. Stop thinking like that. He'd be waiting for me in his room. Probably just asleep. After getting back, he'd been so energized that he stayed up all night, and then slept through the day. Maybe he stayed up to see his mom when she got home from the graveyard shift. That was understandable. That made sense.

As I reached the second-floor landing, two doors were ajar. One was the door to Blake's parents' bedroom, which wasn't a good sign for me. When Adela went to sleep, she blacked out the room with heavy curtains and made sure the door was sealed tight, to help her keep a regular schedule. If the door was open, she either wasn't home yet, or . . .

I couldn't wait any longer. I pushed through the other open door, into my best friend's room, where I'd spent so much time playing games, watching movies, reading, or just hanging out through lazy afternoons. Where he would be sitting, right now, feet up on his desk, staring at his monitor. Except he wasn't. I turned, expecting Blake to be lounging on his bed reading a book.

He wasn't.

"Carl?"

My heart plummeted. Right accent, but the voice was too feminine. Motherly. It wasn't him.

Adela stood half-inside Blake's closet, putting away clothes. She was tall, like Blake, with long light blond hair and an athletic frame, like his whole family. Her face tilted around, stamped with confusion and surprise. She dropped the clothes, jumping in shock a little as she saw me.

"Uhh . . . hi."

"You scared me to death," she said breathlessly.

"Sorry."

She shook her head, bending to pick up the clothes and hang them properly. "It's fine. Are you okay?"

"Huh?" I asked, before connecting the dots myself. Of course she'd ask that. I wasn't at school, like I was supposed to be. "Oh. Yeah, I guess. I just . . ."

"Needed a day off?" She winked. "Don't worry. I won't tell your parents. Your grades can take it, right?"

"Probably." I shrugged. I assumed so, but hell if I knew what my grades were like right now. "I assumed you'd be asleep."

"Thought you'd have the place to yourself, hmm? I decided to get a few things done first. Don't worry, I'll be out of your hair soon." Adela continued to put up clothes while she talked, working quickly through the basket.

"No, it's fine." I sat down on the edge of Blake's bed, looking around. I deliberately bumped the keyboard tray under his desk, lighting up the screen. The conversation we'd had the day before we'd left was still on-screen. Blake telling me what he'd seen. Asking me to come out there. Asking Matt. Getting the whole group together to go out into the woods.

He'd have closed that by now. I could feel the truth sliding into view, but I kept shoving it away. I was begging, pleading with the universe to make it stop. In my head, I was screaming. Let it not be true. Let Blake just be out back or something.

"My son didn't skip, did he?" Adela asked casually, reaching up high to place something on the rack above the clothes hangers. My mind crashed to a halt at her words. She didn't know Blake was missing. Adela would have gotten home after Blake should have left. I moved my foot back slightly, feeling it bump against his backpack underneath his bed, covered by the bed skirt. She had no idea he'd never made it to school today.

That he'd never make it to school again.

That Blake was—

Oh gods. No.

I felt it cascade through me, like a waterfall bursting through a dam after so many tiny leaks. Acceptance took hold and bashed me across the head. I felt the tears beginning to form, but the realization of what Matt had been trying to get across finally broke through that same mental wall.

If we were going to survive long enough to go back, we had to play this exactly right. And Blake's mother finding out her son was gone wasn't part of the plan yet.

Even as my chest felt like it was collapsing, like my heart was threatening to burst inside my throat and tear my lungs to shreds, I had to keep silent.

It felt like an eternity had passed in that single second. I finally pulled together an answer.

" 'Course not. He had a test today."

Adela turned around. She looked suspicious. I squirmed mentally, which felt so strange for me. I'd interrogated the scum of the kingdom, but she still had power over me. Had I hesitated too long in responding? Did she know?

"Carl, is something wrong?"

"What would be wrong?" I answered as innocently as I could muster. Guilt wormed its way inside my body, alongside the raging whirlpool of grief and anxiety. I was lying outright to a woman whom I considered a second mother—who'd been there for me time and again—about the fate of her own son. I felt awful, sick to the core.

She walked over and sat down beside me. There was no way I could lie to her again, could I? Not like this.

"Did you get in a fight with your father again?" she asked quietly.

A bit of relief. Some calm to the storm. She'd picked up on something entirely different, something familiar. Most importantly for my present state of mind, it wasn't untrue.

"Sort of," I replied honestly, glancing up at her. Her eyes were so kind and wise. I swore to myself right then I'd tell her the truth. Not today, but I would. She deserved to know that her son had been a hero. That he'd saved countless lives. That I would immortalize him in the annals of the Scriveners, and make sure everyone heard his name for a dozen generations.

She put an arm around my shoulders, giving me a brief hug. "Carl, I know he can be a bit harsh sometimes, but he does love you."

"Uh-huh," I grunted sarcastically.

"Believe it or not, parents make mistakes too."

"You've given this speech before," I pointed out glumly.

"It's still true," she said. She ruffled my hair, which I'd always pretended bothered me, but was honestly really comforting. "He wants you to be successful, and he's doing what he thinks is best to make that happen."

"I'm already successful though," I muttered.

"As a student, maybe, but there's a lot more to life than being a student." Which I knew, of course. I'd stopped being just a student a long time ago. Hard to argue with results like mine, building a guild from almost nothing, becoming the closest adviser and best friend to the emperor. I was single-handedly responsible for turning the war in favor of the rebellion. Power and success were things I was accustomed to. Here, I was just so . . . helpless.

Weak.

I couldn't change anything. I couldn't do anything. My best friend was—

The emotions roared back into life, and this time I was powerless to stop the oncoming flood. I felt droplets falling into my lap, warm trickles down my cheeks.

Adela looked alarmed. "Carl, what's wrong?"

"I'm sorry," I choked out. I couldn't bring myself to say anything else.

"What for? Talk to me. Tell me what happened."

"I can't." I stood up, a little too quickly. The rush of blood from my weak, old body sent my head spinning. I stumbled a bit, but I brought it under control. I *forced* it back under control. I started for the door. "I need to go."

"Carl, wait," Adela started, but I was already out of the room. I took the stairs two at a time. I needed air. Anything besides the cramped confines of this suburban nightmare. I reached the street, and the sight of trees was enough to quell my panic, if only for a moment. But as the fear dissipated, it was replaced once again by creeping, overwhelming dread and the utter despair of loss.

Blake was dead.

The word finally crashed through my skull. I'd been dancing around it for so long, ducking away, trying to avoid its sting.

My best friend was dead.

I started running. I didn't know where to. I didn't *care* where to. Anywhere was better, but I couldn't get to anywhere.

Blake was dead.

And I couldn't do a thing about it.

CHAPTER 7

JEN

"What have you got for me?"

"Nothing, sir. We're still actively pursuing all possible leads."

"So he's been missing since last night."

"Yes, sir, based on the mother's testimony. Adela Svartholm last saw Blake before leaving for work the night before."

"Leaving for work?"

"Graveyard-shift nurse, sir."

"Chief, kid's been gone for less than twenty-four hours. Doesn't that mean he's not considered missing yet?"

"He's under eighteen, Detective. That rule doesn't apply. Did you get anything useful from the mother?"

"Hysterics?"

"West, do I need to schedule you another sensitivity training?"

"We're not sure about the mother's testimony yet, sir. We have another name or two to run down."

"Well, get going, then. Dismissed."

I know what you're thinking, but you're wrong. Pancake has cake in the name. It's close enough. And I haven't had a really good pancake in a *long* time.

Matt's pancakes are amazing. Okay, you might think it's easy to make pancakes . . . and it is. But to make *good* pancakes, that's hard. Not everyone can do that. My brother can; my mom too. Family secret recipe. One whose ingredients, along with maple syrup, sadly didn't *quite* carry over to Cyraveil.

Pancakes with maple syrup and powdered sugar. That's been our family "breakfast for dinner" treat for a long time. The sort of special surprise we'd occasionally get when we actually had the chance to sit down together and eat a good meal. Tonight's feast was better than any meal I could remember—and that included several *literal* feasts. I'm not claiming Matt's some kind of food wizard, mind you. The meal tasted great, but it was so much better because of the company.

Mom was actually awake and laughing, for one. We told the usual inside jokes, teased Matt about his unexpected new love life, and just hung out. It was like we'd picked right back up where we left off. I felt so comfortable and warm there at our little round table, just the three of us. I felt . . . normal. Relatively. For the first time, I went for hours without a single wayward thought about Cyraveil. Still the occasional glance out the window to make sure no one was there watching, but without the usual hallucination and flash of terror.

The one instance of *real* anxiety cropped up came when Mom asked me how school was going. I passed it off—or at least, I thought I did— but she came back around a few minutes later to pester me again. I knew she was just trying to be a good parent and all, but how the hell was I supposed to answer questions about my classwork from seven years ago?

Matt was no help at all. He'd gotten all moody and withdrawn, when he could have easily deflected Mom onto another subject. It was only through years of experience dealing with my opposites in the ambassador tent that I could hide my emotions and redirect the conversation back where I wanted it to go. Mom was doggedly persistent, something Matt obviously got from her. Once they put their minds to something, they did not give up. Admirable, but *really* annoying when I was the target.

I love my mom to death, don't get me wrong. I wanted to tell her everything, but Matt said no, and he was probably right. Better we kept it secret until everything became clear, and we knew what we were doing, who we could trust.

Yeah, I'm a bit of a hypocrite. Shut up.

Sara is my best friend. And not that sort of best friend where it's just the person you happen to hang out with the most. I mean someone I trust with *everything*. She's the sort of person who's seen me cry, who knows every secret crush and weird thought that has crossed my mind, whom I'd keep awake until three in the morning for weeks straight talking about anything and everything in between. I've never lied to her about *anything*.

Okay, that's a lie too, if you want to get pedantic. But the big stuff. I've never lied to Sara about anything like that, and she's helped me through so much. Like stuff with my father, or when Mom was sick, or stupid school stuff, or my massive identity crisis when I realized what it meant that my last name was different from Matt's.

(Not adopted, by the way. Full-blooded siblings, it's complicated. If you ask nicely, I might tell you the story someday.)

Point is: Sara is trustworthy. She's the best person I know in this world, except maybe my mom. But while my mom has never quite understood discretion, preferring to share everything among the family, Sara would never break a promise to anyone. Maybe Matt didn't know that yet, or maybe he just overlooked people like Sara when he said we couldn't tell anyone.

So why didn't I tell *Matt* about what I'd done yet?

If I had to admit it, I was afraid. Afraid he'd say it was a bad idea. Afraid he'd tell me not to talk to her anymore. Then we'd run into a real problem because there was no way in hell I could ever agree to that. I didn't want a fight with my brother. We'd done that before, and it only ended badly. *Really* badly.

For now, secrecy was the best option. Sara knew just enough to not ask anything yet. That seemed like an okay compromise. Besides, that also kept the rift away from her and Matt.

Yeah, my best friend and my older brother were going on a date, and that was super weird. But they're only a year apart . . . now . . . and I meant what I said. They seemed like a cute couple. I thought they'd be good together. I mean, they're my two favorite people in the world, and they want to be together. That couldn't be a bad thing, right?

Right?

No, I'm not worried. It'll be fine.

I *was* worried about whether or not Matt noticed the box I'd carried in that afternoon. When we'd gotten home from school, I'd run to check the mailbox. Lo and behold, same-day shipping is a miracle of modern technology. I'd rushed the package inside and up to my room before Matt got out to the garage—I hoped. He might have seen me through the window. I dunno. I think I hid it pretty well. He didn't mention it, at least.

After dinner, while Mom was helping Matt clean up the kitchen (even as he insisted she go relax and enjoy her unusual day off), I was very quietly and carefully climbing the stairs. Normally, our entire house creaked and groaned everywhere you walked. It was practically impossible to move around without everyone hearing you. I'd learned a lot about moving quietly though, and a lot of the concepts still applied. My feet were light and quick, and I still remembered a lot of the specific spots where the old wood made noise. Memories resurfaced, of so many nights with Tethevallen and Naeflin, learning how to move through a forest with only a whisper in my wake, how to avoid rustling the leaves and branches, and how to avoid making any audible footfalls without losing an ounce of momentum. Completely different environment, but I could adapt the basics, and I was a fast learner.

By the time I reached my room, I was practically a ghost rushing above the ground, with nary a thump of a door or a heel striking the floor to be heard.

I wasn't sure *why* I was doing it. It wasn't like my family didn't know where I was. It just felt natural. Being able to move silently almost anywhere was a skill I'd honed over the years, and it had been incredibly valuable. I didn't want to let go of it.

Also under the "valuable skills" column was what was in the package I'd ordered that afternoon, using Carl's phone. I'd slid the surprisingly short cardboard box under the bed, and I cracked it open slowly now, trying to avoid making too much noise tearing away the tape. Nestled inside was a handsome three-piece maple recurve bow, built to break down and reassemble easily. A hard leather carrying case with attached quiver accompanied it, along with a set of feathered arrows.

I took the bow out and assembled it, though I didn't string it right away. I didn't want to stress the wood, and I didn't plan on using it anytime soon, so there was no reason to bother with it yet. I slid my hand along the sier, feeling the smooth maple wood and the perfect finish. It was perfect. *Too* perfect. I wished I still had the bow I'd helped craft myself, but I forced that thought away. It was silly. There was no way I could assemble a bow of that quality with the tools and materials I had here. Besides, there were fancier, modern materials to use in place of the traditional wood, and I wasn't exactly a purist.

Case in point, the limbs on this bow were not made of wood—or any material known in Cyraveil—but black fiberglass, rolling back and upward to create a slender curve, increasing the weight of the draw when strung. I shuddered at what Tethevallen might think about such a thing, but it wasn't like I could just strengthen the limbs with an etomala here. I'd yet to feel any connection or resurgence in this world, so I had to make do. Fiberglass would work, even if the shiny black was totally at odds with the pleasant swirls of brown along the maple wood.

Satisfied, I disassembled it and placed the three pieces into their slots in the foam liner of the leather bag. The bag was worn at the waist and had an attached cylindrical case for the arrows. I tried the getup on, testing it out carefully. After a few adjustments, it flexed with my movements but stayed close and firm. It wouldn't swing around unnecessarily and catch on things or hamper me down. I reached experimentally and found I could grab an arrow as swiftly and painlessly as I needed to.

I inspected the arrows. They'd been more expensive than I'd hoped, but they felt solid and smooth, and the fletching was excellent. The tips were broad and they looked like they'd do the job. They'd fly straight too, even if the feathers were some weird colors. I guess solid white and black made them easier to spot when hunting. I packed them away into the bag, not wanting them out in the open in the quiver in case someone went snooping.

Finally, the knife. I had a lot less experience with knives—in terms of materials and quality, anyway. I definitely knew how to use one. I looked it over, and it seemed fine. The blade was sharp, and it was long enough for anything I might use it for. I was satisfied.

The bag went under my bed, concealed under some sheets. I followed suit and collapsed underneath my own blanket. Every muscle ached from exhaustion. I pulled the blanket tight around me and curled up, waiting for the heat to settle in, wishing I had a fire or anything else since I couldn't keep myself warm like I usually did.

You can buy a bow online and have it shipped to you within nine hours. How crazy is that?

With that passing thought out of the way, I drifted off only a few moments later. Real sleep had finally arrived, after one harrowing night of insomnia and an *exhausting* first day back. I was so grateful to finally drift off for real. As I slipped away though, my thoughts were fixated on what I'd just purchased. The weapon.

For the first time since I'd gotten home, I felt safe. That bothered me a lot, but I couldn't help it. I had no logical reason to expect something bad to happen, but my brain decided logic could go screw itself. In my hands, that bow was a deadly, swift, virtually silent weapon, and the knife made a great complement. They'd be perfect at putting a swift end to the fight if I were attacked.

What the hell was I thinking? I didn't want to kill anyone. That's not me. I didn't even want to hurt anyone.

So why was I clutching the knife tight under my pillow as I fell asleep?

The next day—Thursday, as I finally learned the names of the days again—was a disaster.

I mean that in the nicest way possible, of course, but I'm pretty sure I ruined everything in one day. Go, Team Jen.

Let me rewind and explain that a bit, I guess. It *started off* okay. I woke up the next morning after sleeping something like fifteen hours straight, knife still in hand. I ate breakfast, leftover pancakes from the night before. Matt had set them on a plate in the refrigerator and left a sticky note with my name on it. Mom was already gone too, so I had the house to myself for a bit. I spent it mostly just staring out the back window at the woods beyond our backyard while I chewed.

We had a small forest behind our house. It really wasn't that large, but it was deep enough that you could get a little lost, feel like your sense of direction was totally gone, surrounded by scattered tree trunks and thickets of underbrush. Of course, since we were still pretty close to a few big roads, the faint ambient noise of cars rushing by was inescapable. The woods muffled it, but only so much. Cyraveil Forest was much larger and more difficult to travel through, but it was way on the other side of town, farther away from the city.

I had an intense, primal longing for those trees right now—to sit down under the shade of some huge trunk, in the comfortable nook of its thick roots, with scattered sunlight filtering through the layers of leaves above me, feeling the wind rustle through the branches and the layers of ivy and fallen twigs coating the floor, filling my nostrils with the scent of the bark and tree sap and maybe the petrichor from an upcoming downpour.

But I had to go to school.

I packed up my bag and headed out the door. I'd managed to grab a class schedule for myself later in the day (with an assist from Sara), so I actually knew what I had today instead of just blindly hoping my feet took me to the right room. Our school operated on an alternating day schedule, so I had a new set of classes today. Sara had something in the morning on Thursdays too, so I'd be walking to school without her. My other friends were waiting by the gate in the morning though. I said hi, did the usual meet-and-greet, but I avoided conversation the rest of the way. I just let them talk. I really didn't feel it today, especially with them.

Their conversations seemed so . . . I dunno. Unimportant now? I kinda hate myself for thinking that. Does it make me super arrogant? Naeflin would have a few choice words for it, for sure.

I just couldn't get into the gossip anymore, especially since I barely remembered half the people we were talking about. Not much in the way of juicy information when names float by as insubstantially as petals in the wind. I knew I'd later regret not paying attention, but for now it just seemed like too much effort.

Sorry, back on topic, disaster day. Nothing interesting went down in the morning. I'll skip ahead to the notable bits. It happened during the break between my second and third period.

I was just standing at my locker in the hall. Nothing special about it. (Thanks, Sara, by the way, for showing me where my locker was with only a *few* raised eyebrows of pained concern.) I'd been fighting with my bag all day, trying to keep the supplies inside from moving all around whenever I walked. It made way too much noise. I could tell myself it didn't matter, but my instincts stubbornly insisted until I gave in. So I was separating everything loose into small bags, and filling them with cotton balls I'd lifted from the art classroom.

I was feeling clever and satisfied, so *of course* something had to go wrong.

A couple of guys were playing catch nearby. Nice guys, actually. I vaguely remembered the far one from a long time ago. I think we were in the same elementary school class, or something like that. I was paying attention to them, in the same way I was always keeping track of every single person within thirty feet or so. But I got distracted, trying to figure out the contents of my locker and what half of the junk stored in there actually was and if I'd really picked out the lame decorations on the door, and I didn't notice the ball coming until it crashed into the wall in front of my head.

Okay, objects flying at my head wasn't exactly a new experience. Usually they were more pointy. The similarities were there though. The rush of air in its wake as it rushed past my face, the flash of something I only caught a glimpse of. Suddenly, my mind slipped away to a wholly different place as I turned—and came face-to-face with a snarling kapavas, charging at me with eyes drenched in hatred and fists raised.

I struck. *Hard.*

He was taller and much larger than me, but he was unarmed. Something quick and direct, something he wouldn't expect. I targeted his unprotected stomach.

A sharp punch to the lower abdomen, in the unprotected fleshy spot. He started to double over from shock.

Now I could use his momentum and weight against him. As I sidestepped, my strong right foot caught his unbalanced left.

He stumbled forward. His head slammed straight into the locker interior. I spun around to follow him. My hand drew the knife from the belt holster at my back. One knee went right into his spine, pressing him into the ground.

I grabbed his head and put the blade right to his throat.

I had him at my mercy.

"What the hell?"

The real world snapped back into place. I hadn't taken down some racist, hate-fueled warrior of the Empire—just a guy on the football team. He'd been trying to catch a bad throw from his friend, and he got distracted. Nearly ran right into me.

And I'd drawn a blade on him. Taken him down. I'd nearly killed him.

Sheer, icy horror enveloped every fiber of my being. I scrambled off of him, sliding the knife up into my sleeve—praying to every star I could remember that I'd hidden the blade before anyone else spotted it. I offered my hand to the guy, now thoroughly confused on the floor at my feet, head still jammed into my locker. His friend had rushed over, while a small crowd gathered around us, chattering away excitedly.

Oh man. This is bad.

"Sanan," I offered awkwardly. "Self-defense classes, am I right?"

"Uh-huh," he said slowly, but he took my hand anyway. I pulled him to his feet, relieved at the lack of confrontation. He hadn't noticed just how close to death he'd been a second ago. Because of me. Because I screwed up.

"Are you okay?" asked his friend, staring at me.

"Is *she* okay?" the guy shot back.

"Oh, get over it, Chris. You weren't using that head anyway," he snorted. I giggled at his tone, in spite of myself, and the friend grinned. "How'd you do that, Jenny?"

The brief moment of mirth drained away into cold ice again. Okay, don't get me wrong, I dig being the center of attention on a good day, but this sure as hell wasn't a good day. If I was up to it, I could rock the "edgy, mysterious cool girl" vibe I'd suddenly picked up and ride it all the way to the next dance—but right now? I was in volas us manav mode. I had so much adrenaline in my blood begging me to get away that I couldn't keep still. My right hand was playing with the hilt of the knife just inside the hem of my sleeve, fidgeting, waiting to strike.

I needed to get out of there. My heart hammered the inside of my skull with blood.

They were still waiting for me to say something. "I eat my veggies," I said lamely. "Sorry, I gotta run."

Without looking back, I grabbed my bag and closed the locker. In seconds, I was out of the building entirely.

There was *no* way I was gonna make it through the rest of the day. I wouldn't see a single friendly face, thanks to the class schedule change. I felt so weak. I hated that I needed a support system to get through *one day* of high school. I'd never had this problem before. I wasn't supposed to be like this. I was supposed to be normal again, but I still felt like a mentally unstable, emotionally broken wreck of a person.

Yeah, I know, I've got some kind of PTSD or such and such. That's obvious. I can even pinpoint where I got it, and that doesn't do a damn thing for me. Knowing what's wrong with you and actually being able to *do* something about it are very, very different things. I was still stuck on step A, and I had no clue how to get to step B.

It terrified the shit out of me.

So I ran. I sprinted through the neighborhood, retreating to the place I felt most comfortable and safe, where I could feel like myself again. Where I felt home. Where nothing bad ever happened to me, where I'd really figured out who I was and how to actually live in the world.

So, naturally, I found myself deep in the woods behind my house, with the bow and arrows slung over my back and the knife comfortably resting at the small of my back.

Even yesterday, I hadn't actually planned on using the bow for anything. I'd wanted it like I wanted a security blanket when I was a kid. I just needed it, not because I was actually gonna use it as a blanket, but because it had to be around or things just weren't *right*. That bow was gonna sit in its case, under my bed, unnoticed, and I'd probably never take it out again.

Funny how things can change in a single day, right?

No, it's not funny at all. It's fucking terrible. I've had way too many "single days" in my life.

But this, right now? Here in the woods all alone? This was good.

I was deep in the forest, as totally immersed as I could get. The noise of the human world was barely audible, muffled to a faint whisper by the undergrowth and the thick branches. There was almost no wind today, which was a bit disappointing, but just being surrounded by lush green, with birds chirping away and even a squirrel darting along a branch nearby, set my mind at ease.

For a long time, I just wandered idly, no purpose in mind and no real direction besides away from the noise. Normally, I'd be lounging in a bind, waiting for prey to show itself, but I wasn't sure there was any worthwhile game in this forest. More to the point, even though I hated that I couldn't forget it even out here, I was back in the real world. I wasn't totally clear on what the law said, but I was pretty sure hunting in the woods in a random suburb was illegal.

Plus, to be honest, I wasn't really hungry. I just wanted to feel good at something again. Use the skills I'd obtained for something other than fighting and . . . you know. The other thing. But if I went hunting on a full stomach and a well-stocked pantry, Tethevallen would be *seriously* ticked off.

So, yeah. Tethevallen. I know I haven't brought him up much, and I'm sorry. It's still painful. He's the best father I ever had. Okay, the only one, but still.

I found a nice trunk to lean against and sat down. Above, the sky, dotted with puffy clouds, peeked through the forest canopy. I couldn't see a single star at this hour, obviously, but I knew where Tethevallen's would be. I offered him a smile and a short prayer as I started to doze off. Not that he was actually there. He'd roll his eyes at the idea whenever some of the younger Sylves brought it up. But I liked it a lot. It comforted me to think some part of his personality and memories had followed his intelligence back up into the sky.

Man, I sound like a nut, don't I?

I reached into my bag and pulled out a blanket I'd brought with me, wrapping myself up tight, wishing yet again I could do better than just cloth coverings to warm myself up. I pulled up my hood, then leaned back against the nook of the tree and let my eyes slide shut. Just listening. Hearing everything in the woods. Letting my mind wander out into the forest.

For a minute, I could almost hear the whispering of the Sylves in nearby trees. My friend Naeflin played her tulavir, and she was begging me to sing along, even though I barely knew any of the songs yet. She'd laugh as I made up the words to her melodies, and we'd trade off playing the tulavir and singing increasingly provocative songs to the more handsome of the dusylfs across the fire, as we downed cup after cup of talverreth. When we were too drunk to keep playing, she'd break out her usual party trick of catching a ball of flame from the sparks of the fire, making it fly circles around my eyes until I got dizzy and fell over.

All the Sylves would laugh. I'd get embarrassed and snatch the fire right out of the air. I'd multiply it into a dozen licks of flame and spell out something horribly rude to Naef, which would just get the whole lot of them laughing even harder. None of them could match my etovola for fire, so they got a kick out of my party tricks.

Of course, with the entire group drunk off our asses and already playing with fire, it was only natural we got into a vakakka-measuring contest of etola. Most Sylves preferred the water or the wind when it came to etovola, which meant their drinking games usually involved talverreth and screwing around with the actual liquid. Naef and I were the only ones around with any real etolendei of flames, so our fireside contests became legendary in our suunsyl. Dozens of Sylves showed up whenever they heard we were having a gathering, sending Ruvalei scurrying into the shadows in embarrassment over her little sister's antics. They came in droves, eager to see the two masters showing off our skills.

Or maybe they just came out to see two girls playing with fire. I can't say for sure. I was only twenty, after all, and Naef was only sixty or so. (That's young for a Sylf, all right? She looked and acted basically the same age as me. It's totally unfair.) We were prime targets for the younger Sylves in the audience. Plenty of them approached Naef, and a few of the really adventurous ones tried to ask out the strange human girl they'd collectively adopted.

I turned them down.

Oh, don't get me wrong. I was interested. By the stars, some of those guys . . . I mean. Damn. But I had my reasons.

A branch snapped in half nearby. The sharp crack echoed around the trees. My daydreams burst like a bubble, abrupt and terrifying. I tensed up, my hand already grabbing at my knife. Someone was crunching through the leaves scattered on the forest floor not far away.

I slowly reached for my bow, out of pure instinct, prepared for the worst.

I'm on Earth. If I draw and they see me, then I'll really be in trouble.

I fought the urge. I was in the suburbs, and nobody was likely to attack me out of the blue. I was safe. Except I still had the knife in my grip, just in case, as I peeked around the edge of the tree trunk toward the source of the sound.

Relief flooded my mind as I recognized the source—followed by a twinge of confusion. I sheathed the knife and stood up to call out.

"Shasalla, Kalleddor. Dov to dou tolal tona vis sylvec?"

Carl froze in place, eyes narrowing. He looked around and spotted me without too much difficulty. Since, you know, I wasn't really hiding anymore. Why hide from the guy who saved your life a couple of times over? The only guy in the world who could even understand that sentence?

"Hi, Jen."

"The one and only," I added, as he made his way over to my tree. I winced at every loud, crunching step through the leaves. "Weren't you way better at this?"

"Shut up," Carl muttered. He sat down on an overturned trunk that had fallen many years back, while I returned to my comfortable position in the nook of the tree roots. "I'm not used to my old body yet." He paused. "Did you just call me Kalleddor?"

"Yeah," I teased. "Did I leave off your title or something?" I knew full well I had, and that it bothered him.

". . . I dunno. Just sounds cheesy now." He looked embarrassed.

I grinned. "It always did."

"Oh god, it did?" His face turned an even brighter shade of red.

"Don't worry, I'm sure it was just me and Matt who thought that," I said. "It's a perfectly good fantasy name." Carl still looked doubtful, so I changed the subject before he could really start to dig into it. "Anyway, back to the obvious question: Why the hell are you out here?"

"I could ask you the same," Carl shot back, raising an eyebrow.

"Yeah, no," I replied without missing a beat. "This is basically my thing, and we're near my house. You better not be stalking me," I added jokingly.

". . . I kinda was," he answered, sheepish. "I saw what you ordered on my phone. I figured you'd go out hunting sooner or later."

I was genuinely surprised. It took me a minute to figure out how he'd done it. ". . . Oh shit. Browser history."

He nodded. "Yup."

"Good thing I didn't use Matt's computer then, I guess."

"Yeah."

"So you just followed me out here to scare away all my prey?" I added, pointedly glancing at his feet.

"I wanted to talk."

Something in the tone of his voice, or maybe his expression, killed the mood. I'd actually been enjoying myself for once. The conversation wasn't that different from the ones we used to have, back before . . . well, it. Me teasing, him getting teased, good-natured banter. That was our thing. So obviously, it was bound to come to a crashing halt today.

"What's wrong?" I asked, already dreading the answer.

Carl started to respond, but he faltered, his mouth opening and closing a few times without any sound coming out. I waited patiently. I had no idea where this was going, but it seemed so unlike him. Carl didn't speak up all that often, but he was never at a loss for words. I really felt worried. Finally, he worked up to a single question.

"You were there, right?"

Well, that was underwhelming. "Uhh?"

"When Blake . . . When he—" Carl choked up, glancing away awkwardly.

Oh stars. My heart sank. Carl had finally come around to acceptance. I knew it was coming, but still. How the hell are you supposed to talk to someone about their best friend dying?

". . .Yeah," I said quietly.

"I never found out," said Carl, his voice a little stronger, his eyes coming back to mine. "He didn't suffer, right?"

He did . . . I replied mentally, *but I can never tell you that.* "He didn't. It was quick."

Carl smiled. "Even if that's bullshit, vannen dou."

"Selnou."

He picked up a small branch from the ground and fiddled with it. I settled back into my tree, picking up my blanket and wrapping myself tight. The day was getting chillier as the clouds moved in and blocked out the sun, and a breeze had finally started to roll through, rustling the branches and leaves. I loved the sound it made. We just sat there, like old times, Carl sharpening his sword (okay, branch), me watching him and everything else from my spot under the tree. Minutes rolled by, with only the birds keeping us company.

"He loved it there, you know?" Carl said finally. I suppressed a sigh of relief. While I was kinda enjoying the silence, Carl hadn't been the quiet type in a long time. If it kept stretching out, I'd really start to worry.

"Blake did?" I prompted.

"Yeah. I mean, he hated the war and all that, but the world. He loved Cyraveil."

"Oh." I wasn't sure what Carl wanted out of this conversation. I resigned myself to just letting him bounce stuff off me. I hoped that was what he needed. Seemed to be working so far, anyway.

"He found a girl, you know? She was beautiful. They were going to get married, start a family. He asked me to be his best man."

"I thought that wasn't a thing over there."

Carl grinned. "We were going to start the tradition ourselves. Blake was such a romantic. Had to have the picturesque wedding."

"I never knew," I said. "I didn't really get to spend a lot of time with him."

"I'm sorry."

"It's not your fault. I was kinda busy."

"Busy being the Maiden of the Sylvandar?" Carl raised an eyebrow, smirking.

My turn to get red-faced. "Vack, that's so much cheesier. Is that really what they called me in Candir?"

"Well, they had to call you *something.* You were a legend."

"Does that come with a shiny hat?"

"More like the undying hatred of the Emperor."

I snickered. "Now *there's* a badge of honor." Carl laughed. "Undying's not really right though, huh?"

Oh vack. Carl's expression fell, dark as night. I cringed. I hadn't meant to kill the mood. I'd said *exactly* the wrong thing.

". . . Sorry."

"It's okay," he said, but he glanced away again.

"I shouldn't have said that. He was your friend."

Carl shook his head. "Not anymore."

"Carl . . ."

"You know he first met me after I bought out his whole city?" Carl said, starting a story I'd heard a thousand times—but never from Carl himself. "I can't believe I was stupid enough to go out and meet him alone. I can't believe he was even stupider and showed up with just a single bodyguard."

"The two most powerful people in Cyraveil, dumber than a box of rocks," I joked.

"He respected me," Carl went on, ignoring me. "I'd never had that. He could have wiped us out, even as powerful as we were, but he brought us into the Empire. Brought *me* into his confidence. He named me the protector to his *son.*"

I raised an eyebrow. *That* was news. "So you would've been regent?"

"He called me brother," Carl said, voice hard and cold, "and I let him burn."

"I'm so sorry," I said softly, though I was glad beyond belief that Reynir Cellman was dead and buried.

"He made mistakes, and he paid for them," he said. "I can't say he didn't deserve it."

Why, oh, why, Carl, do we always have to bounce wildly between joking and teasing, and painful shared memories? Every single damn time. The silence was uncomfortable beyond belief.

Why couldn't I just keep the awkward bits out and have a nice, normal conversation? Or, you know, whatever passed for normal between two casual dimension hoppers like us.

"You know, I meant what I said," Carl blurted out, looking back at me. "On the phone."

"Huh?"

"I still love you."

That's where he decided to take the conversation next?

"Carl . . ." I started, but he kept talking.

"Even if we're stuck here, even though everything's different, I really do love you, Jen."

I had to stop this confessional before it got way out of hand. "Carl, you don't."

"What?"

"You don't really know me." I sighed. "Before we left here, you didn't even know my name."

"But, that night—"

Oh stars, not that. "Look, Carl. You're my friend, and yeah, we went through some ridiculous, life-changing, terrifying things together. I got caught up in the moment, okay?" I shrugged, red-faced. "At the time, I really needed to be rescued, and you were there. I'll be grateful to you forever, but that's all."

"I—"

"It was just a kiss, Carl." My face lit up like someone had just poured boiling water on it. Stupid emotions.

If you're wondering, I was being honest. I'm gonna be horribly cliché and drop the oldest line in the book, but I only liked Carl as a friend. That night at the inn outside Vennenport was just that—one night when I let my guard down and got swept away by everything else around me. There was nothing romantic going on between us, and even if there was, I had way too much of my own shit to deal with.

And there wasn't. Seriously. Just two friends who spent a lot of time together and kissed once . . . or twice.

I didn't like what I had to do to him though. Carl was my friend, and I was still hurting him. Of course, *of course,* it had to get worse.

"It didn't seem like that," he said, confused.

"I don't know what else to say, Carl." I sighed. "You met someone, but it wasn't really me. I'm sorry."

"You're wrong." I raised my eyebrows at his harsh tone. His eyes narrowed, and he tossed the branch aside. "That was you. This?" He leaned in and picked up a little keychain on my bag. A cute plastic squirrel, something I won at the arcade a long time ago and kept on every backpack I'd had since then. "This isn't the real you. This is just some facade you've put up." He sat back down again. "I'd bet anything you're armed right now, yeah?"

I nodded slowly. Since we'd started talking, I'd actually let go of the knife, but it was still gently pressing into the small of my back as I leaned against the tree.

"Yeah, because *that's* you. You're still her, not Jenny. You're *Jennifer Demovi-Ralaev*." He said it with awe, almost as a whisper. Like it was something inspirational. "You're a fucking legend, not some silly high school girl."

"Seka nara vack do you know my name?" I snarled, shocked. That name was private. Carl couldn't possibly know it. Only the people in my suunsyl knew that name.

He recoiled in fear at my sudden shift in tone. "I—"

"Talk, masasak-la, or I'm gonna get violent."

"Reynir told me," he blurted.

". . . And how the hell did Reynir Cellman know?"

Carl looked down at the forest floor. His voice got very quiet. ". . . Because he tortured it out of a Sylf. Her name was Ruvalei. I think."

I stood up abruptly. The blanket fell away. My hand went straight to the knife. Not to attack Carl or anything, but I wanted to stab something. "Ruvalei Dusylari?" I asked, forcing the syllables through my teeth. I already knew the answer though. There were very few Sylves that spoke enough Linguen to be worth torturing, and I knew all of them. I'd *taught* all of them.

". . . Yes," Carl answered nervously. "I'm sorry."

I started pacing in front of the tree, deliberately crunching the leaves with each step. I needed to express my rage somehow, have some kind of outlet.

I hadn't known where she went. We never found out what happened to her. Naeflin cried for days straight when she vanished. We both did. Naef's sister was the kindest, sweetest person in the whole forest. Super timid, but when she came out of her shell, she was an amazing cook and the most beautiful singer you can imagine. She taught me everything about history and culture, especially music. She wrote her own songs, too, and I'd learned them all.

She went missing not long before the first border raids, when my happy life had finally shattered.

"Did he kill her?" I asked, looking up at the sky, trying desperately to see her star—though I knew it was forever lost to me. It was a whole world away, and she'd died alone in the depths of a dungeon on a torture rack, far from the roots of the world.

"Yes."

"Syldavacka," I growled. I kicked the tree trunk, though it didn't make me feel any better. "I'm glad that dektolal kapar-basal is dead. Blake should've killed him slower."

"Wait, what?"

I stopped pacing. I'd just said something I really, *really* shouldn't have. I turned in place, very slowly, to look at Carl. His face was an unreadable mask.

Well, guess we both learned something shocking and terrible today.

"Blake was there?" His voice was too calm. Unsettling.

Oh stars, don't connect the dots. Don't be logical and smart for once in your life, Carl. "Yeah. Blake and I were both there," I said cautiously, fighting against my own emotions. I was still reeling from what *I'd* just learned, even as I tried to hide the secret from Carl.

"But you never made it into the throne room. And Matt knew what was inside . . ." Carl's face contorted. I braced myself. He'd figured it out. Matt should have known better. "He sent Blake in there to die."

"Carl—"

"He knew. Matt fucking knew," Carl muttered. I could hear the iron in his voice, the cold steel of Kalleddor. "Matt fucking *sacrificed* Blake."

"We *all* knew," I said weakly, but Carl was already up and moving.

"I can't, Jen." Carl's voice was thick and pained, and I felt for him. I felt so much for him I could barely breathe. He turned to leave, and I opened my mouth to speak, but nothing came out. "I just can't."

I watched him turn and walk away. I knew he was starting to cry and hiding it, and I could feel tears forming in my own eyes. I'd screwed up today. That conversation had gotten way out of control.

I fell back against the tree again and pulled the blanket up tight, ducking into my hood and closing my eyes as tears rolled down my cheeks. Memories of Naeflin, and Tethevallen, and Ruvalei, poor Ruvalei, took over my mind. I let them swallow me up, desperately shutting out the real world to hide in the other, if only for a little bit longer.

CHAPTER 8

MATT

Not having my own cell phone was becoming a real problem.

I'd heard from a friend about an . . . *incident*, something involving Jen in the halls between second and third period, but he didn't know anything more than that. Without any way to get in touch with her, I had no way of knowing what was going on. Stress compounded in my head all day. I barely heard half of what my econ teacher was saying. My fears were growing by the hour, but there wasn't anything I could do. I wasn't likely to see Jen until late that night. We didn't share a lunch time today, and she'd be gone when I got home. I wouldn't see her until after I got back from work.

Work. A normal job, where I got paid to do something by someone *else* in charge. Part-time at a convenience store. I'd picked it up for some experience, plus the extra spending money. Mom trusted me with the money she brought in, but I never spent any of that on myself. Most of it was strictly for the family's needs, and the rest went into a rainy day savings account. I only spent my own money on myself.

The job was painfully dull. Endless restocking, reorganizing, cleaning. No matter how many times I went through a section, it'd always be messed up again minutes after I walked away. Somehow, even when the store was empty. It felt like a ghost was deliberately screwing with me.

Not that I had to deal with ghosts anymore.

The store wasn't particularly well trafficked, so I had a lot of downtime. In the past, that usually meant hanging out with whichever of my coworkers I had that afternoon. Screwing around, goofing off, making up games we could play that wouldn't wreck the aisles. Whatever. Of course, whenever the coworker took a break, I'd lapse into boredom again. I used to be so terrible at being idle. I had to be doing *something*. Even if it wasn't productive, even if it wasn't enjoyable, as long as I was engaged I could feel at ease.

Calm, quiet moments were now precious gifts, every last one of them. It gave me time to think. Time to reflect. Time to plan. I'd learned quickly that if I didn't slow down and consider everything, find the best approach I could, I'd end up with even more failures and regrets.

It was a hard lesson to learn. A lesson I learned in sweat and blood, in the heat of battle and the quiet, deadly halls of diplomacy and subterfuge. I'd found a new way. Careful, measured, patient. Taking control whenever possible.

I didn't *want* control. That's not me. I'd love for someone else to be in charge. I'd prefer that. I hate the pressure. I hate what I'd been forced to do, the decisions I've had to make, with lives in the balance—but nobody else was going to do it. By chance, or by fate, or by sheer stubborn resilience, I'd ended up in charge of the whole rebellion.

I had so many things still weighing on my mind. Tasks unfinished, problems unsolved. There were a dozen advisers, policymakers, and members of the court awaiting my decisions. Kings, princes, vassals, dukes, lords, and a myriad of other titles I barely understood, all wanting meetings, jostling for favor. They'd decided that since I was such a great leader, I was obviously the best person to take the keys to the whole damn kingdom.

But that wasn't me anymore. I'd put that part of my life away. It was wrapped in heavy blankets, stuffed into a chest, and shoved under the nearest bed. I wasn't going to worry about it anymore—until the world, cruel and unrelenting, had reared its ugly head and decided I wasn't quite off the hook yet.

I was blissfully unaware for most of my shift. Yes, I'd heard that Jen had done something, but I convinced myself it was something minor. She'd probably just stammered out some long phrase in Etoline, or maybe she'd tried to cast some spells without thinking. It was so instinctive for her, I could see it slipping out by accident. It'd be a simple misunderstanding, something I could paper over, something we could work on.

So it was that my coworker and I were talking about totally normal things, as if another crisis wasn't right around the corner.

"Hey, Kyle."

"Yeah?" Kyle looked up from over by the soda machine, where he was refilling a cup of ice. He came back, chomping through a couple of cubes, and leaned against the counter. "What's up?"

"How are you and Kersey doing?"

Kyle looked surprised. I couldn't blame him. I normally didn't care much about relationships or any of that. I used to be totally apathetic about the whole concept. It wasn't worth the effort to keep up. Cyraveil had changed my perspective completely. Maintaining a network of people, and knowing how they all intertwined, was essential. By now, it was habit.

"Good, I guess?" He shrugged. "We hang out a lot. It's . . . going well. Why?"

"To be honest," I said, "you're kind of my only friend with any dating experience. Got any tips?"

"Wait." Kyle looked genuinely shocked. "*You've* never asked a girl out?"

I laughed. "Not until yesterday." Which wasn't exactly true, but I drew a pretty solid line between dating a girl and courting a princess. Especially when the latter was all about easing diplomatic tensions, maintaining alliances, preventing wars, and keeping our respective armies in line. There were so many rows of dominoes waiting to be knocked over, I had to tiptoe around every word, in public and in private.

Very different.

"Oh man," Kyle grinned. "Who's the lucky girl?"

"You won't spread it around, right?" I asked. Not that Sara was anyone to be embarrassed about, but for Jen's sake, I felt like avoiding any attention right now could only be a good thing.

"Hey, man, you never told anybody about me and Kersey. I wouldn't do that to you either."

"Bit different though, what with your parents."

"I guess." Kyle shrugged again. He was a frequent shrugger. I'd become a lot more attentive to body language and subtle cues. Reading people was a valuable skill and way more universal than one might expect.

I tried to brush it off. I wasn't trying to get some kind of advantage over Kyle. I just wanted his advice. I needed some dating ideas from this century.

"Anyway, what did you want to ask?"

"Just need some ideas. It's either you or the internet."

"The internet's better than you think," said Kyle. I raised my eyebrows, and his cheeks shifted to an interesting tomato hue. "Or so I've heard," he mumbled.

"I trust you more than the internet."

"You're crazy, but whatever. So, who's the girl?"

"Do you know Sara Monaghan?"

Kyle frowned. "The junior?"

"Yeah."

"Not really, no. She's in my comp sci, but that's about it. Doesn't really talk that much. Kind of a loner."

That didn't really fit with what I knew about her, but maybe she was different when she was around Jen. Or in that class. I couldn't be sure.

"You asked her out?" Kyle continued.

"Yeah. We're going out tomorrow."

Kyle clapped a hand on my back. "Nice. Good for you. You really seemed like you could use a break, man."

"What?"

"I dunno. You've just been really quiet, dude. Scarin' me. You okay?"

Our conversation was interrupted by the chime of the front door. A customer wandered in, and instantly I knew something was off. Something about the way he moved. His body language. I watched him carefully in the mirrors mounted up in the ceiling corners. He wandered to the back, out of sight of the register, and visibly relaxed as he seemingly passed out of our view.

The refrigerator door opened, and his hand flickered out. I saw the brief flash of a brown bottle. His hand retracted again into his heavy coat.

A second later, the door chimed again and he was gone, before either of us could react. He was sprinting headlong out the door, almost smashing into it as the automatic slider didn't open fast enough for the speed he was moving at. I wasn't sure what scared him off. Maybe he just felt like he already won.

Lucky for me, the security camera probably got a good shot of his face. I pulled out an asset loss sheet and dutifully recorded the time and date, a rough description, and what we'd lost.

"You're actually filling that out?"

". . .Yes?"

Kyle shrugged again, and I resisted the urge to wince. "You know they never actually bother with anything that cheap. Especially not with a homeless guy."

"We still have to fill it out." The pen went dry halfway down. I rattled it, but not a single drop of ink was left. "Got a pen?"

Kyle shook his head, amused, and tossed me a fresh one. "Man, even the universe is telling you not to bother."

"The universe and I don't get along anyway," I grumbled aloud.

While I finished filling out the form, the door chimed again. Jacob, a friend of Kyle's and a member of his *D&D* group, strolled in, glancing back over his shoulder. "Jesus, that guy was booking it. What did you two do to him?"

"Nothin'. He just stole some beer," said Kyle, hopping up to sit on the counter.

Jacob started pouring himself a soda from the fountain. "Seriously? What an asshole."

"Nah, he probably needs it more than we do."

"Sure, whatever. Anyway, I had something else to tell you guys."

Kyle and I both looked up. "You came here with some actual news? Stop the presses," said Kyle, smirking. I rolled my eyes.

"Oh stuff it, grandma. You hear what happened during APUSH?"

My heart skipped a beat. I couldn't quite remember what APUSH stood for, but Jacob had to be talking about school. Horrible images of anything Jen might have done flitted through my mind, accompanied by visions of white beds and padded cells.

I was paying very close attention to every single word Jacob said now. Every muscle tic in his face, every shift in tone. I wasn't going to miss a thing.

"Uhh . . ." said Kyle, clearly as lost as I wished I were. He didn't sound nearly as concerned as I felt. It irritated me. Completely irrational, but still, the idea that Kyle didn't understand the weight of what Jacob might say next bothered me more than I'd like to admit.

"It was nuts. Carl went psycho in the middle of class, ranted to Mr. Edwards some crazy speech about war."

I don't think I can really convey the emotion that washed through me when I heard Carl's name. Panic, fear, and images of Jen drained away—but at the same time, frustration and a creeping dread slithered in, taking just as tight a hold.

"What did he do, exactly?" I asked, trying to sound casual. After all, Carl and I barely knew each other.

"Oh, he went on and on about how shitty war is. Got pretty dark. He shot down what Edwards was saying with some pretty good stuff, actually. It was super messed up and seriously psycho, but it was still smart, you know?"

My breath got easier. Carl was just letting off steam. Dangerous steam, but nothing was boiling over yet. This was manageable. Jacob kept talking about what Carl said in painfully familiar detail, but I was already thinking miles ahead. I had to consider what to say to Carl when I next saw him. He was getting worse, that much was clear, but I could handle that.

Of course, the next bomb was about to drop.

"So that's why he ditched?" asked Kyle.

It was like he'd just thrown a dagger into the relief growing in my brain, pinning it dead to the wall.

"Yeah, probably. He just stood up and walked out in the middle of class. Straight out the door without a word."

I shook my head in despair. Carl was going to be the end of us.

They started talking about some video game after that, something coming out soon. I might have been interested if I could actually remember the game in question, but video games were long erased from my memory. I'd filled up all that space with too much information about a world I'd never see again—if I had anything to say about it.

I didn't mind that the conversation left me behind though. It let me get back to what needed to be done. My thoughts were preoccupied with fears of what Carl might do next, what had happened to Jen that morning, and what my next move was. There was always a next move to take, a new plan to make. I'd prayed so many times I'd never have to decide someone else's fate again, but it always fell back to me, one way or another.

The rest of my shift passed in no time at all, as Jacob went home and we were replaced by the overnight duo. I drove home with the radio blasting at the highest it could go. The weak, tinny speaker was actually comforting now, a taste of familiarity and stability. It never changed, as awful as it sounded. I appreciated that.

That golden path I'd seen just two days ago seemed so far away now. I'd wanted desperately for nothing to change, for my world to go back to the way it had been, but fate seemed determined to deny me any respite. Even as I'd thought we could just settle in and return to our old lives, Jen seemed haunted and withdrawn. She wasn't adapting yet, and that scared me.

On the surface, she was totally fine. She'd lapsed here and there, but we all had. That was normal, to be expected. I knew her better than that though. I knew how good an actress she could be. Jen could hold in problems as long as she needed to, and she was so much quieter than before. She seemed reluctant to engage with the world now, always hiding something.

She just needed time. She'd spent the better part of six years in a virtually alien culture, speaking a different language, adopting their customs. She'd grown accustomed to using magic, a concept completely at odds with reality. The elves' magic let them avoid so many of life's usual hassles. How could she possibly adjust in such a short time from *that* lifestyle to the mundane grindstone of the real world?

Her old life would reassert itself. I was confident of that—I had to be—and I'd do whatever I could to help her adjust. I was worried about the *other* member of our group.

Not only was Carl clearly just as dramatically changed as Jen, he was in a position I couldn't really support. Much as I wracked my brain for solutions, I came up empty. Carl and I had too much animosity in our past, even with bombshells yet un-dropped. We'd been on opposite sides of a vicious war, in surprisingly influential positions for two twentysomethings from suburban Oregon.

Our forces had been circling each other for some time. I'd known from the modern tactics and total disregard for feudal practices of honor and duty that it had to be Carl commanding the other side. I'd been using the same, since I was running a rebellion anyway. We were trying to overthrow the whole government. Who were we going to bow and swear fealty to? It was ludicrous. I wasn't a lord. My generals were gutter trash, and I was a nobody—and yet we defeated legions of Cellman forces with ease until Carl took command.

In all honesty, I think we both probably would have ended up dead, but for my sister. Carl's men were fanatically loyal to him. They would have fought to the death, even once we started to outnumber them. Between that and Carl's personal abilities—on top of a penchant for assassinating my officers—my neck felt particularly soft and vulnerable for weeks on end.

If Carl hadn't found Jen in that dungeon. If he hadn't betrayed Reynir. If he hadn't pulled his forces out of the war and left the Cellmans to die.

If, if, if.

I shuddered. I truly believe Carl would have sent a man to kill me. He very well may have. My head would probably be mounted on top of the walls outside Candir along with all the rest, a macabre warning to strike fear in the hearts of the next would-be revolutionaries.

I feared him.

At the same time, though, I did respect him. Carl took a situation where anybody else would have probably just died, and he carved out a life for himself. He was strong, he was incredibly cunning, he treated his subjects well. It sounds bizarre to refer to Carl as having "subjects," but he did. There was a reason he commanded such a steadfast, unwavering army.

Most important of all, Carl was intelligent. Certainly smarter than me. I admit that freely. Carl seemed to know more about everything, down to the minutiae of any subject, than I could ever hope to learn. Not only that, but he could actually apply that knowledge—which he did, with terrifying efficiency. As the receiving end of his military strategy, I could attest to that personally.

So, given all that, what was Carl's play now? I turned it over and over in my head, like roasting meat over a fire that stubbornly refused to finish cooking. By now, I assumed, he must have visited Blake's house. He'd be certain Blake was dead now, something I'd already come to accept. Where to next for a man who'd lost almost everything he valued, who'd been forced back to a life he believed long dead?

A man whose entire world had literally been taken away.

I didn't have an answer. I couldn't empathize with Carl. I was eternally grateful for the elf witch, the one who'd given me the way out. I hated Cyraveil, hated what it had done to me. What it had done to Jen.

To Blake.

I'd sent one of my friends to die. Knowingly, deliberately, he'd gone to his grave, on my orders. That odd smile he always seemed to wear was forever fixed in my mind. He looked so confident, so self-assured when I laid out the plan, fully aware what it meant. It had to be him, after all. A foreigner, an outsider like the rest of us. Jen and I were too well-known, but Blake could get inside unhindered, thanks to Carl's betrayal.

Carl could never be allowed to learn that his own actions inadvertently led to Blake's death. He'd never recover. As I pulled into the garage, that single thought became firm and clear in my mind. No matter what, I would protect Carl from that revelation.

My mom was already home, which meant I was definitely running late. I hurried inside. I'd wanted to help prepare dinner, since I hadn't been able to spend much time with her since the night we came back, and last night was so full of worry about Jen and what came next. I wasn't going to waste any more valuable time.

"Mom, I'm home," I called out down the hallway as I kicked my shoes off and into the closet. I sniffed the air. Garlic. "What're you making?"

"Tortellini soup," she said, waving a spoon at me. "You're late, bucko."

"Bucko?" I teased, washing my hands.

"Showing my age?" she asked sarcastically, before she handed me a towel to dry off. "Start choppin'."

"So, school's good?"

"Yes."

"Good." She smiled, pushing aside her bowl for a moment and leaning on her hands. "Since Jen's gone, I figured it was a good time to have this talk."

Jen was at Sara's house, which was a regular Thursday thing. I wondered what she was doing there. I still didn't know what she'd told Sara. I trusted Jen, but I needed all the details if I was going to come up with a plan. I was feeling a bit claustrophobic without one.

Not unlike the feeling my mother had just sprung on me. "Uhh, what talk?"

"About your future."

I breathed an inward sigh of relief. Mom was referring to how I'd always hated talking about my life around anyone else. I appreciated that she never brought it up again, even around Jen, since I'd mentioned it.

"What about it?" I asked, taking a sip of the tomato soup.

"Well, have you made any plans for after you graduate?"

I scoured my brain. *Had* I made any plans yet? It was so long ago. I had no idea. "Not really, no." It was the most honest reply I could think of.

"Well, you need to start. I know it can really suck, but now's the time. College will sneak up on you sooner than you think."

College. I'd forgotten all about it. I mean, not that it existed—I'd actually briefly attended a university of sorts, out in Dekinport. Not for education though. I wasn't there for the lectures; I was there for the cache of gold and magical weaponry a few floors and a couple dozen feet of solid rock below my desk.

While I hesitated, my mother started going into detail about applications, acceptance, funding. "A state school's probably the best option for you, I think," she added, between mouthfuls.

A sudden realization struck me and interrupted my unbidden memory of the desperate chase and fight with the Dekinport city guard. There weren't any state universities near our home. Not close enough to commute, anyway. "You sure you'd be okay without me around?"

"You gotta leave the nest sometime, Matt." She said it so nonchalantly, I was taken aback. I knew I'd leave eventually, but I assumed it'd be way later in life. I helped out with all the household chores, and I helped take care of Jen, and anything else Mom asked of me. It was my job—or so I assumed.

"What about—" I started, but Mom cut me off.

"Look, I've saved up a bit over the years, and I know you've been saving too. You've got enough to cover four years of college if you apply for financial aid, and you won't even end up with any loans. I'll be quitting my job at the mall after this year, thank God. Between my savings and the raise I just got, it's going to be a lot more relaxed around here." She smiled. "Your sister and I will be fine. You've got a whole life ahead of you. No need to spend it hanging around here."

"I don't mind."

Mom laughed. "You're a good man, Matt." She stood up and started clearing the table. There was only a little time left before she had to head off to the mall, so she was rushing already. I should have gotten up to help, but I was still considering everything she'd said.

As she talked, my life plans had come back to me—how I'd seen myself taking care of her and the house for decades to come. I fully expected Jen to leave and make her own way, but I just assumed I'd be here forever. Now, my mother was not only giving me permission to leave, she was practically pushing me out the door—not in a bad way, but it was the impression I got.

She thought she was letting me off the hook. She'd probably been thinking I felt pressured into being the man of the house. It wasn't like that though. I'd just wanted to help. I wanted to be productive and useful, part of the team.

Was it time for me to move on?

It didn't take long for me to reject the idea. It was laughable, in a cold, cynical way. My mother would have been correct two days ago, but seven years had passed her by in the meantime.

Would she still call me a good man, if she knew what I'd done? I've killed, Mom. The first time I killed a man was, gruesomely, with my bare hands, the same hands that helped make dinner tonight. I hated what I'd done, and I desperately wish I could have found another way, but in the same situation I'd probably do it again. I've fought and bled and killed many times. The blood of hundreds—of *thousands* was on my hands. Maybe not personally, but they were forever fixed in my mind, lives snuffed out before their time, all at my command.

There was no way I could even think about leaving right now. I had a potentially ticking time bomb in Carl, and in the long term, I had a sister whom I still wasn't entirely sure how to help, but it was clear she needed it.

I still didn't know what happened to Jen in Cyraveil. I wanted to ask her, but at the same time, I was afraid to. The details were scarce, but I knew that most of the people involved were dead, if not all of them. I couldn't possibly confirm it, but I had reason to believe Carl put them to death personally. Certainly, the discovery had been enough to shift his allegiance, at great personal cost. All I ever got out of him was that he'd found Jen in a dungeon, in the heart of cruel Vennenport.

For what reason she'd been imprisoned, I'd never found out. In fact, I knew far too little about anything she'd gone through. Carl had burned Vennenport to the ground. Even after we'd finally reunited, I'd only been able to spend a week with her before we had to send her away. We needed the elves' support or we'd be crushed by the advancing Cellman forces using Carl's strategy, and Jen was the only one they trusted. When we'd lost her, the elves had broken away immediately. They'd never stab us in the back, but without Jen to interpret and negotiate, cooperation was virtually impossible.

In that one week, I'd seen how paranoid and violent she could get at the slightest twitch. I was the only one she'd trust anywhere near her for over half the week. I'd sleep just outside her room, with a few trusted guards patrolling the outer chambers. She'd nearly killed a poor, hapless servant who'd had the misfortune of slipping inside to trim the lamps when I accidentally fell asleep. The boy never set foot inside that building again.

She was my little sister though. I'd promised Mom I'd look after her and protect her, and I'd keep that promise no matter what universe we ended up in.

The front door opened quietly, brushing my thoughts away. My mom was on the couch reading a book. We both glanced up expectantly, but Jen didn't emerge from the hallway. I assumed it was Jen, anyway.

"Jen?" I called, suddenly worried.

"Yeah," she answered, to my relief. Her voice seemed strangely muffled.

"How was Sara's?"

"Fine."

Something seemed off. I expected some teasing, a jab about the two of us again. I glanced at Mom, but she didn't seem concerned, returning to her book. I went out to the front door, but Jen was nowhere to be found. I glanced around and saw her disappear around the corner upstairs. She'd been utterly silent climbing the staircase.

I followed (making a great deal more noise despite my own efforts) and got to her door a moment before she slid it shut. I stuck my foot out, blocking it from closure. Jen's eye appeared at the crack between the door and the frame, meeting my own.

Her eye was puffy and red.

"Jen?" I murmured. Fear and concern were threatening to over-whelm me.

"Nothing happened," she mumbled. *"Vei torl."* Her foot pushed mine away, and the door closed with the softest click possible.

I stood there for a long time, staring at the wooden door with the cheerful "Jennifer" banner across the top and pictures of Jen and her friends plastered in a haphazard collage. My little sister, the cheerful bubbly teenager, whose biggest regret in life was picking the wrong cell phone and losing all her pictures. Who loved to go to the mall, or take a day trip to the beach, or just sit out in the sun reading a good book or talk for hours on the phone.

Not for the first time, I wondered if that girl had died in a cold stone cell, in a dungeon on another world.

Not for the last time, I wondered if she might be better off in that world.

CHAPTER 9

JEN

"Hello?"

"Portman, it's Clark. Might have something."

"Go ahead."

"There was a chat window still open, between him and the best friend. They were getting together Tuesday night."

"Details?"

"Not much. Just that he'd be picked up around 9 p.m."

"Picked up? Carl doesn't have a car. Or a license."

"So there's a third party here."

"Talk to the mother again. Friends with cars."

———————

". . . I wasn't sure you were still coming," Sara said awkwardly, the front door half-open.

" 'Course I came," I said brightly. "It's Thursday, isn't it?"

"Yeah, but—"

"But nothing." I gave her the best lopsided grin I could manage. "You gonna make me stand out here all day?"

I was just outside Sara's door, at the end of a stone path lined with little lanterns and flowers, plus—no joke—a white picket fence at the edge of the lawn. Could've been a painting. After a long afternoon spent recovering in the woods, I'd finally worked up the courage to return to civilization. I was lucky it was Thursday; any other day, I'd probably still be out there paralyzed with worry.

But it was Thursday. Thursday was dinner at Sara's. I never missed Thursday at Sara's.

It took me a *long* time to bounce back from that conversation with Carl. I'd spent hours just poking the ground with a stick, tracing out long and increasingly incomprehensible rants in Etoline about Reynir Cellman and incredibly specific insults about his henchmen. Worthless stuff, really, since there wasn't a thing I could do about it anymore, but it made me feel better. Scratching out Etoline in the dirt was as nostalgic as I'd allowed myself to be since coming back. I grasped those threads of identity like a drowning woman, pulling myself out of despair.

And it *worked*, dammit. I was here, I was alive, and I was eager to hang out with my best friend.

Sara finally opened the door fully, still bemused.

"Anybody home?" I asked, walking past her and kicking off my shoes into the neat pile by the stairs.

"Mom's out back." Sara shut the door quietly. I glanced around, remembering what the house looked like.

The staircase wall was packed with pictures of their family—Sara and her mother and father. Real professional stuff, every one of them. Proper lighting and framing and all that. Her dad worked in computers as a something-something-engineer. Something really typical for our area, but he was on the upper end. They were rich, but they didn't flaunt it. He drove a normal car, so did his wife, and their house really wasn't that much bigger than ours. From the outside, it was all neat and well kept, but very middle-class.

Inside? Gizmos and gadgets galore. I couldn't tell you what half of the stuff in their house even did, but I knew it was all pretty expensive. Her dad loved his fancy toys.

A hand touched my shoulder.

Despite everything, despite knowing exactly who she was and what she meant to me, I flinched. My hand shot up and knocked hers away.

I turned, prepared to apologize, but her expression was . . . satisfied?

"You're still hiding," she prompted.

"Sara, look," I started, but she just shook her head. Her hand took mine, and she dragged me up the stairs two at a time.

In moments, we were in Sara's room, door closed tight. *This* room I remembered perfectly. Sara's bed, the most comfortable bed I've ever felt, tucked into the corner. Posters and drawings stuck all over the walls (some by me, the better ones by her), and a closet full of clothes, way more than I've ever had. In the other corner, near a window, a wide desk with a line of screens (three, count 'em), along with speakers, keyboards, and everything else you could ask for as a techie.

Her computer, more expensive than possibly everything I owned combined (I'd never asked—don't think I'd really want the answer either . . .) sat underneath, with wires trailing off in every direction. A bookshelf near the bed was stuffed with great novels (my personal borrowing library—the gaps in it were probably books I had back home right now), and "my" laptop sat on top, where I'd probably left it the last time I was here.

Sara let me use it. She called it mine and promised nobody would ever be able to look at it or get into it without my permission. Not even her. Even so, I never took it home. I guess I didn't want Mom to feel guilty that she couldn't afford to get me one.

Sara closed the door behind us, then plopped down onto her chair. I took my usual spot on the bed facing her. For a moment, we were both totally silent.

I fidgeted awkwardly, glancing around, avoiding her gaze. I didn't want to speak first. I wasn't sure what she was going to bring up, or what she'd heard or figured out. I wanted her to make the first move, so I could be smart about what I said. Matt's words about trust echoed through my head. That, along with my own personal experiences with betrayal, meant I was pretty reluctant to open up to anyone—even Sara.

Not that she was gonna let that stop her.

"You know, people talk a lot . . ." Sara said, very formally. Like she was about to give a speech.

"About what?" I asked innocently.

"Screw it," she snapped. "What the hell happened after second period?"

"You're gonna have to be more specific . . ." I didn't know why I was stalling. Clearly, she already knew.

"I heard you took down a varsity football player like it was nothing. Dropped him straight into a locker."

"Oh. Yeah, I did."

"Jen," said Sara, her voice weirdly high-pitched. "Last I remembered, you were scared to slap a guy for being too aggressive a flirt. Now you're beating up jocks for fun?"

"Not for fun," I said quickly. "Definitely not for fun."

"So, what then?" Sara sounded seriously concerned, which made me feel all the worse. "Did he do something to you?"

"No. Nothing. It was an accident."

"That's not an accident," she said, her eyes narrowing. "God, Jen, what is going *on*? You've been acting crazy for days now, and not just you. Matt's suddenly super confident and outgoing, which is great and all but still—*bizarre*. And now that guy Carl, the one you're suddenly super buddy-buddy with even though I've literally never heard of him before?"

I nodded slowly, wondering where this was going. What did Carl do? Oh man . . .

"Well, Carl—a guy so quiet and out of the way that I never knew he was even in my class—suddenly chews out the teacher in the middle of

APUSH. Goes on and on about some really awful things." Sara shook her head in exasperation. "Jen, something's going on with you three. It's obvious. So . . . tell me?"

"I can't," I murmured, as my eyes darted away. I couldn't look at her when I said it.

Sara got up and knelt down in front of me. Her hands grasped mine tight, holding on desperately.

"Jen, please. You're my best friend. I just want to help. Tell me what's going on. No lies." Her eyes were sparkling. She looked like she might cry. All I had to do to stop her was talk.

"You're one to talk about no lies," I snapped before I could stop myself.

Sara flinched backward, as if I'd slapped her. Her hands dropped away. She fell against her chair. "I—"

"You and Matt were together for *how* long?"

She frowned. "That's not fair."

"He's my big brother. You're my best friend. You'd think *someone* might've clued me in here." I really was annoyed. I hated feeling out of the loop on anything. Just imagine how awful it was, stuck in a forest where I couldn't understand a single damn thing around me. This from Sara was hitting all the wrong buttons at the wrong time.

"I thought you were cool with it."

I shook my head. "That's not the point. I just wish I'd *known*. No lies." My voice cracked a little on the last two words. This obviously wasn't just about her, and both of us were catching on quick now.

Sara frowned. ". . . So tell me, then. You know my secret. What's going on with you? Please, Jen."

Oh stars, did I want to. I wanted her to know everything, without me having to actually tell her. To skip right past all that mess, my frustration and fear, and go straight back to being best friends again.

And why not? came the little voice in my head. It's Sara. If there was a single person in the whole world besides Matt I could trust with my secrets, it was her.

I could feel my entire body sharpen to a single point, as if I were about to take off in a sprint. It felt like the entire world was quivering as I turned back to face her. There was enough anticipation in the air to stop time itself.

"I went to another world."

Sara's eyes blinked. They blinked again.

I didn't say anything else. I just watched. Waited.

Would she think I was crazy? Would she believe me?

Did I *want* her to think I was crazy? Maybe I wanted to *be* crazy. To have imagined this whole insanity.

I couldn't say for sure. All I knew was that I wanted my best friend on my side again, with me through thick and thin, us two against the whole universe.

". . . Run that by me again," she said finally. I couldn't tell if she was being sarcastic or serious. Her face *looked* serious. Kinda skeptical, but definitely not annoyed or amused. I decided I'd just go with it. I trusted her.

"On Tuesday night. We—err, me, Matt and Carl—we were all . . . taken. To another . . . *vack*, I can't think of the word."

"Planet?" Sara guessed. "Dimension?"

"Dimension, yeah." I nodded. "A place called Cyraveil."

"Like the forest?" Sara sounded dubious again. She sat back on the floor, leaning against her desk. Her water bottle was nearby, like it always was, and she took a deep sip, still watching me carefully.

"That's where it happened," I replied, nodding again. "We went out to the forest that night. The four of us found a—"

"Wait, *four* of you?" Sara interrupted. I gulped audibly before I could stop myself. ". . . Jen?"

I couldn't leave him out, but I definitely couldn't talk about it yet. It was too much, especially after talking to Carl earlier. *Someday,* I promised her in my head. *I'll tell you, I swear.* "I'm sorry. Do you know Blake Svartholm?"

"Nope."

"He's a friend of Matt and Carl's. Nice guy. Kind of goofy, but really nice."

"And he went with you," she concluded.

" . . . Yeah."

"So where's he hiding then? I feel like I'd have run into him by now with how crazy this has all been."

I looked down at my feet, concentrating very determinedly on my toes while a rushing wind filled my ears. "He didn't make it back," I mumbled. Against my will, against every nerve in my body shouting at me to avoid the drama and keep calm—my eyes welled up.

"Oh . . . oh, God."

Sara was on her feet and next to me in an instant. Even in my current state, even in this place, damn it all, I still felt an instinct to recoil from the sudden physical presence, but I suppressed it. I don't know how I managed, but I am forever grateful to whichever star decided to grant me the mental fortitude in that moment to just let Sara take care of me for a minute.

She put an arm around my shoulders, and my head instinctively found a spot on her shoulder where the tears flowed free. For the first time since I'd returned—for the first time in a very, very long while before that too—someone else actually saw me crying.

Was it talking about Blake? Nah, as heartbreaking as that was.

It was simpler than that. Sara—no matter what she might be thinking right now, even after I'd snapped at her only minutes ago—had seen my expression, and without a second thought, she'd leaped up to try and comfort me.

Do you know what it's like to have a friend like that? Somebody who's automatically on your side, no matter the circumstances? I'd missed her more than anything while I was gone. More than showers or normal clothes, more than microwaves or chocolate cake or anything: I'd missed my best friend.

I sat up again, brushing at my eyes. Sara found a box of tissues and handed me one.

"Vannen," I choked out.

"No sweat," she said, smiling. "I'm guessing that meant 'thanks.' "

"Top of the class."

"So you can speak another language now?"

I nodded. "Etoline. The language of the Sylvandar."

"Sounds super high fantasy."

"Okay, yeah, they were basically elves. I mean, there's a lot more to it than that, but yeah, elves."

Sara raised an eyebrow. "Elves?"

"Well, Sylves. Calling them elves was kind of racist. Sara, it was a full-on fantasy world. Sylves and dwarves and everything. No daphut, I met a dragon once."

". . . How the hell do you meet a dragon?"

"Very, very carefully." I laughed. "They're actually not all that bad. That one wasn't, anyway. I dunno about the rest; most died off a long time ago."

"Hang on." Sara cocked her head to the side. "You said you left Tuesday night. How long—"

"Seven years."

Sara's mouth seemed to stick open in mid-sentence. It took her a while to recover while I just stared at the pile of stuffed animals in a basket in the corner. ". . . Seven years?" she whispered, incredulous.

"I think so. Likav silan."

"You don't look twenty-three," she said, sounding skeptical again.

"I definitely *feel* twenty-three," I grumbled. "Getting shoved back into my sixteen-year-old body really, really sucks, believe me. One silan isn't exactly the same as a year though, so it might be off a little. Plus, when I got there, I didn't have any way to keep track of time. I don't really have a clue how long I was lost in the country before Tethevallen found me."

"So you came back and no time passed. Very Narnia. You're mixing up your fantasy worlds here." She laughed.

"Don't make fun," I said defensively. "I'm trying to be serious here."

"I know," she said, shifting back to thoughtful and relaxed. "It's just . . . a lot, you know? I'm catching up here."

". . . You believe me, right?" I said, very nervous. I didn't know *what* I'd do if she said no. I don't think I could have gone on living if she didn't believe me. But . . . Sara wasn't the type to take people at their word. She always wanted proof. It was a family thing, right in her blood. I couldn't predict how she'd react to all of this, when it was so . . . outlandish.

"It's like this," Sara said, very deliberately. "Either you've suddenly grown a *hell* of an imagination overnight—"

"Vack dou."

"—and you're lying to me, which . . . yeah." She winced again, but hurried past it. "Or you're batshit crazy, which is pretty reasonable, but you don't really seem like it. Mostly." She shrugged. "So, I'm pretty much down to believing you." Sara tossed her hair back from her face, before looking me in the eye. "Sound good?"

I could have kissed her. "Thank you," I said as a warm glow spread through every vein in my body.

"Right," Sara said excitedly. "Now: explain how a girl who basically failed French class two years in a row is suddenly the master of another language."

I shrugged. "I lived with the Sylves for years. None of them spoke a single word of Lingu—err, English. Between that and a bit of magic, I learned Etoline pretty quick. Kinda *had* to."

". . . Magic?" Sara's eyes sparkled. Now she was *really* interested.

So was I. I got to explain my whole world to her, my dearest friend. I always liked to tell stories, even if I wasn't very good at coming up with them. Suddenly, I had a great, *true* story to tell, and the perfect person to tell it to.

"Magic. Etola."

"Details. Right now." Sara spoke so fiercely, I was taken aback. But I felt just as eager as she was. The desire, the longing for a real fantasy. One I'd actually gotten to *live*.

"If you . . . ugh." I frowned. "I can't word it right in this language."

Sara looked sympathetic. "Did you really forget English?"

"I didn't *forget*," I said, a bit indignant, "but I went without for so long . . . I only started speaking English again about a year ago. When I started—" I paused, searching for the right word. "—interpreting. For the treaties."

". . .'Interpreting for the treaties,' " Sara repeated incredulously. "This isn't fair, you just gave me like fifty more questions to ask."

"Well, I was the only person they had who spoke English at all. I was the first member of a suunsyl to ever negotiate with humans. They even made up a special title to mark it."

"Okay, now you're just bragging."

"Yup." I laughed. "No joke, they named the position after me. The ambassador to humans is called the sylajen. Even the sesylf who took over after me, she's the new sylajen."

Sara grinned. "So you got immortalized. Way to go. At least this explains your weird accent."

I suddenly felt very self-conscious. "Is it really weird?"

"Nah. Okay, yes, it is, but not *bad*-weird." Sara tried to give me a comforting smile. "I like it. Don't lose it."

"*Selnou.*" I stopped trying to correct myself after that, to my tongue's relief.

"Wait, aren't elves—err, Sylves—immortal?"

I sighed. I figured this was coming, as much as I hated thinking about it. "Nah, but everybody assumes that. They do live hundreds of years though, thanks to etola."

Sara was too sharp not to pick up on the possibilities. "So if it's the magic, and you were living with them and had access to it . . . were you gonna live that long too?"

I hesitated. ". . . Probably," I said quietly. "Every time I did the ritual, I felt it. You know, healing me."

"But, when you tried it yesterday . . ." Sara trailed off, connecting the dots in her head. "Oh."

"Yeah."

"I'm so sorry, Jen," she murmured.

" 'S okay." Truth be told, I didn't really know how I felt about it yet. It had taken a long time to adjust to the idea of living more than a hundred years longer than normal and staying young and healthy that whole time. To have that suddenly snatched away was pretty unsettling. Plus, I had to take care of myself way more carefully now.

I really hated once again having to brush my teeth in the morning, or watch what I ate, or deal with periods. Don't even get me started on the rest. Sometimes, being human really sucks.

"Wait, so you *could* do magic, then? Etola, I mean?" Sara's eager tone was back.

As she spoke, her cat peeked out from the closet, where he'd been lounging on a pile of clothes tucked inside. It was his customary spot, and the only thing Sara ever left on the floor. Her room was totally spotless otherwise. He sauntered over and leaped up to the bed, where he promptly found his way right into my lap. I smiled, petting him, and was rewarded with a satisfied purr. He was napping again in moments.

"Nuh-uh," Sara warned, "he's not letting you off the hook."

"I could," I said casually. "A bit, anyway."

"Oh, a *bit*. Right."

"Okay, so I was pretty good." I grinned. "Tethevallen said I mastered it a lot faster than anyone he'd ever taught, and even better than some of the legit masters. In some etolev, they called me the best in the entire forest."

"And so *humble*," she teased.

I giggled. "They think it's 'cause I'm human. I dunno. They could last way longer than me any day tossing out etolev. I got burned out way faster than they did." Sara's cat shifted in my lap, prompting me to keep petting.

"So what were you so good at?"

My eyes fell to the cat, avoiding her gaze. "What's his name again?"

"Qwerty. Dad named him. Pretty lame to name a cat after the keyboard but whatever." I could tell I was supposed to know that already, but Sara explained it as nicely as she could. She didn't sound irritated at all. She just looked concerned again. "You okay?"

"Yeah." I cleared my throat. When I continued, I felt a bit more subdued. "I was the best at fire. It was fun, tossing it around, splitting it up and combining it, changing colors, making fireworks and explosions and stuff. Once I studied and practiced and meditated enough, I was really able to get into the etolendei of fire. I could even make it from nothing. They thought that was impossible."

"Etolendei?" Sara asked. I winced deliberately at her pronunciation, although it really was pretty bad. She picked up a stress ball from her desk and threw it at me. I dodged it, grinning. "But seriously."

"Really hard to describe," I said honestly. "It's like . . . the true knowledge of something, I guess? Until you really know something, you can't do anything to it or with it."

"Huh," Sara said, her eyes coolly analytical, just like whenever she was working through some programming problem. Of course, cold analysis wasn't really helpful for magic. After a few moments, she was back again, looking frustrated. "I was hoping for something more concrete."

"Sorry. I can't really explain it well in English."

"Damn elves," Sara intoned. I grabbed the ball and chucked it back at her, nailing her in the chest. "Ouch."

"Did that really hurt?" I asked, worried. I hadn't paid much attention to how hard I'd thrown it.

"No," she said, realizing how serious I was. She squeezed the ball for a minute, thinking. ". . . I can't help but feel like there's a dark side coming here."

I looked away again. "Yeah," I said, talking to the wall.

"Look," she said. I looked. Her eyes seemed so friendly and warm. I hadn't seen eyes like that since I left Naeflin on the field outside Candir, covered in blood, but still ready to give me a hug and tell me everything was gonna be all right. "If you don't want to say—"

"I do." I *had* to. It was the only way I was ever gonna get past the gnawing feeling in my heart. "There's a reason they were so happy about my skills with fire."

". . . And I'm betting it has to do with those treaties you were helping translate," she filled in. Her voice got thin and nervous. "There was a war, wasn't there?"

I nodded.

"And you fought in it?"

I nodded again.

Sara didn't speak. Her eyes studied me carefully. The silence stretched out, more awkward with every moment.

What would she think of me? I couldn't say. Even as my best friend, with the things I'd done? I did what I had to do to survive, right? That's what I told myself every night before I went to bed, every time the memories came to take over my mind for a bit.

Not that I actually got to sleep. A full night's sleep was something for normal people. I wasn't normal, and I sure as hell never got a full night's worth. Naps scattered throughout the day, that was my life now. Even that fifteen-hour stretch the day before was full of panicked moments when I woke up, white-knuckled, ready to slash at an opportunistic cellmate who wasn't actually there. Sleep wasn't relaxing for me; it was a terrifying state in which I was at my most vulnerable.

I couldn't keep going on like this. *Please, Sara. Don't abandon me now.*

I was praying furiously in my head, to all the stars closest to my soul, that she'd accept what I'd become. If you can still hear me on this planet, send some of that wisdom into Sara. Let her know what to do, because I'm clearly not in the running anymore.

"Look," she started again. My eyes found hers, desperately hoping, but I forced my face back into a passive expression. I couldn't let her see my emotions right now. "I can't possibly understand what you went through—but I can try to listen. As much as you need me to. Anything you need to say, anytime. Okay?"

Oh, Sara. how can you possibly exist? How are you so perfect and what benevolent twist of fate delivered you to me? I felt like crying, laughing, smiling. I wanted to dance, I wanted to sing, I wanted to hug her, I wanted to curl up in the corner of her room and bawl my eyes out while she held me. I wanted to pour my soul out for her, confess every foul deed I'd ever committed, the men and women I'd killed, the friends I'd failed, the laws I'd broken and people I'd loved and lost, the entirety of the forlorn existence I'd come to accept. I wanted her to see me and tell me I was okay.

I said none of those things. I did none of those things.

I just waited, staring at Sara, with her guarded, lonely eyes permanently affixed to my face.

"Thank you," I said, and I forced a smile. She smiled back—but she, too, carried a sadness, something I'd never seen in her expression. Or . . . had it always been there, and I'd never understood it? Never recognized it for what it was, because I was naive and believed in a best friend too perfect to ever lie or let me down?

I didn't know the answer, but I could tell in that moment: I wasn't the only one in the room harboring a secret.

Sara's mother called us to dinner. We'd started talking again, and thankfully we'd returned to happier, easier topics. I tried to answer truthfully and thoroughly. Sara loved fantasy books, but even so, I still underestimated just how much she'd want to hear about all of my adventures.

It was really fun, actually, telling her everything else. She was just so *fascinated.* I could have talked about the weather there and she'd probably still eat it up. She wanted every little detail, and I was happy to share. Mostly stories of the Sylves and how they'd adopted me, but also tales of the world at large, of the different people and their cultures (as much as I knew, anyway—Sylves didn't really get out much), and of course, of etola and Etoline.

Despite the similarity of the words, they aren't really all that connected. I mean, saying a phrase related to whatever sort of etola you're trying to cast might help you focus, but at true levels of mastery, speaking aloud is considered amateur. As long as you know *exactly* what you're about to do, in every sense of the word, you don't need to say anything.

Hand gestures, though, are pretty much required. As Sara had noticed, between my midday ritual and the meal ritual, I'd been acting like a very confused mime over the last couple of days. While some etolev don't require handwork, most do, especially anything external. I couldn't say if it was just another thing to help focus the mind or not, but I'd never gotten anything good to happen without a gesture or motion to direct the etola. Trying pretty much just ended up in disaster.

My fingers were singed many, *many* times before I figured out how to move flames around with tiny, precise movements.

I'm sorry, I'm getting distracted again. There's a more important story to tell here, and it's not me fooling around with fire.

Sara and I headed downstairs, laughing and chatting like normal. Her mother was setting out the plates for dinner. I smelled pizza, and I was excited. I hadn't had pizza in—well, you get the idea by now. But seriously. *Pizza.* Is there something more real world than pizza or what?

"Shasii, selaval," Sara called out casually as we walked into the kitchen. I giggled and elbowed her.

"What was that?" asked her mother, glancing up from the oven.

"Oh, nothing," she said very seriously, stifling a laugh along with me.

"Doues danadelasec dena masateva atev Kalleddor," I whispered in her ear. Not exactly true—she and Carl were both pretty bad—but I'd just taught her the line. She managed to still get it wrong just a minute later.

"Huh?" she asked aloud, but I only smiled innocently in reply. "Oh, two can play at that game. *Tu es une pomme de terre avec le visage d'un cochon d'Inde.*"

"Play nice, Sara," her mother chimed in absently as she pulled out the pizza. It was homemade and looked absolutely perfect. Not that I had much to compare it to lately, but seriously, I was frothing at the mouth for this pizza.

Sara's mother started slicing it up while we took our usual spots at the table. Just as she brought a piece over to each of us, I heard the garage door slide open.

Now this was unusual but not exactly unheard of. Her father wasn't normally home from work by the time we ate. He tended to work late more often than not. When he was there, the conversation died down a bit, but he was always polite, asked after my family, how I was doing. He seemed like a nice guy. Yeah, he was kind of cold sometimes, but he was also super exhausted and stressed from work. I couldn't blame him for not wanting to put up with two high schoolers right when he got home, and even so, he never failed to act like a proper host.

This time, though, something was wrong. I couldn't put my finger on it. Some detail had changed. Except . . . I'd been here last Thursday, and on Monday, too, for Sara's mom's birthday. It was just three normal world days ago, and something felt very different. Besides me, obviously.

I looked around the room. Sara was still talking about something that happened at school today. Her mom was nodding along, continuing the conversation like nothing was wrong . . . but I could see it. The way she started moving ever so carefully. She was measuring every single step she took, choreographing every movement, deliberate and cautious.

Sara, too, seemed suddenly guarded. She was staring very intently at her plate—her *empty* plate, I should point out. Her hand fiddled with her fork. As my eyes swept across, though, I could see how tight she held it. It was subtle, and it came and went, but the intent was clear.

It hit me like an arrow to the gut. I was an idiot. How had I missed this?

They hadn't changed at all. I was finally able to recognize what was going on. What Sara had been hiding from me.

They were afraid.

As the door to the garage door opened, it became even more apparent.

"Welcome home, hon," Sara's mom called out. Perfectly normal.

Her father looked down the hallway and saw me at the table. He smiled and waved, putting away his coat. "Evening. It smells delicious, dear."

"How was work?"

"Exhausting. I'm glad to be home."

"Want anything to drink?" asked Sara, still staring at the plate. Her voice was as casual as could be.

"Thank you, Sara, but I can get it. Do you want anything?"

"Coke sounds good. Jen?"

Stars, were they all *acting*? The whole damn time? I spluttered back to life as I realized both Sara and her dad were looking at me expectantly. I gulped, trying to clear my throat.

"Uhh, root beer for me?" I asked awkwardly. Was I supposed to play along with the script? I was a terrible actress. I can hide things if I need to, but I'm bad at faking being normal. I barely even know what normal is anymore.

"Oh, is it Jen now?" asked her mother, sliding a slice of pizza onto my plate. Her hand still clutched the pizza roller, the sharp silver edge sparkling as it caught the sunlight streaming through the window.

"Yeah. Just time for a change." Sara nudged me under the table, trying to get me to focus, but I was still fixed on her own hand clutching the fork like a dagger. "No more Jenny."

"That's too bad. I liked the name Jenny."

"Now, dear, it's her name. She can do what she likes with it," said her father. He threw me a wink. "No more Jenny from the block."

"God, Dad." Sara rolled her eyes. "Please don't try to reference pop culture. Ever again."

I felt so horribly confused by what was going on. I couldn't process the absurd contradiction of the conversation going on, and the physical reactions of everybody in the room. The instant her father had spoken up, Sara clutched the fork again. When he looked toward her mother, she seemed to relax ever so slightly—but when he looked back toward me, her knuckles turned white as she gripped the pizza roller.

If I hadn't had this exact dinner a hundred times in their kitchen, in almost the *exact* same circumstances, I'd think we were about to throw down.

Except this was suburban Oregon, not some back alley tavern or decrepit dungeon. A fight here was as likely as a portal opening up and dumping us all into an alternate universe.

Sorry, bad joke.

It kept going through the entirety of dinner. Like they were putting on a show, just for me. The normal, happy family. They'd tease one another about old habits, argue politics, discuss movies and TV shows. It was so perfectly, totally ordinary that I found myself reaching for my knife, still tucked under the hem of my shirt at my back, the one thing I hadn't told Sara about.

When was the curtain coming down?

It never did. After dinner ended, as Sara's mother cleaned up, I headed straight out the back door into the yard to get some air. Sara followed a moment later, after her place was clear. Only once the door was closed, and we were around the corner and out of the light, did I turn to confront her.

"Dov nara *vack* was that?" I asked, halfway between confused and angry.

Sara looked genuinely confused herself. "Huh?"

"*That.* The whole dinner. All of you." I was on edge. Very on edge. Sara was lucky I couldn't conjure up some flames right now, or the neighbors might've called the firefighters.

"What are you talking about?"

She was determined to keep the charade going, I guess. I wasn't sure how to react, what to do, how to respond. I wanted to be angry at her for hiding this from me, but how could I? After what I'd been hiding from her for the past couple of days, wouldn't that make me a massive hypocrite?

This is different, I convinced myself. This was control and fear. This was actively happening, and clearly had been for some time.

Without warning, I grabbed the hem of Sara's shirt and lifted it up. No, it's nothing like that. Get your mind out of the gutter. I was looking for bruises. Marks of any kind. Evidence.

"Uhh . . ." Sara glanced around, making sure no one could see us. "Well, this is weird."

Mentally, I agreed. There wasn't a sign of abuse anywhere on her. Was I just imagining everything? Had that actually been a perfectly normal dinner?

Was I going completely insane?

"I'm sorry," I mumbled. I let go and backed into the wall of the house.

"No worries. Just . . . warn me next time?" Sara looked weirdly comfortable with the whole situation.

"I'm sorry," I repeated, turning to leave.

Before I could go, Sara reached out and grabbed my hand. "Hey, it's okay," she said quietly.

I felt my eyes begin to well up again. I couldn't even spend a single night with my best friend's family without my past springing up to haunt me. My instincts had almost led me to attack Sara's father, in his own home and in front of his family.

Could I *really* live here again, the way I used to?

For the second time that night, I cried, but there wasn't any joy in it anymore. Joy was reserved for people not actively losing their minds.

CHAPTER 10

CARL

"Portman, I got someone. A friend he plays basketball with, Matthew Westin. Family owns a beat-up white pickup."

"Did you get an address?"

"Mom didn't know it. Maybe the school?"

"They wouldn't just give out that information. Did you check the vehicle database?"

"System's down."

"Of course it is . . . All right. I'll get it from the school. I have a friend in the administration."

"What if the Stokelson kid comes home?"

"I can't be everywhere. You'll have to come cover it."

"Damnit, I hate stakeouts."

"Just don't be obvious."

———

Site: Realms of the Dragons—Fantasy Discussion
Board: Off-Topic Chat

Topic: Fantasy in Real Life
Post #27742: fantasyanon9 (Newbie) [09/12/04]
Friends, I come to you a changed man. I have been to the other side, I have seen the world we all long for. It's real. Elves and wizards, dragons and castles. I stumbled upon a well, high in the mountains, and upon lowering myself into its depths, I discovered a world adjacent to ours, full of wonder and mystery. Come, sit by the fire and ask me anything of this strange new world. I have only just returned and am eager to converse with my fellow compatriots of the internet.

Topic: Re: Fantasy in Real Life
Post #27746: Eldrazor (Loremaster of the Heavens) [09/12/04]
@fantasyanon9: Hi, welcome to the board. So, you're saying you *actually* went to a fantasy world? Prove it ;P

Topic: Fantasy in Real Life
Post #27747: fantasyanon9 (Newbie) [09/12/04]
You dare mock my perelous quest to bring you these tales of adventure?

Topic: Re: Fantasy in Real Life
Post #27749: Eldrazor (Loremaster of the Heavens) [09/12/04]
@fantasyanon9: What can I say, I'm a skeptic ;)

Topic: Re: Fantasy in Real Life
Post #27751: cantstopdabeat (Member) [09/12/04]
@Eldrazor dont feed the troll

Topic: Re: Fantasy in Real Life
Post #27850: Eldrazor (Loremaster of the Heavens) [09/15/04]
Guess I scared him away.

Topic: Re: Fantasy in Real Life
Post #125614: Reynir_Cellman (Newbie) [10/02/10]
@fantasyanon9: I believe you. PM me.

I went back to the house.

I didn't think of it as my home anymore. Of course I didn't. It was a place to sleep and keep my things, but it couldn't be my home. That was a trap. Nothing in this world could ever be home for me.

I'd walked away from Jen. I couldn't bear to consider her new mental image of me. I'd been party, albeit reluctantly, to the torture and execution of an elf. A friend of hers too, judging by her terrifying reaction. Jen would never see me in the same way again, and that crushed me more deeply than any nuisance this world had to offer. I loved her, and she couldn't bear the sight of me in that instant. If she ever found out I was responsible for introducing Reynir to such a strategy in the first place . . . Jen would never look at me again. She was too good, too noble.

Not like me. I was the Traitor. I was worthless. When the time came and Reynir begged me for aid, I'd marched my men out of the city. We didn't fight. We didn't do anything. We just walked away and let Reynir face the wrath of a revolutionary crusade.

I should have died in that crusade. I was just as responsible. Reynir was a good man before the war turned him into something else— turned us all into something else. Years of friendship, of governance and adventure, burned to a crisp in the fires of rebellion. He'd done unspeakable, unforgivable things, and I didn't regret his death, but . . . I'd give anything to turn back time, just as the real world did. I wanted my best friend, my brother, back.

The two people I'd have considered my closest friends, and I felt like I'd betrayed them both. First Reynir, and now Blake. I wanted to do something, anything to avenge him. I couldn't. There was nothing to be done.

Nothing, nothing at all. I was a man adrift in time, lost in space. I didn't belong in this world.

I walked inside. No one seemed to be home. Good, that was good. I couldn't deal with my parents right now. If they saw me, they'd pierce through the shell I'd built. I was vulnerable. I was empty inside. A gust of wind could have scattered me to the corners of the Earth.

I was so . . . cold.

Site: gg-no-rm
Board: Off-topic
Topic: Seeking writers to help develop idea
CyclicalDestruction [09/02/08]
I had an idea for a fantasy story. Alternate world style, with normal high-school kids getting pulled into a fantasy world and having to figure out where to go and what to do. I don't want to play up the fish-out-of-water comedy too much though. This is going to be legit stuff.

Rough ideas: The kids go off into a forest one night, end up getting sucked into a new world. Kids get split up immediately. No supporting one another. They're going to have to end up fighting one another down the line, due to the warring factions and all that. Two of them are even related and still end up on opposite sides of the war. It's gonna get dramatic.

Yeah, no, it's not well developed yet, but I'm working on it. I just want someone to bounce ideas off of. Anyone interested?

Private Message
Topic: Fantasy world you posted about
From: Cyraveil
To: CyclicalDestruction
If you don't mind my asking (I know you abandoned it a long time ago), where did you get the ideas for that story?

Private Message
Topic: Re: Fantasy world you posted about
From: CyclicalDestruction
To: Cyraveil
Holy shit, blast from the past. Haven't thought about that piece in forever. I dunno, I just came up with it one day. Why do you ask?

Private Message
Topic: Re: Fantasy world you posted about
From: Cyraveil
To: CyclicalDestruction
Really? All your imagination?

Private Message
Topic: Re: Fantasy world you posted about
From: CyclicalDestruction
To: Cyraveil
Uhh, yes?

I felt adrift. Even my anchor, the mighty web of the internet and its endless capacity to enthrall and entertain, just frustrated me more. No one could answer me. The few people I found claiming some experience similar to mine had either vanished long ago into the archives of the bulletin boards, or just admitted straight up they were lying.

It was all lies. All but mine.

Why should the internet believe me though? The internet didn't trust anyone openly. All stories are lies, all people are fake, all women and children are desperate men and undercover FBI. How was someone as unimportant as me supposed to get through to the uncaring internet at large?

As the sheer futility crashed down on me, I felt myself sinking farther away. The world and I were disconnected. I turned around in my chair and an object came into view. A cord, in thick black coils, sitting in the corner, beckoning. The rest of the room became a blur. My vision narrowed on that cord, bringing it into sharp focus. I noticed every single detail: the way the light played off of the texture, the white stripe running the length of it, faded and cracked from use. The shining prongs at the end.

Exhaustion defined me. The world wasn't worth the effort anymore.

My eyes followed the circles of the coil around and around. Then, from the end of the cord to the wall, where I found another line I could trace. The frame around the closet door. White wood, elegantly shaped, perfect as usual. Clean. Look, there it goes, without a single scratch on it. Up, up, higher and higher. There, as it crosses to meet the other end.

There, behind the frame. A solid metal pole, embedded into the walls. It held clothes. Nice clothes. Clothes for special occasions, for my father to dress me in and parade me about as his son, his protégé. Someone he could be proud of.

I wondered what he'd think of me if I just ceased to exist? How would my *perfect* father react if I were to suddenly disappear—for real this time? How about my mother? How many people would attend my funeral? What would they say about me?

I didn't care about the clothes back then, and I didn't care about the clothes now. My eyes were fixed on that pole.

I stood, and it felt like the entire world was upon my shoulders. I was so tired. I reached out, my arm heavy, struggling through the thick air. I wasn't tall enough. I looked around and found an empty computer case to stand on.

I tugged on the pole. It was sturdy. I tugged harder, and it didn't yield one bit.

It would do.

I looked back at the cord, coiled up in the corner. Would it be strong enough?

Site: Writers Anonymous

Board: Reading → Fantasy → General

Topic: Anyone ever have an out of body experience?

WikiWarrior (Power User) [04/02/07]

I'm kind of freaking out over here. I can't tell if I was dreaming or not.

Okay, let me explain. I don't remember going to sleep, but I felt like I was in a whole new world. It was like some crazy fantasy world. I met up with a bunch of elves, speaking a language I couldn't understand. They were fighting off this invading army, surrounding their forest and attacking. I wanted to help, but I'm just a normal guy, even in my dreams, I guess. Pathetic, amirite?

ANyway, after they fought off the humans(?), they took me to . . .

Then I was returned to the real world, and I woke up in my bed with a massive headache. I know, probably just a dream, but seriously, it felt so crazy real I had to post something. Anyone else ever have something similar?

Topic: Re: Re: Re: Re: Re: Anyone ever have an out of body experience?

Bottlemurder (Elite) [04/07/07]

@OP Way too detailed for a dream. Sure you're not on shrooms or something?

Topic: Re: Re: Re: Re: Re: Anyone ever have an out of body experience?

WikiWarrior (Power User) [04/07/07]

@Bottlemurder Like I said up in the thread earlier, never used drugs. I'm thinking this may have been legit.

Topic: Re: Re: Re: Re: Re: Anyone ever have an out of body experience?

Rispetto (Newbie) [04/08/07]
fukin liar. probably just stole all this from another site.
[USER WAS BANNED FOR THIS POST: Repeated flaming
~mod]

Topic: Re: Re: Re: Re: Re: Anyone ever have an out of body
experience?
RollingInTheMuffins (Newbie) [04/08/07]
I know he already got banned, but I still want to refute Rispetto's
claim. @WikiWarrior is legit. I went through the same thing.
Even went to the same place. Can you PM me? I want to talk
about this more.

Topic: Re: Re: Re: Re: Re: Anyone ever have an out of body
experience?
SylfSympathizer (Newbie) [10/02/10]
Sorry for the necro, but I might have been through the same
thing. @WikiWarrior @RollingintheMuffins, can you add me
to the PM?

Topic: Re: Re: Re: Re: Re: Anyone ever have an out of body
experience?
Bottlemurder (Elite) [10/02/10]
@SylfSympathizer This thread died out years ago, and neither of
them hang out here anymore. Pretty sure one of them admitted
to it being faked on IRC. It was only archived since it was pretty
fun to watch it play out until they "disappeared."

Topic: Re: Re: Re: Re: Re: Anyone ever have an out of body
experience?
SylfSympathizer (Newbie) [10/02/10]
@Bottlemurder, you wouldn't happen to have either of their
email addresses though? Or any way to contact them?

Topic: Re: Re: Re: Re: Re: Anyone ever have an out of body experience?
Bottlemurder (Elite) [10/02/10]
@SylfSympathizer Sorry man, can't help. Forum rules: no personal information. And I don't have it anyway. Try a PM?

No.

The singular word thundered through my skull.

No.

I froze in place, the cord halfway around my neck.

No.

I wasn't going to give up. Not yet. There had to be a way.

I let go of the bar. I didn't exactly feel *better*; I could still feel the weight pressing down on me. I sat down and booted my computer back up. I needed to be doing something. *Anything* to distract me from what had just happened.

I had come so close . . .

Oh god.

I tried to shake the thought away, but it persisted in the back of my mind. My desktop finished booting up, and I went straight back online. I'd saved every thread that I'd posted to in a neat folder, and the tabs scattered across my screen with a single click. To my dismay, not a single new reply. Nothing at all.

No.

It was time to get back to work. I was going to get back to Cyraveil, no matter what. I realized what I'd done wrong. In every attempt to gain information so far, I'd gone with the polite approach. I'd nodded and smiled along. I'd followed the rules. I was thinking like a normal citizen of the internet, following etiquette and knowing my place.

I glanced at that coil again and felt a shiver roll through my body.

My eyes narrowed. I didn't belong in this world. Why should I follow its rules? My world, my laws, and my *life* were back in Cyraveil. *That* was my mission. I'd go back, and I'd wreak bloody vengeance on the entire remaining Cellman family. Not a single one of them would survive. Once that entire corrupt bloodline was cleaned from the kingdom, I could finally rest easy.

Fuck Earth. I had a real life to get back to.

Site: Warez Hut
Board: Listings → Entertainment → Fantasy
Topic: looking for a series
#5542561 cyric_veil (Fresh) [01/06/09]
looking for a book series about escaping to a fantasy world. one of those where they had elves but insisted on calling them something else just to be different and special. teenagers, kind of a YA series but not really. syra-something. i dunno it just seemed super awesome. wish it could happen to me.

Topic: Re: looking for a series
#5542580 Iceman (Super Moderator) [01/06/09]
Wrong section. This is for posting downloads, not requests. This is your third offense, you have been banned.
~THREAD LOCKED~

```
wget -r -l 0 warezhut.com
pageanalyze.py warezhut.com/*

---

VULNERABILITY FOUND
SQLi on warezhut.com/memberlist.php?q=
Dump? Y/N: Y

Dumping database . . .
**
Done.
SELECT email FROM members WHERE username ==
"cyric_veil"
```

From: fantasy.throwaway.addr@qmail.com
To: cyric.godslayer@coldmail.com
Subject: Fantasy Worlds. Saw you on warezhut
What if they were real? Tell me, do you know anything about
Sylves? Or Cellmans?

From: mailer-daemon@qmail.com
To: fantasy.throwaway.addr@qmail.com
Subject: Delivery Status Notification (Failure)
Delivery to the following recipient failed permanently:
cyric.godslayer@coldmail.com
SMTP: 553 5.1.8: Domain of sender address (coldmail.com)
does not exist. Maybe no longer registered?

Having a solid goal kept me focused, kept my mind off of my mis-
ery. I didn't have a solid path forward, but that wasn't really a problem
for me. I could do abstract, as long as my end goal was clear. In this
case, it couldn't be a more straightforward measurement for success.
Either I'd return to Cyraveil, or I'd die trying. The rest of the universe
was nothing. There was no Earth.

Earth definitely wasn't going to make it easy for me though. Even
as I started delving deeper—breaking more rules, scanning websites for
holes in their security, and finding ways to contact users more directly—
results seemed always just beyond my grasp.

I couldn't stop. I'd never stop.

I wished I still had my informants. In Candir, and well beyond it
too, I had a network. Lowlifes, criminals, everyone who'd helped me rise
to the top. Even after I'd become friends with Reynir and been granted
title and lands, I still kept those connections alive. The pickpockets and
thieves who'd trained me and made me one of their own, they became
part of my personal army. They might not stand up in a straight fight
like trained soldiers, but they could brawl with the best—and more
importantly, every last one of them knew how to navigate the streets.

They knew what to listen for, who to follow, how to keep up with the shifting politics of the city. I knew every power play before it was made, and I capitalized on that advantage whenever I could. I was often working both ends of every agreement made, every alliance formed, every pact broken. Whenever a noble felt like improving his position in the city, his first step was a back-alley meeting with me.

I laughed at the nobles behind their backs. They trusted *me*, even over their peers, because I was a foreigner. I was an outsider, with no apparent ties or motivations, seemingly eager to help out my fellow man. I played on their insecurities, their racism, their scorn for the poor, even as I used those selfsame poor to undermine their maneuvering. They underestimated the true worth of a beggar's loyalty on a street corner, often to their own detriment.

I hoped to use the internet in that same way now. Somewhere, in this virtual city of cities, I'd find that lone street corner, where someone else with knowledge of real magic, of Cyraveil, waited. They'd give me a lead that would be the first step toward going back. In those posts that most would ignore or dismiss, someone would eventually prove to be the real deal, playing it just as close to the chest as I was.

It was just a matter of time and persistence.

Site: The Dark Alley
Board: Conspiracies and Mysteries
Topic: Parallel Dimensions and Modern Application
Error: You do not have permissions to view this board.
(Message from the moderators: Sorry, this board requires membership to view threads.)

```
pageanalyze.py thedarkalley.org/*

---

No vulnerabilities found.
```

Site: prt7g2fngznphqiq.onion
Index: leakdumps
thedarkalley.org_members.db_MySQL.torrent

. . .

```
Download complete.
```

Site: qz2zg6f2lphmblzj.onion
Board: Hash Cracking
Topic: need this cracked
See attached DB. Offering reward in BTC for password to any mod account.

Reply#4:
Username: Lighthouse
Password MD5: 3a0dcc626e016df18014e4fd3251fb0d:g0r489fjglz2
BTC address: 13jiAuLHSzhBNWgfSfnn2mQCrzdNE8QWGa

Reply#5:
@4: Worked, BTC sent.

Site: The Dark Alley
Username: Lighthouse
Password: g0r489fjglz2
Topic: Parallel Dimensions and Modern Application
This was published recently. I'm posting it under this board since it's a paid journal, don't want to get slapped with a takedown.

If you read from the abstract alone, it seems to suggest they may have discovered a parallel dimension when doing teleportation experiments. However, since this is quantum teleportation and only involves the transfer of information, not physical mass of any kind, the parallel dimension theory flies out the window. As such, this thread is purely conjecture into the ideas posed by parallel dimension possibilities and what we might need to prepare for in the event such travel ever becomes reality, as our government would doubtless exploit it thoroughly.

War between worlds would doubtless . . .

I delved into more restrictive boards, smoky members-only taverns where they didn't notice I'd slipped in through the back door. Inside, though, I found nothing but the delusional ravings of paranoid conspiracy nuts. I was starting to spend real money on some of these investigations, and getting nothing back in return. What else could I do? There was still so much of the net to scroll through, and it wasn't like I had anything else to spend it on. This was an investment, and I was willing to make it.

I was so focused, I didn't hear the garage door open, or the heavy footfalls on the stairs.

"Carl?"

I looked up. How was it already morning? The sun wasn't up yet. I checked the time. It was early—but I'd stayed up way too late.

". . . Hi, Dad."

My father was a pretty intimidating man, all things considered. He was tall, fit, and strong. He spent his mornings working out before he headed to his job. In my current condition, there was no way I could conceivably take him on.

He didn't seem to be there to confront me though. He closed the door quietly, then sat down on my bed. It felt like the beginning of a lecture. I spun around in my chair, back to my screens, fully prepared to ignore him and face the consequences. They wouldn't mean much in the long run.

The monitors went blank. I whirled back to my father, fury heating up my skin like the beginnings of a wildfire. He'd flipped the switch on the power strip for my desk. The computer itself was plugged into another strip, so it wasn't affected, but I couldn't see anything anymore.

Guess he was going to force this talk. So be it.

"What do you want?" I asked, my voice hard. I was in no mood to be diplomatic.

"Carl, I'm not here to fight," he started calmly. I was stunned into silence. My dad was normally the picture of overreaction. Sometimes, I wasn't sure if he knew how to speak in a volume below shouting. I'd been prepared to take it and get back to work as soon as he'd gotten his fill, but this was rendering me speechless.

"I know you skipped school. Is everything okay?"

I took a few seconds to compose myself again. I wasn't sure how this conversation was going to play out anymore. If he was going to be this calm, maybe I should try being cooperative. There was some piece of the puzzle I didn't have yet, so I needed to play it safe.

"Everything's fine, Dad. Why?"

"Your grades are good. I understand if you think school's too slow or boring for you. But you still need to attend." He was speaking in a very even tone, with just a hint of anxiety. Was he *genuinely* worried about me?

"I've had . . . other things on my mind," I offered, with just enough of a pause to really emphasize it.

"Do you need to talk to someone?"

"Like what, a counselor?" I really felt hostile to the idea. I'd never liked the thought of lying on a couch and confessing my feelings to a total stranger. They didn't deserve to hear what was going on in my head.

"Not necessarily. Your mother and I would listen, if you wanted. Or a professional who won't tell us anything, if you prefer that. Whatever you need."

"Thanks, but I'm good. Can you turn that back on?" I nodded at the power strip near his foot.

He frowned. "Carl, the police came by today."

If he had pulled out a gun and started shooting, I don't think I would have been as shocked. It was like being plunged into an ice bath. Everything froze. My nerves lit up in fear. I was ready to bolt at a moment's notice. I think my father saw it too.

His eyes narrowed. "What did you do?"

"Nothing. I didn't do anything." In the case the police were probably investigating, that was technically true. I really had zero involvement in what happened to Blake.

"Carl, they wanted to talk. I told them I'd call if you came back, but I want to hear your side first. Your friend is missing."

There, he'd confirmed it. The cops had caught on to Blake's vanishing act. We were on a timer now. They'd be asking questions we couldn't possibly answer. We'd either fess up to what we'd done, or become pariahs of unproven accusations—blamed for the disappearance, but never quite convicted. The only real way out was to disappear from this world once again.

The fuse had been lit. I could run from the bomb, or I could leap atop it and try to protect my friends from the explosion.

Or . . . the third option. I could cut the fuse, leave the bomb ready to explode down the line, after I'd gotten us far, far away. I'd leave it right where it was, untouched. It'd be way easier to convince Matt of the threat and the solution if it were right there in front of us.

"I haven't heard from him," I replied casually, hoping I hadn't hesitated too long. "I've been trying to get in touch actually."

The suspicious look didn't disappear. Even though I'd long since abandoned the idea that he had any authority over me, I still felt like cowering under his gaze. He had a withering glare—one I'd inherited, and put to good use many times over the years, with servants and captives alike.

I wasn't going to back down though. Not this time. "Can I get back to it, then? We're wasting time here."

There, his eyes widened. I'd gotten him to react for real, back to the dad I knew. "You will speak to me with respect, young man."

"If you say so," I said mildly. I reached forward with my foot and flicked the power strip back on. The monitors clicked to life, one by one, each lighting up the room a little more as they warmed up.

"This is serious, Carl. Your friend is missing. If you know anything, you need to tell me. I'm trying to help you."

"I don't. Sorry." I didn't give him a second glance. I was trying to set up automation for the scanner I'd been using all morning to check sites for security holes, anything to give me more information to work with.

He sighed. "If you're trying to protect someone, I understand that. But your loyalty's in the wrong place here. It will be much worse if you don't come forward now."

Loyalty? That gave me some pause. He was going to bring up *loyalty?* Loyalty was what I lived for now. I had an obligation to avenge my friend. My loyalty was to my comrades, my guild, the people of my city. I knew what loyalty really meant.

A lack of loyalty was what started this whole mess. Betrayal.

That was the word. Betrayal. *Matt's* betrayal.

I was having a confrontation with the wrong man. My father wasn't important. Matt was the key to everything. Matt knowingly sent Blake to his death. He'd lied to us, to the people closest to him in the entire world.

Matt and I had to come to a reckoning. Today.

I accessed my remote server and set it up to run the automation script I'd just finished writing. It was in the cloud, away from my house so the police or my father couldn't get to it. Once the cloud machine was rolling, I loaded a script onto my desktop that I'd written a long time ago, just in case. I'd never actually expected to *use* it.

In minutes, my hard drives would be zeroed out. My machine was getting completely nuked.

No turning back now.

I grabbed my laptop and stuffed it into my bag.

"What are you doing?"

In all honesty, I'd half-forgotten my father was still in the room.

"I've gotta head out." I slung the bag over my shoulder. It was already packed with a change of clothes and other basic necessities. I'd packed it right after we'd got back, thinking I might be able to take it across.

Nothing made it across the first time around, but who knew what we might find now?

"Carl, sit back down. We're not done here." Dad stood up, but I was already moving out the door, speeding up as I went. I wasn't sure if he'd try to physically restrain me, but I wasn't going to give him the chance. I made a break for it.

He followed me down the stairs, thumping on each step. I was about to open the front door when it occurred to me.

The police had already been here. What if they were watching the house?

I needed another exit. I turned and ran for the back door out into the garden.

"Carl, if you leave, I can't protect you anymore! Please!" He sounded desperate, but I was already bursting through the door. It slammed behind me as I sprinted across the lawn. Could I still climb a fence?

I was about to find out.

I leaped. My hand grasped the top of the solid wood, and I slammed hard into the wall. Was I still able to move? Yes, I could still move. The bag didn't seem as heavy as it did two days ago. Maybe I was stronger now—or maybe it was just adrenaline. Either way, I managed to clamber into the neighbor's yard.

I hoisted myself over the top and rolled into a bush on the opposite side. I crashed onto the lawn, breathing heavily.

The back door to my house opened. I heard shouting, but it brushed over me like the wind. For one glorious, beautiful moment, I felt free again. Another lawn, another fence, and I was back on the streets I'd spent all day wandering yesterday.

Except this time, I had a mission.

Site: SFFHaven.net - Your Sci-Fi / Fantasy Home
Board: Fantasy General → Tip of My Tongue
Topic: Anyone else remember Cyraveil?
ReynirCellman (Newbie) [10/03/10]

Does anyone else remember Cyraveil? Send me a PM, we need to talk.

Private Message
Topic: Re: Cyraveil [10/04/10]
From: fantasythrowaway626
To: ReynirCellman
How do I know I can trust *you*?

CHAPTER 11

MATT

"What took you so long? I have Westin's address, and school's out today."

"Thought I might snoop Carl's computer."

"And?"

"Nothin'. Kid's got it locked up tight. We'd need an expert."

"Given his father's occupation, I doubt we'd ever get into it. Did he ever come home?"

"Never showed. I watched that front door all day and night."

"Well, start driving. Chief wants an update in person before we head out again."

"Kid's gotta come home sometime."

"I'd rather follow the solid suspect than a murky one we can't find."

———————————

A day off. I'd forgotten what they were like. Days off weren't exactly common on the other side. There was always way too much to do. I never got a chance to just cool off for a day. Now I was eager to enjoy some actual rest and relaxation—but my anxiety wasn't about to give up the high ground. We had a three-day weekend, which I should have been looking forward to, but after Jen's apparent breakdown the night before, I was really worried about my Friday afternoon.

She'd come home from Sara's and locked herself in her room for the night, with nothing more than a single word to me or Mom. By the time I woke up Friday morning, she was already gone, headed out to God-knew-where. I called her cell phone from the house phone, but got an "out of range" message. I assumed she'd turned it off.

I knew she could take care of herself. I wasn't really worried about her physically. But mentally? Emotionally? She was obviously unstable. I couldn't stop thinking about what might happen to her, or to anyone around her.

There wasn't anything I could do, as much as it pained me. I had to believe in her for now, because whatever had happened last night, whatever happened at Sara's house, I couldn't see any way it *wouldn't* come up on my date today. I had to get ready for that.

I was going on a date today. A first date with a girl I'd had a crush on for years and years. Apprehensive was a pretty good word for how I felt.

So, of course, when Sara knocked on our front door, I pulled it open just a little too eagerly.

"Uhh, hi," she said, small fist frozen in midair.

"Hi." I smiled, hoping it would break the ice a bit. To my relief, she smiled in return, although hers was a bit more guarded. I wasn't sure what it meant, but I just chalked it up to her own nervousness. *I* definitely felt nervous, why wouldn't she? "Want to head out?"

"Sure."

Sara followed me to the garage, and moments later, I was backing down the driveway, the truck positively purring as we rumbled away. Or so I wanted to believe; in reality, it probably sounded as terrible as ever.

"So, you hungry?" I asked as I pulled out onto the main road.

She rolled down her window and let her hand dangle out in the wind. "What's on the menu?"

"I was thinking pizza." I caught a wince out of the corner of my eye. "What, not a pizza fan?"

"No, I love pizza. It's just . . . we had it last night, actually."

"Oh. Okay." I had to wonder again what happened last night, but it wasn't the right time to ask. "Well, are you in the mood for anything?"

". . . No, not really."

"All right then." I was trying to stay cheerful. She really wasn't giving me much to work with for conversation. Meanwhile, my mind raced through topics I'd usually bring up in a situation like this, where I wanted to impress or flatter a girl. Stuff I was used to talking about.

It didn't help one bit. I gave up and landed on nothing.

"Where are we heading?" Sara asked, breaking the awkward silence.

"Well, after food, I hadn't really decided. Want to go see a movie?"

"Actually, would it be cool if we spent some time outside? I've really been feeling cooped up. Maybe a walk in the park?"

I felt a chill roll down my spine, as if I somehow already knew exactly what she was about to say next. I couldn't see any way around it though. It was inevitable, unless I wanted to call the whole thing off now.

"Sure. Sounds good."

"Cool. Ever been to Cyraveil Park?"

The chill became solid ice, and yet I kept talking like it was perfectly normal. "A couple of times, I think."

"Shall we?"

Why on earth did I actually agree to this?

We were at the edge of the forest, driving down that same fateful route I'd taken Tuesday night. At least the conversation had gotten lighter; some good-natured teasing and talking about movies, and we were actually starting to bond. I was surprised to learn she was an avid cook too, same as me. I took that as a real success, something great we had in common.

Fate, of course, had no intention of letting us enjoy the rest of the afternoon.

I don't actually believe in fate and destiny. I hate the idea of not being in control of my own life. Even if plenty gets chalked up to luck, at least I can make choices and steer my own free will. But that Friday, of all the days in my life, was the closest I came to believing the universe really had it out for me.

There was a bit of a lull in our conversation while we enjoyed sharing a park bench in the sun. We were still way out on the edge of the forest, where the trees and foliage weren't so thick. I decided I might as well get at least one answer out of Sara, to calm the fears still bubbling away in the recesses of my brain.

"So, and tell me if I'm breaking a rule or something here, but weren't you and Jen supposed to hang out today?" I asked, trying to stay casual.

Sara watched a leaf twirl down from a nearby tree. Her dark, thoughtful eyes tracked it all the way to the ground before she finally answered. "Yeah. Jen called me this morning though, said she had something important to do. Nothing to worry about, just something."

Which, of course, only made me *more* worried. Jen breaking her routine, missing spending time with her best friend, was *definitely* something to worry about. Sleep clearly hadn't done anything to help the pain from the night before.

She wasn't getting better.

"Didn't have a fight, did you?" I asked, acting like it was a joke—though I actually hoped that was what really happened last night. A fight between Jen and Sara wasn't unheard of. That was something we could resolve.

"Nope." Sara stood up, stretching out her arms. She yawned—which I found strangely adorable—then pointed at a trail peeking out between two trees, one leading much deeper into the forest. "That looks like it could be fun."

I disagreed wholeheartedly, but I shrugged. "Lead the way."

"So you're saying you've never watched a *single* episode?"

"I'm not really a TV guy."

"Oh man. I'm bringing over all the DVDs then. You'll love it." She shook her head in mock disgust. "Not one episode. Horrible."

"That sounds nice. Let's make a whole day of it. I'll cook up something special."

"Mmmm." Sara licked her lips exaggeratedly. I laughed. She grinned back—then promptly tripped over a tree root.

In an instant, I closed on her, sweeping one arm under her chest and gently catching her. She never came close to falling down.

I felt my heartbeat quicken. The thick forest seemed to surround us, like we were the only two people around for miles. All I could hear was the birds chirping and the wind rustling through the leaves, and all I could see was Sara's face as she twisted in my grip, eyes wide. I could feel her body moving as she took sudden, deep breaths, still in the midst of reacting to falling.

I didn't want the moment to end, me holding her like that, but I felt like I was already overstepping. I helped her up and let go, stepping back to let her catch her breath.

As she relaxed again, she smiled. "That was your moment, Matt."

"Hmm?"

"Shouldn't've let go." She turned away. I cursed under my breath. "Don't worry. I'm sure you'll get another." She steadied herself, then continued walking, heading deeper into the forest.

Maybe I would've gotten that moment, too, if it weren't for what I spotted between the trees. I'd turned to look away for just a second. I wasn't familiar with this area of the woods, and I wanted to get my bearings, figure out where we were. When I looked back toward Sara, I saw her.

She flitted through the trees ahead, clad in a green jacket and dark pants. She wore a hood, which mostly concealed it, but some of her dark brown hair still spilled out onto her clothes. Over her shoulder was a strung longbow, and on her back sat a quiver of arrows. Her face, which turned to meet mine for only an instant, was clearly my sister's.

Jen's eyes widened. I'm sure mine did too. I wasn't sure what to do. I couldn't call out to her, not with Sara so near. What was Jen *doing* out here? Where did she get a bow? Questions were exploding in my head like fireworks. I had to do something before Sara spotted her.

A single nod. I tried to put as much meaning and emphasis behind it as I could. I wanted to tell Jen I accepted this. Give her some kind of comfort. To my relief, after the briefest hesitation, Jen returned my nod.

A second later, she disappeared into the woods once again, as thoroughly and silently as only an elven-trained huntress could.

I stared after the spot where she'd vanished, hoping she'd come back home someday, but not really sure if she ever truly would. Hoping that we'd actually talk again, like we used to.

"You saw her too, didn't you?" asked Sara.

Any hopes of returning to our date were dashed. I sighed. I didn't see any point in denying it anymore. "Yes."

"She's kind of crazy to be out here hunting, isn't she?" Sara spoke so calmly, so benignly, that I was completely stunned. ". . . Sorry to spring this on you, but yeah, I know."

How was I supposed to respond to *that*? "Jen *told* you?" I hadn't meant to sound so accusatory, but there it was. I was angry.

"Don't you dare get on her case," she snapped. "She was going to crack if she didn't talk to *somebody*."

"She still might," I murmured.

"What?"

"She came home a wreck last night," I said. My eyes narrowed slightly. If we were going to have this conversation, I was going to get answers. Whatever might shed light on Jen's condition, so I could actually get her some help.

"Oh . . ." Sara's eyes shimmered slightly. "I don't know what happened. We were fine, right up 'til dinner. Then Jen . . . snapped? I don't know, really. She got super defensive and twitchy during dinner, then ran out the back door when we were done. She seemed like she might attack someone."

I paused, trying to consider exactly what to say next. "How much did she tell you?" I asked slowly.

"A lot, but I'm guessing that with seven years behind you guys, there's no way she could have told me everything." She spoke so matter-of-factly. I was seriously unsettled. Her voice fell as she went on. "She told me that only three of you came back too."

A complex mixture of emotions was springing forth: betrayal and rage and fear and a whole host of others I couldn't name. I had to force them away for now. Sara knew. I had to deal with that now. There was no way to take it back. It was time to get more information. Whatever she knew, she knew, and I would figure out where to go from here.

"Did she say what she went through?"

"Lived with Sylves for six years, completely cut off from people, got into a huge war, only found you guys again way later. Is that about right?"

I nodded. "Mostly. But Jen went through a lot worse stuff than we did."

"Like what?" she asked. She was direct, which was one of the traits I'd always liked about her. No beating around the bush. Straight to the point. I decided to tell her the rest. She already knew more than enough to damn us; better she know everything so she knew what to look out for. Maybe she could help Jen when I couldn't do anything.

"She was captured," I answered. My voice caught as I tried to continue. I swallowed a few times, clearing my throat. Even now, way after the fact, it was still painful for me to describe, even though it hadn't happened to me. "She was tortured. Forced to fight, I think. I've never gotten the whole story."

"Oh, God . . ." Sara's face fell. "So she has . . . what? PTSD, I guess?"

"I think so. That's probably the best way to describe it. What she went through was . . . well, horrible. I think it's preventing her from remembering how to live in the real world again."

Sara shook her head. "It's not just that. Unless I got mixed up, she was the only one of you who could do stuff. Like, magic and stuff. Right?"

I nodded. I wasn't quite sure where she was going with this.

"So, yeah. Consider that. Not only did she get shoved back into the real world, she's seriously traumatized and she lost all her support systems. Her power, her people. Plus, she's gotta deal with losing hundreds of years of her lifespan."

"She what?" That last sentence was news to me.

"Oh." Sara looked uncomfortable. ". . . I didn't realize she hadn't told you."

"Can you explain? Please?" I had to know.

She shifted in place, glancing away. "Jen told me she had a ritual she did every day, just like the Sylves. She said it restored her, that she could really feel it." Her face twisted into a sad smile. "She probably could've lived to be three hundred or more."

I felt like she'd just hit me in the face with a sack full of bricks. My sister, my happy ray of sunshine sibling, whom I'd spent six years searching for, who had turned the tide of the war along with Carl, was still dealing with so much more than I could imagine, or understand— and in some twisted, indirect way, I was responsible for this. I'd brought us home, and by doing so, I'd cut her life drastically short.

"You're blaming yourself, aren't you? Cut that out." Sara grasped my arm. I looked around, and saw a fire in her eyes. "You saved her. You got her home. You couldn't've known."

"She didn't have to come home though," I said weakly, words I hadn't dared to voice even in my own head.

"What?"

"She could have stayed. It was my decision to bring us all back. I could have let her stay."

"But—"

"She was happy there, I think. She had friends. She had a family. A best friend named Naeflin. And she had a position of real importance. Prestige. She was the *sylajen,* she ended a whole war and united the kingdom." A warm streak rolled down my face. I reached up to brush it away. "I was proud of her. Proud to be her brother. Then I ran away.

I forced her to come back with me to the real world, where she's got no accomplishments, where she's terrified and hurting and I can't do anything for her. All because I was scared to come home alone."

Sara shook her head. "Don't be an idiot. If you came back alone, you'd be in even worse trouble. How could you have explained that to your mom? Or to the world?" Sara put an arm around me, and pulled me into a hug. "Hindsight's a stupid useless thing. I'm super biased, but I think you made the right call." She stepped back and smiled. "Come on. Let's go back."

"Pretty awful first date," I joked, though my voice was still thick.

"As if. I got to see the closest thing to a real elf on this whole planet, and I got to feel up a great-looking guy." She grinned and took my hand. "Just promise that our second date won't involve you bursting into tears."

"Deal," I said, with a rush of completely incongruous joy at the words *second date*.

Despite that happy note, the rest of the date was mostly awkward silences punctured by brief anecdotes of Cyraveil. Sara seemed way more interested in anything having to do with Jen, which didn't surprise me, since we'd barely hung out before. I couldn't blame her for her curiosity—or her concern, since I was just as worried myself.

It was one thing for Sara to insist I didn't get lost in hindsight, but quite another for me to actually follow that advice. I felt like reflection was productive. Looking back on my mistakes was a useful tool for learning. In this case, though, Sara was probably right. My decisions had been made in a radically different situation, in a war-torn land on another world. How could I possibly judge them against my life now?

Yet I couldn't help myself. I ran circles in my head, blaming myself over and over. I wanted desperately to find a solution, anything I could do to help Jen. Anything to help my sister out of the rut of despair she'd found herself trapped within.

For the second time since we'd come back, I wondered if she truly belonged in Cyraveil.

I didn't dismiss the thought as fast as I had before. By all accounts, Jen had taken to Cyraveil so thoroughly that the Sylves considered her one of their own. That might sound merely special, but really, it was totally unique. As far as I knew, including what Carl had told me in his own research, the Sylves were incredibly insular and xenophobic. They were openly dismissive, if not outright hostile to all attempts at contact by human settlers. A rare few traded with humans, but for the most part, they maintained the circle of silence to a man—err, elf.

So how was it that Jen, a perfectly ordinary human from another world, had so ingratiated herself that they gave her a new name and adopted her as one of their own?

I wanted to hear that story, but I knew I could only get it from Jen herself—and since I'd reunited with her, she'd never been in a state to share it. First, it was the negotiations, where she hadn't even recognized me. She was so busy juggling the various dignitaries, generals, and nobles—while still struggling through basic English—that she just glanced right over me without a second thought.

Every Sylf commander present treated her with the utmost respect. An older looking elf with very kind, silvery eyes watched her every move from afar, usually perched in the corner of the tent like a wise old owl (not that he looked a day more than thirty). In turn, I watched him, carefully. I later learned his name was Tethevallen Sylnanden, and that he was the elder of sorts for the forest where Jen had first appeared.

I only spoke to him once, on the eve of his death. I'd asked him, after stumbling through what I'm sure was awful Etoline, what he thought of my sister. He laughed and answered me with a clap on the back and a string of words I hadn't understood in the slightest, even after three tries. When I repeated them carefully to Jen the next day, she looked embarrassed but thoroughly pleased with herself.

Of course, only an hour later, we found his dead body on the side of a cliff, pinned to the wall with a scroll stuffed in his mouth. Jen's happiness hadn't lasted long.

The memory of that event sent me spinning back into the present as I dropped Sara off at the bus stop. How could I have even considered sending Jen back to that place? Where war and pain and darkness loomed large in memory, and our friends were slaughtered by a delusional madman?

Our worlds were separate—and should remain separate. I'd find a way to help Jen, no matter what it took. Once we were united again, we could stabilize Carl, and the three of us would return to a normal life. The path was beginning to clear up once again. I could see the bricks in the road as it stretched out to the horizon. All I had to do was start walking it.

As I pulled into our garage, the first step revealed itself, like fate sending me a signal to begin. Jen had just walked through the front door, probably after taking the bus home. It was time for a talk, and she knew it too. She went straight to the living room as I walked in. I stalled a bit, pouring myself a glass of water and grabbing a bowl of chips before I sat down on the couch opposite her.

"So," I started, but Jen interrupted before I could say another word.

"Yeah, I went hunting. I needed to be alone, and it seemed like a good place to go. Nobody saw me. Got a problem?" Her voice was instantly hostile. I recoiled. I didn't want this to be a confrontation, not at all.

"I was just going to ask how your day went."

"*Keldaphut.* You were getting ready to lay down a lecture."

I raised an eyebrow. "Do you *want* a lecture?"

"Matt, I'm twenty-three years old. No, I don't give a shit how old I look right now. That's where my mind's at. I don't need a lecture from my big brother." Jen leaned forward in her chair. "What I *do* need is some support, because I'm barely holding on by a twig here."

I sat back, unsure how to respond, and Jen took that as reason enough to keep ranting.

"I'm scared, okay? I'm sure you already heard about what I did at school yesterday, since you always know everything."

"Back up a second. What happened at school?"

Jen faltered. She shifted in her chair, glancing away. "Oh. Uhh . . . shit. Well, I kind of went all out on a guy, just for a second. It was a super easy takedown; I couldn't help it. He ran into me and I just . . . reacted."

I shook my head, one knot of tension easing a little. "Well, if I didn't hear about it by now, it probably wasn't that big a deal. What happened last night though?" Her lips squeezed shut. I sighed. "Jen, you said it yourself. You need support right now. Talk to me."

". . . I don't know," she murmured. Her voice cracked as she continued. It was clear she was barely keeping herself from falling apart. "Everything was going great. I felt better than I have in years. All Sara's work, no thanks to me. But then all through dinner . . . I don't know if it was me, or if it was just because there were too many people around. But I felt . . . *vack*. In danger. Uhh . . ." Jen paused, searching for the word. Her eyes always darted around in the same way whenever she was trying to think in English. "Threatened."

I wanted to get up and go to her, to hug her and reassure her that everything would be all right—but I knew, in her current state, that I would only make things worse. She didn't need someone physically by her side. I didn't know what she needed. I just had to hope I could provide it.

"You thought you might attack them," I concluded. Jen nodded, looking ashamed of herself. "But nothing happened, right?"

"Nothing."

"Then it's okay. You didn't do anything wrong."

"I don't want to keep feeling like this, Matt," she cried. *"Vei kilsve dovei nalv vnulvus."*

I couldn't understand what she'd said, but the emotions behind it channeled more feeling than anything from her in English could have.

It was so full of bitter desperation that my heart wanted to burst out of my chest.

What could I say?

Tell her it would get better over time? I believed it would, but the words felt so hollow in the moment.

Should I offer her anything she wanted? Try to provide for her, like I always did?

Did she want me to be stern and commanding, or did she need kind and gentle?

Why was I the father figure? The leader, the general, the commander?

I hated my thoughts for turning back to me again. This was about Jen, not me. I didn't have time to worry about me right now.

An idea struck me.

"Jen, tell me about Tethevallen."

It was a shot in the dark. Something we'd never had time to discuss, but the elf was clearly of great importance, and nearly all her memories of him were positive. He was something she could anchor herself to. Not of this world, perhaps, but right now I'd take anything that might pull her out of this spiral.

Jen blinked furiously for a few moments, looking startled. "About Tethevallen? Like what?"

"Who was he? I mean, he obviously cared a lot about you. I only met him once, but he seemed like a great man."

Jen wiped her eye with a sleeve. "He was my father."

I raised an eyebrow. "Not literally."

"No, 'course not." Jen rolled her reddened eyes, but she smirked slightly at my joke. "But he adopted me, basically, when nobody else would. He gave me a name and brought me into our *suunsyl*. If he hadn't found me that week, when I was starving to death, I wouldn't be here now having this great chat with you."

I was never more aware of Jen's elven accent than in that moment. As she talked about her other family, the one I'd never known, I could hear their culture come through her voice—that unique sound I'd never heard anywhere else. Carl referring to it as a "magical language" might seem crazy to me, but the accent was certainly something special.

"You couldn't understand him though."

Jen smiled. "Not a word. We got some good hand gestures down after a while. He didn't learn any Linguen 'til after the war started. I asked him about it years later, and he said Linguen was forbidden long ago. I was the first in the entire *suunsyl* to 'learn' it, and between the two of us, we started teaching others."

"Sorry to interrupt, but what does *suunsyl* mean?"

Jen giggled. "Sorry. Hard to remember you're an uneducated lunkhead."

I raised my eyebrows exaggeratedly. "How *did* you learn a whole language that quickly?"

"Magic, *duralav-hila*." She grinned. "*Suunsyl* is a . . . *vack*. Shortening. Of two words."

"Abbreviation," I supplied. "Lunkhead." Jen chucked a pillow at me. It slammed into the wall, right where my head had been a moment earlier. "Is that really the best you could come up with?"

"I could do *way* better, but you wouldn't understand it, so what's the point?" Jen sighed mockingly. "Anyway. *Suunsyl* is an abbreviation of *suunis* and *sylvec*, meaning 'our forest.' Really just means a group of Sylves though. Or a home. A community, I guess you'd call it."

"Huh."

"Language lessons with Jennifer Silverdale." She gave a mock bow, twirling her hand. "Hey look, it worked. You . . . *syldavacka*. You manipulative bastard. That's the one." Jen laughed. "I'm all cheerful now, good for you."

In spite of the insult, I laughed too. The best strategies I ever devised were as straightforward as that one. I knew if I could just get her talking, on any subject related to her adopted heritage, she'd regain some kind of peace. Much better than the doubt-filled, angry, fearful creature I'd first walked in on, at any rate.

I wish it could have lasted, but as per the norm, fate's ugly claws were reaching for us once more.

A knock came at the front door. Our heads both snapped in that direction. It was the middle of the day; no one we knew was likely to come calling, were they?

The knock came again. The doorbell rang a second later, and again. Whomever it was clearly had no intention of leaving.

"Wait here?" I whispered. Jen nodded.

I crept toward the door, anxious to get a look at our unexpected guest before I came into view. To my astonishment, I heard a clicking sound at the doorknob. A moment later, the lock clicked open, and the door swung wide.

"Jen?"

I was simultaneously relieved and infuriated. "Hello, Carl."

I yanked him inside and shoved the door closed. His face twisted into an expression I couldn't describe. There were too many emotions scattered across it to name them all.

"You son of a bitch," he growled.

"Huh?"

"Don't you ever play dumb again. This is about Blake."

Did Carl know? How could he possibly have found out? There was only one possible, logical conclusion.

Jen, what did you do?

I went for diplomatic. "Carl, I'm sorry."

"Sorry? *Sorry?*" Carl's voice rose in pitch. "Oh, that's great. Matt's *sorry* he sent a friend to his *fucking grave.*"

Like a curtain falling from the stage, a veil lifted. Carl knew. I was exposed before him. The secret was out, and he was in front of me, with fury in his heart and vengeance filling his eyes like twin bonfires.

"Blake and I made a decision. We did what needed to be done." My own voice rose in volume, as if drowning out Carl would somehow make it right. As if I could simply overwhelm all the guilt and depression I felt in my core.

"If I hear one more crap excuse out of your mouth, you'll be eating the floor, asshole."

Carl's stance changed. I saw it plain as day. While he might still have the mental ability and long study of a dozen fighting techniques, his body just wasn't trained or focused enough to keep up. Anything he did was wildly telegraphed.

His weight shifted. A punch, coming in low. I dodged aside easily, and he swung wide. Carl managed to keep his balance though. He'd never intended for that one to land. Another fist, already on its way from the opposite side.

His punch landed. I rolled with it, letting momentum absorb the blow, refusing to let him make an impact.

"Calm down," I shouted, but Carl's expression only got sharper. His determination was set. He swung again, and I dodged aside. I might have thrown a return punch then, but neither of us got another chance.

A sharp *thwok* of an arrow. The shaft sprouted out of the staircase bannister, right between the two of us, at eye level.

We froze.

As one, our heads rotated to face Jen. She stood across the hall, with another arrow already nocked on the string. Ready to pull back and launch at a moment's notice.

"Are you two done being idiots yet?" she asked, quite calm.

I nodded, taking a step back.

Carl was breathing heavily. His eyes narrowed.

"Carl, *vei torl* I will put this arrow through your skull. *Ovol nos.*"

Slowly, reluctantly, Carl retreated. He leaned against the doorframe, while I waited by the stairs.

"We can't fight," Jen stated.

"No," I agreed.

"But—" started Carl.

"But nothing," Jen snapped. "Arrow. Skull."

Carl fell silent.

"Good," said Jen, still remarkably calm. "Matt?"

"Carl, we have to stick together right now," I said. By Carl's reaction, I'd chosen my words poorly.

"Stick together?" His voice began to rise once again. "That's rich, you fucking hypocrite."

"Calm down," I started, even though I knew it to be futile.

"Se develd!" Jen hissed.

We all fell silent instantly. Carl and I both knew what those words meant—but on top of that, the sudden intensity in Jen's voice sent my mind reeling in fear, back to memories of ambushes in the deep forest.

"Someone's at the door," she whispered, barely louder than a breath.

I turned. It took an eternity just to rotate myself to face the dark brown door. The entire world faded away as my eyes focused on the brass doorknob. I hoped that Jen was wrong, for the first time ever, about the presence of a threat nearby.

Fate wouldn't have that. Fate and I were mortal enemies, from now until the end of time.

Knuckles rapped on the door three times—and in that moment, I knew our lives on Earth were about to be shattered completely.

CHAPTER 12

JEN

"They'd damn well better be home this time."

"We saw the truck heading this way. They'll be here."

"This lawn is really shit. Doesn't anyone mow their lawn anymore?"

"Pay attention. We're about to question a suspect."

"If I ring this bell and no one answers, you're buyin' lunch."

"Wait. Do you hear something?"

. . .

"Sounds intense."

"Do we knock?"

"No, keep listening."

"They've stopped talking. If we don't go now, they'll rabbit."

"Damnit. Okay, let's do this."

———————————

It felt as skin-bitingly cold as winter in the forest all week. Not saying it was *actually* cold out; in fact, the weather was really nice for this time of year. But when you've just spent the last couple of months in the middle of summer and you suddenly drop right into autumn, even in pretty much the same climate, your body takes a while to adjust. It's like how two days that are the same temperature can feel way different depending on what season they're in.

All of this is to say that I was shivering constantly over the last couple of days, but I didn't want to give it away. I wore light clothes like everybody else—although Sara had pointed out I'd been wearing way darker stuff that tended to blend into shadows more. I didn't want to look like a freak though, wearing some heavy jacket everywhere. Instead, I dealt with the chills and the sniffles while at school.

So when I tell you that, even with all that, I still felt the room get colder in an instant, you'll understand that I mean it was like the Arctic in there.

It didn't take me long to figure out why. As I glanced away from Matt and Carl, both still on edge, I saw the outline of a hand, just through the curtains around the windows by our front door. My instincts were right on the money.

I got the guys to shut up. We stared at the door for what felt like hours, but only a second later, the first knock came. A sharp tap of a fist on our door.

Matt immediately took charge. "Jen, hide," he hissed. I didn't have to be told twice. In my hunting outfit, with the quiver of arrows on my back and bow over my shoulder, I was *seriously* out of place. I snagged the arrow out of the banister as I hurried upstairs, ripping out a small chunk of wood in the process.

Matt raised an eyebrow. I shrugged, retreating into the shadows of the upstairs landing. The staircase looked so beat up anyway, it didn't really stand out much.

Okay, it did; there was a big difference between the scratches and scuffs and the sudden gaping hole I'd just torn, but what the hell did he expect? I couldn't just *leave* the arrow there.

For a brief moment of bizarre jealousy, I wondered why Matt had sent me away, but not Carl. It didn't take long to reason it out though.

Whoever was on the other side of that door had probably heard people arguing—two guys in particular. If Matt answered it alone, he'd just look more suspicious. *I* could disappear, since I hadn't been shouting my head off like an idiot, but we needed to seem like we had nothing to hide.

No way in hell I wasn't gonna listen in though. I laid down just beyond the corner at the top of the staircase, pressed into the carpet with my ears as close as I could get to the edge of the wall without showing myself.

I heard the door click open.

"Hello, officers," Matt's voice rang out, quite calm. The staircase groaned slightly as someone leaned against the bannister. I assumed it was Carl. He was still breathing pretty heavily, though he was trying to suppress it.

"Matthew Westin?" A typical cop voice, direct and professional. I decided the guy must have glasses, with a full proper uniform, all perfectly even and pressed. Probably pretty handsome too.

"Can I help you?"

"Detectives, actually. West and Portman," said a second voice. Rougher. He'd be the off-the-rails guy, the plays-by-his-own-rules cop. Shabby clothes, a devil-may-care attitude. Meanwhile, I had to revise my mental picture of the first guy into a plainclothes investigator. Well-dressed still, but in a business suit instead of a uniform.

Shit, did we just stumble into some kind of buddy cop show? Man, why do I remember TV so well but nothing else?

I could have laughed, if I wasn't so terrified. Instinctively, my hand slid down to the knife near the small of my back. Not that I was about to attack *cops*, but there was no way I was getting taken somewhere against my will.

Never again.

I tried to focus on the conversation. My mind kept flying off on too many tangents. They still seemed to be on introductions though, so I hadn't missed much.

". . . and we're here looking into a missing persons case."

"Missing persons?" said Matt, still the perfect tone of control. I knew he wouldn't slip up in front of the police, no matter what they might try. I was much more worried about Carl, who still hadn't gotten his breathing under control. He couldn't *still* be tired from the fight, could he? It was like two punches. He wasn't *that* out of shape. It had to be nerves.

Carl was scared.

"Do you mind if we ask you a few questions?" asked Professional-Guy. It was all so calm and polite. The only thing out of place was Carl's ragged breaths.

"Of course. Please, come in."

Carl's breath sharpened again. He was not ready for this kind of stress, I could tell. Matt, this is a mistake. I know you're doing the right thing for you, but Carl cannot handle this right now.

They crossed into the sitting area next to the front door. I could just make out Matt's face in the corner, as he took a seat. The two detectives followed, flitting through the gap, and Carl stayed on the stairs, watching from the third step up.

"When was the last time you saw Blake Svartholm?" asked Rough-Guy. Straight to the point, as expected. He was doing off-the-book perfectly *by* the book. Even pronounced "Svartholm" wrong.

"Blake's . . . missing?" Oh thank the stars. Matt, you're good. No hesitation at all.

"When did you see him last?" prompted Professional-Guy again.

"Uhh, night before last." No, that's wrong. Matt, don't lie to them. You don't know what they know yet.

"Wednesday the second?"

"No, sorry. I meant Tuesday night." Or you knew what to do all along. Okay, gonna stop doubting you now.

"So Tuesday the first." I heard a scratching sound. Probably Professional-Guy taking notes on a yellow legal pad, because it always had to be yellow.

"Were you aware nobody's seen him since that night?" Rough-Guy said.

"No, I wasn't. I mean, I was surprised I didn't see him at school, but I thought he might be sick or something."

"What were you two doing that night?"

"Just hanging out. Nothing special."

Carl was fidgeting on the stairs. These guys were too good not to notice. "You wouldn't happen to be Carl Stokelson, would you?"

He nodded nervously. I was astonished. To see somebody like Carl—with what he'd accomplished, the power he'd once held—so thoroughly unsettled by a couple of real-world cops was . . . pathetic. I felt sorry for him.

"Blake was your best friend, wasn't he?"

"Yeah."

"And you were there that night as well?"

"Yeah, I was." Carl sounded really subdued. Maybe he had a thing about cops? I couldn't remember, as much as I tried. I still couldn't wrap my head around his defeated posture.

"Where did you go that night?"

"Here. And uhh . . . out for a bit."

"We drove around for a while, went to a few places," added Matt. He was trying to deflect them off Carl.

"Anywhere in particular?" asked Professional-Guy.

"Not really."

"Not Cyraveil Park?"

Shit. Shit, shit, shit. We'd been caught in a lie. Well, kind of. It was enough of one to make them suspicious.

I set my bow aside in the nearest room, along with the quiver. My days of watching way too much TV with Sara were about to pay off big-time.

"We might have," said Matt noncommittally, but I could hear his voice falter *just* a tad. I doubted the cops would recognize it, but I wasn't going to let this get any further. I was already moving.

"Hey, Matt, what's going on?" I called, hurrying down the stairs.

"Jen?" He twisted around in surprise. Carl, too, glanced up in confusion.

"You guys cops?" I asked in what I hoped was a cheerful, upbeat voice. I tried my best to suppress any hint of my accent. Just a normal Oregon girl, that's me. Unsurprisingly, I had their appearances down perfect. Disappointing, but what can you do? More interesting to me, though, was that Professional-Guy looked barely older than I was. I didn't know detectives came that young.

Barely older than *actual*-me, obviously. Not current-me. But still, I'd call him mid-twenties, easy.

Professional-Guy spoke up. "Yes. Detectives Portman and West."

"Neat. Mind if I hang around?" I plopped myself onto the chair next to Matt. Professional-Guy looked taken aback. *Wondering if you're allowed to question us with a minor present, right?* For once, I was actually grateful to be seven years younger.

It wasn't the most elaborate move, and definitely just a temporary solution, but it was enough to stave off the pressure, give Carl some breathing room. So I hoped.

"If you wouldn't mind, we'd like to speak to your brother alone, please." Professional-Guy was polite as can be, but I wasn't gonna let it slide.

"Nah, I kinda do mind. Is he under arrest?" *Estek*, Mr. Detective. *Your move. Will you bluff, or do I take the round?*

"No."

"Then you can't compel him to answer anything right now. And I was promised a good lunch, so if *you* wouldn't mind, I'd like my brother to get back in the kitchen." I was deliberately playing up the bratty-little-sister angle. Anything to get them out of our house, right away. Matt had stumbled hard, and I didn't want to consider what might happen if they started questioning Carl directly.

Obviously doubting his legal standing in the room, Professional-Guy stood up. Rough-Guy seemed surprised, but followed his partner's lead. In typical detective fashion though, Rough-Guy pulled out a business card from his jacket and handed it over to Matt.

"You think of anything, you call."

"Of course," Matt replied, pocketing the card. I felt immensely reassured by the aura of calm that had returned to his voice. The cops were out the door in moments, and I watched carefully as they walked back to their car and then down the block and away. Only once they were out of sight did I turn back to face my brother.

"That was sloppy," said Matt.

"Masal daphut," I snapped. "Why did you lie?"

"I—" Matt started.

"We're screwed," said Carl. We both looked at him, confused.

"I think that's a little premature," said Matt.

"They already came to my place once. My dad told me."

"So they know you and Blake are friends. It's not exactly news," Matt reasoned.

"Yeah, but the bit about Cyraveil. They probably got that from a chat between me and Blake. Off Blake's computer. They'll know I was involved somehow."

Matt sighed. "It's not the end of the world yet, Carl. We'll figure something out."

Carl's eyes narrowed. "Figure something out," he sneered. "Like you always do."

"Yes, Carl," said Matt. His voice was much sharper now. "Like I always do. You guys put me in charge, now you're going to listen." I had been about to speak up in Matt's defense, but his tone reminded me that he didn't need it. I'd forgotten just what he could sound like.

It wasn't really a good memory.

"They know we went to the forest," Matt went on, Carl and I totally silent. "We can't deny that. We'll just have to stick to our story. When we came home, after midnight, we dropped Blake off. That was the last time we saw him. Jen, you were never there. You don't know a thing."

I nodded, but I wasn't sure how well it'd hold up. It was better than nothing . . .

"That's it? We just keep up that lie forever?" asked Carl.

"There's literally no evidence," said Matt. "They can never prove anything."

"What about Blake's parents? Our friends? Are they supposed to believe he just disappeared?"

"Well, he did."

"Fuck you, Matt," Carl snapped. "Blake deserves better."

"And what are you thinking?"

"I . . . don't know. Yet." Carl's voice fell. He hesitated. "I don't know if we can do this. Live here."

"We don't have any other option," said Matt. I could tell he was trying to be comforting, but it didn't work; Carl wasn't taking it. Matt wasn't the right person to help him. Maybe I was, maybe I wasn't, but I couldn't think of anything better to say. So I stayed silent.

Which meant, of course, that Carl's head swiveled to face me. He looked me straight in the eye. So much for staying out of the conversation.

"What do you think?"

I took a deep breath, trying to get my nerves under control. "I think Matt's right."

Carl looked crestfallen. Had he expected me to *agree* with him? Over Matt?

"Carl, I need to know you can do this," said Matt. "They'll be asking you questions, without us around. Can you handle it?"

He didn't answer, not right away. I could see him processing, calculating. He was a planner, just like Matt. Carl was definitely the smartest of us, the most well-read, the most cunning, and absolutely the most successful of us in Cyraveil. But he lacked Matt's self-control, his ability to shut out emotion when he needed to. Matt was an iceberg, stable and floating along, hiding so much more under the surface. Carl was an open flame, bright and powerful, but ready to burn down the whole world if he got pushed too far in the wrong direction.

Worst of all, I wasn't actually sure which of them I really agreed with. My own mind was so mixed up, I just defaulted to supporting my brother. Trusting he had a real plan. Knowing he'd take care of me.

"Jen, can I talk to you?" Carl asked quietly.

I raised an eyebrow. What was he expecting to get out of a private conversation?

"Go ahead and talk," Matt said sternly.

"Alone, dickhead," Carl retorted.

"I'm staying right here," said Matt.

He was trying to protect me. I got that. Normally, I appreciated it, but right now it was all wrong. This was Carl, not the cops or Reynir's armies or the Vennenport Deathblades. Even if he *did* mean me harm, I could take out this weaker version of Carl any day of the week. No sweat.

"Then I guess we're going somewhere else," I cut in. Carl glanced over, surprised, but not nearly as much as Matt. "I'll be fine. Go make us a snack, okay?" After a moment's hesitation, he nodded.

Good. He still trusts me. At least something's still right here.

Matt retreated into the kitchen, and Carl and I stepped out into the backyard. Almost immediately, Carl started pacing. Clearly, he was still way too amped up by the cops to stay calm. I walked onto the lawn, letting my bare feet enjoy the grass. I sat down cross-legged, staring up at the clouds swirling across the sky. They looked like gigantic structures, miles and miles wide. I wondered if I could reach them someday, if I somehow got access to etola again. Maybe there was some way to use the wind, reduce my weight, letting me be carried upward into the sky. I could see myself really enjoying that.

I could *also* see myself plummeting a couple of miles to my untimely death, but hey—nobody ever did anything *really* cool by playing it totally safe, right?

Not that it mattered. I'd never get that opportunity, unless I decided to take up skydiving. Magic was a thing of the past, forever. I was gonna die young, waste away like a human at eightysomething. I was never gonna get to fly like a bird or swim like a fish or tree-shape or mind-meld or any of the other hundreds of things I hadn't done yet. It was gone.

"We don't belong here," said Carl finally.

I sighed, twiddling my toes in the grass. "What are we supposed to do about that?"

"I don't know yet. But I'm trying to find out."

"You're what now?" I was cautiously interested. That's not to say I was *eager* to find a way back. Despite everything I just listed off, there were a hell of a lot of reasons to be happy back here on Earth too. The jury was still out. I just liked having options. Anything to feel less confined in the world.

"I've been sending out messages. Trying to find anyone who might have gone through something similar. If it happened to us, why couldn't it happen to someone else?"

I shook my head. "It's magic, Carl. It doesn't have to be logical."

"I can't believe that. The universe works on rules. We just stumbled upon a new rule no one's documented yet."

"So you think you're gonna figure it out?"

"I'd rather somebody else already did and is just keeping it secret for the same paranoid reasons we are," Carl muttered. I started to speak up, but he kept going. "No, I think you guys are right, and I'm not going to go public or anything. Our lives would get way, *way* worse. But a few anonymous posts on the internet aren't going to set off any alarms."

Made some sense to me, I guess. Matt wouldn't like it though. "Any luck yet?"

Carl shrugged. "Mostly a lot of trolls, or just pure fantasy. But I did get one possible hit. A guy claiming he knows something, and clearly just as scared as we are. I've been talking to him."

I felt a thrill roll through me, coupled with a healthy burst of defensive skepticism. "How do you know you can trust him?"

"I don't. Of course not. It's the internet. But he seems legit from the couple of PMs we've traded so far."

"PMs?" I asked, with a twinge of embarrassment.

"Sorry. Private messages. No one else will see them."

"Okay," I said neutrally. I didn't want to get my hopes up, but I trusted Carl to be discreet. Especially with anything concerning the Web.

"If—" Carl started, but he cut himself off abruptly. I glanced over at him, curious. His face was unreadable, a mix of apprehension and hope.

"If what?" I prompted.

"Would you come back with me? If I found a way?"

I didn't answer right away, because I didn't really *have* an answer, and that seemed to open a floodgate.

"There's nothing left for me. I don't fit into my family, school is worthless, and I can't see myself just going through the usual hoops. Going to college, getting a job, whatever. After what I've done? It would be such a step backward. Nothing I could ever achieve in this world would amount to a fraction of what I accomplished in Cyraveil." Carl's face twisted into a bitter smile. "I still have so much unfinished business over there. It wouldn't be right for me to leave it, you know? And I know you still have people here. You've got friends and family. But do you *really* belong here? Can you really be happy here?"

A couple of days ago—vack, even a *month* ago, I could have said yes. Today . . . I said nothing.

"You should be at my side while we reshape the world."

The way he said it, the attempt at grandeur, I couldn't help but laugh. "Sorry, sorry. But seriously. *Reshape the world?*"

"Why not?"

"Dunno. It just seems nuts to be saying that about a couple of kids from Oregon."

Carl shook his head. "It *is* nuts, but we already did it once. The four of us overthrew the whole empire."

"We had help," I said dismissively.

"Tell me you prefer this world over Cyraveil," Carl snapped.

"You know what? It wasn't all great," I shot back. My own temper was rising, and at the moment, I *really* didn't feel like controlling it. "Cool as your city and your guilds and daphut were, they treated me like shit."

Carl's conviction didn't seem to waver, so I pressed on. "I'm not talking about the Pit. You took care of that. I mean after we won. They *still* didn't want me around. I could walk down the streets and get spat on by any random human that walked by. Just because of where I came from."

"I didn't—" Carl started.

"No, you didn't. Because I didn't want you to know. I was going to handle it. Hard enough being a teenage girl in a medieval fantasy world, but add to that a seriously racist kingdom and my half-Sylf . . . heritage," I landed on the right word after a moment's searching. Hard to give a good speech when I still struggled with the language. "I know you and Matt had plans to try and bring everyone together. But honestly? I was pretty close to just ditching you both and going back to my suunsyl."

It was something I'd never planned to tell them. If Matt knew, he'd be crushed. I didn't ever want to hurt him like that. But Carl, with his rose-colored vision of Cyraveil, needed a serious wake-up call.

When he spoke again, his voice was quiet and unsettled. "What makes this world so much better?"

"I don't know yet," I said honestly, "but I'm not ready to give up on it."

Carl left not too long after that. He confessed what happened at his house, in full, and why he couldn't go home. I had his cell number though (finally), and we'd promised to meet up again soon. He'd be camping out in public places where he could get internet access until we figured out how to handle the police. I felt like I'd gotten him to calm down for now at least. I could only pray to the stars that we'd find a more permanent solution soon.

When he left, though, I could tell something had been lost. Carl didn't quite trust me anymore. A bond we'd once had, something forged in shared experience and the many days and nights we'd spent alone on the run outside Vennenport, it was suddenly walled off. I could still feel our connection, but it was weak and fragile, and I didn't think he'd reach out to me again. Not until he found a real solution to the problem of returning to Cyraveil, one way or another.

The stars sure weren't doing much for me anymore. I blamed it on the night sky I no longer recognized, a void full of strange patterns and a single moon that was far too large.

Did I want to return to the sky I remembered? I couldn't say. Everything I said to Carl was true, and yet . . .

And yet I'd already found I could barely live in *this* world either. As I'd said to Matt, I was barely hanging on by a twig. I wanted to return, but at the same time, I didn't want to leave. I was caught between two worlds full of things I loved, and full of things I feared.

Eloquent, I know. If I could write it out in Etoline, it'd sound way better, but then you couldn't read it, so that's the best you get.

In that moment, I thought of my mother. She had always flitted around the edges of my life, but for one reason or another, she'd never really been a central figure. She and I were family, and I'd love her until the day I died, whether that was in eighty years or a few hundred. Mom had always been closer to Matt than to me. I didn't resent them for it. Matt had taken care of both of us for years, ever since our dad ditched us. He'd gotten more time to bond with Mom, before she'd been swamped with holding down two jobs to provide for us.

It made me mostly a solo adventurer. I spent most of my time out with friends, hanging out with Sara, being a kid. Home was a place to come back to for food and shelter at night. I never brought friends over; I spent as little time there as I could.

I felt so stupid about it now, but I'd been ashamed. I never wanted my friends to find out that we were poor. Whenever we went out, I'd do everything I could to avoid looking like I didn't have money to spend. I'd say I wasn't hungry if we went for food, and just sip water or leech off Sara when nobody was looking. When we went shopping, I'd buy something nice, wear it once, then trek across town alone to return it the next day. Movies? I'd snuck into the movies more than once. Got pretty good at it too, slipping in with the crowd past the ticket guy. Nobody ever came over to my place. I never had to face that judgment.

So ridiculous. So much wasted effort. I couldn't care less now.

Only two people ever caught on. Matt was the first, spotting my clothes cycling operation one day. After I'd finally explained it to him, he offered to drive me back for the returns, no judgment at all, every single time. That was when I knew I could trust my brother with my life. Kind of a silly reason, but seriously. From that moment on, we were always a team.

The other person was, of course, Sara, and we'd been best friends ever since.

Clearly, I should've just let more people in on the secret. Worked out great twice in a row.

I got up from the grass and walked back inside, where Matt was stirring something in a bowl. It already smelled great. "What are you making?"

"Well, you said we needed more cookies." Matt smiled.

"Chocolate chip?" I asked eagerly.

"You got it."

Okay, maybe today wasn't going to be so bad after all.

A few hours later, we were munching our way through freshly baked cookies, out on the back patio in our cheap plastic chairs.

"Did you really have to shoot an arrow at us?" asked Matt, grinning.

I shrugged. "Seemed like the quickest way to shut you both up."

"How do you plan on explaining that hole to Mom?"

"Oh, I figured we'd just blame it on you. This would be what, the third time you've broken the stairs somehow?"

Matt raised his eyebrows. I laughed. It was true—twice before, he'd caused some noticeable damage to our staircase. Once, knocking out a support for that same bannister, tossing a ball around with friends. Heavy basketball and thin aging wood, it wasn't hard to see that coming.

The second time, he'd tripped and actually knocked his head onto the endpiece, knocking it clean off. That time was less funny in retrospect. More heart-rushing-terrifying. Also, the first and only time I'd ever dialed 911. It turned out fine in the end, but . . . *vack.*

Reminiscing like this with my brother felt good though. I felt . . . peaceful. Happy, even.

So, of course, Matt had to go and ruin the mood.

"Carl's getting worse, isn't he?" he asked quietly.

I had to clear a chunk of cookie from my mouth before answering. "Yes," I said finally. "He wants to find a way to go back."

My brother . . . reacted. I couldn't say what it meant, but I saw his eyes twitch. His voice remained steady. "What do you think?"

"Me?" I asked, taken aback. Was he asking my opinion on going back? Or about Carl?

"You know him as well as I do by now, I think. You spent more time with him in the last year, at least." His eyes were studying me carefully. I hated *that* feeling, but I knew Matt didn't mean me any harm. "What's your take?"

I hesitated. "Carl's on the edge. He could go either way. I don't know what I could do to send him in either direction."

Matt sighed. "That's . . . unfortunate."

"No kidding."

"I'll try talking to him again."

"After how well that went *today*?"

He frowned. "What else can I do?"

"Let him be for now," I said. I wasn't sure if it was right or not. It was what I would want though. Time to be alone, time to contemplate. And maybe, *just* maybe, I was hoping his search would pan out. That he'd find a way back. Options.

". . . Okay," said Matt, with an air of finality. He adjusted his chair slightly, then leaned forward to rest his head in his hands, propped up by his elbows. "Now, about Sara."

"How'd your date go, hotshot?" I teased. I was more than happy to shift gears entirely . . . but Matt, *of course*, was still all business.

"You told her," he said. It didn't *sound* accusatory, but I still felt like he was trying to express disapproval. I really didn't think I deserved it.

"Yeah, I did."

"We agreed, Jen."

"If there's anyone, *absolutely* anyone in the world we can trust—" I started, but he raised his hand.

"It'd be her. I understand. In fact, I think you probably did the right thing."

"So wha—"

"You should have told me."

He was trying to be so hard to be calm and understanding, and it only made me more angry. It felt so condescending. I didn't deserve it. I threw caution to the wind. I'd had enough of this. We were home now. "Matt, you're not my father."

"What?"

"Telling her was my decision to make. I don't need your approval on everything I do. We're in this together, yeah, but as equals. Brother and sister."

"That's not what I . . ." Matt trailed off as I stood up. I needed to leave. I needed some space.

"Think about it for a bit." I picked up my bow, which I'd brought out to the yard with us. I felt very attached to it right now. It was a symbol of my identity, even if it wasn't the one I'd made myself, with my own hands, sweat, and magic. The bow was already unstrung, so I just packed it away in its bag, and slung it over my shoulder. I double-checked the arrows in the quiver and my knife at my belt, then pulled my jacket back on tight. "I probably won't be home for dinner, okay?"

". . . Okay."

* * *

I took a bus out to the forest again. I'd covered my bag in a blanket, so that no one would spot the quiver of arrows sticking out. Didn't need the random looks from other passengers, not today. Plus, the blanket was keeping me warm—and like I said earlier, it felt *really* cold out to me.

Even so, I needed to be out in Cyraveil Forest right now. Something about the place was drawing me back. I'd been out there this morning, of course, to get away from the world for a bit. I found myself needing to go there just to get some proper rest. That idea made for a weird disconnect between my mind and my body.

My mind clearly longed to be outdoors, out in nature. In my suunsyl, we usually slept outside, with just a light cover above to block rain and falling leaves, on soft beds built right into the trees. Every single night since we'd come back, I'd had trouble sleeping. The industrial noise of suburbia wasn't a huge deal—I could shut that out if I needed to. It was the *walls*. The confinement. Being cut off from the world around me. I felt like I wasn't able to feel everything anymore, and it disturbed me.

At the same time, when I went into the woods behind our house, or came out to Cyraveil Park, my body was telling me a different story. It practically screamed at me to wrap up, defend myself against the elements. Only now did I realize it was the lack of magic. I couldn't use the etovyla to protect myself against exposure, to maintain a comfortable temperature and fend off the harsher parts of nature while I slept. My body begged for a bed, a roof over my head, and solid walls to keep away the wind and any other dangers that might lurk just out of sight.

Between the two of them, mind and body, I was trapped and totally helpless.

The bus arrived at the stop for Cyraveil Park. I thanked the driver and took off, bounding through the underbrush with ease. The memory of Sara tripping over the tree root earlier popped into my head. I giggled aloud. Yeah, I admit it, I'd been spying on them. Come on, you would have, too, if you had my skills and spotted them wandering around in your forest together.

I'd learned how to get through thick forest without a care in the world. There was always an order to how a natural forest grew, how the roots took hold and shaped the landscape. Once my mind picked out the patterns, I knew exactly where to place every step, where every jut of a branch or root would shoot out. There were a couple of surprises, of course, but for the most part, I always knew exactly where I was, and everything around me.

Which meant I spotted the trail on the forest floor instantly.

I didn't recognize the footfalls at first glance, strange zig-zag lines and evenly spaced grids. It took me a moment to remember that sort of pattern would come off the soles of real world shoes.

Well, this could be fun. I hadn't tracked anything in a while. Hard to track through the cobblestone streets of Candir, after all. A bit of practice would be good.

I set off, following the trail as it faded in and out through the underbrush. I nearly lost the tracks a few times, but other clues kept the chase going. A snapped-off branch, trampled undergrowth. An overturned rock in a stream, wet on the wrong side. I continued along like a wolf on the hunt. I was determined to reach the source, if only for my own pride.

Instead, I ended up finding something truly life-changing.

The trail opened onto to a small clearing, barely wider than I was tall. Still, it was perfectly circular, a brown patch amid the thick, rolling greens surrounding us. It couldn't have been natural. I stopped to examine it, since the tracks seemed to end there anyway.

There was a rock, pure white, sitting underneath a fern at the opposite end. It almost seemed to be glowing, lit by a beam of sunlight that filtered down through the trees above. I crouched down in front of it, curious.

I nearly fell over in shock. There, etched unmistakably on the surface, were words in Etoline—in its native form. There was absolutely no one else in this world who could have read what was inscribed there. I looked up to the sky, to the stars that didn't even exist in this universe, and I wondered.

The rock described, in perfect detail, how precisely three people might travel to Cyraveil. No more, and no less. Forever.

I sat down in the clearing. My mind was still reeling. As if to remind me I was still in Oregon, a shadow passed over the sun, the scent of petrichor filled the air, and soon the world around me darkened in a drizzle of raindrops, pattering down through the leaves.

"What the fuck am I supposed to do with this?" I asked the sky.

The stars, smug in their devious machinations, did not deign to answer.

CHAPTER 13

CARL

"Something was definitely up with those two."

"No shit. Do you want to bring Westin in?"

"I'm not sure. Did we have anything listed about his sister?"

"Nothing at all. Didn't even know he had one. Did you get a look at Carl though?"

"What about him?"

"Kid was sweating bullets the whole time. Practically soaking the carpet. He's our in."

"We still have to actually track him down though. Let's go by his house again. That bag on his shoulder, I recognized it from his room. He's been home since we were there. Figure out if the father covered for him."

"You got it."

If the internet is a marvel of modern technology, free wireless access to it is a genuine miracle.

I couldn't go home. No matter what Matt said, there was no way I could chance the police picking me up, or running into my dad again. I was burning bridges left and right, but I really didn't care. My mind was focused and clear for the first time since we'd come back. Instead of the nebulous goal of finding Blake and figuring out what to do next, I was laser-focused on my mission: returning to Cyraveil.

That might not seem much better, but I'd already been there once. I knew it was possible, so it was perfectly logical to assume it could be repeated. I was following in my best friend's footsteps here. It was the best way I could think of to honor his memory.

Blake had urged us to travel out to Cyraveil Forest that night. I'd gone along mostly to humor him. A weird, teal-colored light flying around deep in the forest? He'd spotted it from his bedroom window, and *nobody* else had seen it? Sure, why not. I had nothing better to do, and it was a good excuse to force Matt out of his house to join us. This was back when I idolized Matt, of course.

Not so much anymore.

I was camping out at free hotspots. Fast-food places, coffee shops, bookstores, the library. I had plenty of money if I needed it, through a credit card tied to my parents' bank account. I'd have to make as much use of it as I could before they canceled it, and keep on the move, not following any kind of pattern if I could help it. Anything to avoid detection.

So far, luck seemed to be on my side. It was already early Saturday morning, and I'd had no trouble with the police nor anyone else. I'd slept in the woods, under a heavy blanket and in the shelter of a particularly thick-rooted tree. Unless someone had walked straight up next to it, they'd never have spotted me.

It reminded me of the weeks I'd spent on the run with Jen, outside of Vennenport. Even with all of my influence and authority, with my friendships in the court and my own personal forces, I'd still become a fugitive in that city. I'd broken up a generations-old tradition that had been twisted into the war effort, and in particularly bloody fashion. As a rule, long-standing institutions like that *really* don't appreciate getting shut down. We never should have made it out alive.

Jen, of course, wouldn't let that stop her. *She* got us away, not me, straight into the fields and forests. We were still within the bounds of the city's influence though, and had to spend our days and nights alone, in deep distrust of anyone we came across. But between my knowledge of the area and Jen's unparalleled ability to keep us hidden and alive, we managed our way across the expanse, back into friendly territory where my troops were assembling.

One word from me and the city burned to the ground, and any ties of loyalty to the Empire along with it.

It *might* have been an overreaction, but I stand by it. That city was foul to the core.

A *ping* from my laptop brought me back to the present. I was seated at a corner booth in an overnight diner, where I'd spent the early hours of the day. I ordered a plate of bacon and a tall soda, enjoying my favorites while I still could. Nothing but underwhelming substitutes for bacon in Cyraveil, and *soda*? Forget it.

I wiped off my hands before popping the laptop open. It was fully charged again, which brought me a whole world of mental peace. I'd run down the battery a ton the night before, and being tethered to a single spot while it charged was seriously unsettling. Even the few seconds it took to unplug might cost me everything if I had to flee—and if I left it and lost access to information, especially my servers in the cloud, my search would get exponentially harder.

The *ping* was a new email from my best contact so far. He was a guy clearly as paranoid as me, and we'd been exchanging private messages on a sci-fi/fantasy forum. We soon progressed to encrypted emails to keep off the site's servers. I was desperately trying to verify his story. Some of the details were wrong, but overall, he actually seemed to have a legitimate grasp of Cyraveil. I was afraid to let my hopes build up. Could this man truly have been across the divide between worlds, as I had?

I had to know. I wanted to meet him, but he refused any offer of direct contact. Every message I sent seemed to take us one step forward and another couple of steps back, as he tried to tease out my own identity in return. Caution was the name of the game, and I was determined to win. If he was some sort of plant, a mole to lure me out into the open to get some leverage, I wasn't going to slip up first.

His latest email was disheartening, to say the least.

Subject: Re: Cyraveil

I think you're just making this up. You haven't given me any real details. Nothing that would be out of place in any two-bit fantasy novel. Until I know for sure you're legit, I'm not saying another word on this. Quid pro quo. Send me back something real and we'll talk again.

I wasn't going to just take that. I began probing for real. My bag of tricks ran pretty deep. I was determined to find out his identity, no matter what it took.

The first step was to get more details on his connection and access logs. To do that, I'd need more privileges on SFFHaven, but I could only get those in one of two ways. Either they'd deliberately give me authority by promoting me to staff, or I'd have to wriggle my way in. In a word: hacking.

There was no way I had time to actually persuade the administrators to grant me privileges. Hacking it was.

Unfortunately, *that* wasn't going to be exactly easy either. The simplest form of attack I had, an SQL injection, required them to have security holes right there on the website front end. To my disappointment, whatever software they were running had covered its tracks properly. All inputs were sanitized, all known back doors were closed. I'd need another vector, besides just brute-forcing my way in and stealing the database.

If the direct approach won't work, I wondered, how about impersonation? No one in power, wealthy noble or server admin, ever really knows everyone in their own hierarchy. I didn't need to yank out the data if I could just have the server hand it to me cleanly.

Rain pattered against the windows as I shifted mental gears. The early morning staff at the restaurant shot me the occasional curious glance, but nothing more. I guess they were used to this sort of behavior, furious typing from someone in a corner booth. They probably assumed I was studying or doing something else schoolwork-related. As long as they had free tables and low traffic, I didn't expect to be disturbed.

Which meant it was time to *really* get to work.

A quick check of the website's public registration revealed the owner of the domain name—and more importantly, his email address. Thanks to the regulations for the internet registry system, this information was relatively guaranteed to be up-to-date. Now I just had to hope he was as lazy as every other server admin I'd ever come across.

I pulled up the couple of databases my automated server had gobbled down over the last day of scanning, and started querying them for matching email addresses. On the second database, I got a hit, and on the third I got another, on a table that didn't properly salt its passwords. Amateurs. Within a few minutes, I had the admin's password—and, as my lucky streak continued, he wasn't as security-conscious as whoever wrote his forum software. His password was the same for his email and his account in the database.

Unfortunately, it didn't match the admin account on SFFHaven, which was my real target. It would take another few steps before I could achieve my goal, and SFFHaven didn't provide password recovery for admin-level. I seemed to be out of technical options, but with access to the admin's email, I was suddenly a great deal more powerful than I had been only minutes earlier.

I opened up his account and started searching. Any keywords related to SFFHaven, moderators, logs, users, and so on. I needed to find someone else with access. Somebody I could dupe into handing over the keys. After some fifteen minutes of digging, I found another administrator who seemed gullible enough. There were multiple instances of a quick email exchange where the second admin had asked my stolen identity to do a quick password reset. They'd even mailed the password back and forth in plaintext.

I tried the last listed password, just in case, but it was a dud. That didn't deter me. I spent a few minutes composing a message before I sent it along.

> need a pw reset. cant get in and im on the road but someones emailing me about something going on. can you log in and set it to changeme123

I hoped the all-lowercase and lack of punctuation would give the message some sense of urgency. Emergencies usually got people to ignore the proper protocol, which was exactly what I needed. Fortunately, my hapless target seemed to be located on the East Coast, so he was already awake and saw the email was almost right away. I was chomping through a cold piece of crispy bacon as a reply came in only a couple of minutes later.

> done. password set to changeme123

Thank god for clueless forum admins. I emailed a quick thanks, after verifying it had indeed been reset. I now had access to proper logs for the entire board, and all the members present. Time to start digging.

There was a ferocious headache building up in my skull. Probably dehydration, or maybe just hunger, but either way, it was seriously hurting my ability to read off my laptop screen.

I'd switched locations to a public library when the restaurant traffic started to pick up. A short bus ride through the pouring rain and I was situated comfortably in the corner of the book stacks. As I arrived just after the library opened, the better chairs were actually open for once. I sank gratefully into one, opened my laptop, and returned to my search.

The email and username of my correspondent were easy enough to find, but they were both throwaway one-use names, with little to tie them to any existing identity. Instead, I hit the jackpot when I used his most common log-in IP address. One check against a locating service and my jaw practically fell off my face.

It traced back to Mellbridge, Oregon. The same suburb we were in.

It *couldn't* be a coincidence. I doubted he just happened to be using a proxy that ran right through my hometown. The IP lookup service wasn't more precise than a dozen miles, but it was enough. I had a way better idea of where this man was, and I could narrow it down further with some painstaking cross-referencing.

It felt like a good sign. I was on the right track. Of *course* somebody who had actual knowledge of Cyraveil would live in this area; Cyraveil Park and the all-important forest were here.

My eyes were getting really sore, on top of the headache. The frequent shifts in light levels weren't exactly helping either. I tried to rest my eyes frequently, but there was only so much I could do when I had to spend an inordinate amount of time scrolling through long lists of time stamps, dashing between social networks, trying to locate a single person in town.

The account my erstwhile potential ally had used to contact me was a throwaway, but according to my research, it wasn't the only one he had on the site. I started comparing log-in times, one by one, between users who frequented the same boards. It was only a matter of time before I'd narrowed it down to a pool of possible matches. One of them *must* be him.

Whenever I found a potential match, I'd trawl their post history. Any sign of personal information, even the *slightest* detail, might lead to an identity. I'd follow through on any clue. I'd sift through search engines and social networks, pick through public directories and records. Anyone I found who wasn't living nearby I filed away for later, focusing on those candidates who were within city limits.

It was frustrating, boring work—and so far, utterly pointless. But I couldn't give up. No matter what, I'd find this man, and he'd tell me everything he knew about Cyraveil. Then, *finally*, we'd go back. We'd leave this place forever.

I leaned back in my chair, closing my eyes for a much-needed reprieve. I really needed better sleep than I'd gotten out in the woods. Thankfully, it hadn't rained, but I still wasn't exactly *comfortable* out there. I wasn't Jen. I didn't love trees like the Sylves. Did they worship them? I dunno. Something to figure out when I got back, I guess.

I wished I could talk to her. Every encounter since we'd gotten back had been painful, marked by loss or argument. When I'd left the day before, after the police, we'd parted as friends, but there was a barrier between us. I couldn't face her again, not when I had nothing to show for my efforts. I had to prove her wrong. Prove *both* of them wrong.

It was physically painful for me to hear Jen take Matt's side. She could have stabbed me in the gut with that arrow and I don't think it would have hurt as much. Not in the long term, anyway. She clearly belonged in Cyraveil. Why couldn't she see it like I could? In those seven years, she'd adapted more quickly and thoroughly than any of us. Was it just because of Matt's conviction that we should stay that she believed otherwise?

I was running circles in my head at this point. I'd been through this same thought process dozens of times now. I needed something new before I drove myself insane. It was painful having no one to talk to. I had my other few friends online, of course, but I couldn't be sure which of them I could talk to. If the police had connected Matt and Blake so fast, and picked up Cyraveil off Blake's computer, who was to say they hadn't also followed through on everybody else in our chat room? My friends were off-limits for the foreseeable future.

I was alone. I hated being alone.

Physically alone I could have dealt with, once upon a time. Conversations online were more than enough social activity to satisfy my brain most of the time, and the rest was filled by attending school. I hadn't lived that way in a *long* time though. I'd adjusted to the constant connections and interactions of my life in Cyraveil, where I had men to command, civilians to keep happy, political affairs, courtships, an honest-to-god fiery romance, and an endless host of things to manage. I'd learned to thrive there, and now that I'd come back, my brain was having a hard time readjusting to the speed of life my old body expected.

I needed to talk to someone before I started really losing it.

I ended up calling the only person I could, the only person I hadn't driven away yet who I still knew I could trust.

After a few rings, she picked up, in a sleepy, confused voice. ". . . Hello?"

"Hi, Sara. Please don't hang up," I said quickly.

Sara's voice got sharper *very* fast. I was impressed. "Wait, who is this?"

"It's Carl. Jen's . . . friend. We met the other day."

"Right," she said, and all sounds of just-waking-up were instantly gone. "So uhh, why are you calling me at seven in the morning?"

"I'm sorry. Did I wake you up?"

"Well . . . yeah. Is something wrong?"

I suddenly realized how utterly pointless this conversation was. Sara didn't know anything. What on earth was I supposed to talk about with her if I couldn't bring up Cyraveil? It wasn't like my current internet stalking would seem like anything other than bizarre and creepy devoid of context.

Okay, yes, in context it doesn't look much better, but it would all be worth it. I wasn't *hurting* anyone. In the end, I'd get the information I needed and I'd disappear from the world with no one the wiser.

"No, nothing's wrong, I just—"

"Look, Jen called last night. She said the police wanted to see you."

Well, I guess Jen had no reservations about talking with her friends. She was braver than me, as usual. ". . . Yeah. Do you know Blake Svartholm?"

"Yeah. Jen told me about him," Sara's voice seemed to get softer, though it was difficult to tell for sure. As nice as my phone was, calls could never quite convey the full spectrum of sound. Nothing could replace hearing someone's voice in person, or seeing body language, facial expressions. Cyraveil had magic that allowed all of that to come through. Yet another reason this world sucked.

"That's why they wanted to talk. They're trying to find out what happened to him."

"Oh." Sara paused. "Do you need help?"

"... Huh? Why would I need help?" I didn't want to get her involved unnecessarily. Jen wouldn't want her to get in trouble, for sure. Besides, if we were going to disappear, it'd be cruel to bring Sara into the mix. Better her friend just vanished once again than for her to have to live with the truth—and the danger it posed.

"Well, you ditched school twice now, and the cops are trying to find you." Sara paused. "Just offering."

"No, I'm fine."

"So why *did* you call?"

"I don't . . ." How could I explain it to her, without telling her anything? This wasn't working at all. I was just making things worse. "I'm sorry. I shouldn't have called."

"No, wait. I'm sorry. Just . . . talk to me?"

What should I say? Nothing came to mind.

"You still there? Carl?"

"Still here," I said.

"Look," she started hesitantly. "I know you guys are going through a lot of pain right now, and a whole bunch of things I can't understand. Just remember you've got friends, okay?"

What had I really expected to get out of this conversation, anyway? This was going nowhere—and worse, I felt awful that I'd dragged Sara into our problems.

"Okay. I have to go. Sorry for waking you up." Before she could get in another word, I hung up. I set the phone on the table, staring at it as if it had betrayed me.

That was unproductive and dangerous, I told myself. You don't know her. Jen trusts her, but can you? Jen's been wrong about people before. You've seen the results of that first-hand, even if the scars have healed now.

Back to work. I picked up my laptop and settled back into the comfy chair. I was going to find this man, no matter what it took.

Faster, faster. I'd set up macros to do some tasks for me. Others were too difficult to automate, and I ran through them manually. Identity after identity, person after person. I'd go through every last one of them if I had to. No one was off-limits; nobody was out of reach. The entire world put their personal lives online, and damned if I wasn't going to abuse that.

I relocated again a few minutes after that disastrous phone call with Sara. I'd tried to soldier on, but I got too uncomfortable. Too paranoid. A change of scenery helped me refocus. I found myself in a fast-food restaurant again, scarfing down fries as I set back up. Soon enough, I was deep-diving databases once more, and suddenly, out of nowhere, I found him.

There he was. It was the closest thing I had to a match. His log-in and log-out times closely matched up with those of the anonymous throwaway I'd been communicating with. He even lived on the other side of town, near Cyraveil Park. Daniel Whitman, twenty-two. A student, with no particularly active friendships judging by his social profiles. Kind of a loner, by all accounts. His feed was nothing but automated birthday prompts and similar posts.

He looked like my man, but I didn't have anything on him yet. All of his privacy settings were properly engaged, so I couldn't get any information without a connection. No way to leverage him into giving me more details, no personal information I could exploit. I'd need to get closer if I was going to force him to talk.

I went back to his friends list. One of them *had* to have something I could use. I started adding people at random, and quite a few accepted almost instantly. People who preferred quantity over quality. I rolled my eyes, but began delving into their posts. It still wasn't fast enough, and I was getting frustrated by the monotony. I wrote a script, and soon my machine was automatically spinning through their entire online histories, sucking up everything like a vacuum chewing through the dust-covered abandoned corners of the internet.

Once I had everything downloaded, it was much easier to search through their pasts, any references to Whitman. There, a mention of his home. Another to his pet. A happy birthday for his grandmother. More little missives, personal information I could use.

I went back to Whitman's profile and attempted to log in. His password was useless, which didn't surprise me, but I had another way in now. I clicked through to his security questions, praying one would match up with the information I'd acquired.

The world was back on my side again, finally. I grinned as soon as I saw the first question—the name of his first pet. The rest was just as easy.

Within a few seconds, I'd logged in as Whitman.

A few seconds after that, I had his home address. His phone number. Everything.

I leaned back against the hard plastic bench, breathing heavily. I felt like I'd just run a marathon, even though I'd been sitting still for over an hour.

What should I do next?

It hadn't even occurred to me what to *do* with Whitman's information once I obtained it. I knew who he was, and where he was, but how could I capitalize on it?

Should I try blackmail?

Worthless. Even with all his personal information, none of it really screamed blackmail material. I had no evidence, no real leverage. He'd been cagey so far, but I doubted just dropping his name into our conversation would do much. For all intents and purposes, he seemed like a pretty normal college kid who lived alone.

Coercion from behind a screen wasn't going to work. I needed something more direct.

My mind was already patching together a plan, even as the thought first formed. I knew where he lived. That was enough to make a move. First, I'd need a few things though, including a more thorough accounting of his life. I had to cover every angle, just in case. I had to be prepared for anything.

Quid pro quo, Daniel Whitman? You're gonna regret that.

I dove back into his account, committing his entire life to memory, a guy who—unbeknownst to him—had suddenly become the most important man in this entire world.

CHAPTER 14

MATT

"If Carl's completely off the grid now, what's next?"

"We turn back to who we can lean on. I got more details about Westin and his sister. She didn't show up in the school records we grabbed because they don't share a last name."

"Adopted?"

"No. Looks like a pretty messy divorce. The father failed to get custody; mother wanted nothing more to do with him. Changed her name and her daughter's and ran out here."

"But why not change Matt's name?"

"Do I look like a psychiatrist?"

"And here I thought you knew everything."

"Not as much as I'd like."

———

My sister and I used to fight. A lot. We'd argue over anything—whose turn it was to watch TV, who got the front seat in the car, what we'd be eating for dinner, and so on. When we were *really* young, it was who got to sit next to Mom whenever we went out. Jen usually won that one, mostly by being smaller and more willing to burst into tears. I'd give in just to get her to shut up and quit embarrassing us in public.

I'm not proud of it, but there were times when I wished she weren't my sister, that it was just me and Mom in the house. She was always getting in the way, even if just by accident. It wasn't that she *always* got her way, of course. Mom tried to be fair to both of us when she could manage it. I was a kid though; to my mind, Jen was always getting the better treatment. It was unfair. I was the older child; I helped out around the house more. I took better care of myself, I cleaned up after myself, I did my chores without complaint every time. I deserved more, didn't I?

One single afternoon changed my mind completely.

Jen was ten, and I had just turned thirteen the week before. We were at the mall, just off the bus, looking around at stores and just generally wandering. I hadn't realized why Jen didn't go with her friends at the time; I only found out about her clothes cycling routine a couple of years later. Mom bribed me to watch my sister there with the promise of taking me to a movie that weekend. I just needed to keep an eye on Jen for a few hours, make sure she didn't get lost or in trouble, and bring her home on the bus again. I wasn't about to turn that deal down, so I shepherded Jen to store after store, impatiently pacing around and trying to ignore the awful mall radio music selection, made even worse by the commercials and announcements that kept interrupting the songs.

The mall was three stories, with escalators dotted all around, and easy to get lost in. Jen was an expert though, and she knew how to avoid the crowds by taking the plain old staircases around the edges of the building. We stayed out on the perimeter, which also happened to be where most of Jen's favorite stores were.

So it was that we ended up on the third story, browsing through yet *another* clothing store, when I finally noticed a clock. It was getting late. Not time to go yet, but there was a show I wanted to watch when we got back, and I was determined not to miss it. If we left now, we could catch an earlier bus.

I began hustling Jen, telling her it was time to go, pressuring her to hurry up. She took her sweet time, prancing up to the register and asking the salesperson question after question. Finally, as the minutes dragged on, I stepped in and forked over the cash, practically dragging Jen away by the hand.

The nearest escalator was packed, so I hurried to a nearby staircase. Jen's shoe had come untied at some point, but neither of us noticed. I was too busy dragging her toward the exit—any exit. I was done with the mall, and all I could think about was that show I wanted to watch. I can't even remember what show it was anymore, but I know I was fixated on it. Another memory took its place, something that would haunt my mind forever.

I stopped near the top of the stairs, distracted by an entertainer. Someone doing street magic with the big theatrical voice. I wasn't really interested, but he captured my attention just long enough. Just for a second.

A single moment of distraction, and a sickening crack and thud.

I whipped around. Jen was on the landing where the stairs turned back around between floors. She was laid out on her side, with limbs splayed out, but all I could see was her arm, twisted in a direction it should never go. I saw her expression, as if in slow motion, twist in pain. Her eyes creased together; her mouth began to open wide. Her entire face seemed to compress in on itself.

I was already bounding down the stairs toward her when something else happened that stopped me dead.

Jen stood back up.

There wasn't a single word from her mouth. Barely even a sound. She just stood up and limped over to me. Jen was clearly dealing with overwhelming pain, but she didn't say a thing until she reached the stairs. Her eyes were sparkling as she looked up at me, a few steps above her.

"Matt, I think my arm's broken." Her voice was pinched and scared, but still she didn't cry. Her words finally broke my trance. I was instantly at her side. I had her sit down while a bystander dialed 911.

The rest of the story is pretty straightforward. Jen ended up in the hospital for a bit, my mother was called in, and everything turned out okay in the end. Honestly, in the larger scheme of things, except for the financial stress it put on Mom due to the medical bills, it really wasn't that notable. I wondered if Jen even thought about it much.

For me, it completely changed the way I saw my sister.

Jen didn't cry *once* through the whole ordeal. There was a bravery in her I felt like I could never muster. I'd thought of her as just something to watch over, a chore to take care of before I got back to my life again, but Jen was so much more than that. Even as young as she was, with the amount of pain clearly wracking her body, Jen acted stronger than I'd ever felt in my life—in *either* of my lives.

The guilt lingered in my head for a long, long time. I'd been the one to rush her, I'd missed her untied shoe, I'd gotten distracted at the last second. My mother tried—and failed—to convince me otherwise. *I'd* been entrusted with protecting her and I'd failed. My sister had gotten hurt when I should have been more careful. I swore to myself I'd never let that happen again. I'd be there for her, no matter what.

As I watched Jen leave the house, bow over her shoulder like a huntress from legend, the guilt came again. I'd failed her a third time. I didn't want to believe it, but I felt like there was some sort of secret tug-of-war over Jen's soul now, with me on one side and Cyraveil on the other, pulling as hard as it could.

Her words struck me to the core, though she probably hadn't meant it like that. She'd inadvertently compared me to our father, a man she'd never really known. I remembered him though, partly from my own memories, but mostly from conversations I'd had with Mom. He'd never seemed like a *bad* person, but in his own way, he scared me as much as any man I'd ever met. A cold, manipulative nature, devoid of emotion. My mother described him as "a controlling, selfish, heartless bastard," though never to my face.

I didn't think I was all like that—but the calculating, manipulative part? I could feel that sometimes. When Jen had told me to back off, I realized how I'd been pushing her in a direction without meaning to, a part of me lurking just under the surface until Jen shined a spotlight on it. I'd started stepping over the line, reducing her to being just someone to protect, forgetting who she was.

Jen was right. She could more than take care of herself. I'd let those years slip by once again. My sister was an adult, even if she didn't look the part yet. I had to step back and let her make her own decisions. I was her equal, not her protector.

And yet . . .

She needed my help. Didn't she?

My mind was conflicted. I wasn't sure what I could do to help her. Would it be better to try and forget Cyraveil entirely? To force the real world into place and try to persuade her to never mention it again? There was no evidence, after all, like I'd said. For all anyone knew, we'd never disappeared. Our minds might tell us otherwise, but by the real world's standards, we were totally normal.

I'd tried to stick to that path, but it wasn't going well so far. Carl was on the run from the police and his family, and becoming increasingly unstable. Jen was an emotional wreck from what I could tell, although I definitely didn't have the whole story from either of them. Something had to change, clearly.

Should I take the other approach? Try to indulge the lives we'd led? I could bring it to the surface, keep the memories alive. It definitely seemed to calm Jen down in a crisis, bringing her some measure of peace and balance. She could revel in the happier times, tell her stories to Sara and me, do right by the people she'd left behind. She'd never forget, and the more painful memories might never get the closure they really needed, but at least she could pull through.

Of course, she'd already tried that with Sara and apparently broken down completely during their family dinner only an hour later. Meanwhile, that approach could only spell doom for Carl. Every mention of Cyraveil—of the world he longed to return to and the betrayals and sacrifices we'd made without following through on the consequences—would only bring him more anguish.

There was a third choice, always lingering in the deepest recesses of my brain—to return. To jump back as if no time had passed on the other side. To fling ourselves away from this world permanently, vanishing into thin air and resuming our lives in Cyraveil.

I'd rejected it out of hand after hearing it the first time, and again every time it had floated back up in my thoughts—but as our lives continued to spiral into chaos on Earth, it kept swirling around my brain as a final option. It was an escape hatch, by which I maintained some measure of control.

"I'm home!" came a shout from the garage. I struggled to my feet; one of my legs had fallen asleep from the awkward angle I'd sunk into. I was still sitting out back, long after Jen had left, and hadn't noticed the garage door opening. I hurried out to help Mom with the groceries I knew she'd have brought home. Sure enough, she was carrying two bags on her arm as I walked past, and I grabbed the third she'd set down to open the door.

"Oh, thanks, Matt. You're my favorite son, you know that?"

"I'm glad I beat out the competition."

Mom set down the bags on the counter and ruffled my hair. I flinched away instinctively, and she laughed. I'd never liked people touching my hair, which of course meant she did it at every possible opportunity.

"How long until you head out again?"

Her eyes flashed. She smirked. "Oh, you want me to leave? Need the house to yourself?"

"I have work too, Mom." I rolled my eyes.

"Oh, so it's not for a pretty girl then."

"Did she tell you?" I asked, surprised.

"So there *is* a girl?" Mom looked equally surprised. "And she would have told me? Ooh, this is getting juicy." She opened the fridge and started putting away the milk. "Do tell."

"There isn't." I sighed. "Or, I'm not sure if there is. We went on a date, but it was sorta . . . interrupted."

"She didn't like your hair?" Mom reached out and plucked at it.

I brushed her away irritably. "No. There were just other things to talk about. Big things." I shrugged. "I don't think you could really call it a date in the end."

"If you say so," she replied absently. She was digging through the cupboard, trying to find something she could eat quickly before she had to head out again. I think something in my voice got to her though, as she suddenly stopped and turned around to face me, very serious. "Is something wrong?"

I didn't want to lie to my own mother, not more than was absolutely necessary. I let my exhaustion show, all the stress built up in my head seeping into my face in one smooth wave. "I have to make a choice about something and I'm having a hard time figuring out what's best."

She looked confused, but it didn't deter her. "What sort of choice?"

"Between two important people, and which one I believe is right. Or if neither of them are. I don't know." I shrugged again. "Whichever I decide, there's no going back. No do-overs. It'll be final."

"Do I know either of these people?"

". . . Yes."

Mom's eyes narrowed. "Is one of them Jenny?"

I almost corrected her on the name but managed to stop myself in time. "Yeah."

She shook her head, still puzzled. "Well, I won't pretend to have a clue what's going on, and your sister definitely isn't right all the time, so I'm not going to tell you to take her side. Just remember, Jenny's your sister. No matter what you might think, you two need to stick together. So she can protect you and you can protect her too." Mom smiled at me. "So take her side if she's right, and if she's wrong, make sure she doesn't get left behind. That she understands why you chose what you did, and that you're still on her side no matter what. Family always comes first."

Once again, Mom's advice didn't really help much. It didn't make my choice any easier, and it only did a little to comfort me. I appreciated the effort though.

"That didn't really help much, did it?" Mom added nonchalantly, echoing my thoughts. She turned back toward the cupboard. "Sorry. Let me say this, then. I trust you, no matter what you decide. I know you think things through, and you always follow through on your decisions, and I know you care about your sister. You'll choose right, I'm sure. You're a good man, Matt."

Tears sprang to my eyes. I still didn't necessarily agree with her, but I needed her reassurance more than a drowning man needed air. I wanted to commit everything she said to memory, because I had felt my mind tick over, ever so slightly, to the other side. Without warning, without fanfare, I'd begun actually considering the third option—going back to Cyraveil.

I pushed it away. I had a real life here. Friends and family. I had school and work and a relationship I actually wanted to pursue with Sara, even if we'd gotten off to a rocky start. I liked the calm and quiet, a life far away from danger and madness. What could possibly drive me to return to that place?

My mother had pointed it out. I *did* always strive to follow through on decisions. Yet, as I'd told Sara myself, I'd run away—from Cyraveil and from the choices I'd made there. When the battle was won, the new alliances formed, when they'd asked for a leader to help them move forward and maintain order in the new kingdom, what had I done? I hadn't worked with them to establish a new state, overturn the terrible laws that had led to the rebellion in the first place.

No, I'd fled. I'd taken an out no one could have seen coming, a portal to another world none of them had ever heard of (or believed in, if they were the few generals I had taken into my confidence). I'd retreated to a place where no one could follow.

I had abandoned them, and worse, I'd dragged along two people who might not have wanted to come with me. I'd told Sara I'd forced Jen home, but that wasn't exactly true. Jen had known of our ability to return, but I hadn't told her that it was entirely up to me—that I could trigger it at any time. Jen and I had discussed it, but we'd never actually made a decision.

I'd finally given in, at a moment when I'd finally been truly overwhelmed. Blake was dead, Reynir was dead, Carl was nowhere to be found. The people were literally at my doorstep clamoring for leadership, and I didn't know what to do. I had no idea how to lead now that we'd won. All I wanted was to run away—and then I'd remembered, I actually *had* that option.

In my chambers, with people banging on the door begging for an audience, I'd disappeared. Now I felt like I owed them an apology. An explanation for why I'd abandoned them in their time of need.

I forced my mind back to the present. Those people were far away, impossibly far away. There was nothing I could do for them now. Instead, I had a sister to protect and a friend to . . .

To what? To confront? To debate? To comfort? To stop?

I still wasn't sure.

I was actually grateful I had work that night. I'd do anything for a reprieve from my thoughts, even if it meant mindlessly dealing with customers. As long as I was occupied, I wouldn't be stewing in my own head. When I wasn't helping customers, I talked about anything I could think of with my coworker, no doubt annoying him to death.

Unfortunately for my sanity, though, I was about to have the entire store to myself. My late-night partner had called in sick, so I was going to have the slowest part of the shift all to myself, until someone else came in to cover. I'd tried to mentally prepare myself, rifling through the magazine racks for anything that looked even remotely interesting to read, but nothing caught my eye. I was about to give up on finding anything to do when our store phone rang.

Now, the store phone almost never rang, and it *never* meant anything good. I picked it up with a bit of fear—only to hear a voice I'd never expected, but one I very happily welcomed in that moment.

"Hi. Is this Matt?" It was a bit crackly, as our store phone wasn't exactly the greatest, but she was still perfectly audible, and a great relief to the endless hum of the machines and beep the front door.

"Sara?" I asked incredulously.

"Yeah. Jen told me where you worked."

". . . Hi. How are you?"

"I'm good, but that's not why I called."

I took a breath. Whatever she said next, I knew it wasn't going to end well. "What's going on?"

"It's Carl.

My heart sank. This *really* wasn't going to end well. "What did he do?"

"That's the thing. I think he's *going* to do something." Sara's voice picked up in urgency as she went on. "He just called me. Talked about the police and about Blake. He seemed scared. He refused to talk about anything in particular, and he just hung up out of nowhere. I don't think he's all there, you know?"

I tried to rationalize it, if only for my own sake. "Well, he isn't aware that you know. That might be why he didn't talk about much."

"You guys didn't tell him?" she asked, surprised.

"We haven't actually talked in a while," I replied, a little embarrassed. "I don't know where he is."

"Matt, that's really, really bad, isn't it? Jen didn't say much about him, but he was a pretty big deal over there, right?"

"Yes. He was a general, kind of. A lord."

"So he's already feeling a loss of power, he's lost his friends, and now he's losing control all over again. He's going to try and get that back somehow."

"I don't know what to do about that," I admitted. Something about her made me want to be honest, or maybe I just really wanted advice from someone who knew what was going on, since my mother hadn't been much help.

". . . I don't either," Sara replied, to my dismay. "But we can't just leave him to wander the streets alone. He needs help."

The door chimed. I glanced up, and a shabby-looking man was there, staring at me expectantly. "I'm sorry, Sara. I have to go. I'll keep that in mind."

"Okay. Good luck," she added as I hung up.

The man just wanted a pack of cigarettes. While I checked his ID, the door chimed again. I didn't bother to look up until the new voice addressed me directly.

"Matt, we need to talk." His tone chilled my blood to ice. It was a voice I hadn't heard in a long time. Not Carl's, but the voice of the Lord of Candir, whom I'd never trusted for a second. The man who'd betrayed Reynir Cellman, to his ultimate death.

"Hi, Carl," I said, trying to keep calm. The customer was struggling with his wallet, his hands unsteady. I prayed he'd get out of here soon, before Carl started talking—but as usual, fate and I were still at odds.

"I'm going to find a way back, and you're going to help," said Carl. There was no anger in his voice, only determination and confidence. Even so, it worried me. I didn't have control of this situation. I was adrift, and danger lurked in every corner, waiting to strike.

"Not sure what you're talking about," I said mildly. The customer finally got his wallet out of his pocket and began to count out change coin by coin.

"I found a guy. Daniel Whitman. He knows about Cyraveil. He'll know how to get there. He even lives in town, Matt! We can go back. All of us." Carl sounded almost deranged. His voice rose as he went on. I had no idea what he was talking about. It seemed illogical. The thoughts didn't flow together right.

"How are you sure?"

"I know he will, Matt. Trust me."

I could never trust you, Carl. "That's kind of hard to believe."

"Okay, look," he said impatiently. He turned to the customer, still counting out nickels. "Hey, get lost?"

"Jus' be a secon'," the man muttered. Carl's eyes narrowed.

"Carl, it's fine," I cut in, but Carl was already closing on him. He grabbed the man's hands and started tossing his money on the counter.

"Hey now!"

"Just shut up. Here." Carl shoved the pack at him. "Get going."

I hopped the counter, landing behind Carl. I grabbed his arm and his shoulder, twisting him around and pinning him to the glass display of lottery tickets next to us. He was too surprised to react in time. "Carl, calm down."

"Matt, what the fuck?" He struggled, but he was too weak to do much to me on Earth. I had no trouble holding him steady.

"Calm. Down." I turned to the customer. "Please excuse my friend. I'm so sorry about this."

"Don' worry 'bou' it," the guy mumbled. He took his smokes and the change, and left in a hurry. Once I was sure he was gone, I let Carl free.

He came back swinging, but it was too obvious. The punch was too telegraphed. I dodged it easily. I stepped back and waited calmly for Carl's next move. He was heaving, but he seemed to recognize finally that attacking me wasn't going to accomplish anything.

"Are you good?" I asked.

". . . Yes," he replied, more calmly than I expected. I entertained the faint hope that he actually was under control.

"You wanted to talk?"

"Yeah."

". . . So?"

"Don't you *want* to go back?" Carl asked, exasperated.

"No," I said firmly—but if I was being honest, I'd never been more on the fence about it.

"But—"

"It was one part of my life and it's over now. I'm trying to move on, Carl."

"You were a general. A leader. A revolutionary," Carl said breathlessly. "You started a movement. You toppled an empire. You were important and powerful. They would have given you anything. Why wouldn't you want to have all that?"

"Did you rehearse that?" I asked, raising an eyebrow.

"Take this seriously, goddammit," he snapped. "That was you, wasn't it? You're a natural leader. Those speeches, man. You said you were just improvising, but you inspired people to fight. To *die*. 'Eternal glory,' wasn't that it? How they'd be remembered, even if they died in the struggle, breaking chains? You'd fight for the silent and something-something."

I shrugged. "I got that from a song."

Carl paused. I saw him twitch a bit, before a *laugh* of all things erupted through him. "Fucking *song lyrics*. You're kidding."

"Nope." I shook my head. "Straight from a song. I barely even changed the words."

Carl laughed harder. I grinned nervously. Maybe he was getting back to normal.

"See, this is why you *have* to come back, Matt!" My hopes were dashed as quickly as they'd grown. "Help me find this guy. We can *all* go back. You belong there, I belong there, Jen *definitely* belongs there. We'll all go back, all of us, and everything will be okay."

Carl wasn't stable; that much was obvious. He didn't know what he was doing. He'd completely jumped off the deep end. At the same time, though, I did consider his words.

Maybe we *did* belong there. I felt like I had unfinished business now. Between Carl's reminders and Jen's recollections, I was brought back to those moments just before I'd decided to bring us home. The people there depended on me to lead them through crises. I was insane to think it would all just work itself out. We'd just overthrown a generations-old dynastic government; chaos was bound to follow no matter how well we handled the transition. We'd only just begun our work there.

Responsible. Everybody called me the responsible one. I don't know how much I agreed with them, but I couldn't deny I felt an obligation to these people. I had a duty to them, after having asked them for so much. Those speeches I gave, the oaths I made. I would betray the spirit of my people's sacrifices if I didn't come back to follow through on what I'd promised.

Not just to the people I'd led. There was another, more personal sacrifice I had to honor. An agreement made in the dead of night, around a low-burning fire in the command tend on the outskirts of the city. A promise I'd made to a dear friend, far braver than any of us, who knew he was going to die but charged forward without regrets. Blake had loved that world and the people within it. He'd made me swear to make it a better place, whatever it took.

As my past words echoed through my head, I looked back at Carl with a cold eye. Even if I felt like I might need to return, I knew Carl shouldn't. He was a far better person *before* we'd left. Kinder and warmer, if a bit annoying. He'd become so cold and distant now. I hesitated to admit it, but I felt like Cyraveil had created a monster in him—one that never should have been woken.

Carl couldn't return with us. I'd seen him betray a best friend first-hand, turn his back and let him die at the hands of a ravenous horde of revolutionaries. I would never, ever trust him again.

"Go home, Carl," I said softly.

His face fell. "That's it? That's all you've got to say?" His voice was as quiet as my own.

"Cyraveil doesn't exist," I said firmly, consciously echoing my words from the night we'd come back.

Carl shook his head. "You'll change your mind. Eventually." He turned and left the store, and it felt as though the room instantly became lighter. I found it easier to breathe, as if the weight of Carl's presence had settled right on my lungs. The release seemed to affirm my decision to shut him out. I leaned back against the counter, once again lost in thought.

Now I had two paths in front of me. One of them grew increasingly dimmer each day. I'd tried to walk down it but had lost my way.

Beside me, another path began, where my sister and a world I thought I'd sworn off loomed like ancient towering statues, silently judging my every move.

I felt my mind turn, and with reluctance and fear in my heart, I stared down that second path.

CHAPTER 15

JEN

"So what's the connection here anyway? History of abuse from the father, possibly passed down?"

"No. As far as I can tell, Mr. Westin was a model citizen. The records of his divorce proceedings with Erica Silverdale are sealed."

"Entirely?"

"Anything worth mentioning, at least."

"Wait, you said was a model citizen."

"Philip Westin died in a car accident, about a year ago. Apparently fell asleep at the wheel and drove off a cliff on the coast. No foul play suspected."

"Huh."

———

The door to Sara's bedroom opened. I snapped upright, the pillow I'd been hugging tossed aside and landing on the floor with a soft thump.

Sara's nervous voice answered. "Uhh, hi?" Her face poked through the door. She looked startled, and more than a little confused.

". . . Hi. I kinda snuck in while you guys were out at dinner . . .
Sorry."

She walked over to shut the window I'd left open. I would have
closed it, but the breeze and the fresh air felt *really* nice. It still didn't
smell right, but it was better than nothing. "Did anyone see you
come in?"

"As if."

She closed the blinds as well, before settling down cross-legged on
her desk chair. I leaned back into the corner of the wall again, letting
my eyes droop half-closed. Surprise all done with, Sara now just looked
concerned again—which only made me feel worse. "Were you sleeping?
You really freaked out there."

"Huh?"

"I mean, you jumped up really quick. You used to be impossible to
wake up."

I'd already promised myself never to lie to her again, and I wasn't
about to break it now. ". . . I don't really sleep well anymore."

"Since you got back?"

". . . No. Before that." I took a deep breath, but Sara held up her
hand before I could say anything.

"It's okay. You don't have to. Just tell me when you're ready, okay?"

I closed my mouth. I wasn't ready. I *thought* I was, but the moment
I tried to summon those memories to the surface, just to talk about
them, they enveloped me like a frozen river. The sounds were the worst.
The chains, clanking on the stone floors as they dragged past. Metal
gates opening and closing day and night without warning. Newcomers
crying through their first night—then the utter silence when they didn't
come back on their second.

"Nightmares," I said finally.

Sara nodded, trying to look sympathetic. "I'm sorry. I wish I could
do more to help."

"You really are. You don't have to be sorry." I tried to give her my
best smile. "Thanks for letting me steal your bed."

"You didn't even ask," she growled in mock-outrage.

"Well, I didn't get to sleep anyway, so all's fair?"

She shook her head, smirking, then twisted around and tapped at her keyboard. The computer screen flicked on. "I've got a paper I have to finish writing. Are you spending the night?"

"Is that cool?"

"Of course. Just . . . we gotta stay quiet. I can't have my parents finding out."

I was puzzled by that one. Sara's parents had always been super nice to me. "Why not?"

She shrugged. "I just don't want to answer questions I don't have to."

"Okay." I felt like I wasn't getting the whole truth, but I trusted her. She'd tell me when she felt ready, same as she'd offered to me.

Okay, I'm sorry. I've been avoiding the dragon in the room. That stone I found out in the forest. I hadn't decided anything about it yet. But it was a way back. All three of us could go back. To Cyraveil.

Did I even *want* to go back? I had no clue. I mean, I'd been leaning toward the idea when it was just wishful thinking, but having the actual possibility suddenly thrust into my hands was way, way different. Now it wasn't a hypothetical anymore, something to comfort myself before I got back to facing the real world again. Now, this world wasn't even necessarily the *real* one anymore. This was just one world, and Cyraveil was another.

Before you start wondering if I was getting all worked up over nothing, I was almost one-hundred-percent sure that the stone was for real. It was written in a language only I knew, out of anybody on the entire planet, and it described—in explicit detail—the exact nature and methodology of casting an etomala for transporting people across worlds. I'd even tried out the first part of it, and for a second, I'd actually felt the connection again. In the core of my being, I felt swirls of energy, beautifully familiar. I cut it off before I went too far, but it was exhilarating.

We'd even be returned to the exact time when we'd left, although I couldn't say for sure where. Stars, if it split us up again . . .

The idea was tempting, I won't lie. If nothing else, having options again made me feel so much more at ease. At the same time, though, my nightmares weren't getting any better, and every last one of them had to do with Cyraveil. How could I just go back to *that*? And Matt— why would Matt ever want to go back? The two of us had a life here, and even Carl could probably find a way through his issues. Go back to normal. If the three of us weren't certain, we'd never cross back safely, and we *had* to have three to make the trip. The stone was very clear on the rules.

When I found it, I stayed in that clearing for a long time. I just looked at it, looked at the trees, at the sky. I barely moved for an hour, if not longer. When I finally did, I left the rock exactly where it was. I felt like it shouldn't be touched, like it was sacred or something. I don't really know why; it's not like Sylves worship rocks or something. Sylves don't worship anything, really.

Anyway, after all of that, I just didn't want to be alone—but at the same time, even wandering down my own street, the neighborhood I'd grown up in, I looked around at every house and realized I didn't know a single person. Not one neighbor. I couldn't even remember ever meeting them in the first place. *Had* I ever met them? Had I bothered to get to know the people right next to my own damn house?

I got out of there. I was scared. Sure, I could tell myself I probably wasn't in any real danger, but that doesn't mean daphut when you're feeling like you're surrounded by strangers with intentions you can't understand, people you don't know, who you can't expect to leave if you just wait them out. My own house no longer felt safe to me . . . so I ran.

Instinct brought me to Sara's. It was a pretty easy climb from a tree near her house to the roof, and from there in through her bedroom window. I'd never tried to sneak in before, but I just wanted somewhere to hide out that felt familiar. Plus, nobody was home. Weirdly enough, Sara's room felt more familiar and safe than my family's house. At least, while it was devoid of my actual family, anyway.

"This is soaked," said Sara, picking at the jacket I'd draped over the folding chair she kept in the corner. "Were you outside this whole time?"

"Oh, you know me," I said airily.

"Uh-huh. Out worshipping trees or something?"

"That's racist," I grinned. "But yeah, I was out in the woods. Speaking of which, how *did* your date go? Matt refused to spill."

"It went . . . *okay?*" Sara tilted her head to the side. "There was a lot to talk about. Things more to do with magic and certain parallel worlds."

"Oh . . . sorry I ruined your date," I said, red-faced.

"As if." Sara echoed my tone from earlier almost perfectly. She even tried to affect my accent. I couldn't help but laugh. "That bad?"

"You sound like a five-year-old dubasal." I giggled.

"Well, you're my teacher, so whose fault is that?" Sara easily dodged the pillow I threw at her. "Jeez, you're so violent now."

The mood was dead. Sara had killed it. I felt utterly deflated by her words. I tried not to show it, but to her credit, Sara realized instantly.

". . . I'm sorry."

"No, it's fine. Please, don't feel like you have to tiptoe around me. I'm good."

She still looked concerned. ". . . Do you want to talk about it?"

Yes, please, by all the stars in the sky. "Seriously, it's fine. No problem." Sara didn't look convinced, but I was determined to change the subject. "Have you called Matt yet?"

"Uhh, yeah. But not about what you're thinking."

"Huh?"

She adjusted in her chair, hesitating for a moment. "Carl called me. I think he's losing it. I thought I should warn Matt before something happens."

". . . Losing it how?"

"He was totally incoherent. Err . . . sorry. I mean, he sounded really confused. Really unsure of himself. Like he might do something really stupid."

I stood up and started pacing. I needed movement. Blood flowing through my brain would help me think more clearly. It usually did, anyway. I wasn't exactly in the best state of mind right then, but I would take anything I could get. *Carl, what are you doing? Are you crazy?*

"Jen?"

"I don't know," I said. The pacing stopped, almost as quickly as it had started. My body stepped in and pointedly reminded me how exhausted I actually was, forcing me to sit down. "He's under a lot of pressure. I think he just needs some time."

Sara looked even less sure than I was. "But . . . the cops?"

"They don't have anything. They *can't* have anything." My face warmed with guilt as I repeated Matt's usual line. "There's no evidence."

Sara shrugged—but before she could say anything else, a light *tap-tap-tap* came from her bedroom door. Her father's muffled voice rang out. "Sara?"

My head twisted around to face the door, and before I could stop myself, my hand took hold of the knife still tucked behind my back. Sara didn't seem to notice. I forced myself to release the handle. Why had I grabbed it? There wasn't any danger here, was there? Sara seemed nervous, but that could be nothing. I was an uninvited guest who snuck in—of course she'd be nervous about her dad finding out.

"Yeah, Dad?"

"I'm coming in, okay?"

Before she could answer, the door opened and her father stepped into the room. I felt the temperature slide up just a few degrees instantly, as everything seemed to sharpen. Something about his posture, or maybe it was Sara's, but I felt threatened. My hand slowly crept back toward my knife, out of sight.

He looked around and spotted me, his eyebrows raised. "Jen? When did you get here?"

"A little bit ago. Sorry, Mr. Monaghan," I said, trying to stay calm. "I needed to talk to Sara about something."

"Well, it's late, and Sara didn't ask to have guests over. I'm afraid you're going to have to leave." His tone brooked absolutely no room for argument, but I still hesitated. I glanced at Sara. Part of me was just feeling rebellious—I *really* didn't like being told what to do—but I didn't want to get Sara in trouble.

She nodded at me, very slowly, very carefully. I raised my eyebrows, trying to get *something* from her, but her mouth was shut tight.

I stood up, feeling very out of place. I mean, feeling out of place was my entire life at this point, but I felt *especially* wrong right then. I told myself it was nothing. I was just crazy. I was a lunatic from another world with some serious mental problems. Nothing about this was remotely threatening. I was imagining it.

Her dad didn't want unexpected guests in his house. That was totally reasonable. He'd even asked nicely.

I started down the stairs, her dad following and Sara trailing only a few steps behind. She still hadn't spoken a single word. I could hear her footsteps. Too careful. Too light. Something was wrong. She was tense, way too tense. Preparing for something.

I couldn't be imagining *all* of this, could I?

"Do you need a ride home?" he asked, opening the front door for me.

I shook my head. "It's not too far. I can walk."

"All right. We'll see you for dinner on Monday, then."

"Night, Jen," called Sara, with only the faintest quiver in her voice.

I gave them a thumbs-up before stepping out into the street. It was cold out, especially with my still-damp jacket clinging to my shoulders. At least it had stopped raining. I set off down the road, whistling a tune Ruvalei once taught me. A bird flew across the road, landing in the trees opposite, chirping madly. I smiled at it, taking it as a sign, though the birds in this world weren't smart enough to carry messages like I was used to. It didn't matter though; I'd made up my mind.

I reached the end of Sara's yard and promptly dove between the two houses, rolling on the slick grass.

You didn't think I was actually gonna *leave*, did you? That song I was whistling was a prelude to war. It foretold the coming of fire and destruction, swift vengeance on any who dared harm the forests. Ruvalei had always hated that song, but she held it as something sacred and beautiful, nonetheless. I had to paraphrase it a bit to fit the situation with Sara, but I was sure Ruvalei would understand. It gave me the courage I needed.

I wasn't done here yet.

I crouched beneath the Monaghans' window, just outside their kitchen. The fence was easy to get over. I doubted anybody had seen me drop into their backyard. I left my bag back in front, near the street but hidden away in a bush. If I had to make a break for it, I could grab it as I went, or come back for it later if necessary.

I could hear someone talking. A deep voice—had to be Sara's dad. The words were too muffled though. I had to get closer.

A few more steps would take me to the sliding door into the living room, where they were probably sitting. I had to stay low or I could be spotted through the kitchen window, but I couldn't just crawl straight to the door. There was a wooden patio deck in front of the door that raised up off the ground. I settled on a kind of awkward waddle that kept me low to the ground, but also let me balance on my feet to take slow, silent steps. The wood creaked a bit with each movement, but I doubted they could hear it inside.

After a *very* stressful couple of minutes of slow going, I finally got as close as I could to the sliding glass door, and I could hear them clearly enough to understand what they were talking about. Which, apparently, was me.

Bizarre.

"I don't mind that you're friends with her. I mind that you let her into our home without asking." He sounded so calm . . . but at the same time, there was an emptiness in his voice I hadn't recognized before. Or maybe it hadn't been there until now.

"She comes over all the time, Dad," said Sara, but it wasn't the same Sara I was used to. Her voice wasn't steady. There was that tiny tremor I'd heard before, except it had grown to an earthquake. I didn't recognize her at all. Sara never let *anyone* boss her around, but now she sounded . . . scared.

I hated hearing her sound scared. My friends should never have to feel scared. I never wanted them to feel that. But this wasn't my family. It wasn't my life. Did I really have the right to jump in? I had no idea what was going on in there. I didn't belong here anyway. I couldn't judge them. I should just leave, go back to my own home, my own family.

If Sara's voice hadn't sounded so afraid, I would have disappeared back into the forests. Possibly forever. Utterly alone. But I cared too much to leave her behind. I had to stay. I had to make sure she was okay, or I'd never have a moment's peace. I'd listen, and then I'd leave.

Thank every single star in every sky in every world that exists in the whole damn universe that I didn't walk away.

"Sara, you are not to talk back to me." *His* voice was laced with ice, a chill I'd not heard in a man's voice in a very long time. How had he concealed that from me for so long? I knew that tone. I recognized that brutality. I'd heard it before, from a man I'd—

No. Now wasn't the time for getting lost in memories. I forced it away. I needed to focus.

"Honey, it's okay. Jenny's gone, no harm done," said Sara's mom. "Let's all just head to bed, all right?"

"No. It's not all right," snapped her father. The volume in the room ticked up a notch. "Sara directly disobeyed me. She disrespected my wishes in front of a guest of the house."

I heard something scrape along the floor. I desperately wanted to see what was going on, but moving even an inch forward would put me in direct view of the couch. All I could see was the near corner, where I saw a vague shadow I assumed to be Sara's, outlined on the wall.

I looked down at my hands. When did my knife get there? I didn't remember drawing it from its sheath. I wasn't about to put it away again though. I clutched it firmly, grip at the ready. Just in case.

Just in case.

Nothing was going to go wrong. This was just a family argument.

"Sara, you understand what you've done wrong?"

"Yes, I do," she replied quickly. Again, that fear. I felt real pain in my chest, hearing that from my best friend.

"Tell me."

"I invited a friend over without asking for permission. I'm sorry. It won't happen again."

"No," he growled. Fire blew through the ice, as his voice became a hot spear. I knew *that* voice too. Knew it all too well. I knew what was coming next, even if I couldn't see it.

No. I didn't know. This was all wrong. People like that didn't exist here. This was the real world. This was the suburbs. Oregon. We were safe here.

"Respect, Sara. You did not respect me. Your *father*."

Another scrape. A chair moving along the floor? Somebody stood up, I guessed.

Sara's mom spoke next. "Dear, please. It's okay."

Thump. Someone slamming something? Maybe a book on the table. I couldn't be sure.

"It is *not* okay," her father snapped. "Don't interrupt me."

Sara's mom didn't reply. I watched Sara's shadow shift uneasily, but I couldn't get any more details just from that. I heard another *thump*, followed by the sound of the couch sinking in. Their couch had a very distinct sound when it compressed, like when someone sat down. That only confirmed my fear that somebody would see me if I peeked around the corner. I had to stay still.

"I'm sorry for disrespecting you," said Sara. Her voice was so small. I'd never heard her sound like that before. I didn't know she was *capable* of sounding so weak and defeated. What the hell was going on in that room?

I don't belong here, I repeated in my head. I don't know what's going on. Nothing's happening.

Thump.

I don't belong here.

A sharp cry. Someone in pain, or maybe just exclaiming something.

I don't belong I don't belong I don't belong.

Another *thump*, and a groan.

Fuck this.

I hooked my shoe onto the lip of the door and shoved. It slid open in one smooth motion. A gust of air whistled over the threshold. I hurled myself around the corner.

Time stopped. *Dear stars, why did I wait so long?*

Her mother was curled up in the corner of the couch, hiding her face, protecting herself. Through the gap between her limbs, I saw bruising. Tears streamed down her face—the kind I knew. The kind you have to learn to shed in absolute silence.

Sara was in the chair nearest me. Towering over her, clenched fist raised, was her father. She was ducking into a defensive posture, something that was really just useless. Instinctive, but ultimately pointless against a man that outweighed her by so much, with far more strength and endurance.

I didn't have long to act. I still had the element of surprise, but every head was turning toward me. I saw the threat, to my best friend and to myself, and I moved in.

Sara's dad was quicker than most to react, but even so he couldn't swing around fast enough. I was smaller and faster. I went straight for his center of mass. I had to knock him off balance. Knock him over, if I could.

My shoulder hit him just below the waist.

His arm was still raised, and it threw off his center. He toppled backward, tripping over the footrest behind him. The . . . ottoman. Another loud *thump* as he crashed to the carpet.

"Jen?" Sara asked, her voice cracking in shock.

I didn't have time to respond. He was disoriented and down, but he wasn't out. Sprawled between the ottoman and the chair, he twisted around. He was trying to right himself.

I leaped over the furniture. My knee connected with his stomach. He grunted in pain as all the air blew out of his lungs. My hand raced forward. A red line appeared across his arm as he tried to block it, tried to fend me off.

"Jen, stop!"

His arm retracted from the pain. I wasn't about to waste an opening like that. My knife plunged down again. The blade sunk into his shoulder. I retracted it and saw red.

Another. I had to strike again. He was still moving.

Something knocked into me from the side. I was bowled over into the nearest chair. I scrambled back to my feet in the best defensive stance I could manage. There was only one threat in the room, wasn't there? What hit me?

My eyes strained to focus again. Sara's mom was suddenly in front of me. Her arms were outstretched. I was breathing heavily as adrenaline surged through me. I was ready to strike, but I knew she wasn't who I wanted. She wasn't the threat.

She wasn't moving toward me, but she wasn't getting out of the way either. Her face was suddenly calm. The tears had stopped flowing. She was resolute, while her husband growled and writhed in pain on the ground behind her.

Sara appeared at my side. "Jen?"

I will never forget the tone in Sara's voice when she said my name. She was scared, she was hopeful, she was grateful, she was terrified. It brought me back. I had to fight off the adrenaline urging me forward. Urging me to fight. Between Sara's mother blocking my way, and my best friend wide-eyed beside me, I couldn't move.

What did I just do?

Sara seemed to recognize I was frozen. She took my hand and bolted for the front door. I was dragged along, my feet following her lead straight out the door and far away. Away from the blood and the pain. Away from the fear and confusion. Away from a house that suddenly loomed like a dungeon, receding behind us in the darkness as we fled into the night.

We kept running until we were *miles* away. I lost count of the streets we crossed. The neighborhood seemed utterly deserted, not a soul to see our panicked flight from Sara's home, which had become a place of terror and bloodshed.

Sara finally slowed, panting for breath. There was a bench nearby. She sat down, trying to catch her breath. A lone streetlight hung above us, flickering gently in the cool night breeze. Darkness had fallen completely, leaving us two completely alone in the world. The entire street didn't have a single other light visible, curving away in both directions. There was almost no moon that night either. It was like we were on an island made of light, and the rest of the world didn't exist anymore.

That sounded just fine at the moment.

Sara still hadn't let go of my hand. I was standing, looking every direction, keeping watch for anyone. Anything. I couldn't shake the fear that we'd been followed, even though I knew no one had. I probably would have started circling the area to scout if I hadn't felt Sara's hand shaking in mine.

That brought me back again. I looked at her and saw her face, pale as fresh snow.

"Jen?" she whispered.

". . . Yeah," I said, but I felt as uncertain as she looked. I finally sat down. She needed me to be with her more than she needed my protection. I scooted over a little and let her lean against my shoulder.

"Are you okay?" she asked.

"No," I snapped, more harshly than I meant to, but I was *angry*. Sara had lied to me again, and this time to devastating consequences. "It's your turn for that. *Dov nara vack* was that back there?"

She looked away, but I saw her face get red again. "Nothing. Don't worry about it."

"Don't— Sara, your dad was—" I couldn't bring myself to say it. I cleared my throat awkwardly. "That was something to fucking worry about."

"I know, okay?" She whirled around, tears in her eyes. "I should have said something. I should have done something. I never did. I broke our promise. I lied to you so many times. And now this. This . . . mess. I'm so sorry, Jen. I should have told you so long ago, but I was too scared. I didn't know what he'd do, or how bad it was going to get. Please." She was talking so fast toward the end, I was having trouble keeping up. Her face was a mess, and she couldn't stop quivering. Fear visibly pulsed through her.

All the rage and frustration I felt vanished into the cold night breeze. I knew exactly what she was going through. I couldn't let her go through it alone.

She shivered with the next gust of wind. I took off my jacket and draped it around her. The outer layer might've been damp, but it was still warmer than the T-shirt she had on. More importantly, I could see, it was comforting. Like how they always gave blankets to people after traumatic events. *If I'd had a blanket or two . . . wouldn't have changed much, but I would've felt a little better.*

I pulled her into a tight hug as she started crying. Tears fell into my lap. I let her bury her face in my shoulder, let her hide from the world. I had to comfort her, however I could.

I began to sing.

Sara couldn't understand a word of it, but I've been told my singing was nice. I don't know if that's true. I can't really say if it's any good. I liked singing and I liked the reactions I got from friends when I sang. I had sung for large gatherings and I'd sung for just Ruvalei and Naef before. I sang every day before the war started and I sang again when it was over, after my friends begged me to. It was fun, the simple joy of being able to create music and convey some real emotions through melodies and lyrics, stuff I couldn't just say. No tools, no instruments, just my voice and the lyrics.

I sang to Sara a lullaby, something I'd learned long before I understood the words. Ruvalei used to sing it whenever I felt *really* homesick, back in the early days when I was still new in the forest, before I'd even joined the suunsyl. She somehow always knew when I'd need it most. When I was lonely, curled up in the little nook of Tethevallen's guest tree, Ruvalei would show up to sing me to sleep, while Naeflin darted around just out of sight, playing my fears away on her tulavir.

I didn't have anyone to accompany me, but I tried to put everything I had into that performance anyway. I wanted to give Sara every bit of comfort Ruvalei gave me, during those dark early nights in the forest, long before I'd understood where I was and what was going on, when I was still a stranger in a truly strange, foreign land.

The lullaby was the story of a young girl who'd lost her way. She'd wandered away into the forests and tripped, falling into a copse of trees she didn't recognize. She cried out for her family and friends, but nobody answered. She was alone, and she was frightened, so she prayed to the stars for help.

The stars didn't answer her of course, because the stars have no voice, but the girl suddenly remembered that she was still in her own forest. She searched for a trail, and soon found her way to another suunsyl. The Sylves there were kind and friendly, and welcomed her as a wanderer to be fed and sheltered. They sent a message to the girl's family, and soon she was on her way home again, where her mother and father and her older brother were all anxiously awaiting her return. They were reunited in their forest, and they were happy again, and the girl felt safe once more.

Cheesy, simple story, but what did I care? It was the first thing that came to mind, and it had a happy ending, *and* it wasn't like Sara could understand a single word of it anyway, so what the fuck do you want from me?

I would to sing to her forever, if she wanted me to. Her hand never let go, and her head slid down until her eyes were buried in my lap, still softly crying. I kept singing as I looked up at the sliver of moon in the sky and the unfamiliar stars that dotted the whole universe around it. I still couldn't find Tethevallen's star, and I knew that I would never see it in this world—and that was something I could no longer accept.

I felt peace. My mind was finally settled. I'd made my decision, and not in a clap of thunder, but in this quiet place, with my best friend holding onto me like a life raft. Everything was finally calm. I wasn't scared anymore.

I was going home.

I went through three or four more songs before Sara finally sat up again. Please don't ever tell her this, but to be honest, the last song I picked was pretty . . . well, let's just say it's not for kids. Horribly inappropriate, but it has a nice tune, and I couldn't think of anything else.

I let go of her hand so she could wipe at her eyes. "Now, why don't you ever do that in English?" she choked out, trying to force a smile while still brushing away tears.

" 'Cause your language sucks." I grinned.

Her expression softened. "It was beautiful."

". . . Vannen." My cheeks flared up in embarrassment.

She smiled again. I liked seeing her smile. Anything was better than what we'd gone through only minutes earlier, though it felt like it was hours and hours ago.

"Are you okay?"

"*Shh*. Don't worry about me," I said. "We're still on you."

"Jen—"

I raised my hand to cut her off. "I'm fine."

"You're not though," she said. Her voice was getting stronger. Not harsher though. Just more confident. More like the Sara I know and love, my best friend. "Jen, I know you went through a lot, but what you just did back there . . . that was . . . something else."

I shook my head. "It wasn't though."

"Huh?"

I sighed. "It wasn't something else. It was me. That's me now."

"You mean—"

"It was called the Pit. They caught me alone and threw me down there. I had to fight people. Lots of people. Most of them were bigger and stronger than me. Stronger than your dad too. I had magic on my side, sometimes, but most of the time? It was just me and the other guy, and I knew I had to come out on top."

"But—" she started in again, but I interrupted her. I had to say it all. I couldn't stop now.

"I fought to win. I had to get out of that place, and for a really long time, I believed the only way I could was if I never lost. So I decided I wasn't gonna lose. And that meant, as I kept fighting, as I . . . progressed in the Pit, I had to face a choice."

She hadn't caught on yet, but it didn't matter. I'd already decided it was time to confess everything. Lay it out, so Sara knew what I was and why I couldn't stay in this world anymore. "It was always gonna be them or me. I chose me, so I was the only one who walked away."

"I don't—"

"I killed, Sara." I choked up a little, but I kept talking. "They didn't deserve it, it wasn't part of the war, but I still killed them." Tears were starting to drop from *my* eyes now. I brushed them away. "All of them. And if I'd just waited. Just a few more days, we might have all lived. But I killed them, because I thought if I didn't, they'd kill me."

So that's why I just stabbed your dad. So . . . you know, you can hate me now. I understand.

"Oh . . . Oh, God . . ." It was her turn to pull me in for a hug, to my surprise.

"Sorry," I added, slightly muffled. "My timing really sucks here."

She shook her head, brushing against my shoulder. "You're okay."

". . . You too," I replied softly.

"What?"

"I'm sorry." I didn't move a muscle, still talking into her shoulder. "For being stupid. For getting mad at you for lying. For all of this."

"I wanted to—"

"Me too," I said, and that was enough. She relaxed.

We didn't say anything else. I just enjoyed the embrace, the first of its kind since we came back that I didn't feel compelled to break out of. I actually felt comfortable. For the first time in a *long* time, I felt real human contact and I wasn't afraid. I wasn't threatened. I felt safe again. *Finally.*

How could I give her up?

I couldn't live on Earth anymore. I knew that for certain. I didn't belong in the clean suburbs. I had changed too much to ever live here safely anymore. I belonged back in the trees and the forest, with the suunsyl I knew and loved, and the people who'd come to accept me as one of their own. I belonged to that world and that era. Now that both doors had been flung wide, I knew which I needed to step through.

I had nothing tying me to this world anymore, except for Sara.

A lightning bolt would not have struck me as hard as the idea which formed in my head in that moment.

The rock specified three. There was no reason it had to be the *same* three.

Before I could stop myself, before I could think through the consequences or the problems, before a single new thought crossed my mind, I was already opening my mouth to speak.

"I found a way back."

CHAPTER 16

MATT

"You'll never guess what I—"

"Just spit it out already."

"Stokelson popped up at Westin's place of work."

"Wait, what?"

"We picked up a security tape from the store at their request after a theft report. Fast-forwarded through it and saw this. Looks like some kind of confrontation."

"Sound?"

"From a dirt-cheap convenience store security cam?"

"Okay, fine. Still, between this and Carl on the run, I think we have enough to bring him in properly."

"So next time I see him—"

"We're authorized to detain him. With force, if necessary."

———————————

It was past midnight, and Jen still wasn't home.

I couldn't sit still. I was pacing the house anxiously. I also had no idea where Carl might be, and no idea where to start looking for either of them. I'd called Sara's house, but no one picked up. Mom wasn't home at least, so I didn't have to explain to her yet, but there wasn't a chance I could even think about going to sleep, no matter how tired I was.

There was a constant hum to the real world. I'd noticed it the second I got back, but it seemed even more oppressive now. Whether it was the steady purr of the refrigerator or the barely perceptible crackle of electricity in every direction, I felt surrounded by suppressed energy. It was like the world was ready to spring into action any second, a rubber band stretched taut and always on the verge of release. To my mind, that release could only spell disaster.

Shortly after Carl left the store, my closer showed up, and I got home without incident. Of course, without something even as mundane as work to keep me busy, I'd fallen right back into stewing in my own thoughts, reexamining every piece of our conversation in detail before it faded from memory.

Carl was crazy and desperate; that much was obvious. He'd crossed the line. He was going to do something, I had no doubt. I had to stop him, but what could I do?

The question was going to eat at me all night.

He'd mentioned a name. Daniel Whitman. I had to figure out who that was.

I went upstairs to my computer and booted it up. It hummed to life, yet another layer of sound pressing on my ears. Carl had built this computer for me; in fact, every single piece was a hand-me-down from his own machines. We'd never have been able to afford a computer this nice. Now I had to use his gift to stop him. The irony wasn't lost on me.

It didn't take too long to find a Daniel Whitman in the area. I might not be as good with computers or the internet as Carl, but it really wasn't hard to look up a person's name and location. Even so, Whitman didn't have much info available publicly. I knew he was a real person and he lived locally, but I couldn't get anything else.

But Carl was obsessed with him. Either he had a lot more to go on than I did, or he was even more desperate than I'd thought.

Or both.

Should I call the police? Whitman might not actually be in any immediate danger. Who was I even supposed to call? I didn't think 911 was appropriate. This probably wasn't urgent. Maybe the police had some kind of non-emergency tip line. Something to rein Carl in, get him back home safely.

The two detectives showing up on our doorstep felt like it had happened weeks ago, even though it was only yesterday. The police made me uncomfortable, though I wasn't sure why. It wasn't like I had anything to hide or had done anything wrong—in this world, at least. Yet whenever I saw a police cruiser on the road or a uniformed officer on the street, I instinctively fell into the most nonthreatening, innocent stance I could muster. I had never interacted with them once until yesterday.

If I called them, was I tossing Carl to the wolves?

Or was I doing the right thing, shining a spotlight on a potentially dangerous man for the authorities to handle?

What if I did nothing?

The last option seemed ludicrous. When it popped into my head, I laughed aloud. I couldn't do nothing. That's what started this whole mess. I went back to weighing my original options, but the idea kept lurking in the background, like a patient hunting cat. As I paced, my mind overburdened by pressure, it prowled back to the forefront again and again.

I *could* just do nothing.

It went against my gut, but the idea was incredibly appealing. Why should I be forced to take responsibility for Carl's actions? He was to blame, not me. I hadn't asked for any of this, and now that I'd finally escaped, I was still paying the price for actions I'd taken under wildly different circumstances. It wouldn't be unreasonable to just wash my hands of the whole thing, and let Carl determine his own fate without my involvement.

I stumbled on the staircase as I walked down it for the sixth or seventh time. I clutched the railing in a sudden panic. Doubt flooded back in. I wasn't that cold, was I? The fact that I'd even considered it scared me. Carl was my friend—or, well, he had been. I couldn't just *abandon* him. If I was actually considering returning to Cyraveil, I had to at least consider whether or not to bring Carl along.

I was getting nowhere. I'd been through all of this before. I'd felt such conviction after we'd run into each other at the store, but now I had doubts.

Leave it to Jen to crash into my thoughts and scatter everything once again.

Just as I reached the bottom of the staircase, the door swung wide, and there she was. My sister, bag and quiver over her shoulder, leading Sara in by the hand.

"It's a bit late," I remarked, falling back into my brotherly role as an escape from my own confusion. I regretted the flippant tone instantly though, as Jen shot me a dark look.

Something was *very* wrong. Sara's face was a mess, and she refused to meet my eyes. Jen looked seriously amped up. She was breathing fast, and her eyes darted around like she was checking the room for threats.

I stood very still, waiting for her to make the first move.

"Is Mom here?" asked Jen. I shook my head. "Good. Sara, come on. Let's get you to the couch, okay?" Her voice softened as she turned to Sara. They walked into the living room. "Matt, could you go make something? Hot chocolate?"

"Sure." I retreated into the kitchen gratefully, while Jen grabbed a blanket. She wrapped it around Sara's shoulders and stayed close, still acting like a guardian for her friend.

I had no idea what was going on, but I could tell it was going to be an even longer night than expected.

I took my time making the hot chocolate. I could hear them murmuring in the next room, and I didn't think it smart to intrude, as much as I wanted to. I wasn't quite sure where I stood with Sara in this kind of situation. Yeah, I liked her, and we'd gone on one date, but that was hardly anything in a situation like *this*. I'd barely hung out with her even before we'd left—and since we'd gotten back, everything had been about Jen and Cyraveil, or Carl and my own fears. Maybe someday I could be there for her like Jen, but definitely not tonight.

"What's taking so long, Matt?" Jen called.

So maybe I'd misjudged a bit. I quickly scooped up the three mugs and brought them into the living room, setting them on the coffee table. Sara and Jen were seated together on our small couch, so I took the chair opposite, trying to relax. Sara's eyes were downcast and her face pale, but nobody seemed like they were in immediate danger. She sipped the drink gratefully while Jen and I shot each other significant looks.

I had no idea what Jen was trying to tell me silently. I don't know if other siblings can do stuff like that, but Jen and I sure couldn't. Especially not these days.

"Are you guys okay?" I asked. Before Jen could answer, her mouth already open and eyes narrowed, I raised my hand. "Sorry, that was a stupid question. What can I do?"

Jen shook her head. "Nothing right now. Sara's probably spending the night though."

I nodded. My mind immediately jumped to offering my bed up for her, but luckily, before I brought it up, I realized how that might get . . . misconstrued. Jen saved me anyway by blowing away any other thoughts with her next sentence.

"More important though, Matt. I found a—well, a rock."

I raised an eyebrow. "A rock?"

"Let me finish. It had Etoline carved into it. It told me how we can go back."

Like a stone through a window. My mind seemed to fall apart, twisting in painful, confused contortions. Even as I'd been agonizing over whether or not to tell her, Jen went and found out anyway. I wasn't sure whether to be glad or worried about what came next.

"There's a catch though."

"A catch?"

"Only three people."

I wished more than anything that Sara weren't in the room. At the same time, I realized why Jen had started this topic in front of us both. "You want it to be us three," I said slowly.

"Well, I dunno," she went on, and my mind skipped another beat. "I thought maybe you didn't want to come back. Maybe you were happier here."

"So just you two?"

Jen looked confused. "No, it has to be three. I meant us and Carl."

"Right. Of course." I actually hadn't known about that rule. All I'd known was where to go if I needed to go back. Apparently, I wouldn't have gotten far without Jen either way.

She looked a bit suspicious but say anything. Instead, as she brought her hand up to her face, brushing away some hair from her eyes, I saw red. An all-too-familiar red.

I lurched forward, reaching for her arm. "Jen, what happened?"

"La se masadalv." Jen pulled away, dodging my hand. "It's nothing."

"That's blood."

"Okay, yeah, it's blood. I didn't want to bring it up."

"What happened?"

"Look, can we not do this right now?" Something in her voice, the weight of emotion crackling just under the surface, set me back. I forced myself to relax in my seat, waiting patiently. I wanted desperately to know what happened, but since neither of them seemed injured, I doubted I was going to get past Jen anytime soon.

I folded my arms and looked her directly in the eye. "Do I need to know anything?" I asked as calmly as I could.

"No, you really don't," she snapped.

"Okay."

That had the desired effect. Jen visibly calmed down a bit. I noticed that her right hand, the one I hadn't been watching, was white-knuckled, clutching Sara's. Sara was still looking at the floor, and I had no idea what she might be feeling.

"Sara," I started, and her head snapped upward. Even though I could tell she'd just been crying, her face was like stone, utterly devoid of anything I could read.

"Hi, Matt," she spoke, for the first time. "Sorry for crashing." It was the weak, jovial tone of real despair, when you're so depressed you have to treat everything like a bad joke so you don't drag everyone else down with you.

"You're always welcome here."

"Thanks . . . but I guess we might not ever see it again?"

"You really want to go across?" I asked, surprised.

"Yes." She said it so fiercely I was taken aback.

". . . Why?"

"Because it has to be better than here," she said simply. She sounded so certain. All doubt fled from my mind. She'd go, regardless of anything I might say. I wasn't going to get anywhere convincing her otherwise, and I wasn't sure I really wanted to either.

"Is this an interrogation?" Jen cut in. "We're all adults here. Well, not Sara, but she's close enough."

"I'm older than you," she pointed out.

Jen shook her head. "You aren't, but the point is, you can make your own decisions."

"But what about Carl?" I asked.

Jen faltered. Her eyes fell. ". . . Yeah."

Silence stretched out for many minutes. In that time, I decided, finally, to commit. I felt it like a lever in my head, a titanic switch that shifted my entire life from one track—where I'd live on in this house, with my mother and the real world I'd never paid much attention to— back onto the other rail. A life I had truly *lived*, with real purpose and meaning, responsibilities I couldn't abandon and people who actually relied on me. I was afraid, I was *beyond* afraid, but I knew I had to go back.

Not only that, but my sister had to go back too. If she was to return to the world that had uncovered her, this huntress of the forest who built bridges between whole races, it was only right that I go with her. I'd made a promise, to both my mother and myself, that I'd protect her. Okay, when I made that promise, I'd never expected just how far it'd take me, but it didn't matter. I'd keep that promise until my dying breath.

Jen doesn't need my protection though, came the nagging doubt in the back of my mind. Look at her. She's more capable than you've ever been. If she goes back, she'll have magic, and the might of the elves, and a whole list of other things on her side. Why do you have to follow her across?

Because I promised, I answered myself, driving that doubt away. Because even when she didn't need my protection, even though she could probably protect *me* far better than I could her, she was still my sister, and I was afraid to live in a world without her.

There it was. I was afraid. I'd raised her when my mother couldn't, and I couldn't bear the thought of losing her. Even if I could be guaranteed she'd be safe on the other side, that wasn't enough. The six years I'd spent in Cyraveil, I'd never stopped looking for her. No matter what else I did, through all the fighting and wars and politics and adventures, my objective was always to find Jen. To make sure she was safe, and happy. We were a team, and we always had been. I wasn't about to give that up.

"We'll go back. Us three."

Jen's eyes widened. I saw joy flit across her face and knew I'd made the right decision. Even so, it was quickly replaced with more doubt and worry. I knew what was coming next. "But, Carl—"

"I know. If I go, he can't."

Jen shook her head in dismay. "Why did it have to be three?"

"Hey, you're the magical one here."

"Oh, *se develd.* This sort of thing is *way* outside of what I learned."

"But you understand it enough to do it, right?" I asked.

"Yeah, I guess it must be because three of us came back. Things being equal, that's important sometimes. But then other times it doesn't mean shit. I don't know."

"It's magic. It'll never make sense," Sara said quietly.

"As the one who actually has to move us *across dimensions*," grumbled Jen, "I'd sure like it to."

"What else *do* we know about it?" I asked.

"Well," said Jen, rubbing her hands together. "I can't guarantee we'll end up in the same place we left from. But I think we'll stick together this time at least. As long as we're touching."

"Well, that's a relief."

"No kidding." Jen smiled.

Sara shifted uncomfortably next to her. Jen glanced over, brow furrowed. "Second thoughts?"

"No," she said firmly. "I need to do this. But I feel like I'm robbing Carl of his own chance."

"You deserve this," said Jen. "More than the rest of us."

"Says the one who's guaranteed a spot."

"And I want you with me," she shot back.

"I think you're avoiding the issue." My heart sank. Sara was right though; I hadn't wanted to come back around to it in front of her. "Carl's seriously messed up, and I'm guessing it has to do with Blake, right?"

I nodded. "Blake was his best friend. We . . . lost him."

Jen's face fell. "And we can't just ditch Carl like this."

I cleared my throat. This was the moment. Everything was on the line now. I had to do it. "I think he'd understand."

"Huh?"

I took a deep breath. The reluctance and timing was critical. They *had* to believe me. "Carl's smart. We all know that. He'd understand why you have to go back. As for me, he might not agree with what I stood for, or the side I fought for, but he knew how important it was. He knows I left so much undone. Plus, I'm not really going anywhere in this world. I don't have anything. I'm just a nobody. Carl said it himself, how much better suited I am to Cyraveil."

"Okay, so we're both great. He was too," Jen interrupted. "He had a whole city that worshipped him, Matt. Not sure where you're going with this."

"*Was,*" I said, nodding for emphasis. "Carl was broken by that world. You saw it yourself. He hasn't been the same since he got back, not at all. Any time Cyraveil has come up, it's totally broken him. Both of his closest friends died there, and he blames himself for it. He couldn't help them. Cyraveil was horrible for him."

"So you think he'd be better off here?"

"I do."

Jen still looked skeptical. "Shouldn't we talk this over *with* Carl?"

"Think about what that would do to him," I continued, still improvising as fast as I could. I couldn't tell if Jen really believed me or not, but I had to make her accept it. "Right now, Carl's finally getting over Blake's death and accepting that he can't come back. He's taking steps forward, returning to his old self, everything. He's smart, and he has a family that can support him, and he's got other friends. He'll be successful in life here for sure, and the skills he picked up there apply pretty well over here too. Carl can recover."

"What about you?"

"I don't belong here anymore," I sighed. It was true, though I did still regret it. "Mom's practically pushing me out the door already, even though I have no idea what to do with my life. I already did my whole life's work in Cyraveil. Everything here would just feel like an afterthought. If I go back, I can continue that work. I abandoned everyone, and now I have a second chance. I don't want to let it slip by."

Jen studied my face, and finally she nodded very slowly. ". . . Okay."

I didn't say anything. I felt like I'd done all I could. Either I'd persuaded Jen, or I hadn't. The rest was all up to her.

Sara, at least, looked convinced. I wasn't sure if it was because she actually believed me or if she just wanted to avoid conflict and get out of here faster. I couldn't blame her if it was the latter. I decided to shift the conversation, before Jen dwelled too long on her decision.

"You don't have to tell me what happened tonight—" I said, returning to my old voice, the voice of the leader of the companions, our group of four. It felt natural, and that only renewed my conviction. I was making the right call. "—but I do need to know if it's something that's going to draw attention to us."

Sara looked uneasy. "It . . . might," she said, glancing at Jen. My sister was staring straight ahead, unflinching.

"Okay," I said. "Then we should leave as soon as possible. Does it matter what time?" I prompted Jen. She shook her head. "Can we bring anything?" Again, a shake of the head. I was disappointed, but I wasn't surprised. When we'd last crossed, we'd kept our clothes, but absolutely nothing else. Flashlights, phones, the works—all gone.

"What about Mom?" Jen asked, glancing at the front door.

"She should be home in a few hours. We'll see her then."

We spent the next few minutes figuring out logistics—when to leave, what to take, what to wear, and so on—before Sara finally gave up on suppressing a yawn. Jen was quick to hurry her upstairs, while I stayed behind to clean up the mugs. I was at the sink rinsing away when Jen suddenly appeared next to me. I jumped.

"You know, it's really unsettling how quiet you are."

"You jealous?" she asked, picking up a plate from the pile and starting to scrub it clean.

"Maybe."

"If you ask nicely, maybe I could teach you a few tricks."

"Could come in handy." I set the mugs aside to dry and joined her in going through the rest of the dishes. We worked in silence for a few minutes, Jen washing while I rinsed and dried them one by one. It was nice. Simple, good work that let us do something together again.

"What will you do when we get there?" I asked.

Jen grinned. "Find Naef, introduce her to Sara, and then throw a *really* great party."

"Don't burn the forest down."

"What about you?" she asked, nudging me in the side.

"I don't know yet," I replied honestly.

"I heard you were promised to what's her name. Kristvina?"

I snorted. "Jen, I couldn't stand to be in the same room as her for more than ten seconds. She was awful. That was all politics."

"You were the best gossip in town though!" Jen laughed. "Everybody was so shocked that the great and mighty leader of the rebellion could see through to her highness's inner beauty!"

I set aside the next plate, trying not to laugh. "Trust me, nothing inside her was beautiful either. She was a moron."

Jen frowned. "Well, that's not very nice."

"Okay, by moron, I mean the worst sort of conniving, backstabbing noble, but totally incompetent at that too."

"Okay, that sounds about right."

"All she had was an important family name. Nothing else."

"Still, that could be useful," Jen mused.

I paused to consider that. Jen wasn't wrong. "You know, you're right. And honestly, she might not be so bad if she wasn't being pressed into marrying me. She hated the idea. Probably why she kept trying to sabotage it."

"*Keldaphut*, are you actually taking my advice for once?" Jen said, in mock-amazement.

"Congrats."

Another few minutes passed in silence as we continued to clean up the kitchen. It wasn't awkward though; if anything, it was comfortable and peaceful. We'd come to an unspoken agreement that we wanted to make the house look perfect before we left. Leave it better than we found it, just like Mom always taught us.

As Jen put away a stack of plates, her shirt lifted up just enough for me to spot the knife sheathed at the small of her back. My mind jumped back to the bloodstain on her hand when she'd arrived with Sara—the blood on her knife hand.

"... Jen, what happened tonight?"

"We had a brother-sister bonding moment," she answered, still up on her toes to put the plates in order. "Don't worry about it. I won't take it too seriously."

I leaned back against the refrigerator, watching her carefully. "Who did you stab?"

Jen nearly knocked the whole stack over as she whipped around. "I—"

"You said I didn't need to know, but I'm worried about you. Both of you. Please."

She righted the plates again and dried off her hands with a towel. She didn't speak for a full minute, while I waited patiently for her to work up to the words.

"Her dad."

I wasn't sure what answer I'd expected, but definitely not *that*. "What?"

Her eyes narrowed, and her voice got very quiet. "He was hurting her. Hurting them both. I stopped him."

"You didn't—"

"He'll be fine," she said calmly. My panic ebbed away, but between her tone and the images in my head, I was still anxious beyond measure. "Sara couldn't stay there, and after what I did . . ." Jen trailed off. She took a moment to compose herself again before she went on. "I thought I could do something for her, you know? Something nobody else could. I could offer her a real way out. She could have a life with me and my *suunsyl*, or any other life she wants. It's a fresh start."

"Did you tell her what Cyraveil can be like?" I pointed out. "It's not like it's easier to live there than here."

"Harder, yeah, but it's worth it. Or it will be. I'll make sure it is," Jen said fiercely. "She won't ever have to be afraid again."

I smiled. "Okay."

"What about you two though?" Jen asked, winking at me. She was trying to change subjects as quickly as she could, and I wholeheartedly welcomed the sudden shift in tone. "You gonna keep going out with her when we go back?"

I shrugged. "Maybe once the dust settles and I figure out where we stand. I'll have way too much going on in the next few weeks, and she's gonna have a lot of adjusting to do. I dunno."

"Careful," said Jen. "Wait too long and she might fall for some handsome *dusylf*. Some of them are *pretty* sexy. I've been tempted, plenty of times."

"I don't need to hear this." I busied myself with putting away dishes again.

Jen snickered. "And we've got *magic* on our side. You're gonna have to work extra hard at keeping her happy," she teased.

"Uh-huh. Why don't you go see how she's doing? I think I can handle the rest here."

"No fun at all," she groaned, rolling her eyes. She vanished from the room the moment I turned away, again without a whisper of sound. Knowing just how much the stairs creaked in our house, I was astounded that I couldn't even tell when she'd gone upstairs.

I might have been joking around with her, but there was another reason I needed my sister to leave the room. There was something I had to do, something I was dreading but knew I couldn't avoid. Not after the story she'd just told me. Every terrible future in my head had to be avoided.

Carl couldn't be allowed to just roam free without intervention. Somebody had to raise an alarm, call attention to him. At the rate he was going, someone was bound to get hurt. I dreaded to think what Carl could do if he truly went mad. To his parents, or his friends, or this Daniel Whitman he'd been talking to.

It wouldn't end well. Not unless I did something. I had to tell someone what was going on. Make sure he got help of some kind. My first thought was his parents, but I dismissed that quickly enough. Carl was already on the run from them; they couldn't really help in any signifi-cant way anymore.

I could try to get in touch with some of his other friends, but I felt like I'd run into the same problem. Carl was still trying to return to Cyraveil, and he felt like he had to hide from both the cops and his family. He wouldn't trust any of his friends. He'd be completely on his own if he could manage it. They might be able to get him a message at least, but it wouldn't be enough. I needed something more direct.

A business card flashed through my memory.

I dug it out of my pocket. I'd stuffed it into my wallet. Detective Clark West, with both the main police line and his personal cell num-ber. I flipped it over idly in my hand, thinking. Considering.

Was this right? It seemed like the best thing for him, under the cir-cumstances. They'd find him and pick him up. They'd take him back home safely. If the cops were involved and they got in touch with his parents, plus whatever warning I could come up with . . . Maybe every-thing would work out. Carl would get counseling, they'd declare him sane, he'd return to society again. I doubted he'd ever actually forget Cyraveil, but he'd be back to normal.

He'd never be able to explain *our* sudden disappearance, but that was something I couldn't help. I had to hope he'd recognize what we'd done, and finally choose to live a normal life, with all other avenues closed off to him.

Was I betraying him, in the same way he'd betrayed Reynir? Did I even have a problem with that if I was? Did I want him to stay behind because I didn't trust him, or because it was the easy way out?

I flipped that card over again and again. I had too many doubts. Maybe my gut feeling was right. If Carl never heard another thing from us, if we just suddenly vanished, that could be just as good as trying to intervene in his life. Maybe better, since he wouldn't get even further onto the cops' radar. He could really return to a normal life.

I didn't have the answers. Everyone always assumed I could come up with them, but most of the time I was improvising. I was always hanging on by a thread. There was only so much information I could gather, only so much time I had to plan things out. I could feel the sand falling away in the hourglass, grain by grain, and I knew I had to make a choice.

The card danced between my fingers endlessly as I watched the stars through the kitchen window. It was a quiet night. The calm before the storm, maybe? Or just the peace after a long battle? Maybe it was all just mental, because I was through with it all. I could just toss the card aside, let Carl be himself to whatever end.

I sat down and buried my face in my hands. I didn't want this choice, with no right answers, but I knew it was the same type I'd be forced to make so many times over in the coming weeks and months. I had to decide, one way or the other. Even if I chose to remain idle, that was still a commitment. That was still conviction.

In that moment, with the pressure of two worlds bearing down on my shoulders, I finally stood up. I knew what I needed to do. I couldn't let things just stay as they were, that wasn't me. I'd made my choice, and I'd live with the consequences—forever.

CHAPTER 17

CARL

"We've got no leads beyond two kids we can't find, and no evidence to speak of anywhere. What are we supposed to do?"

"We go back to work. Hope for a break somewhere, or to find them. We'll go back to their houses every day if we have to."

"That shit's gonna get exhausting."

"It's the job. Do you have anything better to do?"

"Guess not."

"Good. Now what's for dinner? It's late."

"Wait a sec."

"It's your turn to pick, isn't it?"

"Do you see me on the phone? Shut up . . . Holy shit."

"What?"

———————

This is the story of the last day of my life.

Yeah, it sounds melodramatic, but it's true. I was in mental free fall through memories while I went through the motions of preparing myself for my final day on this planet. The sun was already dropping on the horizon as I worked, casting ever-longer shadows through the windows. I didn't dare turn on a single light, even as I carefully picked up the shattered glass on the floor near the rear window I'd broken. I had to get it all before I lost the light entirely. It wouldn't be good for my plans to get screwed up by something as simple as a cut to the foot by a wayward shard.

I'd tried to get Matt on board. I even went out of my way, wasting precious time to visit him at work. He rejected me out of hand. I was disappointed, but I knew Matt too well to resent him. He needed more evidence before he'd commit to the plan. I could accept that. I'd bring him the proof tonight, and I'd bring him our way out. I wasn't going to hold a grudge. Matt could come back with me.

Would Jen though?

That thought really terrified me. I had to convince myself on an hourly basis that Jen couldn't possibly turn me down. I couldn't bear to live in a world without her. Even if she rejected me, even if we never saw each other again, I'd be happy just knowing she'd come home. I could accept anything as long as she was back where she was meant to be.

Was that too presumptuous? For me to claim I knew where Jen belonged, I felt like I was also claiming I knew her better than she knew herself. It felt awkward. I didn't know what to make of it. My gut feeling—overwhelmingly so, like a churning cauldron in my stomach—insisted that Jen must return to Cyraveil. I always trusted my instincts, no matter my doubts. They'd kept me alive through countless dangers and trials. This would be no different.

I continued to go over every inch of the small condominium. It was surrounded by thick greenery, which I assumed was maintained by a gardener based on how well kept it was. The interior of the place wasn't nearly as neat and orderly. The garden also helped to muffle and shade the house from the outside world, in a perfect insulating effect. It almost felt like its own little private island, completely detached from the outside world once the doors were firmly shut.

I glanced at the clock. Time was running out. Had I set up the room? Was the door properly locked? Yes. Everything was ready.

After I got separated from Matt and Blake, and long before I met Reynir, I'd joined—and subsequently clawed my way to the top of—a small guild of thieves and mercenaries. We operated on a strict code of rules that kept us out of the public eye whenever the city guard came knocking. There were no signatures, no calling cards. Violence was avoided at all costs. We were as ghosts, taking only what we'd been hired for, and vanishing without a trace.

By keeping to the code for years, we amassed so much wealth that we became richer than the nominal lords of the city. With my new-found capital, I was actually able to apply some of my knowledge from Earth, working the market to manipulate traders and merchants little by little, until soon I had the entire economy dancing on my strings. My guildmates watched in awe as our investments doubled, then tripled. We ended up buying out the whole city, district by district, until we finally declared ourselves openly as the Lords of Candir.

This drew Reynir Cellman's attention, of course, and his soldiers. Having your second largest city bought out from under your lackey's thumb would be pretty shocking to most Emperors. I was fully prepared for him to send out his personal guard to kill the lot of us, but he surprised me that day. He came out to meet us himself, with only a single guard at his side, and he made me an offer.

The rest is history. *My* history, as soon as I finished up here.

Was the line in place? Crudely, and without much subtlety, but I wasn't exactly expecting resistance. Surprise was key. Surprise, and application of technology.

My mentor would have looked down on this. Old Fredrik always preferred using as few tools as necessary. If you relied solely on your own physical abilities and knew them perfectly, there were far fewer possible points of failure. How could you ever know the true capabilities of a sword, or a crossbow trap—tools that would weaken over time and with repeated use? He preferred the body as the ultimate tool, flexible enough for almost any situation. Fredrik could get in and out of any target with just a single lockpick and the clothes on his back, no matter how many people he might be forced to subdue inside.

I admired that philosophy, but I had to apologize to him in spirit this time. I didn't have the physical ability anymore, nor even the muscle memory or training for what I needed to get done. I had to make up for it with my knowledge and my access to machinery he couldn't ever have dreamed of. Fredrik hadn't even believed in *magic*, not until I'd returned with Jen. He'd always assumed the rumors from the frontlines were straight bullshit.

I swear, his mustache practically fell off when he saw Jen lighting candles with a snap of her fingers, or lazily floating food across the table to herself.

I grinned at the memory. I looked forward to seeing the old fart again, and hearing his endless grumblings on the state of affairs in the Empire—err, the Kingdom, or maybe it was the Republic now. We hadn't really settled that yet. I wondered how Fredrik was getting on, though, after the Cellmans were deposed. We hadn't had the chance to meet up after I sent my guild out of the city.

Fredrik's little cottage on the outskirts of Candir. That was the very first place I was going to visit when I returned. I'd bring him as much *sylvandine* as I could carry, every single drop I found along the way.

The sun had set completely by now. I was just inside the front door, sitting in a little side closet. I wasn't sure when I needed to be ready, but I'd rested as much as I could during the afternoon. Now I was stuck waiting, but I could handle it. I'd learned patience.

I spun a pen idly in my hand, flipping it around my thumb in neat, quick circles. It was nice to see I hadn't lost all my dexterity. I wished I still had the strength and endurance I'd built up over the years. I'd worked hard for it, and Earth had taken it all away again.

This was why I was so furious at Matt, at his blasé attitude to the possibility of return. We'd *earned* our lives there, through work, blood, and sacrifice. Didn't we deserve to keep them? Or at least be offered the damn choice?

More importantly, who wouldn't want to live in a world with magic? *Magic*, Matt. Earth felt so boring and empty by comparison. Hell, we still hadn't even found a single piece of evidence of other sentient life anywhere in the known *universe*. It was just so limited and painful and small. Meanwhile, a beautiful world full of opportunity and mystery and wonder waited for us, a step away if only we could find the door.

I ranted at him in my head, over and over, the words I wished I could have said but never worked up the courage to voice. I didn't want to just persuade Matt, I wanted him to see the merits for himself. I wanted him to agree with me. I wanted us on the same page, without having to drag him there. If I had to talk him into it, I could never truly believe it was his honest desire, and without that, I'd always feel a twinge of guilt about possibly tearing him away from the life he truly wanted.

I didn't want that. If Matt really wanted to stay, it wasn't my place to interfere.

At the same time, it certainly wasn't *his* to prevent my own crossing of the dimensional line once again. Matt had to make a choice. I didn't want to, but I sure as hell would force him to choose if it came down to sides.

Jen and I could return without him if we had to.

I heard a car door slam. I tensed, as I had for every other one I'd heard as I waited. I couldn't afford to relax for a single one. Only one opportunity, I reminded myself. Don't miss it.

Footsteps. Those *were* footsteps, weren't they?

Was I really this bad at recognizing footsteps now?

My heart was racing. Somehow, I knew this was the moment. I felt my adrenaline surge. My vision pulsed with the blood pounding through my skull. I felt every muscle in my body loaded with anticipation, waiting to strike. I was a coiled spring held tight against the floor, a snake about to hurl itself at its prey.

The door handle twisted. The room was pitch-black, the sun completely gone and the moon along with it. He hadn't noticed the streetlight behind him covered up in black tape.

There was no light to help him.

The door swung open, and Daniel Whitman stepped inside.

I tensed up. Every millisecond suddenly felt like hours.

He took another step forward. In the near-total darkness, his eyes hadn't yet adjusted, while mine were as good as could be. He didn't expect anything. He walked forward, to where he knew the light switch would be. Not a care in the world. Just an ordinary night for him.

His foot caught the taut fishing wire.

I watched him fall and I made my move. His hands obeyed his instincts and flew forward to catch himself, and I struck. I took out the object I'd been saving for this very moment.

I squeezed its buttons and the stun gun crackled to life. In an instant, the contacts found Whitman's falling neck.

His body spasmed. It was mesmerizing to watch as he slumped to the floor and began twitching. This sort of power in my hands, at the touch of a button, was beyond anything short of magic I could ever accomplish, even in Cyraveil. I held it on him as long as I could while he fell, trying to ensure he was completely incapacitated. Seconds later, he was groaning on the floor, still twitching uncontrollably.

Might not be as clean as you like, Fredrik, but you can't deny it's effective.

I dragged Whitman through to the back room, which he happened to have already lined with blackout curtains. A sort of low-budget home theater setup. I'd made a few modifications to block out sound as well, and rearranged the furniture a bit. I hoisted his limp body onto the chair, and quickly wrapped his wrists and ankles with plastic zip ties.

This was all precautionary, of course. I didn't actually intend to harm him. Well, nothing more than zapping him with the stun gun, but as I understood it, the voltage was low enough that there wouldn't be any permanent damage. Barring an unforeseen medical condition, he'd be just fine. I knew everything I possibly could about Daniel Whitman. I was confident he'd end the night in perfect health, except for the scrape he'd gotten from the floor as I dragged him in.

Now I just needed to wait for him to recover.

He'd know what I needed to do. He'd practically confessed to it. Out of all the people on the internet, a man who happened to live close enough that I could reach him by bus had shown some actual knowledge of my world. Of Cyraveil. But through whatever reluctance or paranoia, he'd decided he didn't trust me. He wouldn't reveal the details I knew he must be concealing.

Whitman had to talk.

Is this wrong? A voice had popped up in the back of my mind. I'd forced my way into his home. I'd assaulted him. I'd crossed a line here, and it was one I couldn't easily walk back from if I didn't get the information I needed tonight.

The thought only redoubled my determination. I *had* to get results. There was no turning back.

I'd expected it to take Whitman ten minutes or so to recover, but he was still out of it after twenty. Was his constitution *really* that weak? Or maybe I'd misjudged the strength of the shock? I was beginning to worry I might have caused some permanent damage.

To my relief, he started to move more deliberately. He was getting control of his body again. Time to start the real work.

"Daniel Whitman." I stood behind him, his chair facing the television, tuned to a dead channel. The dancing snow of signal noise on the screen played out on the walls as a flickering light show around us. It was all a show, all an act, but one I could play well.

Whitman tried to twist his head around to get a look at me, but he couldn't quite turn far enough.

"The fuck is going on?" His voice was surprisingly low-pitched. A deep baritone that would have worked wonders on a radio show or a podcast.

I wanted to intimidate him. I wanted to get the information I'd come for, and nothing more. I wasn't trying to make an ally. I wasn't trying to create a new resource or contact. This wasn't usually the case, but in this circumstance, I didn't much care what happened to Whitman in the end.

"You live alone. Probably a poor choice."

"Uhh, okay?" He continued to struggle in his chair. I stayed calm behind him. I was confident in the restraints, at least for the length of time I needed. He wasn't going anywhere soon.

"It's time for you to start talking, Daniel."

"About what?" He sounded less confident now. Good. He was wearing down.

"You've been emailing with someone lately."

"I email a lot of people. That supposed to mean something?"

"About a certain fantasy world called Cyraveil."

Whitman stopped struggling. "Wait, you're that guy?"

"Yes. So start talking."

"Dude, what the fuck is this? Some kind of hardcore RP shit?"

"You think this is role playing?" I snapped. I felt my temper flare. My chest got hot; my face burned. I didn't move on him yet, but I thought about it.

"Wait, wait, wait. Don't tell me you actually believed all that?" Whitman said, his voice uneasy. "Okay, listen. None of that was real, all right? I was just messing with you. Ha-ha, good times. Now untie me, okay?"

"Tol deka danedek so vei!" I roared. I'm sure I got the pronunciation a bit wrong, but it wasn't like Jen was around to correct me.

"Uhh . . . what?"

"Don't you fucking lie to me." I punched him in the back of the head. Not too hard, but enough to cause some pain.

"All right, dude," Whitman snarled, recovering faster than I expected. "Soon as I get out of this, you're in a world of pain."

"Whatever you say. Now, talk to me about Cyraveil."

"It doesn't exist, you idiot." His head twisted back and forth, but he still couldn't turn far enough to see me.

He was lying. He *had* to be lying. My mind wouldn't accept any other conclusion.

We could be here awhile.

This went on for an hour at least. I would ask him to elaborate on some part of Cyraveil, reveal more of his knowledge. He'd claim ignorance or spit some insult, and after a while, he just stayed silent. I didn't threaten him physically, or attack him again after the first strike. I hadn't intended that. I wished I hadn't escalated so quickly. I might have gotten what I needed much faster, with much more cooperation, if I hadn't been so reckless.

I knew if I could just outlast his patience, I would win. I wouldn't allow Whitman any sleep, or any respite whatsoever from the questioning. I'd done this before, more than once. Sooner or later, he'd have to give in and answer my questions, and I'd be on my way home.

"Did you ever come across any of Feindorf's Tablets?"

"Nope."

"When you crossed, did you end up in Caladi or Laodrannen?"

"Crossed what, the Willamette?"

"Did you ever meet up with any Sylves? Maybe get invited to their forests?"

"Depends, were they cute?"

It continued like this, flippant responses that irritated me, but didn't set me off. I had interrogated men before, and I had the patience necessary for this kind of work. Men always broke, given enough time. Some men required far more work than others, but it always came down to finding the one thing they couldn't live without. Could be physical, could be emotional, but every man, without exception, had a weakness. I just had to uncover it, through sheer force of will.

Jen and Matt could never know, but I'd engaged in some less . . . noble tactics while we were campaigning, both on Reynir's side and on theirs. It was a fucking war, okay? For all Matt's sentimentality and righteousness, he was a fool when it came to gathering intelligence. Sure, he might win the hearts and minds of the people as we "liberated" villages, but it was thanks to my men and my network that we weren't ambushed in the ass at every turn. Reynir and I played the same games. Hell, he basically *taught* me how to wage war. Fight smarter, not harder; that was my shamelessly stolen catchphrase.

Smarter was the key, and gaining intelligence came down to two simple steps: Find the person who knows what you need to know and get them to tell you. Could be anyone, and here's where most people screw up: it could be *absolutely* anyone. Nobody's out of bounds. The hooker hanging out by the tavern, the kid playing on the street corner, the old hag who rarely leaves her front porch. Any of them could be valuable, and I couldn't afford to have reservations about who we picked up and . . . questioned.

I wasn't needlessly cruel. Most of them got off pretty light, unless I had reason to suspect they knew more than they were letting on. Even the ones we had to slap around a bit were returned to their lives as if nothing had happened. No, it was the small few, the true loyalists to the Cellmans near the end of the campaign, who brought out the worst in me.

I'm not proud of it, but it got results. It probably shortened the war by weeks, if not months. It was worth it. I saved lives, sent men home to their wives and families sooner, prevented pain and tragedy. I don't regret what I had to do. One of those interrogations lead me to Jen, deep in the Pit at Vennenport. I'd rescued her against all odds, on a longshot hunch and the mumbled confession of a man who'd just lost every single one of his teeth.

I'd never regret that man's death. I couldn't forgive myself for not moving on him *sooner*.

I was beginning to get impatient with Whitman, even as I continued to ask him question after question about Cyraveil.

"What's the best place to get *sylvandine* in the Saenvalands?"

"Is that a Sylf thing?"

Yes! I'd caught him in a lie. "You know about Sylves. You've been lying this whole time."

"Man, you mentioned them earlier!" he protested.

"Wrong!" I cried. I pulled out my phone, shoving it eagerly in front of his eyes. "Not once." I scrolled through every message we'd sent, one by one. "I've never used 'Sylf,' not one time. I only called them elves. Where did you hear that term?"

"You said it yourself!" Whitman shouted. "Like an hour ago!"

"Stop lying to me, Daniel." I walked around and crouched down in front of him. Some vulnerability now, since I'd caught him in a lie. I would play off this anxiety, this fear, and offer him a way out. A friendly gesture. "Just get it over with. Tell me what I need to know."

"Holy shit, you're young." I suddenly realized I hadn't actually shown myself until now. Was that my intention? Did I just make a mistake?

No, of course not. I was an expert at this. I didn't make mistakes.

"I can be a friend, Daniel. You remember Cyraveil. You remember what sort of place it is. Tell me you wouldn't want to go back there."

"You're fucking insane." Daniel resumed trying to rock his chair back and forth, but it was surprisingly sturdy, and I'd reinforced the sides a bit too. He didn't move more than an inch.

"Once you tell me, I disappear, and your life goes back to whatever you want it to be. This doesn't have to be hard."

"I told you already, I made all that shit up. I was bored, and it was better than just trolling some random image board." One particularly hard shove and he began to tilt off to one side. I reached out and caught him, righting him before the chair tipped over completely.

He couldn't have made it up. I needed the truth. I needed my way back.

"You weren't lying. Tell me how to go back."

"I don't fucking know!"

I slapped him across the face. Hard.

"Answer me!"

"I don't know!" he cried. Tears were forming in his eyes. I felt awful, sick to my core. I didn't want this, any of it, but I'd burned every bridge. I knew I couldn't continue living like this. I couldn't face my parents again. I couldn't face my friends. I certainly couldn't face Jen again. Not without a way back. I had to keep going.

My foot slammed into his chest. The chair tilted over backward. With a sickening thud, his head smacked into the floor. My heart was racing.

Instantly, I was at his side, checking for bleeding. Thankfully, my hand came back dry. *What was I thinking?* Why did I actually *attack* him? He groaned underneath me, his feet still tied to the legs of the chair.

"Please, let me go," he moaned. "I won't tell anyone. Promise."

I couldn't take that chance. He'd seen my face. There was no reason for him *not* to tell the police, tell anyone who I was and what I'd done. They'd lock me up. They'd put me in a mental ward. I had to leave this world *tonight*.

"You know what I want," I said slowly. I hated myself.

I hated everything about this.

It had to be done.

"I don't know what you want. I'm sorry. Fuck." He tried to reach up to cradle his own skull, no doubt throbbing in pain, and the plastic cuffs scraped hard against his wrist.

"I just need to go back."

"So go back, you fucking psycho!" he screamed at me. His eyes flew open wide. "Go back!"

"Tell me how!" I roared. "Quid pro *fucking* quo, Daniel!"

I was losing control. Worst of all, I could *feel* myself losing control. It was like I was watching myself on video, as another me took charge of my body. This new me stood up and dropped his foot onto Whitman's chest with a thud.

What if he really knows nothing? the old, reluctant me cried out.

He has to know! this new, vicious me snarled in response.

I watched as my body began to beat Daniel Whitman savagely, and I felt helpless to stop. He tried to roll away, but the restraints kept him anchored to the spot.

I saw blood. Why? Why couldn't I stop?

A banging sound. Raised voices.

Was I imagining them? Whitman hadn't yet answered me. I had to keep going.

Had to keep going.

Had to force him to answer me.

It was best for everyone. Once he told me the truth, I could return home and be gone from this world. No more trouble to anyone. A quickly fading memory.

My foot swung for his face. He twisted away, trying to avoid the blow, which I'd telegraphed too much. It never landed.

I was tackled to the floor. A man in a plain suit, with a rough face and beady eyes.

I knew this man, didn't I?

He was shouting something, but I couldn't hear him. My mind was still transfixed by the sight of Daniel Whitman, battered and bruised, bleeding all over the floor. My eyes were pulled wide, as if a sheet of fog had suddenly lifted away. I saw him moaning, saw his beaten face and terrified expression.

As I was dragged to my feet, handcuffed and restrained, I remembered—I *had* mentioned Sylves to him. It sprang to my mind as I was manhandled out the front door. I'd screwed up. Whitman was just an innocent bystander, whom I'd brutally assaulted out of some insane fixation on an impossible quest. Blake would hate me if he saw what I'd become. What I'd just done.

"I'm sorry," I cried out. "I'm sorry. I'm so sorry." I needed Whitman to hear me. I wanted to give him something, anything to show I regretted what I'd done. That he hadn't deserved it. What I'd done was unforgivable, and he'd paid the price.

*   *   *

I barely heard a single word from the uniformed officer.

The back of the cruiser was hard plastic, with a small space for my handcuffed wrists. They transported me through the dead of night, the rain coming down hard and creating sheets of distorted light as we passed through the empty streets. I watched each flash of color as we rolled along, felt every bump in the road as shockwaves through my throbbing skull. My head was pounding, reliving every moment of what had just happened over and over again, searching desperately for answers on how I'd sunk so low.

I'd known it was coming all along though. In some distant corner of my mind, I'd known I wasn't long for this world one way or another. Either I'd manage to escape or I'd burn out trying. I could never coexist with these people, knowing what I knew, having seen what I'd seen. At some point during the last few days, I'd given up hope of ever living here again. I'd assumed my life would end soon. I had just hoped it wouldn't be like this.

Never like this.

We reached the station, and I was processed. My body felt numb to the touch. I could barely comprehend the situation unfolding around me, even as they tried to explain a half-dozen times. I think they assumed I was insane, the way they were handling me so gently. Maybe I *was* insane. I couldn't exactly disagree. I was surrounded by tall, faceless shapes in vaguely defined uniforms, with deep booming voices that only allowed every third word or so to be understood. I had to string together sentences from the scant clues context could afford me.

I was taken to a smaller room, completely isolated, and given a cup of water. They left me alone. At first, I assumed they'd gone to fetch a parent or guardian, but then I remembered: I wasn't a minor anymore. They could do whatever the hell they liked with me.

There was no doubt I was being watched. I tried to find the camera, but all I could see were thick stone walls, rising up as the first of no doubt endless cells I'd be thrown into. *Ah, Reynir. I'll be doing your family line proud.* I'd end up in a cell just like his great-grandfather—but unlike the Cellman patriarch, I doubted I'd be breaking out anytime soon, much less conquering a whole slaving kingdom as I went. Not much to conquer out here in the middle of suburban Oregon.

A man came back into the room, wearing a plain suit. Perhaps they were afraid to leave me alone for too long. I couldn't blame them. He looked kind enough, but I was in no mood for games. I didn't acknowledge him at all. My eyes were fixed on the upper corner of the room, unmoving. I had a vague sense that talking to the police would only make things worse for me in the long term. I didn't see how much worse things could get, but for now at least, I was determined to remain silent.

I heard him droning on, but I stayed resolute. I wouldn't be broken again. I'd hold out.

So, of course, he played a trump card.

". . . recommend you be committed."

How could he have known? My deepest fear, and he struck right at it, sending the whole of my being into cold shivers. I felt my body seize up at just the words, let alone the terrifying images that accompanied them to my mind. I snapped back into focus and looked him straight in the eye.

"Can I make a phone call?"

"Well, we've already attempted your father, and his listed legal counsel. Until we can make contact, unless you have another form of legal counsel—"

"No."

"Then I suggest you keep silent, kid." He looked sympathetic. I didn't need sympathy though. I needed my exit. I needed to make sure I did *not* end up in that hellish place.

I needed someone to vouch for me. Vouch for my story. Make me credible.

I needed someone nobody would ever doubt.

I'd get him here. I'd use this cop's sympathy to my advantage. No matter what it took, he'd come and he'd find a way out of this mess. Like he always did.

Matt would know what to do.

CHAPTER 18

JEN

"Look, what harm could it do? The kid's a mess."

"You saw what he did to Whitman."

"He's desperate, and things will go a lot smoother if we can get him to start talking. Anything we can get on record."

"I'll get him to—"

"Let him call his friend."

"Sir?"

"A friendly face might do him some good."

"You're starting to sound like a broken record."

"Who's in charge again?"

"Yes, sir. Right away, sir."

"I saw that."

———

Dear Mom,

Matt and I had to leave. We're not running away from home, so don't worry about that. You didn't do anything wrong. You're the best.

But . . . something's come up and we have to go. We might not ever come back.

I wish I could tell you it's nothing dangerous, but it might be. Just trust me, okay? This is something really, really important. I want to tell you, but I

"Masasak nara volavus sel nara kelendil," I cursed under my breath. I wanted to comfort her, not send her into a blind panic.

"What's up?" asked Sara, leaning over my shoulder. I tried to crumple up the letter, but she laid out a hand to stop me. "Jeez, your handwriting has gotten awful."

In response, I flipped the sheet over and wrote out a long, elegant string of Etoline—something *very* rude I'm not gonna repeat here.

"I'm just going to assume that's an insult." She frowned. "What are you trying to write?"

". . . A goodbye," I said quietly.

Sara hesitated, glancing over her shoulder at the stairs. Mom still wasn't home and wouldn't be for a few hours at least. "Aren't you going to talk to her in person?"

I sighed and leaned back in my chair. "I don't know."

"Huh?"

I glanced at the clock, which put us well past midnight. Mom still wouldn't be home though. Last call for drinks wasn't until two thirty in the morning, *and* she had to stay after a bit to close up. I used to try to stay up late waiting for her to come home, but I rarely made it that far. I'd wake up the next morning with my alarm ringing in my ear, or sometimes with the sunrise, having been magically transported back into my bed, nice and snug. On the rare occasions I'd actually seen Mom come home, she'd greeted me with a warm hug—and then grounded me for staying up so late.

"I have a feeling I'm never gonna see her again."

"Because of what Matt said?" she asked. "About us needing to leave soon?"

I shook my head. "I think we're gonna get rushed out of here. If your parents call the cops—"

"They won't."

I wasn't so sure, and definitely wasn't willing to bet my entire future on it, but I let it be. Sara didn't want to stall any more than I did. "Well, that phone call was still super weird."

Sara nodded, just as puzzled as I was. Matt had gotten a phone call about half an hour earlier. They called the house, he picked up, and five minutes later he was in his truck. He'd promised to be home soon and told us to start packing. I had no idea why he'd said that. It wasn't like we could take anything with us. Probably just instinctive.

I shivered as the pieces clicked together in my mind, one by one, slowly uncovering the puzzle. There was another reason that I felt like I wouldn't see my mother ever again, one I didn't want to think about, and I was afraid to speak it aloud. But this was Sara. I needed to say something before it was too late. "That's not everything though."

"Are you afraid to talk to her?"

"Seka nara vack are you so smart all the time?" I asked incredulously.

"Jen, it's okay," she said, obviously trying to be comforting. I only felt worse, like I was hiding from my problems again.

"I feel like I'm running away," I said, echoing my thoughts. "Like maybe I'm just giving up too easily. I'm afraid she'll talk me out of going. Does that make sense? Am I making sense?"

"Yes, it makes sense." Sara shivered too, and it made me feel infinitely better about myself, that she wasn't exactly comfortable with this either. "I feel exactly the same."

"You do?"

"I just ran away from home," she added, wincing. "I'm going to disappear from the whole world just to get away from my problems. I still think it's the right idea, but I'll be worried about it right up until we step across."

"Well, it's not really a step—"

She coughed. "Not the point, Jen."

I glanced over at her. She was sitting cross-legged on my bed, my stupid frilly bed with a mismatched dinosaur blanket on top, picked more for warmth than because I liked the design. At least it was comfortable. More on topic, Sara's eyes were fierce, her expression set and determined.

"I'm never going to know if this is the right thing to do," she went on. "All I know is that something has to change. I've got an opportunity no one's ever had, and I get to share it with my best friend in the whole world. It's not an adventure. I just get to start over. All the good and the bad, but I'm gonna take it." As she spoke, the confidence in her voice grew with each word. By the end, I was convinced.

"I'm glad you're coming with me," I said, and her face lit up like the sun had suddenly popped into my room.

"You'll have to teach me more Etoline," she added with a small smile. "I can't wait to meet Naeflin."

"You two are gonna get along great," I said, feeling so much more cheerful and at ease than I had a few moments earlier. "Oh, there's so much I can't wait to show you. And my suunsyl. It's so gorgeous there."

Sara just smiled as I began to describe it in minute detail. It really is a pretty amazing place, but I won't bore you with the specifics. Honestly, it's actually not all that different from most other forests—though the trees are older and much larger, and then there are the homes we build into the upper levels below the canopy, and the magically lit fields for crops to provide food when hunting is scarce. Okay, so it's pretty different, but none of that mattered compared to seeing my best friend's *reactions* to it. She was just so excited and optimistic, and she took in every detail like a parched woman consuming water in the desert.

Meanwhile, I felt accepted. Unlike the first time I'd told her about all this, when our conversation teetered on the edge of regret and loss and pain, I could actually speak openly. Passionately. I wasn't just telling her memories and dancing around the issues; instead, I gave her visions of things to come. New experiences she'd get to share in. I was giving her hope and, in return, filling myself up with the same. The world felt just a little bit brighter with every single thing I remembered.

We could have talked for hours, I'm sure, but a feeling of responsibility came back around and knocked me upside the head. I'd been telling her about how we sent letters between different suunsyls (carefully bred and magically trained flying squirrels, no joke) and the crumpled note behind me on my desk popped back into my mind. I trailed off as I slowly spun around, picking it back up.

". . . Do you still want to write her a letter?" Sara asked.

"I have to," I said quietly. "She's my mom. I can't just disappear. She might not get home in time, and even if I say goodbye in person, she deserves an explanation."

"What will you say?"

I shook my head. "I still don't know."

She sighed. "Sorry I can't be more help."

"It's okay." I leaned over, pulled out a new sheet of paper from the drawer, and set my pen to it once again. Behind me, I heard Sara attempt to stifle a yawn. I don't know why—maybe it was exhaustion, or just the image in my head of a ridiculously oversized yawn swallowing up her face—but I giggled. I couldn't help it, and it quickly turned into a full-on laugh.

"What?" she asked, indignant.

"Nothing," I choked out. I forced myself to calm down. "Sorry. You should take a nap."

"But I—"

"I promise I won't leave Earth without you," I said, smirking. "Besides, *someone* should probably get some sleep. Matt and I definitely won't."

"Okay," she said as another yawn overtook her. "You don't mind if I use—"

"How many times have I slept in *your* bed?" I glanced over my shoulder with an exaggerated eyebrow raise, as high as I could get it.

"Fair point." She grinned, and pulled up the nearest blanket. "Wake me up if anything happens?"

"Duh."

Within minutes, I heard her breathing steadily, and I knew she was already falling deep into some crazy dream. Sara was a *really* heavy sleeper. I could never get her to wake up with just sound, no matter how loud. She'd only wake up if I shook the bed or tapped her on the face or something.

I took out my phone and turned on some music. Anything to help me concentrate a bit more. Once again, I set pen to paper and tried to write. Something more reassuring this time, I hoped. Also, something Mom could actually *read*.

Mom,

You're probably wondering why we've been acting so weird the last couple of days. I'm sorry I didn't get a chance to explain. Both of us really wanted to, but we just couldn't. We're not in any danger, we haven't broken any laws or anything. But we've gotta go now, and we probably aren't coming back. I wish you could come with us, but it's just not possible.

We were always gonna move out though, right? And Matt's coming with me, so there's nothing to worry about. We'll be okay. You taught us to take care of ourselves, so we've got that covered. We're going somewhere far away though and we might not ever be able to talk again. I swear, though, if there's ever a way, you'll be the first person I call.

There's a lot I want to say, and I wish I had said it in person, but I just didn't know—

Way too sappy. It didn't feel like *me*. I crumpled it up and tossed it into the bin next to my desk, along with the first one. There was a slight amber glow to the curtains on my window, cast by the streetlight outside, and I watched as the shadow of a bug flitted across it like a gigantic monster. I'd seen something like that before, in the mountain crossing to Windmere—except this was actually a tiny beetle, not a real monster. I tried to compare the idea to my current situation, but I came up empty. Not everything ends up making for a cool symbolic comparison.

I leaned back once more, almost tipping over in my chair as I rubbed at my eyes. I was still *really* behind on sleep, though I'd been adjusting to it little by little. As long as I didn't need to do anything super physical, I could deal with it. I was sure, somehow, that once I found my way home to my suunsyl, I'd sleep more peacefully than ever before.

Speaking of sleeping peacefully, Sara was out like a light. I smiled at the sight of her wrapped up in my cheap dinosaur blanket, totally peaceful. After the events of the day, I was just glad she could actually get some sleep—that she felt safe and comfortable enough with me there to let her guard down. It said more about our friendship than any words ever could, and for someone as insecure and uncertain as me? That meant a *lot*.

No lies. The promise we'd made sprang back into my head. I let the chair slam on the floor as I leaned back in, grabbing another sheet of paper. It was the same thing as before, the same as agonizing over Sara. Why *couldn't* I just say what I really meant? Why did I feel like I had to lie? Mom deserved to know. I wasn't ever coming back. I'd tell her everything I could.

Thanks, Sara.

Hey, Mom,

So, here's the thing. This is gonna sound crazy, but I swear to you it's the absolute truth. No jokes.

Matt and I went to another world. Through magic. Also, magic is real. Funny story, I can actually use it too. Cool, right?

But seriously. It's not all fun and games. People got hurt. People died. We fought in battles and almost died ourselves, plenty of times. I'm telling you this because you should know what we went through, and what we're going back to.

Yeah, we're going back. I'm sorry, but we have to. We were gone for more than seven years, but because of magic time stuff, we came back exactly the same. Only . . . we weren't the same. I don't even remember who I was back here on Earth. Seven years is a really long time. Especially when you spend it with people who aren't exactly human.

I'm not sure I'm exactly human anymore either. I'm probably gonna live way longer than you or anybody else, and I'm still kinda freaked out by that. I mean, I'm not gonna be alone, and it also means I never have to worry about getting sick or anything like that, but it's still insane and hard to wrap my mind around. Kind of cool though, I guess. I dunno. Still figuring it out.

Look, you're probably wondering what you did wrong. Or maybe you aren't, hell if I know. I've never been a mom and I'm not sure I ever will be. But you didn't do anything wrong. Trust me. You raised us better than you could know. Matt turned out amazing, seriously. You'd be proud of what he's accomplished. He's saved thousands of lives. Hundreds of thousands, actually. And now he's going back, to make sure they stay saved. He's a great guy, and a good brother. So, that's one out of two, right?

Ha, ha, yeah, I know. Bad jokes.

Mom, Matt and I both agreed this was for the best. I hope you can understand that. Most important though, you can't ever tell anyone where we went. Best case, people would think you were crazy. Worst case? They'd actually believe you. Do you know what people would do to get access to magic? Because I do. I've seen it firsthand, and it can turn anyone into a monster. I lost friends that way.

I'm sorry to do this, but I also have to ask you to help me out with something. See, Matt and I aren't going alone. Sara's coming with us.

She asked me not to tell anyone why, and I promised I wouldn't. Just believe me, she's better off getting the hell away from this world. Her disappearing isn't gonna be so easy to hide like me and Matt though. It's gonna be hard, but you need to protect her just like you did us. Sara really needs this.

This is stupid and horrible and selfish and I'm sorry. I'm asking you for this when I'm running away without even saying goodbye.

Well, this letter is a goodbye, I guess, but you know what I mean. I'm so sorry, Mom.

I'll miss you, and I'll remember you forever, even if I end up living to be nine hundred and seven. If I ever find a way to send a message back, you'll be the very first person I contact. I promise.

I love you, Mom.

I'd started to cry toward the end of the letter, but I'd already decided it was what I needed to write. I had to take a break a few times to make sure I was spelling things correctly, and painstakingly made sure the handwriting was good enough. I didn't want it to look terrible if this was the last time I'd ever communicate with her. I'd made up my mind halfway through that I couldn't face her. Maybe that was cowardly, but I knew in my heart that I couldn't say goodbye in person. Hate me for it if you want.

At the bottom, I signed my name twice—once in Etoline, once in English, as close as I could get to the original pronunciation.

Jennifer velae nara ralaev sel demovi.
Jennifer from the dale of silver.

It was the full name that had only ever been spoken twice; once by Tethevallen when I'd asked him about names, and once by Valen Syldarei in the ceremony to adopt me into the *suunval*. It was super literal and awkward, and way too long, but I treasured it like nothing else. It was a part of me as much as anything else. It was the proof that I'd found a place where I belonged and people I belonged with.

I began to roll up the paper, then I remembered I didn't actually need to tie it to a squirrel's leg this time. I dug through my desk to find an envelope instead. I found a few, but they were either too glitzy and covered in sparkles, or just rumpled up and messy. Stupid. I glanced over at Sara, still fast asleep, and grinned. She'd laugh at me for this, insisting I find the perfect envelope for my running-away-from-home letter.

I took the letter downstairs to hunt for an envelope—or anything, really, that I could seal it in. I wasn't *that* picky. I just needed to know it'd be safe, it'd be noticed, and she'd read it in the morning. Long after we'd left.

How the hell could Sara be snoozing right now, anyway? Even if I didn't have so much trouble getting to sleep lately, the anticipation in my stomach was overwhelming. Maybe it was because I was the one who actually had to move us across the planes, but I couldn't keep still for the life of me. I felt like something momentous was about to happen, and I still wasn't sure if it was a good thing or a bad thing—only that it couldn't get any worse than staying here.

As soon as I sealed the letter in a plain white envelope, with *Mom* scrawled on the front, I heard my cell phone ring. To say it felt "fateful" would have been a huge understatement. My cell phone ringing at two in the morning, on *this* night? It had to be something earth-shattering.

I picked it up. I didn't recognize the number. Who the hell would be calling me right now? Did I usually have late-night chats with friends? I couldn't remember, but I doubted it. If there was anyone I could see myself talking to way past midnight, it was the best friend fast asleep in my bed upstairs.

I flipped open the phone and raised it to my ear.

"Hello?"

"Jen?" His voice shook and trembled.

"Carl? What the—"

"I need your help."

I shook Sara awake and gave her the briefest explanation I could about where I was going and how long it would take. She gave me a sleepy nod and fell right back into bed. I left her a note on my desk, just in case, but I hoped to be back before she woke up again.

I grabbed my bike and bolted into the night, pedaling desperately through the rain toward the police station. Carl's words were still ringing in my ears. They planned to take him away? Shut him up in some psych ward or something?

What the hell was going on?

Was this where Matt ran off to? Maybe he was there already. Yeah, that had to be it. Matt was there, trying to figure out a way to get Carl free. I just had to show up too. Lend my support, vouch for him or something. I had no idea what I could do, but with the way Carl sounded on the phone, I couldn't just *stay home.*

I was pretty unsteady on the bike at first, but I remembered how to ride it quickly enough. The streets were utterly deserted, and I booked my way through intersections, ignoring the lights entirely. Street lamps flashed above me in a hazy blur of rain as I practically flew over the asphalt. I felt like I was going a million miles an hour—and it still wasn't fast enough.

I didn't see a single car the whole way there. It was so quiet, the only sound that of the faint trickle of rain. The whole world seemed to be anticipating what came next. I didn't know what to expect when I got to the station. Carl hadn't been specific. All he asked was that I come, quickly, before they took him away.

And he told me he was afraid.

Hearing Carl—*Carl,* of all people—admit he was afraid sent real shivers down my spine, my back, my arms and legs. Whatever part of me, pick it, I was terrified. Carl was too stubborn to ever voice fear aloud, yet I'd heard it, even through the hiss and crackle of my crappy cell phone. He was really scared and he was desperate. I had no choice but to rush down there.

Ever been to a police station at night? There's a really weird feeling to them when the sun's gone. I mean, I'd never *actually* visited one before, but I'd watched enough TV to have a vague idea what to expect. I didn't trust the cop shows to be accurate or anything, but I figured they had to have some bits of truth, right?

Well, here's the thing: At nighttime, you're dealing with the cops who *really* don't want to be bothered, even more than usual. *Especially* if they don't usually work that shift. Everything about the place just seemed hostile. I noticed it the moment I set my bike in the rack outside, as an officer heading out glared at me like I'd just kicked his dog or something. I tried to look as innocent and unthreatening as I could as I walked in the door.

And promptly ran right into Matt.

Well, that explained for sure where he'd run off to earlier. If he'd hurried out to talk to Carl, he'd probably been in the same panicky rush I'd just blitzed through. Not that Matt looked panicked in the slightest, but still.

Wait . . . what the hell am I thinking? If Matt's here, and he's leaving, then why would Carl call m—

Oh.

Oh *stars*, no.

"Jen?" he asked, sounding perfectly calm.

It was all so wrong.

"Matt, why—"

He held a finger to his mouth and beckoned me into a small waiting area outside the main office. I saw groups of abandoned desks inside, under dimmed hanging lamps, and a single bright room spilling light out from the opposite end of the building. As my eyes adjusted, I could see a door cracked open just slightly, leading into what was unmistakably an interrogation room.

I followed Matt into a corner, under the lazy watch of the officer on duty at the front desk. He returned to his newspaper a few moments later, without much interest in us, which gave us enough privacy to talk. When we sat down in the uncomfortable chairs in the very corner, Matt finally took the finger away from his mouth.

I was all too eager to break the silence. "What the hell is going on?" I whispered.

"I was going to ask you the same question," he said, raising an eyebrow. "Why are you here and not getting ready to go out to the forest?"

"Carl called me. To come help."

Matt shook his head. "He really shouldn't have done that."

"Why the fuck not, Matt?" I struggled to keep my voice low. "He's our friend, isn't he?"

"Look where we are!" he hissed. "Carl's way over the line. He attacked someone."

Carl did what now? ". . . Who?"

"I don't know. Some guy. Daniel Whitman. I have no idea who he is. You?"

I shook my head. "I've never heard of him."

"Apparently, Carl beat him half to death. The guy's in the hospital. They're talking about sending Carl away."

"Jail?"

"Psychiatric care."

I shuddered. The idea of getting locked up in a padded white cell, I knew Carl would hate that just as much as I would.

"Look, I know how that sounds—" Matt started.

I shook my head to cut him off. I definitely didn't need any more images in my head. I needed to take action. "What are we going to do?"

Matt sighed, and I saw a look in his eyes I hadn't seen in a long while. A soul-crushing burden, lurking in the darkness of his gaze, my brother carrying the weight of the world on his shoulders once again. He was working through a terrible decision right before my eyes, feeling like he had no good options, only better or worse.

He was about to choose wrong. I knew, before he said it, what he'd decided. I hated him already, for words that hadn't even crossed his lips.

"Vack dou," I snarled. I almost stood up right then, but his hand clamped down on my shoulder. He forced me back down, to sit still and listen. I struggled for a moment, before I remembered that starting a scene wouldn't help Carl either. I let him talk, though my head pounded and my blood boiled with fury.

"We can't help him, Jen. No matter what we might say, Carl almost killed the guy with his bare hands. He knew what to aim for to cause the most pain and damage. He's done this before; we've both seen it.

We have to deny everything to get out of here tonight. We barely even knew him as friends and we *never* knew about anything like this."

"But—"

Matt's calm, assured voice overrode any chance I had to speak up. "They're going to take him away, and maybe that's for the best. He'll get some real help. He's not going to prison; he's going to a care facility where they'll actually try to help him."

Oh *stars*, Matt, do you even believe what you're saying? Is any of this shit coming out of your mouth the truth? Or do you want to abandon Carl just to save yourself?

Matt, are you ditching him so *you* can go back?

I felt my stomach churn. If I wasn't actively forcing it back as I'd learned to do, I would have thrown up all over his shirt. There wasn't much that could really make me vomit anymore, but this? This was disgusting. Horrible. Awful. I wanted to yell at him, to rage about how he'd sacrificed Blake, how he'd helped drive Carl to this end, how he *knew of a way back and didn't tell any of us.*

It hit me right then. I'd never told Matt where the rock was. It wasn't a lucky guess. He knew. He'd *already* known. He'd kept it from us, setting all the horrible events of this week in motion, putting the three of us in this police station in the dead of night.

And I was going to let him get away with it.

I saw it coming. I was letting this happen. I heard Matt ask for some kind of confirmation, and I nodded. My face and hands went numb. I felt my mind contract in on itself, like I was retreating from the world again. I knew this feeling. I'd feared it ever returning. It was a survival instinct, a way to hide myself from my own actions.

Matt stood up and offered his hand. I took it, though I couldn't feel anything. My brother may as well have been made of ice for all his hand did to help me. I followed him back into the main room, where I waited silently as the door across the room opened.

I no longer had to ask. I understood why Matt was choosing to do this. I understood why I had to support him. If I didn't, if I stayed even a moment longer, if the cops discovered what I'd done that night . . .

I still hated it. Hated myself, hated him, hated everything.

Matt was forcing me to lie for him.

Carl was a mess. His eyes were puffy and red from the tears, his hands bandaged and bloody. I could see a bruise sprouting on his face. He was handcuffed, a personal guard pushing him forward. Behind Carl, I spotted the two detectives who had come to our house and saw recognition flit across their faces as they noticed me.

Damn you to the ends of every earth, Matt.

Carl made his way across the room. The guard stepped away, as did Matt, allowing Carl and me a bit of privacy. Between the hum of fans and machinery, I was relatively certain we wouldn't be overheard, but still, I wouldn't dare risk anything.

"Hi, Jen," he mumbled. I could barely hear him.

"Hi."

"Sorry you have to see me like this." He gave me a weak smile.

"Could be worse," I said. Was joking appropriate? How the hell should I know? What do you say to a friend you're probably seeing for the last time, when you're lying to him and about to throw him to the wolves while you run for your own life?

"Jen, you've gotta tell them."

"Tell them what?"

"Everything. What we went through. Who we are. It's the only way to explain . . . what I did."

"Oh, Carl . . ." I whispered.

"I know. I have to go away. But I'm not crazy. *We're* not crazy. You gotta explain that."

I shook my head and I knew it was a blow right to his heart. His knees buckled; his eyes widened.

"Jen, please. I can't be taken away. I'd never see you again." Carl's voice rose in pitch, no longer whispering.

"Carl, I'm sorry." My voice threatened to break, but I held it steady. I had to hold it in. I couldn't let any vulnerability out. I had to be strong.

One crack and I'd shatter into a million pieces.

"No, please. Don't say you're sorry. Tell them."

Oh stars. Please. If there were ever a time to grant me a blessing of some kind. Anything at all. This is the moment. Give me resolve, give me bravery, give me something.

The stars didn't answer. They'd probably never answer me again. I don't think they take too kindly to traitors.

Carl's eyes got even wider with my continued silence. He raised his hands, still cuffed and chained. I saw the stains on the bandages up close and I deliberately recoiled. I had to act like I was scared, or disgusted, or whatever I needed to do. I couldn't follow my instincts, to try and comfort him and heal him. I couldn't go anywhere near him.

He took a step forward. Instantly, the guard was at his side, pulling him back.

"Jen, please! Talk to them!" Carl blurted out. There was no pretense of secrecy anymore. "Tell them about Cyraveil! About the world! You're a *Sylf*, for god's sake! Matt took over an empire! Explain it! Matt?" Carl's head swiveled around for a new ally, since his closest one had just abandoned him without a word. I looked over too, watching Matt's reaction.

". . . Carl, none of that is real. I don't know what you're talking about." Matt responded so calmly, so naturally. I believed every word he spoke. Everyone in the room would have believed him. He just looked like a concerned bystander.

Carl struggled against his restraints. The guard was pulling him back out of the room, and he began to shout for help, for anything to save him.

Which, of course, meant it was my turn. The world fell into that slow motion state, when you know something terrible is about to happen, and you can see it coming from miles away, but you're helpless to do a single thing about it.

Except I wasn't helpless—because that terrible thing about to happen was me.

Carl got the guard to stop pulling him away. His eyes locked with mine from across the room. I felt my heart harden to ice in my chest, preparing for the worst. My hands flew up to my mouth, as if I could prevent what came next. Like anything could have stopped what was coming next.

"Jen, you were there. You know. The Sylves, Jen. Everything. We were together, Jen. You and me. I rescued you, remember?" Carl was raving now, struggling to keep his composure.

I shook my head again. Tears tried to spill from my eyes, but I wouldn't let them. I refused to let myself cry. *Strength*, I told myself. I had to get through this. I stared straight at Carl, with the rest of the world still frozen in place, and I opened my mouth.

"I'm sorry, Carl. I don't have a clue what you're talking about." His face fell, and my heart with it. But I made it through, right? Carl would be taken away, and I would be free once again—for all the good it did me. This night would be seared into my brain forever. I knew that already. I'd never forget what we'd done.

Then I heard his voice once more from across the room, calling out in perfect cadence, perfect pronunciation. As if he'd memorized it just for me.

"Vei illum dou, velae envil 'svil tosilandar, ta nal erreth ala venand slasev."

My heart shattered. I was *almost* overwhelmed. *Almost* completely overcome. I had to fight through a surging wave of emotions swallowing up every sense in my body to force out four simple words.

Four words that would finally condemn him.

"Carl, you need help."

His eyes, which only a moment before had been filled with hope and love and promises of a life together, hollowed out to nothing. There was a despair so total, so utterly void of feeling, that there wasn't a person inside anymore. He slumped in the guard's arms, and was slowly dragged back into the interrogation room. The two detectives gave us another curious glance before they followed him back in, and the door snapped shut.

I felt Matt's hand drop onto my shoulder once again. It was like he'd flipped open a tap. Tears erupted from my eyes as I turned and fled the building. With every step, I ran farther away from a man I'd just sent to his worst nightmare, all to save myself.

It was raining once more, harder than ever, and I welcomed it gladly. I fumbled my way back onto the bike and started pedaling. Maybe it could wash away the guilt and the pain now consuming me, but I doubted it. Surely, I was damned forever.

By the time I got home, Matt and Sara were already waiting for me in the garage. Matt was holding the envelope I'd left on the kitchen table. I pulled up silently and carefully placed my bike back on the rack where it belonged. Sara watched with worried eyebrows, but Matt wore an unreadable mask. Had he been so distant and terrifying? Was this a new side of him, or a side I'd always pretended wasn't there?

I'd finished crying. I knew there was nothing more to be done. Instead, I had a new choice to make—one just as important to our future.

Sara was the first to speak, cautious and hesitant. "Everything okay?"

Matt hadn't told her, of course. I didn't answer her right away. I turned to my brother, staring him down with all the determination I could muster. I had to know, right there, what sort of person he was. Who the man I was taking back into my world really was under the surface.

"Matt, did we do everything we could for him?"

Matt opened his mouth to answer, and I held up my hand. I knew what he would say and I couldn't ever let him voice it. I could already tell what the answer was, and it sickened me to my core. But I'd made my choice. If I confronted him, if I disowned him for what he'd done tonight, our lives would fall apart completely. There was only one way forward, and it was united. I needed him, and he needed me. If we were going back to Cyraveil, there was no way we'd survive unless we were on the same side again—no matter how much it disgusted me.

It had to be three.

Without another word, I walked forward and took Sara's hand. I led her around to the other side of the truck and got in, deliberately placing myself in the center, between Matt and my best friend. As she got in, I reached over and closed the door behind her. I watched as Matt carefully placed the letter on the door to the garage, wedged into the handle, and turned the lights out one by one.

He got into the truck, turned the key, and backed out down the driveway. The garage door slid shut in front of us, closing off my old house for the last time.

My fingers tightened around Sara's as I kept my eyes fixed straight ahead on the road. As we took the first exit, I turned around to look out the rear of the cabin, up into the stars barely visible through a gap in the rain clouds, and I prayed.

Maybe I was doomed to regret this forever. Maybe I should have told Carl long before I ever talked to Matt. Maybe I shouldn't have volunteered in the war. Maybe I shouldn't have ever left the comfort of my little home up in the trees. Maybe I shouldn't have begged Matt to take me along that night to see whatever Blake had found.

Maybe, maybe, maybe. My life was always full of maybes. I hated it. I was done with it. I was getting the hell off this planet.

And I was traveling back to my own, where I'd live with guilt and the knowledge of what I'd done for the rest of my considerably long life. Where I'd probably never be able to trust my brother completely again, even as I lived side-by-side with him for the years and decades to come, a smile on my face and laughter on my lips, pretending we were a team.

You probably hate me a little, don't you? Or maybe you're sympathetic. Fuck that. I don't deserve it. Save it for Sara, or Carl, or anyone else. I'm just one nervous wreck in a large collection of nervous wrecks hanging around, but I put myself up here. I did this to myself. It's up to me to dig my way back out.

The headlights flickered as we bumped off the main road, and the sign for Cyraveil Park flashed up in front of us. I felt my own hand squeezed in return, and finally, I allowed myself just a little bit of hope. I still had Sara, and I still had myself.

There was still some magic in the world—damned if I wasn't going to use it.

Time to go home.

Epilogue

"Did that convince you at all?" West asked.

Portman shook his head, as Matt departed in the beat-up old truck. The rain drizzled off the awning above the doors to the station in a curtain. Portman felt perplexed as he shivered in the cold night air. He'd not been sure what to expect from letting Carl talk to his friends, and it hadn't exactly flagged any real triggers, but it had still been bizarre to say the least.

Back inside, he had a high school kid with insane delusions of magic and a fantasy world he'd supposedly traveled to, plus a missing friend whose disappearance Portman believed he was responsible for to some degree. He couldn't make heads or tails of Carl's demeanor though— not after the confrontation with his friends.

Portman was never one to just let a case go. His dogged determination to follow threads to their very end, when he could just walk away at the first opportunity to clear a number and bump his statistics, had driven away more than a few partners in his career. West was just the latest in a long line.

"I don't know 'bout you, but—"

Portman interrupted him. "I'll take care of Stokelson. Go get the car. We're following them."

West grinned. "Just what I was thinkin'."

Portman smiled as he hurried back into the station. West seemed like a good fit.

They didn't bother with sirens or lights, not this late at night. The roads were calm. Most people were asleep. West sped through hazy strings of green lights shining in the rain, then took them into the maze of streets that made up the suburbs.

Just as they pulled up to the Silverdale residence, Portman caught a lucky break. He tapped West, who'd slowed to a crawl, and pointed farther down the road. Past the sheets of downpour, they could just barely make out the taillights of the pickup, turning the corner and disappearing from view. A few seconds later and the detectives would never have seen it.

What followed was the quietest of police chases. There were no cars to be seen anywhere, and barely a sound beyond the pouring rain and the purr of the engine. *Surreal,* thought Portman. Like they were cruising through a dream, with faint patches of color glowing through the raindrops from the red taillights, the light yellow beams of their headlights, and the dim street lamps above them. The moon hid behind a thick cloud layer, and as they drove farther and farther off the main roads, even the streetlights vanished.

West killed the lights, and their car was black, so Portman didn't expect to be spotted—if Matt was even checking for people following him.

If the kid was innocent, why was he driving out this way at three in the morning? Portman couldn't figure it out. Was that another silhouette in the cab in the truck? He couldn't be sure, not at such a distance and with so little light.

As they rounded another corner, rising up into the hills, Portman glanced around in surprise. He'd been so busy trying to make out the details of the car, he'd not kept track of their location.

"Where are we?"

"Outside our jurisdiction," grumbled West. "Wait . . . Holy shit."

"What?"

"I think . . . Yeah. We're going to Cyraveil Park."

An alarm bell rang furiously in Portman's mind. "Are you sure?"

"Can't think of anything else this way worth mentionin'."

Carl's story pushed his way back into Portman's mind. *Was it possible?*

No. It was absurd. It couldn't happen. It was the wishful, escapist thinking of a kid who'd seen something terrible and couldn't cope. Carl was disturbed and needed serious psychiatric help.

Yet Portman couldn't explain what he was seeing. They just had to keep following Matt, wherever this was going. Maybe he'd lead them to a body, buried deep in the woods. Portman shivered at the thought. Was he about to catch a murderer?

He placed his hand in his coat pocket and double-checked that his pistol was still there on his hip.

"Careful," hissed Portman.

"I hate the woods, okay?" West picked himself back up from the dirt and shot him a glare. "Just go ahead without me if you have to."

They were a few hundred feet back from a bobbing lantern, traveling deep into the forest. The pickup had pulled off the road a short while after the sign for the park, and three people had gotten out—Matt, his sister, and a girl neither of them knew. Portman's paranoid brain instantly jumped to the conclusion that Matt and his sister were about to murder the girl, but he brushed that thought away. The body language was all wrong. They were helping her through the woods. Matt's sister led the way, just outside the lantern light, while Matt took their friend by the hand through the more difficult thickets.

West had no such companion and tripped over every root and bramble in the near-total darkness.

"Just keep that lantern in sight," Portman whispered, seriously annoyed. He surged ahead while West struggled to keep up. The light was fading away, but Portman was determined not to lose them. The chase went on, deeper and deeper into the woods. He was getting thirsty and tired, having spent *far* too much time awake, but he still refused to let them out of his sight. He'd figure it out and close the case, no matter what it took.

The forest had grown quiet, he noticed. There were no crickets, no frogs, nothing. Only the wind, rustling the leaves around them. He felt anticipation knotting in his chest and knew something was going to happen—sooner, not later. Just as the feeling struck him, he saw the lantern swing to a halt.

How close did he dare get? Portman crouched low, trying to move as quietly as possible. He could hear murmuring ahead as the light shifted around and shadows moved all about. From what he could tell, they'd set down the lantern behind a tree, blocking out the light from the clearing they were standing in. *Why would they do that? What are they planning?*

He needed to get closer. He edged forward, step by step, his feet crinkling the sheets of ivy beneath him. Finally, he could make out a few words.

". . . and I stand here?"

"I don't think it matters. We . . . to hold hands."

"You aren't sure?"

"*Vack dou*, I've never done this before."

A nervous laugh. What was going on in there? He tried to move closer, but he could see thick patches of ivy and leaves in front of him. They'd make too much sound. The risk was too great. If he revealed himself now, he might not hear everything important. He could only trust that he would hear them if they started moving again, or if anything seemed about to happen.

"Ready?"

"Can you *ever* be ready for something like this?"

"Oh, stop grandstanding. Let's just do this."

"Okay."

"You two are gonna be a bundle of fun. Okay, hang on tight."

More muttering, and this time in what sounded like a foreign language. It was too quiet to hear the words—if they were even words he could understand. Portman spoke a few languages fluently, but this definitely wasn't one of them. Wasn't even in the same family.

Abruptly, the voices stopped. Everything stopped. All he could hear was the wind.

He waited. For minutes that dragged on and on, he waited. The lantern light flickered in front of him. He watched carefully for any sign of an escape attempt. Finally, with West creeping up behind him, Portman could wait no longer.

He burst out from the underbrush, rushing into the clearing.

It was empty. Completely empty.

The lantern flickered again from behind the nearest tree. He looked down at the ground, at the tracks scattered in the dirt floor. There was a small depression at one end of the clearing, where a heavy rock might have sat.

"The hell?" asked West, looking around at the forest. Tall, dark shapes surrounded them, thick trees and indistinct shadows alike.

Portman crouched down and picked at the grass in the clearing. The dirt was already dry, though the rest of the forest was still soaked from the rainfall. He sat down, and looked up at the circle of sky above them. Directly above, through a gap in the clouds, he could just make out the twinkling stars.

"They're gone."

Afterword

This book exists in large part thanks to two very close friends of mine—one who was there when the story was inspired, and one who inspired me to finish it. The story of *Epilogue* and of these three troubled people first came to my mind back in February 2016. The year holds some significance—at this point, I was nearly seven years out of high school, and I *still* had no idea what I was going to do with my life. Seven years had flown by in what felt like an instant, and I was stuck in the same dead-end retail job I'd been at for nearly that whole time.

So, quite naturally, when I decided to try and write a "post-fantasy" story—or "post-Narnia" if you prefer—I settled on seven years as my time span. A bit escapist? Yeah, definitely. More autobiographical details made it into the story as well; I learned from a favorite author that characters ought to always have a bit of the writer in them, or else relating to them is too difficult. To save myself the embarrassment, I'm not getting any more specific than that, but feel free to speculate on how Jen, Carl, and Matt all reflect me in some way!

It's funny, I usually write far longer stories than this. Readers of my main series, *The Last Science*, can attest to my long-winded nature. At the time of writing this afterword (September 2021), it is nearly ten times the length of *Epilogue* in only two volumes, with no signs of stopping—yet *Epilogue* popped out fully formed in less than a hundred thousand words. I'm incredibly proud of this book, and a lot of credit must be given to the people who helped it take shape.

First and foremost, my friend Josh, who was the first person I mentioned at the beginning of this afterword. He was standing right next to me when I said idly, "Hey, what if that Narnia epilogue was a whole book?" It is *entirely* Josh's fault that I didn't stop there, so you may blame him for any rage you might hold toward Matt, Jen, and Carl. Josh has been the first person to read every single chapter I've ever written—which often includes barely coherent messages in my chapter share emails at two in the morning—and still provides one of the greatest sounding boards an author could ask for. Josh, thank you.

Second, my sister, Michelle, who deserves the world and then some for everything she's done for me (and for putting up with a little sister as obnoxious as I was . . . ouch). Her editing work is all over the first versions of this story, and she was key to helping me craft the ending, which was wildly different originally. I also must credit a walk with her out on the beach for solving a major issue with character arcs for this new edition, which I felt vastly improved the book as a whole. Michelle is a thousand times smarter than me and I owe her more than I can ever repay. Love you, sestra.

Finally, I want to credit someone whose name I'll probably never know. This story was originally posted on the website Royal Road in November 2018. *Epilogue* qualified for the National Novel Writing Month contest at the time and ended up tying for first place! In all likelihood, that—and any readership of this novel—would not have occurred without one particular review. The writer, who I must assume has some journalism or English background from the quality of their prose and structure, posted this review well before the book had gained any traction. I've no idea how they found *Epilogue*, and they don't seem to be particularly active on the site, but they took time out of their day to craft an incredibly touching piece. This was the first formal critique I'd ever received, and I hold it very dear. So, whoever you are, thank you so much for the review. I would absolutely not be here without you, and I hope you read this someday.

As for Jen, Matt, Carl, and Sara—well, I'd never say their story is done. After all, the entire point of this book is telling the story you don't usually get to read, the one that takes place when you thought the story was over. But I'm letting them rest now. They've been through enough, and I have other characters I need to ~~torture~~ develop and grow. I hope you'll join me.

If you want to get in touch regarding this book or other works, please contact me at etzoli.mail@gmail.com, Discord via https://discord.gg/yY6738dAUK, or visit my website at https://etzo.li (assuming it's still up and the internet still uses the domain name system). I would love to hear from you!

Thanks for reading <3

—etzoli

Lily Lashley

I love you, Mom.

About the Author

Lily Lashley, aka Etzoli, is an IT girl in healthcare from Oregon who loves to write long-form sci-fi and fantasy in her downtime. Lily loves cyberpunk, magical realism, and all other sorts of complex genre fiction. She also watches far too much TV, and she's hopelessly addicted to pretzel sticks. There's nothing Lily loves more in the world than cuddling up on a warm couch with thick blankets and disappearing into another world for the day.

DISCOVER
STORIES UNBOUND

PodiumAudio.com

www.ingramcontent.com/pod-product-compliance
Lightning Source LLC
Chambersburg PA
CBHW021812110726
47902CB00006B/1749